2121

Baroness Susan Greenfield, CBE, is a British scientist, writer and broadcaster. Find out more at www.susangreenfield.com.

2121

A TALE FROM THE NEXT CENTURY

SUSAN GREENFIELD

HEAD of ZEUS

First published in the UK in 2013 by Head of Zeus Ltd.

9 7 5 3 1 2 4 6 8

A CIP catalogue record for this book is available from
the British Library.

ISBN (HB) 9781908800572
ISBN (XTPB) 9781781850145
ISBN (E) 9781781853559

Printed in Germany.

Head of Zeus Ltd
Clerkenwell House
45-47 Clerkenwell Green
London EC1R 0HT

www.headofzeus.com

For Winston Fletcher

Chapter 1

FRED

My name is Fred and I've never done anything like this before. Not that there's any problem of course, quite the opposite. I feel extremely privileged being instructed to make this recording: they've told me that only those of exceptional value to our society are approached and that I must discuss it with no one, not even with my immediate superior, Hodge. It's hard though to entertain the thought of Hodge not knowing everything that is going on, of me telling everything to powerful, faceless people I've never met. While Hodge is excluded … . Sorry, I'm already deviating into proscribed areas: it's just that it will take some time to adjust, speaking without feedback into a void like this. I realize I cannot delete anything once I've said it, but I'll start again none the less.

I have grown up in the purest of possible societies, having been born into an age when human existence has never been more stable. My life is completely fulfilling. When I wake each morning, I can anticipate a day ahead as exactly predictable in its unfolding stages as yesterday was and tomorrow will be. Life nowadays is perfect because it is completely ordered, and it is ordered because we recognize that everything and everyone should have their time and their place. The world about me is just as it should be, and as I want it to be.

No one is alive now who can remember first hand how the great, transformational crisis gathered its momentum so very slowly well over a hundred years ago: it was of course unprecedented and no one could have guessed what was to happen. They tell us that things changed so gradually, so imperceptibly, that no one at first realized that the biggest threat to humanity was going to turn out, after all, not to be what was known then as 'Climate Change'. Since everyone had finally to concede to cutting carbon emissions, it was only a matter of time, resources, and scientific ingenuity, to pull the planet, and our species with it, back from the brink of annihilation. The technologists of the last century were confronted with problems that, while complex and difficult, could be at least objectively defined. Everyone became familiar with what kinds of solutions were required, while the urgency of impending disaster ensured the specialists and experts were at last allocated the budgets and facilities to perform their jobs as quickly and effectively as possible. Meanwhile, sensible lifestyle laws such as the banning of all cars, were accepted reluctantly at first, but understood as necessary. So Climate Change was slowly diluted into insignificance: and the threat shifted silently and unnoticed from the global, to the individual.

And this is precisely why I'm now held in such high esteem: I research on the human mind, more specifically its expression in the mechanistic operations of the physical brain. I fully accept that isolating myself routinely like this and narrating all the minutiae of my daily life, will take up valuable amounts of time each day which should of course be devoted to my work in the lab. But perhaps the insights generated by revealing my subjective inner thoughts, may be as important to our society as my actual objective discoveries about the secrets of brain cell functioning. After all, this is what we hold at premium, central to our philosophy before all else: the power of thought and the uniqueness of each individual human mind. Yet we must never ever again lull ourselves into a complacency that it is inviolate.

Over a hundred years ago, people were enthusiastically adapting to living their lives through screens, with replays and fast-forwards and editing and airbrushing, mingling the virtual and the real until eventually no one knew the difference. Slowly, the skills required for cyber-living, such as fast, multitasking information-processing, were at first exaggerated and then just different from normal life, then dominant, then finally monopolizing all brainpower. Back in that previous century, the screen was still a separate entity, requiring fixation and the exclusion of the peripheral press of the real world. That innocuous-looking little angular epicentre of the previously wide visual field succeeded in grasping and holding attention because it offered the thrill of fast responses to actions, a hectic pace of ill-considered, snapshot decisions, of immediate, easy judgements. Bright sounds and sights saturated the brain and readily outcompeted the slow, haphazard, muted three dimensions of the real world, eventually consigned to the shadows of a mere background reality.

The upcoming generation of the twenty-first century developed an unsurpassed working memory, short-term memory, higher IQ, fast reaction time and astonishing sensory-motor coordination, as the human brain obeyed its evolutionary mandate and obligingly adapted to the environment in which it was placed. As a consequence the skills honed by video-gaming and information-processing gradually edged out those other human talents, such as understanding and wisdom. The very experience of the cyber world was transformed from being a mere means to an end in itself, more exciting and important than anything else.

If the facts that splashed up on the screen before you had no deeper meaning any more, then by definition it didn't matter what you actually chose: the importance now was all in the strength of the image, the loudness and rapidity of the sounds at your fingertip touch command. Since the playing of the game, or the clicking on streams of facts started to provide all that was needed, the snap, fast judgements of what were now meaningless options, gradually lost their purpose.

So, as the twenty-first century moved into its middle years, the majority of humanity changed yet again. The early decades had witnessed the transformation of brains to efficient information-processing devices. People had, in effect, become computers themselves. But of course, they were humans and not machines: their responses were of no value in the infrastructural machinery of existence. Rather, it was the subjective inner experience, accumulated over a lifetime, of making those responses that distinguished the human brain from any synthetic counterpart. And because this latest generation no longer had time to think – to reflect, to question, to find fulfilment in finding meaning – the raw feelings, the sensation of immediate experience, became all that there was. Gradually, the thrill of making quick decisions gave way to the thrill of the increasingly vivid sensation in and of itself. The machine-like mind was transformed further, into the mindless and sensual joy of the infant. Feeling was paramount. There was no point in waiting, thinking, planning or remembering. Hedonism was at a premium.

Such was the scenario by the middle of the last century which can now be regarded as the end, yet also the start, of civilization. I still remember vividly the occasion when I was very small, of hearing the story of what transpired next. The evening had commenced as always. We were sitting round our table partaking of the evening meal. At the time, I did not realize how this everyday ritual in itself was actually an indication of how much our society had achieved, how much damage it had had to repair: dining together in a Family Unit had been reintroduced only as my great-grandfather's generation had taken matters back into their own hands. Until then people had increasingly eaten alone, like mindless animals, as and when their appetites demanded – merely snatching easy and quick tastes, grabbing strongly salty or sickly sweet experiences just as they grasped quick fixes, fast excitements from unreal worlds flashing around them in cyber-space. Eating had become again simply a matter of sensation and physiology, no longer of any greater symbolism or metaphorical significance in establishing relationships.

Three generations ago, the founders of our society had realized that we were losing this essential part of being human – of communicating not only in real time, but of having a fixed time, a narrative to the day, when an event such as eating had its own place and significance. Eventually they were able to reinstate the human practice recognized for millennia as a basic component of civilization: sharing bread, literally being companions. As well as the importance of the symbolism, our society has become acutely aware that communicating while eating is like communicating while walking. The natural rhythms, the acceptable reasons not to look someone constantly in the eye, the inevitable calming effect of the gentle rhythmic motions of cutting, lifting, chewing, swallowing, all contribute to optimal thinking and the development of ideas.

I still remember that evening meal so long ago. My father and mother were seated at each end of a dark-wood oblong table, myself in the middle. Then, as now, there was only one child to a Unit. My mother dark, my father fair and greying. My mother cupping her chin in her hands, elbows on the table, encouraging and half-smiling above the leftovers on her plate, gazing at my father. My father pensively sipping his water, playing for time. But the time had come: I stared from side to side, from one parent to the other, knowing that my father was about to say something especially important.

'Fred, you're getting to be a big boy now. You've had your Helmet for quite some time, haven't you?'

All I had to do was nod. The Helmet was my great pride. Being able to wear it to help me learn showed that I was growing up. But there was no reason to talk any more about it: my father had something new and different to say and I was already fascinated and waiting.

'Let me tell you a story, Fred. A true story. It's all about your great-grandfather, and how he helped make our world as wonderful as it is now. Once upon a time, when your great-grandfather was young, life was very different. Everyone had gradually stopped thinking, because they were having such exciting feelings all the time.'

'What's an exciting feeling, Father?'

'It's when you feel so funny inside that you cannot concentrate on learning things, or on what someone else is saying. When you put your Helmet on tomorrow, I'll make sure you understand more about how you have to be careful not to let strong feelings take you over. Otherwise, you'll no longer be Fred …'

'At least for a while,' he added with a nervous smile, conscious he had spoken too obliquely for my young logic.

'So great-grandfather stopped thinking because he had feelings, and so he stopped being who he was. Why?'

My father grinned widely, truly delighted with my comprehension and my curiosity.

'Your great-grandfather and his colleagues were not like everyone else. They realized that terrible, dangerous things were happening to people's brains, because of the way they were living. It had started without anyone really noticing sometime in the early part of the previous century. Screen devices were not restricted in those days to workplaces, as they are for us nowadays, but had gradually become the most important objects in more and more homes.'

I already knew all about screen devices. Ever since wearing the Helmet I had been learning how a long time ago computers comprised a fixed screen that you used to sit in front of, with separate keys that you tapped for control. This was the time my father was now describing.

. 'Fred, you must understand why we now forbid any cyber-devices for domestic or personal use. Even as far back as the second half of the twentieth century, an unprecedented way of life was emerging, one that was cyber-based. Increasing numbers of people spent greater amounts of time sitting alone, effectively living in a two-dimensional world devoid of touch and smell. But the audio and visual inputs were sufficiently fast and intense to keep them fixed for hour after hour in front of a screen, either to access information quickly, or to communicate with each other, or sometimes just to enjoy themselves by playing games or even by living out a second, fantasy existence.'

I couldn't really understand what my father was saying. I wasn't sure what a game or a fantasy was, but I wanted him to carry on with his story: so I just stayed silent and continued staring back at him.

'Things had already become really bad as computers evolved into being not just portable, but part of the person. Small hand-held devices that could fit in your pocket rapidly became an extension of who you were. These objects were known as 'phones' because one of their many functions enabled you to speak to anyone you liked over any distance, and to see them

7

on your little screen. But the big difference was that people could now walk around as they used the devices, so they started seeing them as extensions of their bodies in a way that the bigger computers could never be.

'By that time, almost everyone had started to venture away from just sitting in front of screens: until then the world had been compressed into the small two-dimensional space that excluded the world around them. But now they could navigate three dimensions as they listened to music or talked with each other. However, they needed their phone device with them at all times because they now interfaced with them rather than directly with other people. Gradually, as you've learnt from your Helmet sessions, it became possible to embed the silicon unit under the skin, and to activate it with voice commands.

'For the moment, Fred, your implant is programmed only to the voice patterns of your mother and myself: you haven't learnt enough yet to be able to control it. But when you're big, only your unique voice will control your implant. And you'll have a watch as well. Well, we call it a watch, just because it wraps round your wrist like the old devices for telling the time used to do. Really, the watch is a means for you to program, select, filter, analyze all the inputs and outputs from your implant: it is more detailed and powerful than the simple voice. Once you receive your watch, you must never, ever take it off, or switch it off.

'But back to how our society was created. By that time people were used to everything happening immediately: they had become used to strong sensory stimulations that made them excited, and they wanted to feel like that all the time. Your great-grandfather and his colleagues decided they needed to find a way where at least some people could be saved and continue to think. Because that is what we humans, as a species, do better than any other.'

My father reached for his water and sighed. He was dog-gedly doing his duty. I was to learn later how this was no casual, chance opportunity for my father to explain the history of our society: rather a clear, recognized rite of passage, a milestone in the prescribed development of a child was, indeed is, for the parent to tell The Story. In a year or two, I will be doing the same for my son, Bill. Although the learning of facts and the induction of understanding can be achieved with the Helmet, it is a story, a story told at an early stage that remains by far the most potent means of ensuring that it persists, unquestioned and unchallenged, in the interstices of the brain's neuronal connections.

'So what happened, Father?'

'They fled. They left behind a way of life that they saw had become a mere fragmented, distracted existence in which humans could not flourish, could not reach anywhere near their true potential. They came to this place, where we can have an existence in the real, three-dimensional world without any physical contact with different ways of life. We are not so far away, but there are enough mountains forming natural barriers to exclude the Others.'

The Others. That's what we called them because we held them in such contempt: they didn't merit a more detailed, descriptive name. They stood for everything that we had aspired to vanquish: which is why, as the great crisis of the twenty-first century had loomed, we had splintered off, as my father had recounted, and set up a society that would protect and preserve the most precious commodity we ever had, our minds.

It was the very concept of the individual mind that had first attracted me to study the brain. My real goal: to formulate the big idea for how to address what had been known for over a century as 'The Hard Problem'. What actually *was* consciousness? How was it generated in the brain and body? And, most urgent of all, what kind of evidence or type of experiment could ever be devised or even simply conceived to answer these questions satisfactorily?

When I was growing up I came to recognize that people were extremely diverse, despite all dressing in grey, and acting out similar behaviours at the same times of day, just as I did of course myself. But behind every pair of eyes, each individual was having a unique, first-hand, subjective experience in some kind of inner world that no one else could share. How could the brain achieve this feat? Surely we needed to treasure the human mind before anything else, and that would mean understanding it as well as we could.

For the first time in human history, we are building a society based not on an ideology, be it religious or political, that is imposed from outside, that forces each person to conform to a rigid pattern of behaviour. Yes, indeed, our way of life might well have been viewed by some historians from previous centuries as stereotyped, oppressive – 'totalitarian' they might even have called it – but it is actually the polar opposite. The whole point is that we don't wish to suppress individuality, but to harness it. The force that we revere derives not from outside, but is generated from within each one of us. It is that force, the unique thinking of each individual that is so utterly central. By devising an environment and lifestyle that is optimal for thought, we are actually maximizing the chances for individual human brain power to reach its full potential.

For example, by walking everywhere, by planning home bases near enough to work bases, risks of high arousal and overstimulation are reduced. The distance between each person's home base and work base has been calculated precisely to maximize an individual's particular potential for exercise, just as food intake is carefully preordained. Of course, the strict personalized dietary regime that we are all given from birth has in any case long eliminated the almost unbelievable fat deposits on the bodies of those now captured only on archive records – our predecessors a century or so ago. In addition the very act of walking sustains physical health further: but of even greater significance, motion itself, one step giving way to the next, enforces the all-important thought process. Ideally, the walking should be with someone else: someone else would readily provide the checks and balances to an argument, would keep you on a rigid, linear cognitive path. Being accompanied would remind you that you were never actually alone, that you should see your individual thought in relation to the wider context of the society in which you were integral.

As a scientist, however, I have a greater ration of solitary time, am allowed to walk back to home base on my own. My superiors recognize that completely new concepts, such as those required to understand the brain, usually incubate better when not subjected immediately to the ruthless and uncompromising interrogative dialogue that we all have to use now to perpetuate the all-important trains of thought. But since a scientific mind such as mine is already acknowledged to be one that is not particularly solipsistic, we are allowed more time than most on our own. So, more than anyone else, I can think on my own in innovative ways.

The man with the diamond-hard eyes and thin white beard paused the recording and sighed. He noted with approval, but not with surprise, that here Fred had been meticulous in his duty, in fulfilling the requirement for thought recordings on a daily basis. It was still the most effective way of gaining insight into how the minds of such key people were developing. He knew he would need to spend a protracted period of time going over and over Fred's story:

11

he needed to understand exactly when and why events had then taken such an unforeseen turn. By listening over and over again he became alert to every breathing space, every shift in voice tone that might indicate a drift, however small, away from acceptable trains of thought. So far everything was normal. Fred, a highly competent neuroscientist, was living out his daily life in an exemplary fashion and in his intellectual prime. The man resumed his task.

Of course, I've always known what a car was. But it is difficult to imagine from a first-hand perspective what it must have felt like actually being encapsulated in a hot little box that could travel through trajectories in real three-dimensional space at speeds so much faster than mere walking, while all the time layers of fat thickened in your blood and your blood pressure escalated. Similarly, it is equally difficult to comprehend at a visceral level those heavily used words from previous eras such as 'passion' and 'abandonment'. The old adjective 'sensational' would be an obscenity now. Loosely formed, unpredictable relationships, sustained at least initially by physical appearance, make me shudder to contemplate. So perhaps we should actually pity them really, those other people who are still living that way. The Others.

Chapter 2

ZELDA

Sunset: the deep gold light streams through the open door of the Dwelling, kissing the dreary little square of screen, then seducing my gaze away and up and outwards. I have no one to talk to, so here I am talking to myself, again. Pretending someone really is listening, that they like hearing my voice, especially on such a glorious night. The beauteous twilight: it should have been the time to sigh from the deck of a yacht, to slip away down cobbled Parisian byways to an illicit, shuttered encounter, to slow down and distance the daytime turmoil with the chilled sparkle of champagne. Time to change clothes, change priorities, change mindset, change your life: be someone different. Up until my grandparents' time, this slow descent of the day was magic. It was the limbo time, the day on hold, the bridge between work and play.

How odd such a distinction seems now, when 'work' no longer exists, and the word itself means so little to most people. So much has changed even across two generations: some events could never have been foreseen and overtook the world like a flash flood. The biggest shock was the mass exodus of the N-Ps. Even the silent articulation of those two simple initials in my mind is enough to make me pause – then quickly, immediately, think of something, anything else. I look away from the natural light, gushing through the oblong of the entrance, towards the artificial garishness of the inner recesses of the Dwelling, the nearest I have to a home.

Familiar figures are drifting around as usual, some dancing, some just wandering in dreamy circles. All young, all half wearing neon clothes, floating and still flimsy, embedded yet unfettered as they are with technologies so light as air: hair gleams bright and long, flicking and swishing around smooth faces that see nothing, seek out nothing. But I study one or two of them, tracking the meaningless trajectories weaving under the precise, perfect panes of the expansive dome: my mind can only wander.

Most transformations have been gradual, hardly noticed, but cataclysmically fundamental to the way we now live. As technology has increasingly provided for us, so first our muscle power and then our brainpower has become barely necessary for devising the means by which we are sheltered and fed. We remain permanently like children from earlier eras, when everything was given through love within a family. But now all is automated and – as befits the eternal infants we have become – beyond our control.

Food appears each day, delivered automatically in a quantity and of a type that complies with the read-out of our implants. My delicate garment is exquisitely smart and will change its ability to warm or cool me in conjunction with the read-out via the embedded thermo-sensors: it also has self-cleaning powers due to bacteria impregnated into every silky fibre of the fabric that survive, indeed flourish, by feeding on any dirt. So nothing needs to be changed or washed in the old way in response to changes in ambient temperature or daily use. No, no ancient ritual of laundry need delay me: my routine of endless stimulation and amusement is there just waiting to engulf me as soon as I speak or move, and as I wake. So, like everyone else here, my needs are actually simple and do not require a complex and straining economy to service them, like that which so bedevilled the previous century.

We no longer need to own objects: after all, what would we do with them? All anyone wants is to feel good, and the all-pervasive and invasive technologies ensure that we do: a multitude of devices, either implanted or embedded, incessantly monitors the continuous maintenance of physical health alongside endless cyber-experiences to fill otherwise empty heads. All physical work involved in food production and body maintenance is performed by automated services, in turn controlled and sustained by still more automation. No resources are needed for hospitals or schools or transport; no quaint, old-fashioned salaries required for providing obsolete goods or services. So why would we need or want to work?

But I alone remember when work was important, not just to earn the means for buying things that in turn enabled you to have experiences, but because it gave a sense of purpose and importance to life. My grandfather and grandmother had worked, before I was born. Although they had long stopped, as they had aged and society had no further use for such as they, they still spoke of the past with smiles and a slight shaking of their heads, in slow, gentle disbelief at how everything was transforming around them. They had been teachers, communicating with children in real time and face to face. It apparently gave them a sense of identity and their lives a meaning. My grandfather wasn't just the passive recipient of his senses as is the only destiny for us now: he could say he was something, someone.

'I was a teacher, Zelda.'

15

I was ten years old, and eager to learn more.

'I was a teacher, Zelda, as was your grandmother. Each day we left our home to go to school, returning at a fixed time every evening. We had to plan ahead, what we would tell the rows of eager faces in front of us, and how we could get important ideas across to them effectively. Often we were tired or angry or sad as, especially towards the end, we were given less and less opportunity, as our pupils spent increasing lesson time in front of a screen. And when we did have a chance to speak with them, even back then it was becoming harder to establish any rapport. But things got worse. Soon all learning was derived from the screen, and conducted in homes. Schools as such ceased to exist, and eventually learning in terms of internalizing and understanding information, turning it into knowledge – eventually, even that ceased to be necessary too. We predicted early on, your grandmother and I, that we wouldn't be working indefinitely. But we never imagined how things would turn out.'

The lines around my grandfather's mouth were turning down, his watery eyes looking at a distant, solid classroom where I could never go. Concepts such as 'rapport' and 'knowledge' were as incomprehensible to my young ears as 'work'. How much more to the current generation would these words seem like some strange, alien language? But 'imagination' – I knew all about that, I still had that. My generation was perhaps the last one that could use a word to conjure up an inner place, to look inwards at the scenes in which my grandparents had once lived, before the screen technologies had taken over everything, forcing us to look only outwards. Yes, of course, we learnt from screens back then, but we had also played, and listened to stories of adventures and love. I grew up just at the time when three dimensions of reality were in the last stages of phasing completely into the two offered by a screen: of course, mobile technologies long ago reversed that flat existence, at least bringing liberation from staring all the time at some two-dimensional oblong.

But back to now: I'm still stuck in that past time where science has contracted global space to the screen in front of me. No one else alive today would sit like this, interacting with a single, large, external device. Of course, 'screen' is a term that no longer describes a little grey object that you tap with fingertips or – even more primitive – control by pressing separate flat keys on a board in front of you. The old term stayed as the technology evolved beyond recognition from two dimensions, back once again to three, our control moving from fingers to voice.

As cyber-interaction became the preferred means of communication, and as the limitless need for personalization of inputs and outputs became more effectively met by clever, perceptive software, so the final and best 'computer' was one truly personalized to you, and indeed itself looked and spoke like a real person. The final generation of these were Talking Heads. This particular technology had started by displaying a head on the two-dimensional screen, to which you would address all commands, at first by a touch menu, but then by voice activation. The end result was a unique individual on any flat surface: your choice could be idealized to whatever face gave you most pleasure or, less often, perhaps representing those long dead, either real or fictional. These were less popular however as fewer and fewer people were aware of any historical or literary figure, or even less likely still, had strong personal attachment to anyone recently deceased.

But unlike everyone else, I remembered my dead family, my grandparents. Yet even though I could so readily have requested heads that looked and spoke like them, the prospect was unpleasant and unnerving. They belong to a different context, another time, somewhere I visit often, but not here. They would be out of place. Here is the present, the Dwelling where I live and where there are many Talking Heads. As you walk around the Dwelling, looking around, 3-D life-size Heads are in fact the most conspicuous and consistent feature, necks protruding from nothing, each waiting to talk, to display, to serve. They are there to provide easy, large-scale audio-visual displays that are not practical from the arm implant and the omnipresent Fact-Totum. Look around and you'll see some males, some females, some dark, some fair, some soft-spoken, some loud and laughing. All inevitably beautiful.

But no one talks to the talking heads because nearly everyone else hates to be still for so long, static in one position, eyes fixed on a flickering image displayed with a commentary by a disembodied Head: they prefer to jump and dance around in their enhanced three-dimensional personal space. But I still enjoy it – sitting and focusing on one central target reminds me of earlier days, before the mobile, embedded technologies took over. And I still miss the opportunity, now gone forever, of running my finger across the thin, hard screen, and of experiencing real touch, to make things happen. Of course, in the interactive, fast-paced world of the embedded and the smart, every moment rushes at you, leaves you breathless, drenches you in sensation: it drives you. You are no longer in control. This way, at least – with this older, gentler strategy of staying still in front of a screen, of deciding myself what happens next – here and now, I can pause for a moment and reflect on the sunset.

No one in the Grouping likes talking to anyone else because no one else has ever spent much time in naked face-to-face iterations that are fast, unpredictable and expose all of the real you, along with the possibilities of the sweaty palms, the squeaking voice, the hot blushing. No wonder no one would want to experience that nowadays if they didn't have to. But for me the mobilization of all of my body in three dimensions, engaging with and responding to other bodies twisting and turning, frowning, grimacing, grinning and guessing – for me, that would be wonderful.

My Grouping is just as you would expect. About ten of us could be said to be fully physically matured, with another ten still clearly growing: 'children' my grandparents would have called them. They in turn would have termed me 'old' by now, since I was born long before any of the others. In general, I think there must be very few people left nowadays who can be as 'old' as me, although it would be hard to know anything about those in other Groupings. No one needs or wants to communicate even through their implants with anyone else in different Dwellings. What could anyone say to you specifically, that might improve still further your ongoing experience? If anything, it could only distract and dilute, and therefore diminish. They have nothing to tell me, and there's nothing I can share with them.

While it is unlikely that I'm truly unique, it would be very hard to discover anyone else like me, other throwbacks from a bygone time, now tossed about in a vast sea of heightened emotions devoid of passions. How would we identify each other among so many who were not like us? An obvious problem would be that we all look the same age after all, homogeneous adults with perfect faces and pristine bodies. The still bigger issue of why I'm so unusual and isolated arises from those simple, irrefutable facts: my imperfect genes and my perfect face.

When I was young, I lived my life by looking ahead to the next stages, to the end of growing up, and to the end of each day. And after that, there would be the next new experience, always a tomorrow: I would tingle trying to imagine what might

19

happen, trying to plan ahead, to reach a goal. I watch the sunset blackening into the void of night and, increasingly, turn away from the emptiness of the present, to work my way backwards into the reassurance of the past.

Chapter 3

FRED

I am making this next recording at the end of another day in the lab, now that I am on my own at last. Tom, my assistant, had been staring at me as he always does, standing motionless waiting for me to address him. His silence was hard to ignore, and I wanted him gone.

The man with the thin white beard pauses briefly to add this new name to his list.

Tom's freckled white face yawned wide open, his short ginger hair, now in need of a further shearing, was a jarring element of colour in our monochrome world. I threw him a cursory glance.

'Time then, Tom.'

He blinked, then looked away, unable and unwilling to engage eye contact.

'Yes, sir.'

My peripheral vision registered his slight shape turn and exit the lab swiftly, leaving me to my domain of straight lines of benches, shelves, books. No curves to be seen, nothing here that is not linear. Everything direct, to the point. The evening sun has now also left with a final, fleeting imprint on the grey wall of the lab, translating it transiently into something to notice. So at last the time has come when I can stop trying to make sense of the neuroscientific information bombarding my brain. The experiments are finished until tomorrow: now I am alone, at least for a brief while. But, as always, I've been meticulous. Before I could take advantage of this time to think and talk, my final task has been to complete the log as always: exactly what has happened, what I have done; and what hasn't happened, what hasn't worked, and why.

For hours, I've been inspecting scans of the brain as they lay before me, trapped in a thousandth of a second of time: then occasionally I would zoom in to peer at single brain cells magnified to the size of my face, now reduced to abstract circles, strands, blobs. Image after image danced before my eyes, forming secretive, mocking patterns while I tried to put together a bigger picture across different space scales and over different time windows – that elusive bigger picture, of how the brain was working.

Following the procedure for which I'd been trained all my life, my priority was to focus on documenting the mental excursions up and down each blind alley that were leading me first sideways, then perhaps a little forward, imperceptibly towards answers. Tom and I had spent all today, as for every day, posing hypothetical scenarios that would test different theories, feeding them into our powerful informatics systems so that the range of possible outcomes was spread out before us almost instantaneously. But such speed and automation could never diminish or alleviate the most important aspect of the task: piecing together what it all could mean. But, now, at last I am freed from the remorseless process of inspection: instead I can legitimately use time and space just to look inwards.

Our people recognized very early on in the crisis that we had to harness technology rather than be consumed by it. As a special and personal testimony to this turbulent, transformational moment in our history, I have treasured always a missive my father sent to me when I was small, on precious paper, in the old-fashioned way. It tells a story that has become as familiar to me as breathing: an amplification, an anecdotal example often repeated, of the wider issue: the Exodus. I keep this single, delicate sheet safely in the lab, and I'll read it out now:

Dear Fred,

I'm writing to you about something that means a lot to me, and that one day will be equally significant to you. By setting it down in this antiquated fashion, I'll know it will remain as a special document, easily distinguishable from anything else. It's important that you always remember that your great-grandfather was one of the first. He was one of the first who realized that he and anyone who wished to preserve their humanity, would have to leave. What triggered this revelation? It was a little thing in itself, but as is often the case, minor events can have major consequences. It happened one morning when he decided to go for an early walk. It was mid-summer so the day was bright and full of potential. As usual, your great-grandfather was enjoying taking the air clean and deep into his lungs, escaping from the screens and mobile devices and the bleeps and buzzers that he was finding increasingly intrusive and ubiquitous. Unusual perhaps at that time, especially for someone as young as your grandfather was then, for him not to see the point of the cyber-lifestyle: but he had been born into a family of philosophers, and so his early life had been spent with his parents' colleagues surrounding him in rarefied, abstracted views. As the press of the cyber-culture became more strident, so your great-grandfather and his friends became an ever more close-knit group. As the world grew increasingly instant and literal, so significant numbers of scholars and intellectuals became attracted to this circle: but still they were relatively few in number, and by then viewed as a very strange minority because they questioned everything and seemed incapable of relaxing.

However, your great-grandfather did find fulfilment in other ways, not in having fast-paced fun, but simply in slowly interacting with the real world in all its three-dimensional, natural complexity by walking. He claimed it helped him think. Anyway, early on one particular morning, he encountered one of them, an Other. This Other had become the norm, the type of person you were most likely to see, even that long ago. Heading straight towards your great-grandfather, the Other didn't see him. But your great-grandfather noticed the figure immediately. Drawing nearer, he could make out another male of about the same age: a young man immersed in the usual other-world, looking everywhere and nowhere, singing to himself, half dancing. They drew closer. Your great-grandfather was a stubborn man, keen to prove things, if only to himself. So he kept walking in a straight line, even though the Other clearly hadn't noticed him. Inevitably, they collided. But despite planning this, your great-grandfather couldn't have predicted what would happen next.

The Other finally registered what was happening in reality. 'Piece of shit,' he spat as he focused on the silent figure in front of him. And then he drew a knife and casually, apparently very slowly, went to stab your great-grandfather. As a reflex, your great-grandfather raised an arm, which caught the blow. It was a deep enough wound for blood to spurt, for your great-grandfather to fall to his knees in pain – but luckily not fatal. The Other simply shrugged, then resumed his trajectory, swaying away, once again oblivious to the world around him. That was the moment when your great-grandfather knew he couldn't continue living with these kinds of people. All around him his colleagues, the minority with a similar outlook to him, were relating comparable experiences. There were escalating numbers of deaths – murders, actually. Bloodstains were increasingly flaunted on people's clothes, unwashed, as signs of status. People lay collapsed in the street, and no one cared but just stepped round them. Ever larger numbers carried knives, women as well as men, children as well as adults. Hostility towards anyone you met had become the default. Everyone seemed angry, and if provoked this low-grade aggression flared more readily into what had once been called psychotic behaviour: gratuitous violence for no obvious reason. This is why the idea of the Exodus gained momentum.

Always remember this incident Fred. Always remember your great-grandfather and his colleagues. They made you and I who we are.

Your Father.

Every time I read this letter, I feel an affirmation, just as my Father had intended. He is still alive, but in accordance with the way things are meant to be, I hardly ever see him, apart from perhaps at the Rallies. But back to my main point …

So, that early generation had made a stand, and then escaped. And now we were flourishing. We put cyberization in its rightful place, extirpated it from the home and channelled it only into work. Our people contribute to a true literal knowledge economy that makes our society perfect. Everything each of us does is directed solely to the goal of nurturing ideas, be it from informatics to education, to the continuous improvement of DNA and quantum computing. I am particularly lucky being able to spend my time in the most exciting work possible as a neuroscientist, exploring the mind.

Just now I closed my logbook, feeling, if not affection, at least a sense of familiarity combined with awe. How many scientists for hundreds of years now had finished a day as I have just done? Most times, the feeling is that of a relentless journey, knowing where you wanted to be but not quite finding a direct route. But that notion of a quest, of finally, eventually understanding incrementally more with regard to the objects, events and people around you, was what drew you onwards into the next day, the future. And how comforting the unbroken thread of continuity with the past, not just in the enduring scientific mentality but even at the simple level of physical objects.

We now realize that the twenty-first-century silicon pervasion had actually been a perversion of human nature: so we have come full circle. In the lab we use logbooks with precious paper pages and write in them with pens like those used at the beginning of the twenty-first century, and recognizable as such even in the dusty eras of the start of real scientific experiments centuries before. They are worth the huge cost. Books, logbooks especially, are important. Compared to the cheap, casual power of the silicon technologies, these exotic objects cannot be falsified: their contents cannot be reversed. Because they defy time, are unchanged and unmodified, they have significance in a way that the constantly updated, ever-changing words and images flung through cyber-space never could. When I have written a word, a sentence, it is indelible: even crossed out there is never a simple un-happening, an un-doing. That crossing-out exists forever.

In the past, though, books such as these would have told a different story: every day, right up to the middle of the last century, logs recorded real experiments conducted in real time.

When I first started in the lab, I was fresh from my advanced science training. After so much time wearing the Helmet that is a key part of our education system, I was keen to have my head bare, and to be in a real work environment. But Hodge, my supervisor, had shaken his head,

'You're in a real lab now, Fred, but real experiments that take hours, days, even months, are thankfully a thing of the past.'

How did they have the patience, our predecessors, to repeat the same procedure day after day, or to conduct a study where the final result couldn't be known for months? And those early twenty-first-century records report endless small-scale catastrophes – equipment failure, spillages, contaminations – all indicating a day, a week, even a month, had been wasted. Even when the procedure took its course as intended, the frustration had seeped through the passive, impersonal prose: that the experiment had 'failed', the idea being tested could not graduate into reality. Nothing to do but try again tomorrow, to continue on your quest.

Now all experiments are virtual. We have no spillages, no human error, and hundreds of hypothetical procedures can be performed in a day. Actions are faster because they no longer need to occur. And yet ... and yet, thoughts still progress at the same atavistic zigzag. Even though the experimental scenarios with their complex interactive parameters can now be foreseen rapidly in silicon, the thoughts that prompted them and the interpretations they inspire – namely, the part played by the human, the scientist, by me – are down on paper. The precious logbooks are as unique and personal as the individual scientist who writes in each one: they are real and – even more important – effectively an extension of one's own brain. These solid little objects fit into the way of things, *our* way of thinking and the way we live nowadays.

'You're here not because you need to plod through a tedious methodology, but because you can now access the latest technology that would be way too dangerous to have in the home.'

I knew that Hodge didn't mean that the powerful DNA, quantum and neurocomputers that we now use literally endangered life: but they could endanger the human mind. We were all too aware of what could happen if the human mind had unfettered opportunity for continuous cyber-living: it could be utterly destroyed, and almost was.

Such a negative and now impossible prospect, however hypothetical, should be terminated immediately. I shall carry on recording while I walk back to Home Base. I pass my arm quickly over the exit panel of the lab door, and it emits a soft bleep on opening. The double security system will now also have a timed check, registered at the door. So that is me logged, leaving, just as I had in turn logged on ancient paper my observations of the chemical traffic down the highways and byways of neuronal connections in the brain, documenting what caused them to twist and turn, how they pushed the mind on to change every moment. I monitor a microscopic, internal system just as a colossal external system monitors me. Chemicals, neurons or people, all of these function within an ever larger context of cause and effect. The process and principle is the same, irrespective of the vast difference in scale.

All the other scientists, along with Tom, and now me, are leaving at the same time: we have no real choice. Not that we had ever contemplated any alternative to the established pattern of laboratory work. The lives of scientists are like those of everyone, completely ordered to ensure no unpredictability. None of us, of course, believes in chance or luck or accidents: but we are fully aware that unless life has as close to zero degrees of freedom as possible, then the consequence of the mere flap of a butterfly wing – as had been explained well over a century ago – could cascade into multiple and momentous unexpected events. No: if we are to focus, to journey in an efficient, linear direction and to achieve, then we must eliminate meaningless distractions which would dissipate precious time before we were back on course.

My life, as for everyone, is lived according to reassuringly prescribed steps, to maximize thought and fulfilment. Each day has its stages, so that everyone knows what everyone is doing at any one moment. My colleagues and I are currently transitioning to the next stage, obviously marked by the change in location, as evening grows nearer. We all walk slowly: why should we rush? We are never late because nothing unexpected could ever occur to prevent us being on time. And, in any case, each time has its own value. In particular, walking time is important to aid thought processes, developing and consolidating ideas without the press of specific outside stimulation from the data on which we concentrate during an experiment.

The grey interiors of the Institute give way to the external beige of the building, and the darker grey slabs that spread everywhere, as I set off on my short journey back. Hard to think of a time when people didn't walk everywhere, but used cars. Terrible to contemplate the rape of the environment that they had caused, and the carbon-based apocalypse they had almost triggered. But the problem wasn't just environmental; it was also biomedical. The obesity, the sluggish hearts, the hideous mental strain and excitement with the unpredictability of a driving experience – all so vigorously antithetical to what we believe in now. Now the world is muted, hushed and monochrome. Now we all turn inwards with reverence for the most important part of our lives, the key to everything: ideas.

I glance around at my colleagues. We are of varying sizes and ages, but unlike in the last century, we are all healthy and with normal-range body-mass index: the regulated food technologies are doing a good job. Irrespective of gender or time of life, our clothes are uniform: shades of grey, slack and soft. Again, no chance of distraction from physical discomfort, unnecessary colours or trite attempts at expressions of superficial individuality. We gesture at small, closed smiles to each other as we file out. There is no reason to talk at this precise moment. On other occasions, at other times of the day, we would be rapidly exchanging dialogues in order to validate and evaluate ideas. But our research is now suspended until tomorrow, and there is therefore nothing else to say. On the way to our various Home Bases, the expected pattern would be to form taciturn groups of two or three in case some thought or suggestion needed feedback, to be kept on track. But I relish being on my own.

The man with the diamond-hard eyes and thin white beard leans forward slightly, breathing more heavily, paying close attention.

Chapter 4

ZELDA

How much nicer it is to spend time in the past, thinking out loud about it now so that it is more real than the actual present. Back then most people would have thought this the behaviour of a mad woman. Now no one cares.

When I was seventeen, life stretched out in front: but still back then something had to be done for, and to, me and my contemporaries.

'What genetic treatment would you like, Zelda?'

My grandmother was calm and her voice was slow and soft: we were discussing my life. My grandfather put his arm round her: they formed a unit, caring and complicit. I think back to the faces that I looked up to when I was small: they were incredible, truly unbelievable as real people. Sagging folds of flesh draped around what could still just be discernible as noses, eyes, necks. My grandparents looked like this, both with corrective glasses and thin lips, both grown to resemble each other, leaning into each other, almost indistinguishable and de-sexed by the passing years.

My grandfather explained it all. 'We want the very best for you, but whatever happens, things are going to be hard. Not just for you, but for all of you young ones. Everything is changing so fast: we would never have imagined it could ever get to this, when we were your age. I suppose we weren't surprised when the schools shut down, that everyone stopped learning on their computers and just played games instead. But of course we are not medical people, and we were fortunately never seriously ill, so we just didn't keep up with what the doctors and scientists were up to. So suddenly, Zelda, here we are. Your generation is the last not to benefit from pre-implantation genetic screening, repair and improvement. It means everyone, even those just a little younger than you, will live much longer, be healthier and –' my grandfather looked me fixedly in the eye – 'will carry on looking much younger while you age normally.'

So there I was, seventeen years of age, and genetically imperfect. Genetic profiling before birth was rolled out wholesale for the first time while I was growing up with my grandparents. I, and what would have been called my generation, had only narrowly missed out on having our genomes screened, remedied and enhanced before being implanted in the womb as a fertilized egg. This procedure means that all potential diseases to which an individual might be prone have been prevented by the new bespoke pharmacogenomic treatments, so that early or slow death is truly a thing of the past. Everyone is born medically perfect and there is hardly any time spent after birth correcting the caprices of nature. The complete dominance of IVF makes such safeguards for longevity not just easier, but automatic and mandatory. Yes, the genetic technologies have made life so different from when I was born, when my grandparents were recognized as such in the way they lived, when they had worked, and how they looked.

At seventeen, the original face with which I had been born, was good enough. I was pretty enough that in my grandparents' heyday I would probably have attracted some men, eventually a husband. But like everything else, courtship, bonding, relationships or whatever we called them, were changing quickly. Long-term partnerships, such as my grandparents enjoyed, were already becoming rare. It was routine technology by this time not just to freeze, but also to thaw, a woman's eggs. But because of my unscreened pre-birth history, my un-vetted eggs were not considered optimal for either genetic extraction or IVF. Then again, because egg harvesting was still an uncomfortable process, this system wasn't universally adopted. My grandparents still hoped, while I was growing up, that I might find a life-partner and be happy, as they were. They talked about it constantly with me. Perhaps that's the real reason I'm so different now from everyone else.

My parents were killed when I was small, so, unlike my friends and contemporaries, I was exposed to a different, older view of life, one that few of my age would have experienced so vividly and personally, albeit second hand. Genetically imperfect I might be, but as I grew I still dreamt of finding my perfect partner as I witnessed daily the true intimacy of my grandparents.

And then, just a few years later, there was another great breakthrough. Any cell of the body could be deprived of half its genetic content, to become therefore just like a sperm or egg. Once fake sperm and eggs could be made in this way, from any cell, irrespective of age or sexual orientation or gender of the cell donor, then anyone could have a baby with anyone else – be they same sex, or not yet fully grown. So the Universal IVF Program really took off, avoiding the need for actual sperm or eggs to generate the genes. All that was needed then was for a female to donate an egg that would be emptied, and another woman to contribute incubation in their womb. Since neither activity now required either of these donors to have perfect genes and, more significantly, since such donors were now given priority on all gene-technology upgrades, there was no shortage of those providing eggs and wombs. But not me: I was seventeen and intoxicated by my grandparents' romance. I decided to donate nothing, but to wait for the real, the best.

What was I waiting for? Someone like my grandfather to offer me the kind of life, the love story that he had given my grandmother. But no such man existed any longer. Paradoxically, as everyone became physically more perfect in both their health and their looks, they shrank in fear from physical contact. Sadly, the only times people touched each other was when they were attempting to inflict pain, in violent arguments. Communication or, more simply interaction, found expression in the lowest common denominator, the simplest language of all: physical attack. Everyone began to find even direct face-to-face conversation, and especially touching with their hands, so difficult that the all-embracing physical act of genital interaction became unbearable and unthinkable.

Sex, in my grandparents' time, had been one of the most reliable ways for 'letting yourself go', and for 'blowing the mind' – the ecstasy of the 'little death' as some once called the climax. But the thrill of cyber-activities meant that raw excitements were there for the taking so much more readily and unconditionally. Then came the biggest upheaval, arguably since humans ever evolved, when the Universal IVF Program gave us all the freedom to reproduce without committing the sex act. The growing cultural distaste for sex could now be appeased by removing the final reason for it. At last, the complete termination of romance, love, marriage: but I'm still trapped in the past.

I was seventeen and sitting in front of my loving grandparents, aware now that people were not only learning less as they thrilled to cyber-fun, but were preferring to do so on their own. Fewer men would want a real, three-dimensional woman, and those who did would look to the screen for their level of expectation: they would prize sensuality and physical perfection. They would look at those girls just a little younger than me but with perfect genes, who were destined not to have old faces.

The old faces of my grandparents were expectant. They truly cared about what I was feeling, what I wanted to do, and what I should do. Every time now that I remember how it felt to have people care about you, a deep lump forms inside me, of sadness and sickness. But then, at seventeen, I took it for granted, thinking instead about my options, or rather the one option – that of having cosmetic enhancement. I beamed brightly back at my grandparents, voicing the need to make up for my unbeautiful genes.

'I'll have the procedure on my face as a priority. I gather it takes some time, so I should enrol almost immediately. I would so love to find someone and have children, just like you did.'

My grandparents glanced at each other, knowing even then that I was being foolish. But they wanted me to be happy, and that meant being like everyone else – which increasingly meant looking as young and perfect as everyone else. The way the world was going, I wouldn't have work, or a husband, but instead would have continuous happiness. So, even now, when I am older, I can stare into the mirror and see a normal adult female human. The face that stares back at me is smooth and even, perfectly proportioned. Thanks to Dr Grant.

Dr Grant was one of the last of the traditional, mid-twenty-first-century type of doctors. Even then, telemedicine – treatment from a distance, with surgery or drugs administered by robotic arms – meant that technicians and engineers had started to replace medical doctors. And, as informatics databases grew more reliable, accurate and extensive, so the automation of medicine proceeded rapidly. The end of professional medical practitioners occurred when the Genetic Optimization Program became established with the shift to bespoke medicines, administered through molecular biologists, to cater for individual genomes. As a result, fewer people actually succumbed to illness: eventually, no one needed to be treated.

Dr Grant, though, knew nothing of this, could not foresee how he might be the last of the line, as he explained to the seventeen-year-old me what he would do. His consulting room was harshly white and bright, like his teeth. But his eyes were black, inscrutable and professional. His smile didn't reach his eyes as he explained, in a flat, factual tone, what he had explained to others many times before.

'Since you are genetically imperfect, it would be best to focus on your genes. But you have 100 trillion cells in your body, so it would be impossible now to access the genetic material in every one. Of course, that's exactly what we're able to do when, before fertilization, we can target the cells that have had half their genetic content extracted so that, in reproductive terms, they are the equivalent of a sperm or an egg. But, as I've said, that's way too late for you. That's why you're now defective, of course, and we must lower our sights to more local targeting.'

I stared back into the black holes of his eyes. No, this man was far from the one I was seeking. But still, I remember the conversations with my grandparents when I was small: I think I would still like to know what it must have really felt like, not just to have someone's body joined into yours, but actually to join minds too.

'So what will you do, Doctor?'

'Well, we've known for a long time now that the reason why sperm and eggs, and indeed cancer cells, do not age, is because the genes are protected. And, if they are protected, they can still work to keep the cell in top condition. All cells in the body have coat hangers as it were, for the genes, the chromosomes. Each and every chromosome has a cap on the ends. The cap is called a telomere, and the longer it is the better. As you age, the telomeres shorten, rather like frayed shoelace ends, and this eventually leads to degradation of genetic material within the cell.'

I tried hard to imagine an old-fashioned coat hanger – my grandparents still had some – but a fraying one, fraying like an equally old-fashioned shoelace which I had also seen in my grandparents' home? No, the two images together just did not coalesce.

'But apart from cancer cells and sperm and eggs in your body, all cells will soon age as the telomeres deteriorate too, so that the genes become damaged. The only reason why cancer cells and gametes, that is eggs and sperm, do not age in this way is thanks to a special enzyme, telomerase, which only they possess and which keeps the telomeres nice and long.'

I thought I could see what he was about to suggest. 'So you will be able to insert telomerase into the cells in my face?'

'Exactly.'

'Will it take long?'

'Yes.'

'Will it be painful?'

'We shall try and reduce discomfort to a minimum.'

It hurt very much and it took a long time. The technique involved mixing the genes for promoting telomerase with small metal particles; in my case it was tungsten that was then fired from the equivalent of a kind of medical gun, at high speed, into small numbers of cells in turn. Other women, I later found out, gave up before the end of the treatment, some because they couldn't bear the pain, and others because they didn't have the patience: for many, it was both. But, unlike them, I had a dream that made it worthwhile. It was even worthwhile to have stem-cell implants in my body: stem cells also have telomerase, and they have long been known to become whatever kind of cells we wish, when placed in the right context and treated the right way. I was willingly swept along on tidal wave after wave of medical advance: I now look and feel ageless, am ageless. I'm the same, or at least I look the same, as everyone else in the Dwelling, so long as I forget my past.

But now I am alone. Quite a few who had also put so much hope on the new treatments had gained infections from doctors less skilled than Dr Grant, and did not carry on to the end of their treatment. Others grew depressed and anxious as they aged in a world of ageless young. Some killed themselves as worthless and useless due to their age and appearance. Most didn't have good enough genes to survive as long as the slightly younger ones who were genetically screened. But I was different, genetically imperfect perhaps, but good enough and healthier than many. As they dropped away, I stayed the same, constant and consistent, as the world whirled around me with everyone else on the move.

No, it's not odd that I'm still looking as I do at a time in my life when, in my grandparents' era, I would have been their age, perhaps a grandparent too, with my current thoughts of finding love regarded as sad and silly and undignified. But now we are all treated under the hormone extension program, so that no one ever experiences that ancient threat to the primeval female identity, once known as the menopause. And the program is so important, not so much to enhance reproductive potential – which no longer needs authentic sperm and eggs anyway – but rather to ensure that we all continue to look ideal.

Treated genes or treated cells, everything is optimized. The rationale is that to feel good, you must look good when you glance in the mirror. Perhaps that's true: but we have come on a long and complex journey if so. In any case, we now have perfect faces and bodies, not to attract a mate by the visible signs of good genes, but rather the other way round: we have modified genes in order to have perfect physical appearances for no one other than ourselves.

The old distinctions of reproductive status, appearance, health, and even work, that would have previously demarcated the generations, with the different stages of life, no longer apply: they have disappeared. We are homogenized across generations. Even our faces reflect less of the individual lurking inside: no longer are we contorting in our personalized grimaces, raising our eyebrows in a characteristic manner and frequency, smiling at someone in a special way. Devoid of exaggerated imperfections – the large nose, the crooked smile, the scar, the moles, the puffy eyes – we are all standardized.

We are also similar in size: there was a terrible phase of obesity in the past, when the screen-technologies were sedentary. But now the norm is to be on the move as attention span is so much shorter than I remember it used to be. The hyperactivity, the endless running after a new millisecond of experience, every moment – this incessant contraction of muscle after muscle throughout the body translates into the wiry, the jumpy, and thus the thinner shape of the younger ones. They take food as and when they want: but there is so much else to do, and sustained eating for more than a minute or two soon loses its novelty. Perhaps it's that which, if anything, belies my longer life: my slight plumpness due to the indulgence of the old screen way of living, and my sedentary disposition.

But, in general, we are homogenized as individuals as we converge physically. Are we converging inside too? I think that must be the goal, if there was indeed some kind of plan – but I don't think there can be. Who could have planned for this to happen, and why? Perhaps it's just the next stage in evolution:

39

having devised ingenious technology, we have evolved into interacting with it, being part of it, rather than part of a society. There was the terrible transitional phase of clumsy, inexperienced interaction that amounted to the easiest and least ambiguous form of communication: simple, mindless aggression that was laden with excitement and the thrill of the moment, when hurting someone no longer meant anything. At least now, if we are on an accelerated evolutionary path, we have moved on to some newer and better stage. Now we are so much in our own space, so in tune with our smart devices, that there is nothing to be angry about. We have everything, all the time. But even though we ignore each other, we all do the same thing in our isolation, and all look the same, identical in a way that our individual minds surely never can be. Unless, of course, we were to devise and live in an environment that is mind-less. I look around me and once again, as so many times before, acknowledge to myself that is indeed what has happened.

Chapter 5

FRED

Ever since I could remember, that single word 'consequences' has suffused every moment of my existence. Nothing real can be erased or reversed: linear chains of cause and effect make up existence. Time moves in one direction only, with everything in sequence, following on in order, whether it is a sentence, or the trajectory of one's life. Thinking is everything, and thinking always, *always* involves a sequence of words, sentences, narrative. And just as with a sentence, so my life, anyone's life here, is compelled to follow the clear guidelines that we have always known, and known not to question.

For example, the Family Unit: the very mention brings to mind Tarra's grey, reflective eyes and pale skin.

The man with the diamond-hard eyes and thin white beard does not need to pause, but emits a deep sigh.

Just like everyone of my age and stage in life, I was allocated a breeding partner with whom I would have one child. Tarra was within my age band, had been matched with me for her brainpower quotient, and after that the consequences were

41

inevitable. A formal partnership was the only option: it was the unquestioned rule. Random, physical contact outside of the Family Unit was truly a thing of the past, at least for those of us privileged enough to live a meaningful life in a society that optimizes the human condition.

Tarra is a scientist too, engaged on further improvement of food intake, personalizing diets with ever more accuracy: the calories and balance of essential nutrients are attuned with an individual's energy expenditure on a constantly read-out basis that will eventually be incorporated into the centralized database held on each of us. This information is continuously updated, and read out to, the embedded ID arm implant inserted at birth.

Tarra has a demanding job that transcends single disciplinary boundaries by drawing on detailed knowledge of both physiology and silicon technologies. But she is completely competent and capable and I am very proud of her. We are perfectly matched as intellectually compatible, to enable the most productive conversation. This optimization for dialogue is the most crucial factor in the selection of breeding partners. Physically, it is of no relevance whatsoever whether outward appearance conforms to long-outdated notions of 'beauty'. So long as each individual is healthy, it is only what is behind the eyes that counts, not their colour or size. But the other very important issue is to be matched in age, so there is no confusion of generations under one roof: we all have to journey through our distinctive stages in life, of child, parent, grandparent and great-grandparent, and to optimize each very different stage.

It is vital that both sexes within each generation are of a similar age, so that each breeding pair has the greatest probability of living and dying together within a similar, congruent time-frame. A Family Unit always only consists of a contemporary breeding pair and a single child, so the upbringing of that child is as controlled as possible. Hence the older generation will live together as a couple, far apart from their grandchildren. It is the best way: mine and Tarra's intentions are to raise our son Bill and develop our minds for the benefit of our greater society. Other relations with older generations are even more peripheral than with work colleagues. We just do not have the time or the need to see our own parents any more: Bill will have a perfect start in life.

The Helmet is, for all children, the first big step in one's life narrative. I actually worked on developing the latest generation of these essential devices that enable us, literally, to shape the minds of the next generation. The idea of merely monitoring brain activity is far from new, with the earliest forerunner having been devised several centuries previously. In those days, electrodes placed on someone's head had simply picked up the patterns of 'EEG', the electrical waves generated by large networks of brain cells that could be, in much muted form, detected through the layer of skull bone as electrical signatures of different levels of gross brain activity, crude levels of arousal.

Since these different patterns reflect various states of arousal, it was relatively straightforward to specify that only certain patterns, certain low levels of excitement, would enable the activation of a cursor on an old-fashioned computer screen. The feedback to the child of what kind of arousal level was effective, and what was not, soon ensured that children with socially unacceptable levels of hyperactivity would readily condition themselves to a maximally receptive frame of mind.

Before long, all teaching facilities were characterized by rows of garishly coloured, primitive Helmets, allowing for this kind of mind constraint. In those days bright colour still counted, before we realized just how important it was, especially in the early years, to reduce sensory distraction to a minimum and ensure that even at an early age the correct cognitive values were installed. But that was just the beginning. We wanted and needed to progress further: if the output of the brain could be monitored, then perhaps eventually it could also be manipulated. But, at the time, the technology was limited because events in the brain were impossible to track with a timescale and sensitivity commensurate with nature. Yes, for ages, non-invasive 'brain imaging' had been used routinely in labs and hospitals as far back as the turn of the twenty-first century. But not only were the time-frames for capturing what was happening at least a thousand times slower than what was *actually* happening, but also the space scales were a thousand times larger than would be needed to see the functioning of single brain cells within a network.

It was particularly frustrating, not being able to monitor specific brain events in real time, or to detect spatially the interaction between individual brain cells. All this was long before I was even born: but Hodge, who came from an earlier generation, recalled being told by his then supervisor of the frustration for scientists of those bygone days. The real challenge was that it had been known for many years that the brain had evolved to adapt exquisitely to the environment: so-called 'plasticity'. Indeed, the human brain has a superlative capacity for this plasticity, which is why we have always occupied more ecological niches than any other species on the planet. We learn from experience: and if you had individual experiences, then that was what made you the individual you were. Hodge's forerunners had spent much of their time with animal brains, and dead brain slices, fascinated at how the delicate, tree-like branching connections between single brain cells so quickly and accurately reflected the adaptations to every moment of conscious experience. But how to monitor that as it happened in real time in the human brain?

That was the great breakthrough: our new technology of Helmet brain-imaging on a space and timescale of real brain

44

cell activity. At last we could actually see the individual brain cells hooking up with each other, at the level of each and every connection, 'synapse', as it actually happened, as the learning process was taking place. I remember so well the first time I saw this process during my early research: only shortly after I was myself becoming habituated to spending the entire day Helmet-free and bare-headed. I was at last properly trained and in need of no further direct instruction, with an understanding that was now all my own – just as it was meant to be.

In those days Hodge had been darker, and his face smoother, without the grey lines that now streak his cheeks and forehead, dragging down his eye sockets and scraping lines from the sides of his nose to his mouth. But back then he almost smiled, almost warmed you as he spoke,

'You of all people, Fred, will know the value of stimulating the brain directly through the Helmet, of improving and speeding up the learning process: and when I say learning, well, I don't just mean delivering the correct responses when required, I mean real understanding. The sort of understanding you now have, have had ever since your first Helmet was set even to minimal mode enhancement. But now … now, Fred –' Hodge leant towards me, pushing the cropped black hair impatiently and pointlessly back from his high white forehead – 'Now for the first time we can see it, actually see it …'

The subject was a small girl of about the usual age for her first fitting, around thirty months. Her name was Mary and, like all our children, she sat silent and calm as the adults spoke in hushed cadences over her head. Her chubby little pink hands lay resting downwards and still on her lap, her grey smock folded round her like a blanket. Hodge knelt down in front of her, an unusual gesture, and spoke with a softness I'd never heard before.

'Mary, today is a very special day and you're a very special girl.'

Mary dutifully met Hodge's gaze and waited, as would be expected, for him to continue.

'Today, Mary, you're going to have your Helmet on. It will help you become very, very clever. And we are going to watch you becoming clever. So you have to be very good and do exactly what we say.'

For the first time, Mary seemed to come to life and nodded her short, curly brown head. How much was she actually understanding? Almost in slow motion, Hodge reached to the bench at his side and picked up what looked like a conventional Helmet. As always, it was as thin as eggshell, as bright as quicksilver. Its secret, its prototype uniqueness, could not be discerned here, but rather in the touch screen that Hodge was operating, and which suddenly burst into coloured life, meaningless, mercurial rainbows racing and chasing each other.

'Just setting baseline calibrations.'

Then, at the same unhurried pace, he approached Mary once more.

'Lift up your chin, there's a good girl.'

With surprising gentleness, Hodge placed the Helmet over Mary's curls, fastening it into place. Returning preoccupied to the screen, he touched and touched again with deft movements that knew exactly where they were going. Then he stood back and gestured silently for me to observe. Displayed in bright and high definition was an image I knew well, could have recognized anywhere: a synapse, the thin gap between two brain cells. At the bottom left of the screen was the rounded, not quite spherical main part of a brain cell, the cell body: but more arresting still were the bifurcating branches growing out and up, filling most of the screen like a tree. This was where connections would be made, where other cells would reach out and make contact, or rather stop just short, creating the tiny space across which the all-powerful chemical messengers, the transmitters, would burst. How many times I had stared at this, at a brain cell. But always as a static, second-hand image. This one was different; it was alive and at work right now, inside Mary's brain.

'Teach her something very simple, Fred, just a quick single fact.'

I moved to face Mary, and knelt down as Hodge had done. I wasn't used to children at that time, and lacked his ease.

'Hello, Mary, shall I tell you my name?'

Mary looked back at me, even at such a young age seeming surprised at the banality of the question. A breathy voice, almost a whisper: 'If you want.'

'It's Fred. Fred is my name, just like Mary is your name. My name is Fred. Fred. I am Fred.'

At last I stopped. Surely that was enough?

I looked over at Hodge and he nodded, again silently, and gestured, indicating that once again I should look at the screen. He was almost smiling – at least, his lips were drawn outwards.

'Just look.'

And there on the screen was the most astonishing sight I'd ever seen. There was movement on one of the branches: Hodge zoomed in for a closer view. Sure enough, a tiny protuberance was growing out of the branch, a minuscule little spine. I knew this was the beginning of a new synapse, that now an incoming cell could make a new contact on to the spine, that this was part of the learning process, the 'plasticity' of the nervous system. But never before had I, or anyone, witnessed it in real time, inside the head of a living and conscious human being. This breakthrough would make a real difference in how we taught with the Helmet: now, for the first time, we had precise and immediate feedback as to how a young brain was learning. Soon after that the imaging technique was miniaturized rapidly, standardized for the instruction sessions, adopted as a matter of course to enable the read-out of the brain cells of the child as they absorbed information. But then came the biggest advance of all. We could reverse cause and effect.

Now that we could pinpoint the actual moment and brain location where an adaption, a learning of a fact, took place, we could stimulate that place directly at precise coordinates through the Helmet, to an accuracy within a thousandth of a millimetre: we could now actually drive the neuronal connections as we wished, while all the time watching the 'understanding' take place. This procedure wasn't to be used for learning facts, such as my name – that could easily be achieved, as it always had been, through sending information through the five senses. No, this learning was accelerated into wider 'understanding' by the direct stimulation of specific groups of neurons so that they connected with each other. The more connections you have, the more you can understand something by seeing it terms of other things. By driving the formation of connections and watching how they developed, we could monitor exactly what was happening in the child's brain, and extend their understanding as more and more connections were stimulated under our view. So, while a child could learn in the time-old way a line from Shakespeare such as 'Out, out, brief candle', the Helmet stimulation would enable them to see how this was really a way of talking about death. In their brain, that is their mind, the connection would be formed between the extinction of a candle and the extinction of life.

The whole point was to enable the young mind, as effectively and quickly as possible, to make sense of the world about them and to 'understand' it as deeply as possible. The aim, however, was not to homogenize neuronal connectivity, not to pulverize the brain into an identical pattern of networks: this scenario would have amounted to the brainwashing of obsolete old ideologies, and in any event would simply not be possible, given that no one lived exactly the same life experiences as anyone else.

Instead, the Helmet system is based on the simple reality that no two people occupy exactly the same time and place coordinates as they travel through their lives: everyone is on their own trajectory of life-story, unique in the 100,000 years that humans have stalked the planet. Each individual will have individual experiences, safeguarded and constrained, of course, by our carefully planned lifestyle. But even so, since every action, however mundane, has a consequence, and since all actions form an unbroken sequence, it follows that from a very early age the iteration between outside events and internal brain plasticity will diverge for every individual brain, making each person increasingly unique.

The Helmet system aids and abets this iteration by providing with maximal efficiency a personalized extensive conceptual framework from which individual thoughts will eventually be generated. In technical terminology, it ensures the most effective transition from what has been long been referred to as a 'fluid' intelligence, where the emphasis is on mere mental agility and speed of processing, to a so-called 'crystalline' intelligence, characterized by real understanding, of seeing one thing in terms of something else, of making connections. But only when nothing would be left to chance, only when the brain has crystallized into a mind that is perfect for our society, only then are you at last bare-headed and acknowledged as an adult.

As a brain scientist, it was inevitable that I would work on the Helmet at some stage in my research career: only by taking a Helmet apart, could you really understand precisely how it worked and hence how the minds of all those in our society function. And, conversely, it is important that all new talent, all newly trained researchers, will have the opportunity to input their particular skills and insights into this essential technology, without which our society would be in jeopardy. As always, the guiding principle is to encourage and then harness individual thought, not suppress it. My first assignment had been to perfect the next generation of Helmets for, as it were, the youngest generation, Bill's age. Once a child started to have language, it meant the initial connections were matured enough to make further connections, enabling them to see one thing – an object or a person – in terms of something else, a word. I contributed to this 'early cognitive enhancement program'. And now Bill was to be in the next wave of young brains to benefit.

After the fitting of the Helmet and the telling of the Exodus story, there is a third milestone: the first Rally.

'Fred is ready for his first Rally.'

I remember blinking up at my mother. 'What's a Rally?'

She registered no response, but then answered in a monotone. 'Fred, you already know about Rallies. You know your Father and I attend them regularly, and that now you're getting to be so big, you must come to them as well. I know that you've learnt all about Rallies in your Helmet sessions. So *you* tell *me* what they are.'

I closed my eyes so that I could recite still more perfectly. 'Rallies enable the maximization of idea sharing and the shaping of optimal ways forward.'

'And what does that mean?'

I wouldn't have dared say I didn't know, and in any case the Helmet had already helped me understand. 'If we all meet together, then we can decide what's best.'

'Precisely.' My father had appeared and joined in, pulling his outer grey coat around himself, and handing my mother hers.

'But I still don't know what a Rally is, what actually happens.'

My father again. 'Well, you're about to find out. Maud, do you think he should wear the Helmet?'

My mother tilted her head to one side, considering. 'There will be so much new and fast inputting that it may overload him to place everything all at once into greater contexts. If he doesn't wear the Helmet, though, we'll have to explain manually moment by moment, and that will impair the value of our own contributions. Let's put it on, but to minimal mode.'

She was already reaching for my Helmet and I tilted my chin up, now already a reflex, for her to fasten it. I knew that we all had to attend Rallies once we were old enough: perhaps we might even meet my grandparents there. I had been told about the parents of my parents, but could not imagine in any way what an encounter with them would be like. I had nothing from which to extrapolate apart from the Story and the subsequent, many mentions of my great-grandparents, themselves the parents of the grandparents I had yet to meet, who had escaped from a great danger. The three of us stepped outside, me in the middle, holding one hand of each of my parents in each of my hands: a chain of three links, a triumvirate of the perfect Family Unit, purposefully walking towards an unknown that was known. I had to half run to keep up, but I still understood no more than I did previously. Because there was no further sensory input as yet that related to Rallies, my only knowledge came from what I had learnt already. Since the Helmet was on minimal mode, I would not be stimulated directly and had to rely on input from my five senses. So I would understand nothing further until we were nearer, or if some new and relevant event occurred.

After not very long, it happened. By now night had fallen but I could just make out more and more grey-clad couples converging, many with a third smaller figure of varying size. I realized we must be almost there. But now too much was happening. It was all so different from anything else. So many people in a great throng crowded in on me, pushing in and on, thick, fast, endless grey figures towering above me pressing forward: a great moving wall of humanity. All of us moving purposefully in one direction. Towards the bright light in the darkness, towards the noise. A single, slow drum beat was getting louder now as we entered. I had never heard anything like it before: relentless, dominating, demanding all attention and obedience. I had never been out so late either. So many of us were amassed in the dark night. I felt it hard even to breathe at the sight of them: all grey but all with different faces, endless cropped-headed variations on the theme of the human face. Expectant, silenced by the drumming, the pale faces were lit up by flames from torches that some were carrying, tall and strong, burning bright, casting long shadows on the faces, turning them skeletal with haunted black eye sockets and hollowed cheeks. I had never seen real fire before, though of course I knew what it was. No one jostled anyone, but I felt the close press of so many bodies unsettling. We were swept along into an enormous, apparently limitless space, the biggest I had ever seen, surrounded on all far sides by banked rows of grey figures, silent now and interspersed with smaller figures with silver heads: children like me with Helmets. I was glad that everyone could see how much I was growing up.

The flames, real fire, were leaping high from overhead containers and now casting a glow over the faraway lines of dots that were faces in a way that I would have described as magical if I had ever heard the word and known what it meant. But I knew without asking that the screens and speakers, at fixed and frequent intervals around the vast perimeter, were to amplify any sound and sight. Just as it seemed there was no more room, so a clear chanting sound began from everyone present:

'Sequence, Con-sequence; Sequence, Con-sequence; Sequence, Con-sequence …'

I understood already that I had to learn this before anything else: that everything is caused by something; everything that happens has irreversible consequences. I had chanted it myself many times, with my parents and when I was having the daily Helmet instruction. But now things were different. Being among so many people, I felt frightened and excited at the same time. I was doing what everyone else was doing: I was doing the right thing. I was obeying the rules, being a good boy. So I felt safe. So long as I did what I was told, I would be safe among all these people. Slowly, I began to breathe more easily.

The shock of the immediate assault on my ears and eyes abated slightly and I started to look around. Even at that young age, and even though I couldn't have articulated it, I could appreciate just how individual each person was. It was not so much that they had different faces, and were of different sizes, shapes and ages, but the tone of their voices, their gestures, the facial expressions and the varying ease and enjoyment which radiated from them – all this told me instantly that each person was unique. Why and how? What was going on behind their eyes? What kind of experience was each having right now? That was the moment that I was to recognize, much later, as the crucial turning point for me, the deciding moment when I would want, from then on, to study the brain and, more significantly, the mind.

For all of us in that huge, grey mass of humanity, I learnt when I was older, this was the one outlet allowed. This was the one time we could shout. The Rallies were not really for deliberation at all: that would have been as impractical as it was unfeasible as it was unnecessary. No, the key issue was affirmation: it was the one time we focused on the moment, a sensory over-laden moment, to be as one with everyone else. To feel safe and to realize one's small place in the vastness of the larger scheme: to be reminded of exactly what you were, a node in a vast network, albeit one that was individual, special.

Before any other form of instruction, I was to learn from the Rallies that we, individuals though we might be, were more important as a collective abstraction. We were all playing an interactive part, as individual as different words that none the less conform to the structure of a sentence, which in turn says so much more than a single word can. There was, and is, no room for even one small component to jar. As such, we are striving, always moving forward to develop thoughts, aiming to attain the apotheosis of the human condition. We were, are, Neo-Platonic, Neo-Puritan: the 'N-Ps'.

The man strokes his thin white beard, the diamond-hard eyes glisten.

Chapter 6

ZELDA

I suppose the only proper conversations I really have, just occasionally, are with Ciro. He is my partner – well, the male carer. Most newborns have six 'parents': the gene donors, the two separate donors of egg and womb, then finally the two carers, those with an appropriate disposition to actually handle the post-natal stage in a new human's life. I am one such: no strong nurturing emotions are demanded; indeed such a tendency would be hard to find nowadays. Instead of womb or egg donation, the role of a carer simply requires the skill to perform functions that enable new humans to stay alive and be comfortable. With no other option, that is what I have to be. I routinely share out the physical needs of feeding, watering, washing and drying with Ciro. But Ciro is not the man I could love.

I have little in common with Ciro, other than our allocated responsibilities. He looks like most other males: a smooth face as to be expected, thick hair which happens in his case to be brown, and a slack mouth and open eyes, waiting to receive, to take. We talk little because there is little to say, little to report: one day is so much like the rest. I don't have feelings for Ciro in the sense that men and women used to 'feel' something for each other, an attraction that made one individual special. Like everyone else, Ciro is just there. He is familiar and therefore less of a threat or difficulty to interact with in real time, in the old-fashioned way.

But I don't want to be here in the present: I want to go back to when I was much younger, though not by then that young. By the time my face and body were ready, time had moved on and my fate was far from certain: the future I had dreamt of was now a thing of the past. I had to face this new reality the day that first my grandmother, then, very quickly after, my grandfather, died.

'We're sorry. But that was often what happened, the second partner passing away soon after the first, even when living and dying was so much more variable and less predictable. Deep condolences.'

It was by then not a doctor who spoke to me, but a remote voice through the screen. I was reporting the second death: the voice had been programed to interject small extraneous comments that would make it sound compassionate. But it neither helped nor worked. I had initially spent time stupidly emailing my dead grandparents, taking advantage of software that could extrapolate from previous correspondence of the deceased how they would respond to current, new missives. If I didn't try too hard, I could almost have been fooled that they were still with me. However, this pointless activity just delayed acknowledging the undeniable fact that we would never smile at each other or hug each other ever again. The only real comfort was that my grandparents had lived to a good age and died a reasonably quick death: a massive heart attack for one, a cataclysmic stroke for the other. I was grateful for this at least, especially when I thought of my parents, killed in an ancient type of car accident – perhaps the last of its kind – when I was five. An accident caused by the N-Ps. A shutter came down. I will not think of that. Better to think instead of the woman I have become.

When I finally left the security of my grandparents' home, I already did not fit into the lifestyle expectation of unremitting well-being. No one seemed in control any more, nor would they need to be. There was nothing more to change, no problems to solve. Evolution had come to the end of the road. We needed to do nothing as a species other than exist in our healthy, perfect bodies: pampered household pets that no one has to care for. Nor do we care about each other: no one wants to spend time with anyone else.

Instead of catering for the old-fashioned family, at that time Dwellings were starting to appear on a grand scale, of a size to make the most of ground usage – a maximal area under minimal geodesic dome roofs, with sanitation outlets, tele-medicine facilities and energy and so on. After all, these designs were simply the result of combinatorial architectural programs developed in an appropriately automated way to ensure the most efficient functional units that were at the same time as stimulating and fun to be in as possible. And once the Dwellings were there, so the number of occupants adjusted to the size of the house, not the other way round as in previous centuries.

Quite quickly, Dwellings with twenty or so occupants became more logical than homes with families. Bright geodesic domes dappled the landscape as the old homes, dreary square little boxes, decayed and crumbled. In the past, up to my grandparents' time, the old idea of the family had been to nurture the next generation. But for over a hundred years the family had been disintegrating, merging and contracting and expanding every time the reproductive activities of the adults capriciously changed. So the Grouping system had much more to commend it. As well as an enduring stability in the organization, there were more adults to share out the few tasks that could not be automated, while the increased size allowed for the differentiation of conception, pregnancy and parenting that the new technologies had enabled.

Now that anyone of any age could have a child, everyone was effectively of the same homogeneous generation in their young adult prime: what would be the point of taking sole responsibility for bringing up another human being as though they were something special, when they would be the same as everyone else. Why would they need highly personal care? And what would be the point of communicating, especially with a baby? What was there to tell them, to pass on, to own as yours and no one else's? Now all that counted for anyone, irrespective of their date of birth, was bodily needs, and that was what Ciro and I attended to until the infants were self-sufficient. There was no reason to pass on the wisdom of grandparents, no knowledge to be gained from experience, since we all had the same standardized, instantaneous experiences all the time. The Grouping way of life evolved to fit the changing times very quickly, until no one could remember or consider seriously any alternative. Apart from me.

There was a centralized database for registering that you needed accommodation. I'd had no choice but to submit my name. The composition of Groupings would be organized and an applicant would be allocated either to an existing Grouping, or instructed to be part of the constitution of a new one. So there I was, twenty-five years of age and sitting alone in the empty old home of my grandparents. I remember staring at the screen, having registered first the deaths, then myself, for accommodation. Already, though, I was part of the system. Lurking beneath my skin I had the mandatory implant. This device is nowadays placed in the arm at birth, by robotic telemedicine procedure: it is a simple smart means for logging physical details, both long- and short-term, ranging therefore from age through to current stress levels or any aberrations or emergency deviations in bodily signs. In the unlikely event such occur – after all, why should we ever be stressed – evading action is instructed immediately.

By pressing my arm implant against the screen extension, I had been instantly logged and spoke my requirement from the list of possible needs and queries I might have. Finding a life partner had not been an option: it never would be in this world ,least of all for me but neither for anyone else. But just whisper 'new Dwelling', or indeed 'new Grouping': instant response.

As a result, within the hour, I'd been standing in the rain outside, enjoying the fresh, natural, unexpected and spontaneous experience of getting utterly wet. I'd looked at the surroundings of my new home, noticing how the landscape around me had changed so much in just a short time, while I'd been growing up. Most old-fashioned houses, like the precious, dear one I had just left, had decayed into rubble all on their own, while others were being actively demolished. Even as I stood inspecting the outside of where I would be living forever, I'd imagined the explosion, controlled and remotely detonated through a chain of automated commands: all those years and hopes and conversations blown up in a choking cloud. Now those dreams from previous times lay smashed in the dirt, alongside the ever increasing numbers of luminescent and fluorescent geodesic domes: vast, bright-coloured hemispheres like disembodied and inverted giant insect eyes. They clustered together as Dwelling spaces, the new focus of our lives.

Back then, as our Grouping had convened for the first time inside our particular Dwelling, I had finally to force myself to accept the old way of life had gone forever. As various people of different sizes and colour of eyes flitted by, no one had spoken, at least not to each other. Everyone had been preoccupied with singing or speaking, removed in their personal bubbles of space.

For a fleeting moment, I'd sympathized with the N-Ps and why, a few decades earlier, they had fled. But then the rationale for their actions had been overwhelmed by my hatred and fear of who and what they were. My grandfather had spoken of them to me from time to time, ever since I was old enough to understand:

'They are strange people, Zelda, not like us. They have no warmth or love. They cannot laugh or do anything that isn't planned with precision in advance. All they care about is thinking, not feeling. But their fixation and determination are more zealous than any passion. They still want to work, even if it isn't necessary, and that's one of the reasons they left. They've all gone to the remote place, over the mountains. They have technology that might well be as good as ours is becoming, but they want to use it in a different way. They want control over everything. Just as well they left: they knew that not many of us agreed with them, that no one with any sense would give up the pleasures that were coming even then, so thick and fast, that made life so easy. Of course, back then, your grandmother and I couldn't have predicted what would happen to education as we knew it, or to marriage and childbearing. We thought we could live as we had always done, but in greater physical comfort and without worry. We hadn't realized that would be impossible. Perhaps the N-Ps had seen ahead – it's all they do anyway: think about the consequences of everything.'

I'd been given my Fact-Totum at about that time: it was a means to liberate you from the screen, which was still in use then, enabling you to interact via the embedded technology. It told you everything you needed to know. One of my first queries had concerned the unfeeling and powerful N-Ps, and what my grandfather had told me was confirmed. Shapeless grey figures had flashed up on the screen. Men and women were indistinguishable: all had cropped hair and sagging flesh, and straight lines where lips should have been. By then, they had become a different type of human.

Remembering what my grandfather had said about them wanting to control everything and everyone, I had shuddered. They had, after all, killed my parents. When she'd thought I was ready to know what had happened, my grandmother had sat me on her knee. After all, it had been her daughter, my mother, who had perished.

'Your father always liked to drive in a car.'

I had not seen a car, of course, since I was very small: but I knew from the Fact-Totum exactly what these ancient machines had been, what they looked like, and how they had risen, then disappeared, over merely some hundred and fifty years.

'Even though cars became increasingly unpopular, despite technology having reduced their carbon emissions, your father kept a car.'

'Why, Grandmother? Why didn't most people want a car like Father did?' How I'd enjoyed saying that word, 'father'. My father.

'Because most people didn't see the need to travel anywhere. Even then, most people already preferred sitting at their computers. Their computers gave them everything they needed, from shopping to information to fun. But your father and mother were different. Perhaps it was the way we'd brought your mother up: because we were both teachers, we gave her more attention than most of her friends had from their parents, and we told her more than she needed to know, explained a lot more. We were careful about what she learnt and how she learnt it. We so wanted her to understand the importance of a relationship, of being close to someone, like your grandfather and me. We told her all the things we tell you. But not many children then, and certainly not now, would have this kind of upbringing.'

My grandmother sighed. 'So your mother was very lucky when she met your father and they fell in love. It was a dream come true and they were so happy together. The car enabled them to go off on their own, in a little world that shut out everything and everyone else.'

'Even me?'

'Sometimes. Your parents loved you very much. But some-times lovers have to be on their own: just a man and a woman, fitting closely together like a handshake. Besides, your parents knew you were safe with us, that we could pass on lots of ideas that were already vanishing. That's why you escaped their fate.'

I waited. Even the fraction of pause as my grandmother drew breath seemed too long a time.

'So they went for a drive one morning. It was a day during the time they called 'The Exodus' when many N-Ps were leaving. But by then few people drove on roads, so your father and mother could drive very fast, which they liked to do, – especially swinging round sharp bends. They enjoyed being together, moving so rapidly that no one could catch them up, – not that this was likely as the roads were already empty and in disrepair. The very old narrow ones had been less used and were more functional, the ones with lots of curves that snaked up the mountains. On this particular day, they were speeding down one such ancient, tortuous highway. As they turned a bend, they suddenly must have come across a large crowd of N-Ps, walking right in front of them, blocking the way. There would have been a great crowd of them, a great grey wall of people, many of them carrying away large heavy cases of books, large black boxes slowly being transported like coffins. They could not have dispersed easily or quickly. It was too late to brake, the term used then for stopping the car quickly. Your father must have had no choice, if he was not to kill many N-Ps: he had to swerve off the road. The area where this happened was the start of the steep region where the N-Ps were headed, and there was a sharp precipice on the side. Your parents had no chance. Their car overturned and crashed down the slope. We were told they both died instantly.'

'So my father and mother died to save the lives of some N-Ps?'

'That's right, Zelda.'

That's why I continue to shudder at the thought of those cold grey people who want control and who live because my warm, loving parents died instead of them.

About to start a new life in my new home, the Dwelling allocated to me, I had shuddered again as the rain, soft on my face, flattened my hair, but only because I'd felt expectant and hopeful. I had also met the man I was to live and work with: Ciro. Yet he'd looked through me, distracted, at a loss what to say. No, he could never be the man I seek. He was no soul-mate. I could tell immediately he had no soul, just a perfect face and body. Ciro's smooth face and vacant eyes, even more than his subsequent lack of conversation, told me that he would act as expected and perhaps even feel things, but that he would not think. So we had both gone inside, ready to meet the others with whom we'd share everything and nothing.

That was the last clear, identifiable episode in my life. Since then every day has been the same. Ciro and I coexist as carers for ten non-adults. Our charges range in age from a newborn boy to Sim, a young female who is actually now fully grown. In turn, the womb, egg and gene donors drift around us. They have no responsibility to do more. A Grouping is defined, after all, as simply the social unit for eating and sleeping in the same shared space. But, this evening, my idea has been for us to converge and actually interact in space and time, however briefly. We need to attempt something highly unusual: to discuss the future.

Chapter 7

HODGE

I've decided to start this diary because I consider that I'm about to be part of something very important, transformational not just in my own professional life, but in the potential impact on our society as a whole. I feel a compulsion to make sure my version of events, my role, is completely clear and acknowledged: indeed, enough has happened already for me to be sure this exercise is worthwhile and that I am truly writing for posterity. Besides, I can't articulate sufficiently the pleasure it gives me to be writing with a real pen, even though it's a once humble biro, on real paper. But I must write it all down, get it down forever.

It all began on an unseasonably warm spring afternoon some months ago. I had been summoned to Centrum, a building I obviously had never before entered. Setting out exactly on time, I had walked from the Institute to my destination, from where all government, all the running and secure continuity of our society is directed. There is of course usually no contact ever made directly between those within the deceptively bland walls of Centrum and the rest of us on the outside. Normally, instructions are indirectly conveyed from them for the continual refinement and fine-tuning of our lives.

What need had they to hear back from us on the outside? Since our lives are so ordered, little happens that has not already been anticipated, and therefore there is little need for sudden action or indeed conspicuous or inspirational leadership, in the old early twenty-first century sense, from our rulers. Rather than a governing system of flashy, old-style charisma, the N-P practice has always been one of long-term forward planning, of ensuring that our way of life enables the human mind to flourish in the best way possible, and be sustained unthreatened. Those in Centrum do not need to govern us, lead us as such. Rather, they run the system that enables us to flourish. And they keep their distance. It is completely unprecedented, therefore, to appear before the Elders, to actually meet them as real people. Because I've never been able to think of them in that way, and still can't. I was feeling what I knew was a reaction to raised adrenaline levels, but had never previously experienced first-hand. I hope I never have to go through that again.

There were unpleasant sensations in my stomach, my throat, my mouth, my chest. The real problem was that, for the first time in my life, I didn't know what to expect. Despite my outwardly purposeful gait, I was in turmoil, still making the most of the brief period of solitude to try and predict, for one more time, why my presence had been demanded. No plausible explanation offered itself. At that moment, no one had given me the slightest hint: I could only and inevitably anticipate the worst. Were they about to shut down our Institute, terminating all our work on the brain? Unthinkable. Well ... Was I personally in some way at fault? As I strode on in my outward attempt at confidence and with more attention than usual on the unusual, unfamiliar route, I could think of no obvious misdemeanour. This surprising, perhaps privileged, contact could, I reasoned to myself in an attempt at reassurance, be due simply to the very great importance that the

Elders placed on brain research, just as they should. But why the face-to-face interview?

The still weak sun disappeared in and out of insignificant little clouds and happened to beam down just as I turned the last corner and caught a glimpse of Centrum close up for the first time. The light temporarily brightened up a building that, like all our constructions, was designed deliberately to be unremarkable: monochrome oblongs or squares in a variety of permutations and combinations. Centrum would not in any event have been a destination for the pointless 'sight-seeing' of bygone eras: I had sometimes wondered how merely seeing something could change anything about how you saw the world. Our whole society focuses on thinking, not letting your eyes just wander where they will: we have ensured that in our cityscape and landscapes, there is nothing anywhere noteworthy at which to stare.

However, as I drew nearer, what I noticed now that *did* distinguish Centrum from all other buildings were the antennae that bristled from it: we had never stopped listening in to the traffic from the Others, banal and strange though all of it was. We could not attribute the signals to particular individuals, since much came from external nodes, while those read-outs that we deduced were from invasive individual implants were almost exclusively concerned with generic-seeming biological data about the different states of various physical bodies: nothing about the minds. None the less, these interceptions, having arrived first in Centrum, would immediately be filtered and categorized.

The cryptography required was colossal for deciphering the endless deluge of information: accordingly, we had at last perfected the quantum computer. Since the quantum computer works on the principles of quantum physics, it differs from conventional computers in being able to work on millions of computations at once. However, the biggest problem had been that any atom within a quantum computer that collided with any other would count as a measurement: we had now circumvented this problem by improving on a technique, 'nuclear magnetic resonance', which pushes the nuclei of atoms into alignment with externally applied magnetic fields. Initially, this had only been possible for a few seconds at a time: but by the time we had established our independent society, quantum computers within their special magnetic fields were up and running for as long as we wished. No coded messages would ever be secure again. Never.

Any information relating not to the general physiology, but specifically to the brain, mindset and psychology of the Others, was then passed immediately on to us at the Institute. Our Department of Field Interpretation was kept very busy, not least because the signals came so thick and fast, monotonous in the extreme, and very rarely making any sense in terms of activities or lifestyle. Everything appeared disconnected and yet homogeneous: but eventually, in any event, meaningless.

With professional curiosity, I noted that I was still feeling what might be described as a heightened emotion. Perhaps it was getting worse: indeed it was. Normally, I can safely say, I feel truly nothing. Well, obviously, everyone always feels something – some inner subjective condition – unless they are asleep. But in my case this everyday experience of my existence will usually be projected forward, back and forward again over time as I ponder and reflect on the facts, the questions, the resolutions: rarely do I notice the immediate environment, and am not prone to the perturbations, be they negative or positive, that it might impose on me. I am well beyond the pure sensory processing of the small child, and hence of the hectic emotions that we have for so long contrived to minimize. Given the seniority of my position and the familiarity and usual routine of my life, there was usually never anything to trouble my thought processes. But today was different. Today my palms were wet, my breathing difficult and shallow, my heartbeat banging through my ribcage. I had to admit that this unpleasant but obvious sensation could only be called anxiety. I propelled myself forward into the unknown.

Because everything we do is well planned, meticulously to time, I was not kept waiting in the cavernous blinding white and glass reception area. Grey figures with cropped heads paced purposefully in criss-cross trajectories from and to unmarked doors on all sides. No one was speaking. I could have been invisible. The silence was only punctuated by the percussive sounds of many footsteps, the occasional cough. I cleared my throat.

It seemed that this entrance area was meant entirely for immediate transit, since there was no furniture at all to cater for the waiting visitor. Weaving between one blank-faced figure after another, I tracked across the emptiness that smelt distantly of disinfectant towards a solitary small desk, behind which was seated a young woman with slightly waxy skin, black hair the regulation two centimetres in length, and flat brown eyes. She didn't smile, or need to ask who I was.

'Dr Hodge, go straight up to the top floor, level 20.'

She gestured to the high-speed pod, still recognizable as a distant descendant of its predecessors from a century or two ago, and without any further attempt at communication, looked down to activate something outside my range of vision to alert those waiting of my imminent arrival. So a few seconds later I found myself standing at the heavy grey door, the only one visible, as I stepped out on the top floor. It slid back and I stepped forward. A sea of grey faces in grey clothes, just like my own, were lined up on the other side of a long table. They were seated, but I was obviously expected to remain standing.

There was nothing to lean on, no podium to stand behind. Just me facing them. No preliminaries.

'The Others are starting to rise in priority for concern. We shall soon need to take action: the question is, what is the best course? We, of course, start with no presumptions but review all options. So what we need to know from you, Hodge, is, er, not so much whether, but to what extent, brains can change.'

The hesitancy in speech of this Elder with a thin white beard – their names were known by no one, used by no one – belied his apparent subsequent speed of thought and the hard of his eyes. He was seated in the centre and clearly the spokesman. If anything, I concluded that his overtly and exaggeratedly reflective manner was either a mildly self-indulgent affectation – as though he was acting out a crude stereotype of the old university professor from over a hundred years ago – or he was using that persona as a deliberate ploy to put any potential protagonist mistakenly at ease with a false sense of superiority and hence security. But however contrived his mannered, hesitant speech, he could not conceal the piercing brightness of his eyes, hard, like diamonds.

'Could we ever aim to, er, let's say influence the brains of the Others, so that they are converted into our way of seeing the world and living with us in an expanded society? If so, then we'll need to plan how we set about implementing the transition on a large scale. It's not obvious how we might best do this. I'm against subliminal, environmental modification via the indirect doctoring of their cyber-world software: there's far too much of it and it would take far too long, with non-uniform and unpredictable results. Or are the changes that have already occurred in their brains, er, too far-reaching and too entrenched? Should we just think of them as infantile creatures only fit to be gene donors or a form of household pet?'

The notion of a household pet is actually not as bizarre as one might have thought. All N-P homes have a pet: the idea is for children to learn to anticipate the needs of another, by starting to learn how to understand a simpler consciousness than their own. The most usual choice is a rat: these rodents are highly intelligent, economical and easy to feed, yet small enough to be kept in a confined space, a cage, thereby enabling the most controlled interaction with the child. However, in the homes where the child had grown and left, and would most likely no longer be in close contact, a pet serves for the 'past-parenting', older N-Ps as a substitute object for nurturing. Now that my daughter Amy has set up a Family Unit of her own, I rarely see her, as is to be expected. In any case, I could now concentrate even more on my work thanks to the reduced domestic distraction. Then again, my latest in a long line of white furry charges is a valued part of my home life.

Perhaps the Elders had in mind as one scenario that instead of a pet rat, we might all accommodate a single Other in each of our homes. My mind immediately reeled at the vast range in possible outcomes and the concatenation of consequences that might ensue: would they also be kept in cages? If deprived of their cyber-culture, would they become emotional, frustrated, even violent? Or would we have to intervene directly with drugs or constraining neurosurgery first? But I did not have time, as I would have liked, to savour each possibility as even a hypothetical situation: each seemed so implausible, so at odds with our current, calm and well-organized lifestyle. I looked back at the line-up of faces: this was one of the few occasions in my life when I felt truly at a loss, completely unable to understand what the Elders wanted.

The faux professor was inscrutable, even more than a typical N-P: his whole demeanour, including the lack of undulation in his voice, was completely free of any apparent emotion at all, as his next suggestion illustrated.

'Simplest of course, er, just to exterminate the whole decadent insult to what human beings should be. We could, er, keep the DNA by extracting it from a sample section, then immortalize it in cultured cell lines, could we not, Hodge?'

'Sir, yes, the process is a very old and simple one: we just need samples of cells from their bodies, so that we can extract the DNA, introduce it to cells we keep alive in isolated "culture" dishes, then use it in an IVF process when we wish.'

But this suggestion would have been approximating a scenario more like the one we understood to be rampant among the Others: it would go against one of the basic tenets of N-P society. The Elder pretended a frown as though he had only just considered the disadvantage.

'Hmm, the only problem would be, er, compromising on our fundamental view of birth: it was the, er, dissociation of reproduction from copulation that our forefathers saw as the start of the deterioration in human relations, and an increased cyber-onanism.'

'Indeed, sir. On the other hand, the DNA supplementation via IVF need only be used under controlled and occasional conditions, when we wish to boost the gene pool. The individual with the new genes could then live in the true N-P way. IVF would not be needed for them or their family for several more generations.'

Professor linked his fingers at the back of his head and leant back, crooked elbows protruding from behind his skull like vestigial horns or wings. His wispy white beard was just long enough to move up and down, seemingly as a separate entity, as he spoke.

'Mass extermination would require technologies we have never prioritized, which would take time to develop. Moreover, it would take significant amounts of time and resources, and could be seriously detrimental to those of our people who had to organize it, both in terms of distraction from the real N-P life as well as the negative consequences ensuing from the project itself. But, in any event, we're getting ahead of ourselves, Dr Hodge. We can keep, er, all options in play at the moment: conversion, pets or annihilation. The crucial issue to establish first of all is, er, the state of their brains, the way they think and what potential they may have.'

He looked around him with a cursory sweep of the head, without really seeking eye contact with his colleagues, but going through the motions of gaining approval and agreement.

At last another Elder leant forward. 'We pride ourselves on being careful, on anticipating all outcomes: sequence and consequence above all. Let's see first how readily their brains can be modified, and then address the possible consequences.'

The other five Elders, three women and two further men, just nodded. Such supremely powerful people never needed to assert themselves: who was there to oppose them? Their single aim was to ensure that the best possible plans were formulated. Their lined but immobile faces and their uniformly monochrome outfits blended into the pale grey walls. Each waited politely for someone other than themselves to articulate to me the desired strategy: my instructions. At last one of the women, with the inevitably cropped hair of both sexes, but distinguished from her two counterparts by the lack of corrective glasses, spoke up. She looked at me with hard blue, small bird-like eyes, unmagnified by lenses and wreathed in the wrinkles of her years. She attempted a small smile that was unsuccessful, presumably through lack of practice.

'Dr Hodge, can you devise a strategy by which we could have first-hand information on the malleability of the Others' brains?

The need for complete secrecy probably means that the initial operation should be something of a pilot, very small scale. We could then escalate operations once we have a clear idea of the situation.'

I thought quickly: not an exercise I enjoyed, was used to, and certainly didn't consider optimal. But the Elders wanted not so much a detailed answer as an indication of direction and feasibility.

'We will need someone actually to go over there, back over the mountains to gain first-hand and full information. I know just who to send, a model N-P who is utterly trustworthy. He is, needless to say, also one of the most brilliant brain researchers of his generation.'

The Elders glanced from side to side at each other, silently raising interrogatory eyebrows, then wordlessly nodding in accord. They looked back at me. One of the men this time, not the professorial one but a small-boned, dark-haired younger one, spoke for them all.

'We are all agreed then, Hodge. You have complete authority to proceed as you deem best. But we shall, of course, await your reports and results with keen expectation. Such reports will be oral, in person, in this room.'

My audience was over.

Chapter 8

FRED

Today my recording will be devoted not to reflections of the past and generalizations, but on a momentous single event which has just happened, something for the first time totally unexpected, and which will change my life forever. What would have, should have, been a routine day in the lab has not resulted in the usual comforting continuity and predictable daily narrative that is so essential for bold excursions of theorizing: I have made no scientific advance at all. There are no results. Nothing has yielded new insight that could undermine the continuing, mocking riddle: how the meticulously measured and now so accessible objective, physical occurrences between brain cells translate into the subjectivity of personal experience. But, then again, at least I could give a good reason for the day's scientific stagnation: I can easily supply the requisite cause and effect.

Today my work was, very unusually and without any warning, interrupted by an unscheduled interview with Hodge. I couldn't recall the last time I was surprised in this way by the completely unexpected. No, it had never happened before. I had grown to maturity with the reassurance that everything was planned, organized, and had a clear order. But now there was an alien and intensely unpleasant, watery feeling in my stomach and my legs that I couldn't control or explain. And, as I approached the room where Hodge worked, dryness clenched in my throat. I was finding it hard to breathe.

Hodge has grey hair and a grey suit and an even-toned voice. He is, naturally, of perfect weight and with the steady gaze of someone with a secure past and a clear direction for the future.

'I know that the request for this interview may have interrupted your daily schedule, Fred, and I apologize.'

We sat opposite each other in the calm area of his simple desk as he ignited his explosive.

'I couldn't discuss this earlier because the implications, were it to be widely known, would defeat the aim we now have. But you may tell Tarra as she will obviously need an explanation.'

'An explanation for what, sir?'

'Fred, we need you to pay a visit to the Others.'

The world tilted. What Hodge was saying just didn't make sense.

'The time is coming when our society, we N-Ps, will need to ensure the safety of the human mind everywhere, not just here. It is our ultimate mission, is it not?'

Hodge's voice was a long way off, muted by fevered imagined scenarios running through my mind. We had moved on since the last century when everything was visible and watchable, remorselessly recorded and available to the 'viewer'. In those days, cameras in every corner of the planet recorded activities of so-called 'interest' because they were actions, decisive one-off events, that in some way would impact on the observer, if only in the effect on their thinking or mood. But now humanity had regressed to the isolationism of centuries long ago, where remote events had no significance for daily life or views. The notion of openly recording and 'broadcasting' (as it had been called) the ongoing existence of the Others appeared totally absurd now.

First, we N-Ps had fled from them precisely because they did nothing, said nothing, thought nothing: what would there be to watch? Second, we had valuable and important ideas of our own to nurture, a whole new society to build: there would be no time for the distraction of looking back over the mountains. Third, we did indeed already monitor any valuable information they might be giving away, the only data they could generate: what their bodies were doing, the physiological read-outs from their biological processes transmitted as radio signals. But these signals were collective, a gross index of mass arousal. We had no insight into what went on, if anything, in their brains. Fourth, there was no one left over there, actually living with the Others, to report on what they were like now.

This systematic list had calmed me somewhat until I came to this fourth point. I forced myself to concentrate on what Hodge was now saying. Was he really implying that I should physically remove to the Others, actually in person travel over the mountain? Surely not ...

'Yes, of course, we are deluged with traffic from their airwaves, both the diminishing stuff sent via old external nodes as well as to and from each personalized implant that they have, not to mention in and out of the enhancers they all wear. But it's just information overload, as it stands. We need to be able to interpret the data. Before we can make any large-scale move, we need to make sense of everything by putting it into a context, and we can only do that from a first-hand perspective.

'We need direct, informed reports from someone who understands how the brain works – someone to clarify what has happened to their minds from a direct, physical perspective, the perspective of neuroscience, your perspective. You will be a pioneer in every respect and, like all pioneers, you'll be unnoticed.

No one there is likely to question you. Remember the Others live in the moment, the infantile products of an organic, viral automation that operates on homeostatic principles to maintain everything as it is: physical ease and well-being. We are taking the calculated risk that the Others whom you'll meet at random will no longer ask probing questions of any sort. Even several generations ago, when our forefathers left, they had already lost the habit. No one over there is in control, no one wants to change anything. But we do, and we must.'

Hodge's opaque grey eyes had been thick and clouded in his grey, wrinkled face. He had paused again, obviously waiting for these scenarios, with their different contingencies, to gain purchase in my neuronal circuits, to ripple out across the synapses, strengthening connections, evaluating against the checks and balances of previous experience that were there already, laid down long ago by the Helmet. One of the most basic tenets: focus not on the self, but the idea.

'But surely, sir, it is unlikely that anyone's mind in our society could be in jeopardy. After all, have we not foreseen every eventuality in a child's development – every moment they are awake, and indeed asleep. For example, the deep psychological effects of sibling rivalry have been carefully catered for, by restricting breeding pairs to one progeny apiece. Then we all acknowledge that the Helmet technology is very impressive. And I'm convinced the enhanced cognitive program that I've been working on for infants is very powerful, especially considering the younger age of the brain we can target now.'

Hodge stared through me.

'Fred, never underestimate the ability of humans to "blow their minds", "let themselves go" or create a "sensational" time. Those phrases are very old, but very revealing, and that is my point. The desire to abrogate the sense of self is deep-rooted and hard

to eliminate. The ancient Greeks knew it: just look up Euripides'
Bacchae, where a king gets killed because he doesn't offset the
"bread" force of reason with the "wine" force of abandonment.
What did "wine, women, and song" and the subsequent later
variant of "drugs and sex and rock 'n' roll" all have in common?
A regression to the time of infancy, of becoming merely the passive
recipient of sensory inputs, a suspension –' and here Hodge almost
trembled as his voice had wavered – 'of individual identity.'

'Yes, sir.'

He was telling me what I knew, of course, the basic N-P credo.
Individual identity was what counted more than anything as it
led to individual thought. Individual thought is at its best when it
makes its unique contribution to a dialogue, which in turn feeds
into collective thought – new, and by this stage, abstracted ideas
unsullied by personal feelings or idiosyncratic imperfections:
pure thought. But while, in the past, misguided ideologies started
with an idea that suppressed the individual with all their flaws,
N-Ps were the first in realizing that the opposite had to occur.
Individual identity, with all its imperfections, had first to be
harvested just as it was, and only then distilled in the system of
living and lifestyle that we alone had perfected.

But always, as Hodge had just reminded me, we had to be
vigilant, because of those other deep and dangerous forces that,
for no obvious explanation I could offer, could suddenly surge
within the brain, hypothetically at least, even in mine. Although
I had heard much of this before, for the first time I had paused,
mentally as it were, to take a breath. I wondered for a moment, just
briefly, what kind of person, therefore, I actually was. What was
my own, my very own identity, independent of the N-P dialogues?

*The man with the thin white beard frowns and the diamond-
hard eyes narrow briefly.*

What a stupid, self-indulgent and pointless thought. In any case, I had quickly to pay attention once more as Hodge was continuing.

'Even if their presence was not a constant danger, an alternative to our way of life, however improbable, just think of the waste in human brainpower. Science has finally given us the potential for an unprecedented opportunity to see just how far our minds and individual talents can progress. Biomedical technologies have delivered to all of us healthy life spans with a longevity unthinkable a century or so ago. And, of course, we have the technology that has freed us from the absurdity of repetitive and uninteresting activity to ensure income for acquiring things we don't need. So we have the time, Fred, time to see just how far we can go.'

'Yes sir. It will be fascinating and vital for our N-P society to see how far the human mind can stretch when it's exclusively and entirely in the cognitive mode, when the sensory-driven loss of self really doesn't distract or dilute. I wonder what we as a species really could achieve. Euripides was, I'm sure, wrong: we're hardly likely to be killed just for being individuals and for thinking.'

This was not intended to be a joke; nor did Hodge respond to it as such.

'Well, remember there was a time, just before the great Exodus, when our side actually did think that death, mass annihilation of the Others, that is, might be the answer. Recall that they were, are, still more numerous than us. They could therefore have coordinated their resources and technology, and have easily suppressed us. But even then their craving for momentary good times, for fun, had corroded their thought processes. They couldn't plan ahead or predict different scenarios or consequences. Their priorities had shrivelled to one consciousness, their own, at one point in time, now.

'There were those of our forefathers at the time of the Exodus who had wanted to intimidate them, frighten them, and show them that they were doomed to lack of fulfilment and eventual misery. But the Others thought we were ridiculous, even laughed at us to our faces. That made the forefathers angrier and more desperate still. We were fewer, but because we believed in our ideals, while they just wanted to enjoy themselves, we could at least have upset their lives – at least those of some of them – by random killing: this strategy had been used a lot in the previous century.

'But, as you know, they were already too far gone: they didn't care and couldn't think beyond the hedonistic moment. They couldn't be influenced or swayed by what might have happened to anyone else: they already had conflated conceptually the death on screen with real death. What would have been the point, therefore, of ending the lives of a few of them? Real events no longer had any meaning for them. It was better for all of us just to leave. And it has worked well. We are flourishing: and for that very reason we need to protect what is good and clean and pure.

'But we've now reached a stage when we cannot any more let the Others just exist independently in parallel. We have achieved so much over just two generations: the time is coming to neutralize any threat to what we have perfected, which such a different type of human could pose. We are much changed, as they must be too. Now is the time to find out exactly what they have become. Only then can we decide how to deal with them for the optimal benefit of our own people.'

As always, iterating the ideas and facts, even familiar ones, with someone like Hodge, had led me to take the train of thought further.

'Of course, sir, the Others may be in the majority but they are now much weakened, and we are not oppressed. The idea of re-engaging with them, especially for all the right reasons, is inevitable and unavoidable.'

Hodge had just inclined his head: all this was obvious to him.

'And one final point, Fred, just in case you needed convincing of the importance of what you are about to do: our gene pool. We are, as you correctly say, in the minority. Although our policy of monogamous sex and one child is the best and the only way forward for humanity, our gene pool is not optimal. The Others are numerous and could enrich our genetic diversity enormously, once they had been persuaded to comply with our way of life. It's the means of actual interception that we need to work out in detail: how best to get into their minds and shape them to our purpose. We need to make sense of all that biofeedback and arousal that they generate. After all, so few of them appear to speak nowadays.'

While we do little else, I had thought, and smiled to myself, too fascinated now to be frightened. The thought, the idea, had captured me completely, as new ideas always did. But this was the first abstract concept that had an application, a direct impact on my everyday life that was unpredictable. Perhaps that was the cause of the strange feelings in my stomach, my chest, everywhere. This was indeed a new experience that made the previous notions of excitement that I'd nurtured seem silly and sad. But I had to focus: Hodge had still more to say.

'Remember, our forefathers came on foot. A very long journey, a hard one over the mountains, and taking a very long time. But, as we all know, it was worth it. It gave them all time to reflect and organize. But, above all, it gave them time to cleanse themselves of all that Yakawow.'

He was using a shorthand, derisive term, which encapsulated for us all the empty hedonism of the Others: even at the time of the Exodus, they had reduced their reactions to whatever they encountered to either a simple reflex negative or positive response: 'Yuck' or 'Wow' – Yakawow.

Hodge was gently nodding to himself, seemingly oblivious to me. 'The mountain air had purged the forefathers' thoughts. And as they walked, step after step, so they were at last able to specify clear sequences of action with the possible consequences. The Exodus was a very special time, arguably the start of our history – or rather our future.'

Hodge tilted his head slightly, tried to smile tightly, and looked at me.

'If we were being purely idealistic, it would be very appropriate now for you to retrace those important steps and walk on foot, back into the mindless squalor of Yakawow. But the aim is not to honour the forefathers, rather to accomplish our vital work as effectively as possible. We do not have the time, even though such a procedure would fit most with what we believe. Besides, you'll have equipment, the Helmet in particular.'

It was undeniable: I had minimal personal clothing and necessities, and always wore my watch, while most of the interface technologies were embedded in either my body or garments. But if I were to give accurate reports, I would need direct access to brains: I would ideally need to record the read-out of a Yakawow mindset and see how tractable it was to manipulation. The Helmet would be an essential part of my mission and I was thrilled at the science involved, my personal and logistical considerations overshadowed by the prospect of a totally new type of experiment involving a living human subject, just as in days gone by. But Hodge had cleared his throat, bringing me back to the present. Leaning forward for emphasis, his weight on his folded arms, he had riveted me with his grey gaze.

'So, Fred, we need to be practical. A century ago you could have jumped on a plane, or into a car. But since the entire globe has become effectively cyber, there is no need for literal, long-distance translocation. Everything we need to learn is instantly available in front of our eyes in the laboratory. Our informatics databases have shrunk space and time. Just as we no longer need to perform real-time experiments, so we no longer need to translocate. We can view the far away, or the far-away past, at a spoken command. This is why your mission is so different: it is in real time, and in a physically remote location to which you will need to travel in person.'

Hodge was, of course, reiterating the obvious, what he had already made clear. But it was only as he repeated the truly unprecedented scenario that the reality of it impacted on my mind. I, who was so used to a controlled life of observation and thought within the safe confines of my muted reality, would now need to embark into a terrifyingly new unknown.

'So we've never before had to tackle the question of transport that I'm about to discuss with you. We can and do and should walk everywhere, while of course the Others go nowhere.'

The double meaning had been clear to both of us; there was no need to acknowledge it overtly.

'However, for your special mission the engineers have put their ingenuity to work on a solution. They were surprised to have a practical project, as opposed to an informatics-based one, I can tell you. Still, this potential difficulty has been the limiting factor in planning the mission and actually informing you of it.'

'But, sir, surely you could have let me in on the secret earlier?'

'It's not an issue of trusting you, Fred. I would never for a moment doubt your integrity, which is one of the reasons of course, that you were selected.'

Hodge leant back in his chair and stared reflectively through the open window.

'But it *is* a security issue. That was why I could not tell the engineers the reason why we had suddenly given them such a new type of problem. We cannot assume that the Others are just what they appear to be. The longer you walked around with such an important secret buzzing in your brain – perhaps emitting signals they could pick up, or indirectly and subliminally reflecting those thoughts in your speech and behaviour patterns – who knows whether they might have detected the plans.'

'I doubt if they have such sophisticated technology, sir, if we do not. We have no evidence that they have anything approximating our DNA- or quantum-computational power. True, their technology appears to be very fancy for what it does, and seemingly well run and organized: but it just keeps them well fed, physically healthy and amused. They are not intellectually geared to learning or planning and drawing conclusions. In that regard they are way behind us, so how would they do it? How could thoughts intercepted in air be attributable to any one person, located in any specific brain? Much as *we* aspire to pick up particular brain patterns from a single individual without any interface technology, it will be a long time before we can do that without the Helmet. How could they be any different?'

Hodge's face tightened with irritation. 'Fred, please do not tell me what I know already and, above all, please do not be uncharacteristically stupid. It is *very* stupid to underestimate the enemy. Remember, that is what they are, and that extreme vigilance and caution is always the best policy, irrespective of however fanciful or paranoid the assumptions on which it is based might be.'

'I'm sorry, sir. Please tell me what form of transport the engineers have devised.'

Hodge had sat forward again in his chair, steepling his hands.

'I'm very pleased because it is not at odds with our ideology, and it may even have wider applications for enabling anyone, if there is ever a special case again, to travel further or faster than simple walking allows.'

The scientist in me immediately sublimated any smart from Hodge's admonishment to the curiosity of a novel solution to a problem. I too had leant forward from the other side of Hodge's pristine desk, and the air between us became conspiratorial, charged with expectation.

'Well, our first concern was to adhere to our principles and come up with something energy-efficient. You obviously know of the old bicycles? Of course. Well, recall that thanks to global cyberization, bicycles fell into disuse because no one had to travel any more, and the devices were too slow, too much effort and too unexciting for recreational Yakawow. But we should remember bicycles were excellent and energy-efficient devices for medium-distance travel. Unfortunately, the Others are more than a medium distance away, plus much of the route is steeply uphill over the mountains. So our engineers have devised a powering of a bicycle-like machine by bringing together two technologies.

'First, they rethought the design and structure of the original bicycle, which was already almost perfect, in ergonomic terms. So they reproduced the original design, but using the latest nanotechnological material, NanoMat, which incidentally has a distinctive lilac colour we have not had time to try and mute: this new metal fabrication means that this version of the bicycle is fifty times lighter than its old twenty-first-century counterpart.

'Second, they adapted fuel-cell technology to amplify your pedalling ability some ten-fold. Because everything is so light, the bicycle can now afford the additional and incidental weight of a feature that will literally empower you: a biocube. As you'll see, this cube is basically a streamlined box where algae exposed to sulphur become anaerobic – no longer needing oxygen – and, as a result, emit hydrogen. As you'll know from your early general science training, it has always been the sheer expense of hydrogen that has posed the biggest drawback for fuel cells: otherwise, they are truly ideal as a source of energy.'

Hodge drew breath. I doubt he was used to talking so much, and about such unusual issues.

'Basically, all a fuel cell comprises is a battery, the design for which was first conceived way back in 1839. The erstwhile precious hydrogen is passed over one old-fashioned electrode, and oxygen over a second one. The ensuing flow of electrons provides the electrical power you need, while the subsequent combination of hydrogen and oxygen yields water as the only by-product – which you can drink.'

Hodge had actually beamed, and I felt my facial muscles configuring into a similar, unfamiliar position. For a moment the scientific beauty of the solution had eclipsed the seriousness of what lay ahead. But both of us were too well trained not to return immediately to the job in hand. I have never been so focused, so clear as to the sequence of tasks, goals and sub-goals that lay ahead. Every sinew in my body was tensed and ready. I'm eager now to leave.

The man with the thin white beard knows that from now on the recordings will not be such good quality. The subsequent recordings had not been generated in the free time and free space of a benign home environment. Even worse, the still later ones had not been submitted immediately after their execution. This much sought-after material had not been made with external devices in the normal way, but in a separate section of Fred's implant. They had finally come into the man's possession at last, after enormous problems and much waiting. In the light of what had happened, he was impressed by their still viable condition.

Chapter 9

ZELDA

Today is different. Today I have the luxury, one that I took for granted when I was young, of anticipating and planning for a specific event to come. For so long now, everything has happened immediately. For so long, there has been no future: we have no need of it. But I alone can remember what it is like to have a past, a time that is different from right now, but that shapes the present. Now moments are homogeneous, all of us existing in a single time-frame. But unlike everyone else, I still know what it is like to have the passage of time differentiate one moment from the next, one episode from another, yet in a way that is related, as steps moving forward.

Now the special tingle has come back because there is something to plan for: a real meeting, in real time. Through the Talking Heads, I've accessed everyone who lives in the Dwelling, with the Heads spontaneously shouting out every so often that we need to gather together. Will the others listen and actually remember? Probably not: but there can always be a final summons just beforehand. Everyone should be there since they have nowhere else to go, and nothing else to do. It will be a rare moment when everyone in the Grouping is together, at a particular time and place that will stand out from all others as we coincide at a specific intersection in real time and space, without the buffers and barriers of the usual enhancements.

The meeting tonight will not be long: no one in the Grouping will find it sufficiently exciting to be in the same place, especially in real time and in the real world, for what would seem to them an achingly long period. But at least I'll be talking to people rather than just into thin air like I'm doing now.

There is just time now for me to walk out into the enveloping night and declaim loudly, to shout or whisper into the air, swathed in the cool blanket of nothingness. Tonight, the outside – even though it is merely composed of the natural phenomena of blackness and wind – promises an encompassing sensual experience: it wouldn't seem that unappealing in its abstraction and extremity, even to anyone else in the Dwelling. But I have come out because I feel more than a need to let the darkness bathe me or feel real air on my face. It is only by being at one with the night that I can dream of that other time, the grandparents' time. I crave hearing their stories again, the romance of life stories with problems and their solutions. For a while now, this need to draw breath, to probe, to search, to grab at something non-existent yet more substantial than all the luminescent, fluorescent objects in front of me – that hunger has been growing. It's not enough just to be excited and stimulated and beautiful. It's not enough to be healthy and satiated with food and hormones and free time. So what more do I want? Everyone else assumes that we have everything.

My embedded implant is trembling discreetly: time to go in. Most of them are already there. Ciro is actually sitting down: he needs to because he's holding the smallest baby, and the second smallest is clinging to his bent knee. Both stare as I come in, or rather stare through me, abstract conglomeration as I am to their new eye of visual patterns, colour and sound: I mean nothing. But still I lower my voice: I'm muttering now, to myself.

As my eyes adjust to the brighter interior, I can see more of them: three of the half-grown young ones are not actually interacting, but they are all doing the same thing. In unison they are playing with palm-pads, images projected on the flesh of one hand that can be tapped with the fingers of the other: predominantly visual stimulation is now quite rare as it doesn't keep pace with being on the move. But it's fun enough to do, especially on rare occasions like these when people are in the same room, in real time. One of these half-grown palm-people is actually one of the genetic donors of the baby on Ciro's lap: it turned out his genome was almost perfect, needed virtually no tampering. The other, another male called Austin, is a bit older and was selected for the same reason. But he's matured enough now to swagger, to sneer slightly, arriving just after me, almost the last there – save one. Sim.

The remaining handful of half-growns are present, but in a sense not there: each is mouthing words or songs, chanting and instructing, according to the dictates of the game permeating their virtual-reality contact lenses and their embedded enhanced hearing aids. Or perhaps they are 'fact-finding' through the Fact-Totum software that we all have embedded in all our clothing. Just ask anything, and immediately that familiar soft voice will answer. Apart from the novelty value of surprise at the mere randomness of a fact, the Fact-Totum is less and less accessed nowadays and I think that few use it at all: what do we really need to know and, even more telling, why would we need to know it?

The fully grown figures are less obvious because they are marginally less animated. Flo, a womb donor, is also sitting down because no technology, no cyber-virtual substitutions, can as yet offset the weight of a thirty-five-week foetus. But the rest are on their feet, as would be expected of anyone not pregnant and not of my time of nostalgia for a sedentary, screen life. There is the second womb donor, Avril, a darker version of the fairer Flo, and three egg donors, not with the impeccable genome of the two younger gene-donor boys, and without the desire to invest enormous amounts of time either in pregnancy or, even worse, post-natal care. They give their eggs to be emptied as the first stage in IVF. Then they are free to go, to move, to wander, to feel good. They have little that would bring them close to each other, these three young women, and yet nothing that would distinguish one from the other. I interact with them hardly at all, as they are always too preoccupied with their own worlds. I can't even be bothered with their names, and think of them just as A, B and C. To the rest of the Grouping, or to Sim who hears me speak these dismissive letters most often, they will actually sound like real names: after all, I am the only one who even knows the alphabet, let alone how to read.

Are we in any way similar to what used to be called a family? Obviously not. No one sleeps in the same bed as anyone else, let alone intertwines their genitals and bodily fluids in that ancient process that ceased two generations ago. And no one eats in that old archaic way round a table. Yes, we share a common food supply that for everyone's convenience is ordered in bulk by the smart storing device that keeps it in optimal conditions until accessed whenever wanted. But feeding is nowadays highly personal, almost the only special feature in your life, that might differentiate you from everyone else: where, when and what you choose to put in your mouth.

The food supplies ordered for each Grouping are logged, monitored, under constant surveillance for deviation in previous patterns, or deviation from a very liberal norm. Food is the high point of my day. After all, it's food intake, the taste and texture and smell of solids and fluids in your mouth, that offers one of the few chances to indulge senses other than hearing or vision. And since atavistic coupling is not a part of our lives, the almost constant craving for sensory stimulation is best of all met by what you taste and smell. For me, the otherwise constant stream of music, images or games lacks that same sharp sense of being alive: the images get ever brighter, the sounds louder, but they do not satisfy the way food does.

Perhaps the newer mobile-embedded way of life is far better than the static of living in a two-dimensional screen world. By actually moving the body, relying on the less predictable interaction of your body with the outside world, combined with the cyber-enhancement, the thrill is restored once again. But I'm not so sure. As I look around the room, as the temperature cools to accommodate the unusual number of bodies constrained in one place for an extended time, and as the walls, in response, tone down in colour from heated purple to cooling turquoise, I'm not convinced. There is still something missing that merely substituting three dimensions for two does not resolve. Increasing the degree of sensation, merely transforming the ordinary world into one of enhanced sensation, may be more potent than static screen outputs: but neither gives what my grandparents had.

There is no sense of time or continuity. Everyone seems on the move, even if they are not moving, and no one looks at anyone else. Only the two smallest ones, clinging to Ciro, are actually looking at what they are seeing. Everyone else is somewhere else.

'We need to talk about us, the future of our Grouping.' My voice, projected to reach the ears of others, sounds unused, unhappy. Because it is, and I am.

'This is also our chance to try out real-time interaction, to show the young ones what used to happen, what real-time reality is like.'

Silence, of a sort. Muted bleeping, jangly sounds meant for piping directly into eardrums alone, a sigh. What I'm saying is nonsensical to them.

'Doesn't anyone else want to say anything?'

'What is happening about Sim?'

Dark Avril cradles her swollen belly, less advanced than Flo, but there for all to see what she does.

'Sim must leave,' Flo mutters, twisting her hair, switching her weight. Already wanting out.

Ciro nods. 'It's certainly time. She'll soon have to give something to another Grouping: womb, eggs or genes, – it doesn't matter. But in any case, the adult quotient is full here.'

Of course, I knew this. And everyone needed to be informed about what was happening, because it will change the balance of our physical coexistence. Not that it's important, nothing ever is. Nothing and nobody means anything any more. Except Sim.

I'd known for a long time as an unacknowledged and vague fact of life that she had some significance for me, but never faced up to explicitly admitting such a strange, primitive idea. Now, in that cold turquoise chamber with eight other human beings of assorted size and gender – all glowing perfect in their prime, and all in incessant motion, twirling, tapping, swaying – I realize with the clarity of a clear sky that Sim has an impossible importance: I don't want her to leave.

Perhaps it's because she was the first one I had to care for. Once again, I happily abandon the present for past memories. She had been given to me as damp and warm as babies have been for tens of millennia. We'd collected her from another nearby Dwelling. In those days, the screen still instructed and called out when something had to be done: nowadays it would be via the improved implant. It was all simple enough. A womb donor had given birth in a Grouping that was sufficiently constituted with very small infants: our Grouping was just being assembled and needed its first baby.

When I first saw Sim, I felt that the circle that had been broken by the death of my grandparents was once again completed. Once again, here was someone with whom I could interact, and to whom I would have a special significance. I inspected her plump, perfect, pink little face with its small wet red mouth, her starfish hands and the blond fluff creating a halo around her small fragile head. She was the still point, a reality in the turning, artificial world. I planned for us to love each other.

Those first few days we all just got on with our lives, each of us preoccupied with our own pleasures and needs. Although Ciro was there from the outset, available as a carer, I gave him no share of Sim. She was mine. The womb donor Avril had arrived early on and was followed quite soon after by a genetically impeccable male, who joined us from yet another Grouping that was getting too large: a male with the expected pristine appearance but actually quite old, as we later discovered. He had died not long after.

Death. An unusual occurrence, compared to the old days. Of course, it still has to happen, but now it is swift, sudden and total – the sharp end to a life living every minute to the full, without the brain rot that cursed my grandparents' time, without the creeping, weakening illnesses that have all now been eradicated. We no longer need the hospitals of a century ago: you are either healthy or dead. At death, one of the organs simply stops working: so you cease to exist, just like in a game. This is the only reality in our lives now, the unique feature that can't be reversed. And so I suppose that matters. But then again, I sometimes feel that life doesn't matter and that I will not mind dying.

But Sim matters and I'm surprised at the sickening sensation deep in my gut even at the thought of her leaving. I had anticipated some kind of negative feeling, one very different from the excitement of everyday life. But this sensation is almost like in the previous era, almost like the notion of true love. I turn the unusual thought with difficulty through the interstices of my unpractised mind. Yes, a sense of meaning has always been important for me, starting with a separate identity, a difference from everyone else. In itself, this is an unusual and inappropriate approach in a world where all that is needed, wanted, is just to be, to consume, to enjoy, to pulsate. Not only are we tending to all look the same, but to feel the same, reacting in the same way to the same inputs that have no personal meaning.

What is the point of being what was once referred to as 'an individual'? My Fact-Totum tells me it only led to depression, a terrible flat state of emotional numbness, the very opposite of what we all experience these days. Now I realize things are worse still: I want not only to be different, but for Sim to see me as different, as I do her. I want something utterly unusual now: I want us to have a relationship, one that lasts a lifetime.

Then again, I have to admit, Sim isn't objectively that extra-ordinary when compared with any other female born currently. Of course she's perfect physically, fairer rather than darker. But what makes her so special? Nothing if I'm honest. And most of the time she's away from me, in her cyber-world. When she was very small, though, and she and I were all there was, before other babies arrived to care for, I let myself pretend we lived long ago, and I was her mother: in my very special scenario, I had given her everything – my womb, my eggs, my genes and my time. In my fantasy, I defined myself as Sim's mother so that, as in my grandparents' era, I became important with a clear and vital role, recognized and revered as the central focus of the family.

But as I was given those other babies, as Ciro and I settled down to a functional, loveless rota of tasks, the pretence became much harder to sustain. And, in any case, it all started to change as Sim grew from infant to child. She began wanting to say things, to tell me things, even though words meant little beyond being the literal names for the objects around her. But as I was taken over by the demands of still younger charges, so she had to spend more time on her own in front of the screen, a Talking Head that was becoming a better, more exciting substitute for me. She enjoyed placing her chubby little fingers on the eyes and the nose and calling out, then seeing immediately the images dance at her command. She gurgled and trilled at the colours exploding every second at her control. And then, more than anything else, she wanted to dance and move faster and faster to the beats that were pushed into her little ears.

All too soon, she was of an age for the embedded implants in her eyes and ears that would provide competition to the screen – and win. I had been too old for this technology, which was normally fitted by telemedicine robots around the age of three. Within an hour, Sim was looking back at me with a slight film over her large blue eyes, and the smallest incisions behind her ears that rapidly became unnoticeable. Soon she was perfect once again. Moving freely in an enhanced world would always be more powerful than passively interacting with a Talking Head or even immersing yourself in a standardized hologram experience. Soon it was impossible for Sim to sit still: and once she was given the embedded, mobile access, she was away, running away.

But I never forgot the early time, before she could escape from my arms. She had been real and permanent, needing me as I did her. So I too had been more real and more alive than I have ever been since. But since Sim I've been careful, and it's been easy to keep the next generation, the endless succession of screaming, vomiting, incontinent later ones, at arm's length.

Sim's presence is enough to keep me going, to remind me of how it used to be. She is my lifeline to the elusive thing that goes beyond the daily excitement and ecstasy of current life, even though I'm not sure what it is. I know that I need it, and I don't know what will happen when she goes. It will be the third big episode that charts my otherwise empty life story: my grandparents dying, Sim arriving, Sim leaving.

There is nothing else to be said. The restlessness in the room is mounting. Ciro's two smallest have understood nothing. Everyone else, partly grown and full grown alike, has come and gone, in and out of their own cyber-spaces. The talking, the interchange, was feeble competition for their senses: desultory words dropped like pebbles in a pond, a stagnant pond with no ripples. Sim wasn't there and no one really cared, apart from me. They didn't really care about anything. So the simple fact of her absence was mentioned, value free, the desire being that she should be permanently absent. It has been actually stated, voiced out loud. Then forgotten, at least by everyone else. But the ripples spread out through my particular brain alone, my special, different mind. I have thoughts and they are ebbing beyond the here and now, beyond the diffident turquoise alcoves.

The meeting is over, if it ever really began. All the bodies start to melt away and the walls become consequently warmer, deepening into lilac then pink. But I am thinking ahead: the ripples push on through my mind and take me to the unusual, unvisited place, the future. What will really happen when Sim leaves? What will happen to her? I'll never be able to find out. I realize just how much I care. I care so much that I consider ways to stop it happening. And I care about what will happen to me, alone. But weren't we all alone, always? Nowadays, yes: in my grandparents' time, hardly ever. How I ache to be part of then, instead of this.

I am alone indeed now, in the room heated up to an accommodating deep red. The prospect of returning to another screen game holds no appeal: I don't want to sit and stare and react and receive, I want to give. I am dying for it. Outside, the square of window is black, unanswering and unhelpful. A storm is beginning. The idea of venturing out into the wild, drenching wet, even with the cyber-embedded devices, threatens too much unpredictability. So the prospect opens up, as it usually does, of the strong drugs designed with stunning accuracy for a single purpose, one that will take me into welcome oblivion. It is the only way forward.

I am almost running to my personalized sleeping space. The walls welcome me with cheerful yellow: my body sensors have transmitted my sadness. For some reason, no reason, I whisper 'mountain' from the infinite range of options for a simulated sleep-inducing scene. Now I'm in the fresh, caressing air, looking up at a clear, starry sky. But my eyes will not close. And so I reach for the slick vial of pills that will indiscriminately and immediately dismantle my brain into oblivion.

Chapter 10

TARRA

They've asked me to give a testimony of everything that happened, as I personally saw it, right from the beginning, that evening Fred came back with his news. Even now, it's hard and painful to recall every moment: but I *do* remember everything in sequential freeze-frame as immediately and automatically as breathing. It's as though those past events are still more real, more vivid, than the way I live now. So, I'll start from the very first night that everything changed.

Fred came home at the same time and in the same way that he always did. He didn't need to call out as it was his designated return time. The instance of his arrival, as usual, had been at the exact minute it always was, and I heard his steps turn up the short path to where the three of us lived. This Home Base for our Family Unit is distinguished from all the others only by its demarcating number. Inside everything is, like for everyone else, organized for the effective and harmonious functioning of brain and body. The walls are all pale grey and completely unadorned, the floor tiled black and the ceilings always white. We have only the necessary furniture: a big enough bed for Fred and me and, in the adjoining smaller room, a smaller version for

Bill. We only need three chairs in the main room, steel and black netting designed to maximize good posture and breathing, as we know no one will ever visit. But dominating the main room is the large, plain wooden table that is pivotal to both mental and physical activities, and which already I had prepared for eating and talking. That night, as on all other previous nights, two white plates waited for Fred and me, a jug of water, simple white ceramic tumblers: accoutrements for eating that would have been recognizable as such many centuries ago.

Once I heard him, I went slowly forward to greet him just as always, pausing and leaning lightly on one of the chairs, watching him approach me, still happy just to stare at the face that was so familiar. As soon as his face appeared around the door, the usual comforting warmth suffused me. Fred was my complement: the reassurance I needed that my thoughts were going in the right direction. My consciousness could once again be interactive and collective, my thinking appropriately linear.

'Greetings.'

'Greetings.'

'All as it should be?'

'Of course. Bill learnt ten new words. I think he'll be ready for his Helmet very soon.'

Bill, our statutory single progeny, now fast asleep: Fred would not disturb him by going into his room. That would have been bad for them both. As a neuroscientist, Fred had told me how important sleep, especially dreaming, was. For a long time we had known that periods of learning were associated with increased periods of dream sleep, and that if you were deprived of your chance to dream, then memory could be seriously impaired. Above all, Bill's thought processes had to be protected and maximized.

'Yes, let's enrol him for the Helmet as soon as possible.'

I nodded and felt myself frowning slightly.

'He's certainly good enough with words and cognitive connections, but he still has moments of spontaneity and distraction. And now he has words, he's in danger of being too self-referential, self-centred, unless we act as quickly as possible.'

Self-centred: Bill must never be that – not in the sense of the dreary solipsism of that previous, terrible era. But, for the first time ever, I noticed Fred hesitate, nervously licking his lips. I could tell he was uncertain whether to share his thoughts with me, to actually say something out loud that concerned him. He looked past me, over my shoulder, eventually speaking slowly as though the idea itself was being brought together and assembled into a final form only then.

'But if you don't see the world through the prism of your own particular life narrative, if instead you are a component, however individual and special, contributing to a greater, abstracted, disembodied idea – then, after all, who are you?'

What a strange thing to say. The silence swelled ominously between us. I could think of no immediate response. I was too shocked. No one, least of all Fred, ever normally spoke like that. But just as I was about to say something, anything, still unsure how he wanted me to respond, or indeed still searching for what was the right thing to say, Fred seemed to shake himself mentally. With a small, tight smile, he sat down on one of the chairs, and with obvious relief sought less frightening territory, safer, more familiar ground.

'Yes, and once he has words, he might well start to play games, unless we're careful. Let's give the boy some meaning to his life as soon as possible.'

As I knew it would, Fred's mind locked into perfect agreement with mine: that's what the Family Unit was about. But the abnormal silence between us started to thicken once again.

Something was still very wrong. I looked away, reached for some water. Fred clearly had something to say, something very different from our normal easy, evening conversations. He stood up. Neither of us had been brought up to give or receive surprises, especially potentially negative ones on a cataclysmic scale.

'Hodge asked to see me today, outside of our usual schedule.'

'Has there been a big breakthrough?'

We faced each other, each standing behind a protective chair, both knowing we would not be discussing a new discovery about the brain.

'He has given me a really significant job.'

His words were all wrong. They seemed to stick in his throat, almost gagging in his mouth so he could hardly breathe. Everything he did was significant, and neither he, nor I for that matter, had ever had a single, simple 'job'. What a silly word, what a stupid phrase: it meant nothing, didn't help in any way with what he needed to say.

All I could do was remain motionless, looking down at the table, leaning heavily on the chair.

'It's a completely unusual project, but one that makes sense, one that will help us all.'

That was a little better, just a little. But almost as a defence, I thought of the worst possibility I could. 'It's something to do with the Others, isn't it?'

'Yes.'

I felt my whole body stiffen. Time slowed, juddered to a halt. Fred flapped his hands helplessly in vestigial little movements at his sides. He opened his mouth, then shut it again. Because he was an extension of me, I knew he could accompany me in my thinking as I wordlessly conjured up different hypothetical scenes, different justifications, alternatives, reassurances. And, after each mental foray, there remained the same, devastating truth. Fred was talking about the unknown, having something as yet unspecified to do with the very people who had once almost destroyed not only us and our children, but evolution itself, almost reversing it by turning humanity back to mindless, useless beings cluttering the planet.

'But we've always had nothing to do with them. We're safer that way. Our whole lifestyle is so perfect, we make such progress all the time. Anything to do with them would slow us down, or, or –' I was pumping out words without taking breath, at a loss for the right phrases to match accurately the improbable, the impossible possibility – 'or defile us in some way.'

I waited for Fred to reassure me, even though he was at a loss himself. The whole tenet of our lives was normally a predictable chain of events, spontaneity of any kind being as upsetting as it was unusual. But he wasn't looking me in the eye, just down at his hands now again grasping tightly the back of the chair as though he might otherwise fall.

'It's a field trip like they used to do a century ago, an investigation simply to understand how their brains may have been changed by their here-and-now, Yakawow technology.'

As a reflex, I felt myself wildly, stupidly, looking around the room, seeking some kind of familiarity, a rationale, a way out. Could he mean that he, Fred, was actually going to visit the real Others, physically, in real time? Surely impossible, but he was already making it clear ...

'And you can't get what you need from the usual simulated scenarios, informatics, or by simply intercepting their radio signals?'

'No.'

'When ... when do you leave?'

'In a few days. Soon. As soon as possible.'

Chapter 11

FRED

It was only a matter of three days before I left. I realize that from now on, these recordings will only be accessible once I've returned: but of course I'm determined I should continue normally, setting down events as frequently as possible and as I've just experienced them, while they are fresh in my memory.

As soon as the first bright streaks of dawn scraped across the sky, I set off. I'd practised balancing on the bicycle immediately after the interview with Hodge. Surprisingly, I discovered I was quite well coordinated and efficient in mastering the strange device: within a few hours the air-light invention felt like an extension of my own body. So then I was ready to go, concentrating single-mindedly on the journey that, despite the complete novelty of my newly acquired travelling speed, would still take me several days.

I started out deliberately blinkering myself, focusing first on the immediate journey over the mountains, with no time for recording this as I went along. And anyhow I wanted time to reflect, without immediately packaging my thoughts into finalized, cohesive, spoken sentences that might give them more certainty than they warranted. It was going to be a special time, and one that I planned to savour. There was no precedent, after all, no experiment to plan, no theoretical question to share in dialogue, no prescribed activity for the particular time of day, and no place to provide the expected and familiar context. No one else had ever done what I was doing now: I was retracing the journey of my forefathers, and totally alone for the first time in my life. My mind was freed up, and it eased its way around its new expanding space, tentative and unsure.

I didn't wish to dwell on the previous evening with Tarra and her uncharacteristic distress. Both of us were unused to, and uncomfortable with, excessive emotions: on this rare occasion, she was frightened at being frightened, while I felt guilty, I suppose, for the perturbation and unforeseen anguish I was causing her. For the first time she hadn't immediately understood and empathized, and for the first time I couldn't convey what I was feeling. I can see all that now, how I had experienced personal culpability for the first time. In calm retrospection I can make sense of it in a way that I couldn't when I had needed to, when I had been with her and needed to explain and understand more.

I shivered: was this the way that the Others might be all the time? Did they live so carried away by such self-absorption and turbulent churnings inside that they could never make sense of the world around them and the other people in it? Dead end, again. Think about yourself instead, in the here and now.

And so I imagined the absurdity from a third-person perspective: a single man, even on an empowered bicycle, heading over the mountains all alone, for no less a purpose than to ensure the continuing safety of the human mind. As always, such a description showed that facts on their own could be misleading without the context and background. And the life, the story, the knowledge and the people behind me, pedalling along, all of these were vast and powerful: I hoped to catalyze great things. I knew I could. I was the first step in a wonderful journey, both for my people and perhaps for myself. I was conscious of the wider context of who I was, linking a past and a future.

Next, I tried conjuring up scenario after scenario as to what it would be like arriving back among the Others. In the previous century, surveillance was everywhere as everyone lived a completely interconnected existence. It would have been unthinkable back then not to have known exactly what a country or a society looked like, how they spoke, what they believed in and what they did. Every moment of the day or night you could have known what was happening. There would have been no need for a mission such as this current one of mine, back then. Everyone watched and listened to everyone else. In the end, by the middle of the last century, that's all they ever did, and it was their undoing. Because everyone spent most of the time connecting themselves in cyber-space, they stopped living their real lives. So there ceased to be anything novel to watch: there was nothing different from you yourself in an infinite regression, like mirrors facing each other and bouncing back the same image to infinity. Monitoring equipment fell into disuse: it was easier, better, more fun to be on the move without endlessly reporting back or being watched by everyone else reporting back again to you.

As the mobile technologies gave back to everyone a three-dimensional life, so they also gave back the experience of an individual body moving around in space: but now such actions lacked purpose, planning and consequence. There was no longer any meaning to life. That was when the forefathers knew they had no choice but to leave. However, when they finally did so in the great Exodus, they were giving up any direct means of knowing what might happen in the future among the Others. The mindless, meaningless, endless quest for sensation was really taking hold, leaving only echoes of mechanical body physiology for us to intercept and study. By the time we were established as a society, with our technology in place, all we could do was monitor mass trends in heart rate and blood pressure over the airwaves ... But now my train of thought had nowhere further to go: it juddered to a halt again. Where next?

So slowly I started to focus just on the immediate present: for once, actions didn't need to have meaning. I started to look around me. As I skimmed along, I began to marvel at the unusual use of my legs and the heightened gearing effect of their gentle pedalling: then I realized that my facial muscles were pulling upwards and that I was smiling at no one. I felt some kind of strange inner warmth, suspended in this fragile bridge of time between a secure past and a future fraught with unknown dangers and novelty. For this brief snap-shot there was no immediate goal, no meticulously staged sequence of thought of action. So long as I arrived at the other side of the mountains, this brief time spent getting there was my own. My own. For the first time in my life, ever, I could let my mind freewheel. No feedback. No checks and balances. No relationship to anyone else. No symbols or metaphors. I was simply alive, as myself, where everything fitted around me: trees, distant mountains, green and sky. In my perfect and rightful place in the world. At the centre. In my element.

The diamond-hard eyes narrow to thin black slits.

Then the slope started to get steeper, but the wonders of the bicycle fuel-cell technology could cope, ensuring I felt nothing but a gentle effort that was truly a pleasure. The next few days I had no contact with anyone. Never before had I been freed from the demands of communication for so long. I slept under the stars, drank the crystal water my pedalling energy generated, and savoured stepping back to look around as I moved forward. There were no external or immediate problems to solve, only unprecedented time to … to be … Fred, the man. The complete man. Then the ground started to slope downwards.

I discovered quickly that I didn't need to pedal at all, just balance. But apart from that, I wasn't aware of being anywhere different. At first the landscape was similar, since on both sides of such difficult terrain human habitation had never been prominent even in the last century. The only non-natural feature remaining from that bygone time, the roads, provided the first sign: unused and thus fallen into pothole neglect. I wove round these minor obstacles, still marvelling in the thrill of true travel for the first time. Until then I had only walked sensibly on the clean, dark, even surfaces that joined the short distances between my home, my work, and the Rally Place. But now I felt a strange sensation that I could best, though bizarrely I suppose, describe as freedom.

But surely I had always been free? I tried to think through what could be so negative about the life that I had always accepted as perfect because it was a constant quest for perfection, for absolute truths. I had always been content with that. But now, rather than calm acceptance, I was finding exhilaration at being alive. I was more than just an N-P or a scientist: I was Fred, alone, fast and free: a real, multi-faceted man who was starting to see himself as complete and independent, defying definition. Like the destination to which I was cycling, I was a whole new country, a whole new subject waiting to be discovered and explored, by just me.

Normally, everything I did, even on the short, permitted solitary interludes between work and home, had always involved placing my thoughts in a more generic context beyond myself – the context of a theoretical problem in general or a neuroscientific issue in particular. Now I looked up at the vast clear sky and felt I was part of a connected universe that didn't need explaining, and certainly not reducing to a model, a principle, an abstraction. I was in the right place, and as Fred the man I had my own special place there. All I had to do was be aware of it and enjoy it. Day after day of solitude, freewheeling down mountains and round potholes, the air on my face and liberated from the shackles of conversation – it all meant that here I didn't need any contrived connections at all to any other time or any other person or society.

Then, as the land flattened, so evidence of the Others started to become apparent. A few hardly noticeable signs at first, such as the occasional obstinate relic of some smashed gadget, left by an era long gone but not cleared away. Gradually, such detritus no longer whispered but screamed, as I found myself cycling not any more in clean, unspoilt countryside, but through what must have been the exploded ruins of some twenty-first-century settlement. The wind was whipping up and carelessly blowing dirty plastic bags in pointless circles, still visible as such in the gathering gloom of evening. Then the rain started, and I knew I would soon need to stop, and indeed that I had arrived.

I first caught site of it all from a long distance. Nothing could have prepared me for it. Despite the growing darkness, the bright glowing colours were defiantly visible, beckoning me on to come and wonder. As I drew nearer, my first reaction was shock at the contrast between the old twenty-first-century leftovers and the blindingly bright onslaught of the twenty-second century. Scattered among the debris were large geodesic domed buildings, some emitting bright multicoloured lights flashing in the night, while some glowed luminescent artificial fuchsia pink or bilious yellow. I tried to reconcile the beige squares of my own home as existing on the same planet, in the same universe, the same reality as all this – and failed.

I felt the heady inspiration of the last few days being sucked out by the demanding and unforgiving assault on my senses. The ubiquitous lurid neon colours with their strident glare and incessant flashing posed too many questions, while at the same time snatching away any chance for proper thought, taking me over and trampling on my mind. My hands slammed over my ears and I screwed my eyes shut, but there was no escape. I pedalled away more furiously. At a loss in every way, I must have been cycling in circles, even though I had nowhere to go. I felt I needed to be in motion in case, if I stopped, I would be drowned, overwhelmed by all the flashing glare and blare: submerged in Yakawow. But my senses were satiated to the point of real sickness as my head started to swim, heavy with overloaded inputs. I finally had to stop.

There, in that demented landscape, conspicuous by its unique naturalness, was a single, ancient tree: perhaps it had been too large and too much bother to remove, too uninteresting to defile. Without any conscious decision, I was drawn to it like a homing pigeon, and propped the bike against this ancient, eternal feature of landscape. My back pressed against its indifferent bark as I sank down with fatigue, and my fingers felt around for the reassurance of real, solid earth. What was I to do now? Where was I to go? In all our planning, Hodge had left this part vague simply because we were unaware of the level of actual experience, of the daily substance of the Others' lives. After all, this was precisely why I had been sent here, to find out what happened to them as people, beyond the endless read-outs and logs concerning bowel movements and calorie consumption that we could intercept remotely: as the Others had apparently used traditional, sessile technology less and less, it had been impossible to place their actions into contexts such as education or social conversation or work.

We had both known that I would have to tap into an unrehearsed skill of using my initiative, of improvising in response to whatever I found. Perhaps we had assumed wrongly that, superficially at least, everyday simple interaction might not be that different from our own – inevitably less meaningful and sustained but enabling me to have introductory conversations of a sort. After all, that is how it had been at the time of the Exodus. But, as I opened my eyes and ventured to look around from the steadying influence of the tree, I realized just how different these people had become, and how much more difficult my task would be. Even though it was raining quite hard, with raindrops swollen with lurid colours from the polyhedron roofs and walls of the domes, there were figures still outside. They were clearly oblivious to the elements, in some world of their own. Strangely, some were singing, others talking but seemingly to themselves, others mute but apparently in some kind of altered state. I got back to my feet, swung my leg over the lilac frame, and cycled slowly forward, into the unknown once more.

No one was interacting with anyone else. In the N-P world, it's usual to see groups, or most usually couples, walking and talking in dialogue so that not only can they stay physically fit, but actually maximize the process of developing thoughts and ideas. But if it were not a designated time or purpose for dialogue, I was accustomed, as was our way, to avoid instigating pointless conversation. At such times, I was used to passing by other N-Ps in the institute or on the street. But even then, always there would be a brief nod of the head, a glancing exchange of eye contact.

However, *this* world was different: even though I already realized how conspicuously alien I must look compared to the gyrating figures around me – not least thanks to my gleaming bicycle – no one seemed to register any interest at all. I was just an object in their visual field: something at most to dance around if I placed myself in front of them, an obstacle at worst, an object at best. Here, none of the inhabitants appeared to be in any way conscious of anyone else. They seemed oblivious to their strident backdrop: most appeared to be not so much looking inwards but outwards in an utterly insular, strange travesty of privacy. One or two swayed to a silent beat, some were laughing and giggling to themselves, some were just smiling, eyes creased, lips wide and open. Why would they worry about me, my bicycle, or my reasons?

They would never accost me. I would have to stand on my own feet and somehow explore for myself what best to do. By now I had a dull, steady headache. However, the nausea had subsided and I needed once more to try and make sense of it all. Unlike our own soft, muted vistas, where such colours as there were, were the green from leaves and grass, here all things natural had either been subjugated, neglected or out-competed by the Others' fabricated world. The multicoloured, sprawling fluorescent domes seemed to laugh at me in their screaming incongruity with the windy night. They were not arranged in neat rows, like our own homes, but in rambling disarray out and around each other. I concluded that the very large size of these buildings must mean that the Others lived in a far less structured way, in far bigger groups, unlike our own tidy trio family units. What was going on in contrast, on the other side of this glowing lime-green facade? Inside were Others, living some sort of lives. And, inside their synthetic, neon palaces, I wondered whether they too, at the end of each day, felt that they had come home.

Chapter 12

SIM

Sim is running. As she does on most evenings. The dark, cold night cuts into her senses, escalates the music in her ear, whisking everything up with the enhancing lenses filming her eyes to take her into beyond. She doesn't know where she is, or where she is going. But she must get away from Zelda. The running is what counts and the new sights and sounds, changing every moment. No past or future, no Groupings, no time and no place, no anything. The black night holds no dangers: after all, it means nothing other than that it is night and it is black. Just reach out and take: on and on, higher and higher, moving for more and more as the moment stretches on and on and on.

Once upon a time, there was a time when she had to be still: a long-ago hazy, endless moment, smothered within clammy, soft, large arms. She jabbing with both outstretched unpractised hands, all fingers splayed at once, reaching out to the lure and promise of the big bright screen that was just out of reach. And the thrill that she knew would come, of commanding up colour, exploding sounds, all for her delight: the tingle of making it all come alive. The screen was part of her, part of her body, as her fingers, thumbs and eyes came together in a whole, infinite moment of experience.

And as her podgy, budding infant limbs had slenderized into legs, so the muscles were stretched and hardened by the newer way, the embedded mobile technology. Just at the time that she was wriggling within Zelda's grasp, and could have grown sluggish and demanding, so the static artificial screen way of life was giving way to the saturation of reality-enhancement via the nano-technologies crouching in clothes, in body prostheses, under skin and within the nervous system. No longer the repetitive limitations of simple games with the Talking Head and snap decisions, choices, evaluations between meaningless options: no more pre-scripted hologram experiences where the apparent third dimension turned out to be a mere illusion. Now the entire outside world had been transformed into cyber-space. No real time or real space, just this moment. The past and the future were indeed long gone: but the new present is different, even better than before.

So Sim runs and runs. Invisible within her arm, the implant that is her biosensor is as much a part of her, as unremarkable as her wild blonde hair, as is the implant in the ear and the thin film over her eyes. She is never alone ever: all the time her voices are whispering or singing, sad or loud or excited, but always there, always close. The Fact-Totum voice is pleasant enough and constantly ready and willing to help: but Sim rarely turns to it to find things out. She has no questions to ask. Other sounds, and clearer and simpler voices, give her all she needs.

When she was smaller and Zelda was there all the time in the background, she never had to ask. All she had to do, wanted to do, was look at the Talking Head, to stare at the fast little coloured happenings on a tiny central image that glowed with importance and was the focus of everything. That focus, though, contained so much: a mosaic of options, so many ways to go with each and every fingertip press. Sometimes Zelda would force her to look away, to the boring, boring slow spaces around her.

'Come on, baby, just look how the shadows grow longer as it gets later, as the day becomes older.'

Sim still has shadowy memories of how silent and slow and dark it all was. Trapped and imprisoned, desperate for escape. The most enduring feature, the only means then of running away, was the daily performance of bodily functions – a distraction that was obviously necessary, just as it still is, accessing all five senses in machine-like three-dimensional motion: a coordinated manipulation of clothes, fingers and faeces. Emptying bladder and bowels was fun. The wash-waste sessions were special because they were different – this was the one place and time when Sim had to inactivate her enhancers and where her implant and Fact-Totum didn't work.

She would go to an area of the Dwelling bathed in still much brighter lights, colours and sounds, and saturated with heavier, headier masking fragrances than normal: at such times, all the experience she would have, unusually and uniquely, had to be driven externally. Then Sim would shed her garment so that her flesh all over could gleam and glow in the light. It was the one time when she needed to be naked as she exchanged the indifference of the element of air around her for the intrusive one of water. Then she would let everything out of her body as the thick, fast steaming, scented streams sprayed her from all directions, washing the waste into the waiting detector-tubes that would instantly analyze for any possible medical threat, from diabetes to incipient heart disease.

Sim particularly liked these wash-waste sessions when she was small, not because of the sounds and nice smell – those were everywhere all the time in any case, albeit less obvious: no, the novelty was the fast, slithery feeling of the water streaming over her skin, everywhere. She also the liked the voice that spoke to her at the end.

'No signs of infections or malfunctions. All in good order.' The voice never, ever said anything else.

Next best, after wash-waste, was eating. Thick lumps of food squashing in her mouth and squirting through her teeth. But above all was taste, a strange process that was special because there was no cyber-way to simulate it: Sim had to put real food into her real mouth and make it perform real, mechanical movements. Unlike everything else, however, it was impossible to continue indefinitely with this action of eating. She had tried once, to keep putting more and more food in her mouth, rolling it around with her tongue and her teeth, then swallowing and reaching for more all at the same time. After all, food was always available and everyone just took it and ate it on their own, whenever they wanted. So Sim had grabbed handfuls of bright, purple-coloured triangles called roast beef: they unleashed multi-flavoured tastes, triggering one after the other different layers of moist depth charges to explode in the mouth. She felt the thrill of a direct, indescribable experience that couldn't ever be accessed from her enhancers. More and more of these wonderful things from outside, these food shapes, but now inside her and part of her. Food blurred the body boundaries. But then her implant had started to bleep, and that had brought Zelda running.

'Sim, you mustn't eat so much: you will become sick.'

Sim had no idea what 'sick' meant, but was angry with Zelda for wrenching the triangles from her weaker, smaller fingers. That was one of the earliest times when Sim had really wanted Zelda to leave her alone, but then that wish occurred more and more often. Sim liked tastes and smells, not suffocating cuddles and silly talking. Why did Zelda want to talk so much? It wasn't the same fun as running.

As soon as she could, whenever Zelda needed to tend to the smaller ones, Sim took off: she ran away, liberated and entranced by her new embedded mobile, to see the world as never before. Now she could spend less and less time with the Grouping, restlessly moving around each other, avoiding eye contact, avoiding any sort of touching or talking, on and on in the rooms of ever-changing hues.

Zelda tried to interest her by telling her about earlier times, when things were not always just happening over and over, but only once, real stories that would never happen again. But why should empty words telling of someone who had done something once, that had then already been and gone – why should that be more important right now? Zelda's busy but empty one-sided conversations could easily be screened out, ignored. They were just sounds that really said nothing, changed nothing, excited no one.

Zelda also taught her 'facts' – the names of things and what those things did. Sim had listened unconditionally: she had tasted the fact, swallowed it whole, just accepting. A fact could be fun, could surprise her and make her laugh or scream. All she had to do was hear it, not simultaneously upload things that had gone before or after in some kind of slowed-down game-like 'story'. Above all, Sim didn't have to answer anything back when she was told a fact. Facts were easier to deal with because they didn't mean knowing other things at the same time. Easy, but not worth putting on hold all those sounds and smells and bright fast colours. In any case, what was she to do when she had heard the fact? If it was new or unpleasant or funny, she might have an immediate reaction. But there was nothing to do with it once she had heard it. It was just there, stored away in the Fact-Totum.

She remembers the time when Zelda had first told her about wrinkles and grey hair and baldness, and because these words sounded so strange she had looked them up by asking the Fact-Totum: such phenomena had been as hard to imagine as a part of life as she knows it, as other funny words that Zelda used, such as unicorns or bombs or books. Unreal things from some strange, early time that had no meaning, dreary distractions that took away all the fun. Increasingly, Sim has become irritated at Zelda displaying her imperfect, non-cyber biomemory: why was she bothering to load up herself all the time?

Still, when she had been small, trapped in Zelda's arms, squirming on her lap, Zelda had tried to tell her facts that she herself was supposed to upload into her own biomemory. Facts, but even more often, stories, seemed important to Zelda, even more important than the screen games that she otherwise played most of the time. Perhaps it was because she was fully grown: but then Sim couldn't see why having a larger body like Zelda's would change what you liked to do. Sim also realized that for Zelda to talk in this way about things that had happened just once, or to download facts, someone had to be there to receive her outputs. That someone was her, Sim, always: for some reason Zelda chose her out of all the other small ones in the Grouping. Why didn't she keep pulling on *their* arms, snake her arm round *their* waists, squeeze the air out of one of *them*? But it was always, always her. And when Sim had to listen to Zelda, she felt like screaming for something more to happen, right then.

But Zelda closed her eyes and, in a strange, distant voice that wasn't really meant for Sim, mixed up facts and stories in recounting a different time from now: Sim didn't really need to be there anyway as Zelda just spoke out loud to herself. She called being small 'childhood' and, strangest of all, told Sim that when she was small she had only two grown members in her Grouping. Zelda kept saying that the real name was 'family'. She described to Sim how a male gene donor called Thomas and a female, Emma, had supplied the genes to make Zelda, but only from very specific parts of their bodies, not as it was done now.

No, it was actual eggs from inside Emma and some very special milky stuff that came out of Thomas that locked into each other once they were both inside Emma's very own womb, without any IVF. And if that wasn't hard enough to understand, Thomas and Emma even looked after Zelda all on their own, in a Grouping of just the three of them. But when she was still small, younger than Sim now, Thomas and Emma were killed by very bad people. So then Zelda lived with Emma's own mother and father, but still in a small Grouping of only three people. Zelda had sighed as she often did, and her eyes had looked into some other place that Sim couldn't see.

'It was what most people did, or tried to do: have a nuclear family, as it was called. Even in my childhood, it was already getting rarer though. No, it wasn't a problem just living each day, but in my grandparents' time it was very rare not to want something else. So after a few years, sometimes more, sometimes less, people tried again with different partners, as they were called then.'

Sim never sighed, and felt uncomfortable when Zelda did it so much; nor could she really follow what Zelda was trying to say. It all seemed so unlikely, so unexciting, and nothing to do with her. But Zelda had gone silent and Sim guessed it must be her turn to say something. She had tried hard to focus on Zelda's glassy face, her reddish curls, her pink lips, now flat and pressed together, her eyes very shiny.

'What else did they want?' Sim asked the wide, flat glassiness.

'They never really could put their finger on it: that was the trouble. People were searching for something but didn't know what. But my parents, Thomas and Emma, had found it.'

Sim was pleased that this story had a happy end, and was especially happy that it was over and perhaps she could now go. But at the same time she wondered what 'it' was that Thomas and

Emma had found, and how indeed they had discovered where it was. Was it a special hologram experience, or maybe a new grade of enhancer? But Zelda was holding her down, tighter still, pulling Sim hard against her body, pinning down her arms with insistent affection, yet watching scenes far, far away. It wasn't over.

'Once the cyber-culture took over everyone had something else to do, something that stopped them looking around any more. First, screen life meant that you could communicate and learn and have fun without feeling threatened. But because nothing lasted for very long, nothing was important. Then people couldn't see the point of communicating with each other at all, or learning anything: next, they couldn't even see the point of thinking about tomorrow because they knew it would be the same as today, and so they just wanted to have excitement. Before I was grown up, so much had changed: things moved very fast. It was a combination, I suppose, of the screen technologies and the genetic ones all finally coming together to give us a chance of the kind of life we all have now.'

Sim had not known what she was supposed to say. This game that Zelda often played had no rules, no template, no goal. But Sim did know about screen technologies, and gene technologies such as IVF. Everyone did. The Fact-Totum started off with facts about what was happening to you and other people in your Grouping, and what was going to happen. The Fact-Totum confronted you with the facts as soon as you asked what a gene was, or a cell. But it was just a way of finding out the names of things, and that was all Sim needed or wanted. The facts, what things were called and what they did. Sim didn't want to know anything more about genes, for example, apart from the fact that that was the name for things that caused lots of other things to happen, such as babies arriving in the Grouping. Zelda was not so helpful or good at supplying Sim with information just as she wanted it, in the small bits that would be just right; nor in doing so quickly. Unlike the Fact-Totum she didn't show Sim pictures and instead spoke for a long time, just into the air. There was nowhere to look. And many of the words she used, and things she spoke of, didn't fit anywhere in Sim's life.

'Things were moving just too fast for me, all the technology was rushing in at once. And my genes weren't that special, at least not the ones that gave me my first face. It was taking up time and it also hurt, having my face and body corrected: why should I want more of that sort of thing from the new gene technologies too?'

'What does "hurt" mean?'

'It's when you are in pain.'

'What's pain?'

'Something no one feels any more.'

'Is that good or bad?'

'Both.'

And Sim had just stared back because there was nothing else she could do. She had listened in those early days, trapped on Zelda's lap, aching to turn back to making the screen do things at her fingertip say-so. Zelda was really just a dull presence, in the shadows, the person who made Sim touch solid, uncommunicative objects around her. Within the Dwelling, most things – from furniture to food to the walls themselves – would transform or at least react in some way at the whisper of a word or a touch. Nothing was just a simple un-smart thing, performing just one function by virtue of a permanent physical shape and continuously doing so irrespective of whether anyone was operating or commanding or using it. So Zelda made Sim go outside and smell real flowers that, unbidden and defiant, were emitting colour and texture and smell outside the Dwelling. But they were hard to find: outside there were usually just

125

other Dwellings and very large trees, tough and old enough to have survived the decades. Flowers were frailer and much less usual now.

At first, Sim liked these excursions, because they were different, at least when she was small. But as she grew, the smells and the textures were always the same, predictable, weak compared to her enhancers, and no longer surprising. She grew to hate repeating the same activity over and over, especially when it was so much less forceful than the screen experiences. Almost as bad as Zelda's real-time talking into air. But Sim had nothing to say, nothing to give. How could she? Instead she wanted to take – take the strong, bright, fast things right now into her body. Or let them out in the wash-waste sessions. Or, best of all as now, let her body spread and merge and run into the streams of sound and colour. Just being. No boundaries of space or time ...

Right now is just right. She is blurring. The darkness lapping round her eyes is enhanced to abstracted iridescence by her lenses, powered as her pounding feet feed them energy through the transducers in her sparkling footwear, converting the pounding mechanical to necessary electrical. She races on, over neglected scrubland in the wasteland between spattered Dwelling areas. The darkness hides ancient broken glass bottles, a dead bird, a hungry rat. But all Sim sees is loveliness. A tortoiseshell glow shining down, with pulsating rainbows all around and swelling to the ever faster beat in her ears. This is the ultimate reality. Sim isn't scared of the darkness. It is just something black to run towards, to fling herself into, to be part of. So on and on until the tired spikes of scrubland and earth underfoot give way to harder, non-natural surfaces: the surfaces of a Dwelling zone.

Suddenly, Sim's arm implant starts to emit a low whistle that indicates she is becoming cold, despite her fast pace: the physiological balance isn't holding. She has run too far and too fast on too cold a night. And even though her smart clothes are now responding by switching on their thermal sensors, the additional energy required from her running would still not be sufficient. Usually that is plenty, but not right now, not tonight. The whistle grows louder and more strident.

Sim has been conditioned from an early age always to obey the biofeedback implant. It is the one real and important fact that Zelda has told her over and over, the Fact-Totum has told her, and the message has been constantly repeated, flashed up on the screen between games. She stops and switches her enhanced display to simple location information. For the first time, she realizes how there is no light at all tonight, and she is now very, very cold.

She has come a long way from the Dwelling of her own Grouping. Obviously, she isn't lost in strict geographical terms: that would be impossible as the location information could obligingly also provide the fastest route back. But beyond the electronics, Sim feels very lost in the most real sense of all: she is actually now unsure what to do next.

This sickening feeling of uncertainty is made worse by being completely unprecedented. Sim usually makes decisions about what to do next instantly on a spontaneous feeling, not by needing to weigh up options by comparing possible outcomes. Normally there is no choice, and no consequences. Nothing Sim has ever done in her life has, as far as she is aware, actually led to anything good or bad as a result. Each moment has been self-contained, atomized. Now for the first time her instinct just to *do*, fails.

Rain has started to fall very heavily, like a wash-waste session unexpectedly turned ugly with harsh sounds, cold water and no entrancing fragrances or mesmerizing voices. And no end, no stepping back into folds of soft, shiny cloth. Her garment is now stuck to her skin, strands of wet hair in her eyes, and her whole body tense with adrenaline. The Dwellings are winking and flashing amid the old silhouetted trees. She has to do something very hard, unpleasant and unusual: Sim has to think.

She switches off the enhancing facility on her lenses, and looks around at reality. The groups of Dwellings are predictable and similar to those for her own Grouping: bright fluorescent, colossal insect eyes that are incessantly changing their hue, even in the dark. As Sim stumbles up to one, emitting her cold temperature to the external surfaces, a bright pink glow suffuses the nearest dome in a gesture of warmth and welcome. Her approach is heralded by a soft bleep, the trigger for a door panel to glide up. Standing silhouetted there's an adult figure. As Sim staggers nearer, she can see it is a male: regular features, thick brown hair, smooth face, empty blue eyes. Normal.

'Yeah?'

Her arrival is sufficiently novel in itself for him to turn off his enhancing options. They are actually meeting face to unenhanced face, in real time.

'Er. My temperature is dropping.'

'Wow.'

'I must be warmer soon.'

'Yeah.'

'I want to get warm inside your Dwelling.'

'No.'

'Why not?' Sim starts to feel an unusual sensation.

'Because you don't belong here. Go away.'

'But I'm cold.'

'Don't care. Go away.'

The smooth-faced man switches his enhancer back on, looks at her with his head to one side.

'Wow.'

He turns back into the brightly lit entrance and disappears

behind the panel, which then closes him off in his care-free world.

Nothing. Nobody. Nowhere. The terrible feeling inside is mounting, spreading, seeping throughout her body. She is shaking. Now she is screaming. Tears streaming, hair tangled into a sobbing mouth, blowing into unenhanced, stinging eyes. The whistle on her sensor is as loud now as her cries. The devices are also starting to pick up sweaty palms and a dry mouth, the whistle changes to a siren wail. This is serious: Sim's body is undergoing, for the first time, an extreme negative state. She responds in the only way she knows, she moves: but this time, all she can do is stumble.

In the darkness, she is not alone. Other figures are running round in small circles and dancing outside, but looking through or swirling around anything or anyone else around them. Their arm biosensors, though, are silent. Their bodies are comfortable and their brains happy. Warm with well-being, they smile dreamily through Sim as her wretchedness and misery mount. They are where they want to be, doing what they want to do. They are embracing the velvet night and the silver rain, skipping through each moment. They stay out of each other's way: what is Sim anyway?

Sim sways between and around the gyrating shapes. She needs to escape back into comfort, to warmth, to fun. Why? Where? How? Help. Help. Help.

'Where is Zelda? Why isn't she here?'

But no one is listening or answering. Sim's legs are aching now, another new sensation. Her heart, usually deliberately made to pound for the good feeling it brings, is now betraying her, turning against her, working too fast to be fun. A burden. Sweat is everywhere, but the tears have dried. The wailing of her biosensor cuts out abruptly. No more energy at all from Sim's feet to power it up. She stands stationary and silent, and knows fear for the first time, though she would never be able to name it.

Of course, she has been scared superficially and for fun many times in her games. Before she spent so much time in the purely sensory world of the embedded mobile, when she was smaller and immersed in screen activities, then there was plenty to fear. The chasing and the fighting and the killing were scary, especially when she was out of control. She could also make them scared too, those kings and dragons and spacemen and monsters that she in turn chased, and fought and killed. Yes, they screamed, and sometimes the princesses, especially, would cry. But not like this, not like this.

'Zelda!'

Chapter 13

FRED

'Zelda!'

'I'm sorry but I don't know who Zelda is; nor indeed who you are. Let's start at the beginning: my name is Fred.'

'I'm S-S-Si-Sim.'

A fairy princess in distress. How silly. She was everything that Tarra was not: obviously stupid and superficially beautiful. Fair hair clung in damp tendrils around a face that was all perfectly proportioned, with delicate bones scaffolding a smooth, translucent pink skin: but that's all it was, a face that could be broken down and analyzed aesthetically in terms of constituent parts where each feature was appropriately large – the eyes and mouth – or pleasingly small, like the nose and teeth. Looking for more substance, my eyes skimmed of their own accord down the rest of her body and took in a firm, caricature female-shaped frame emphasized by the flimsiest garment. I had never seen a real-life creature like her: but then she didn't seem real. She stood before me, clearly shaken, twisting her hand round and round the damp, dangling hair, darting looks around and over me. I wasn't even sure how or where to start to communicate. After all, she was an Other.

'Can I help you? Please let me help you.'

'Get me Zelda.'

'I can help you find Zelda, but you'll need to give me more information.'

I tried to catch her eye, the first rule for a dialogue, but she wouldn't, or couldn't, look at me. Her head still darted nervously around; her hands moved incessantly, screwing up the fabric of her thin, pointless garment, then flying up to her face, and back and round again into her hair. She left me totally unmoved in terms of personal hormonal attraction, but I was quickly astonished with myself even for considering the absence of sexual urges towards her. That very special physical bonding was after all, and in any case, reserved exclusively for Tarra. With Tarra, the only person with whom I'd ever copulated, the physical act was an acknowledgement and extension of our mental compatibility: it was an inevitable consequence of our being completely attuned. It was how it was meant to be.

The first time I met Tarra, I knew just how meticulous and accurate the authorities had been in their judgement. Once a young N-P has reached the critical age and stage in life where initial training is complete, it is his or her duty to register for a breeding partnership. In the carefully plotted course of a life, this is the time when professional performance can be evaluated for brainpower quotient, yet fertility is still satisfactory, in the case of females. Meanwhile, for males, frequency of copulation would still be high enough to maximize the chance of conception. This was the stage in life when you conspicuously moved up a generation, from being the child living at home with the two parents, to turning into a parent and having a child yourself. This was the time to identify, as effectively and efficiently as possible, that crucial other parent: your breeding partner.

I registered at the stipulated time with neither excitement nor hesitation. It was what you had to do. What was there to either fantasize or worry about? The process was completed on a cloudy, tepid day long ago when I arrived in the lab one morning and therefore had access to the technology that was banned from the home: my ID implant had bleeped a quick, soft summons that I was to log on to the Breeding Partnership Scheme. Sitting at the nearest network node, I noticed with gratification, but frankly little surprise, that my brainpower index was within the highest band. That was all there was to say about me in terms of selection in the scheme. The age matching would be automatic, easy and merely the first permissive criterion. There were many, or rather a large enough number, of my generation now to be qualifying for breeding: what mattered was the much more selective process of the matching of minds.

None of us worried about appearance, because none of us had ever been trained or encouraged to notice it. We lived to think, to plan, to talk, to discover: we don't dissipate time and energy just indulging the senses, indiscriminately processing whatever we might have stumbled into without thinking. We are led from the inside, not driven by the outside. We minimize possible distraction by reducing unpredictability and controlling every possible aspect of the environment. So, on that grey morning an age ago, I had no hope or worry about what my breeding partner would look like: rather, I was certain that now I was about to meet someone of a similar intellectual rigour with whom I would be not just compatible, but continuous.

Tarra looked me right in the eye as soon as we met, and carried on gazing right into my head. She spoke in a smooth, calm voice, clearly articulating her sentences, pausing when needed. Taking her time. I was delighted that she didn't smile gratuitously and that when she had finished making her point, she tilted her head very slightly on one side as she listened to me without any interjections: her eyes still held mine and I knew that we were as one. Her brain lapped on to mine like waves on a beach. I knew more or less straight away, that we would be content together.

I was in any case ready to leave my parents' Family Unit. They had done their job, a good job in giving me the ideal environment in which to flourish. Yet three adults together do not have the symmetry of a partnership; nor the counterbalance that a child, but only a child, can add. Three-way adult dialogues become conflicts for dominance, where bids for attention, for holding the centre, eclipse the true reason for talking in the first place. That was how it had become between me and my parents. They had done their duty, and I had been grateful. Now it was time to move up to the next rung in the societal ladder.

The N-P doctrine was now well established and accepted, that the one dimension that mattered in breeding partnerships was a compatibility of thought processes. With Tarra, I could extend my individual thinking in ways and to places that my parents would have hampered with the cross-currents of their own earlier ideas and mutually agreed assumptions. But with Tarra I could challenge everything: we could start on our own, to have our own dialogues and think from a different perspective from my parents. She was almost immediately a part of me. My new stage in life was just as it should be, calm but worthwhile: physical well-being combined with mental dynamism.

Tarra provided a near-perfect complement both mentally and physically: with her thinking and then with her body, she extended me, pushing back my boundaries. She carried on my ideas, helping me work towards the logical conclusions we craved: meanwhile, every morning when we copulated, I was for a brief moment each time unaware of where I ended and she began. Inevitably, then, her body started to swell and Bill arrived right on time. We loosened our tight link a little to include him too, and that made the chain stronger. Bill and Tarra were my base: I set out from them every morning and returned to them every evening. They, not the physical beige box that accommodated us so efficiently, but they – Bill and Tarra – were my true and actual home.

'I don't want to talk to you. I want Zelda.'

How long had I been looking inwards, ignoring her? By now the evening darkness had smothered much, and thrown into sharper contrast the improbable fluorescence of the buildings. Unlike the dwindling number of silhouetted figures still dotted about, she was demanding action, needing the present to deliver more. Needing me to do something, stop her being frightened and take her to a specific person, presumably called Zelda.

An astonishing insight struck me: perhaps Sim had never experienced a real, important and, above all, one-off event like this. The scientist in me was curious to know what kind of emotion she might actually be feeling right now. Then again, why should I care? Someone would eventually come and help her, or this Zelda person would come out and look for her. Or surely she would eventually find her way back to wherever she normally lived. But then I thought again.

Before approaching the Sim creature, I had been trying to make sense of the dense habitation area, wondering and wandering. It was hard to know exactly how to proceed given it was obviously going to be much harder than Hodge or I had ever imagined to instigate any form of dialogue. No one had questioned me, or even seemed to find me worth inspecting: perhaps my remarkably unremarkable grey clothes, my functional hair and falsely purposeful propulsion on the bicycle were so intrinsically under-stimulating, in purely sensory terms, that I was simply not worthy of attention.

'Remember,' I explained to myself, 'that these are people living in a world stripped of all cognitive content. What you see is what you get. Grey clothes and cropped hair do not signify anything to them, any more than they would to an infant. Their world has no meaning, nothing stands for anything else. If you are not bright or noisy they will stare through you at things and people that *do* activate their senses.'

I had approached the Sim creature because it's what an N-P would obviously do if they saw another in distress. Then again, such a scenario was purely hypothetical since we would never have felt, let alone displayed, overtly strong emotions. Nor would there ever be any conceivable cause to do so: our lives gave us no reason to be so out of control with the despair I now witnessed. None the less, I was there because of my ability to adapt, to learn, to report. I could respond appropriately to this very unusual situation of comforting someone I didn't know. Hardest still, an Other. Yet I had a further, clear motive. Despite the initial difficulty of communicating with her, I needed quickly to establish some kind of contact. In this casual, uncaring place, this Sim creature would probably be my best chance for finding out about the Others. But where or how to start?

Then I noticed her arm, which had started to emit a soft electronic hum: of course, she would have an implant. I pulled up my own baggy grey sleeve and in the dark gloom showed her my pale upper arm, rotating at the shoulder so my palm was upwards, my still firm biceps deflected away: I could afford the gesture of the vulnerable supplicant, because I knew I wasn't.

'Let's just synch implants, then we'll know all the vital facts about each other.'

For the first time, she seemed to react: one word seemed to have done the trick. 'My implant's been activated to danger mode. Then there was not even power. But it's coming back now.'

It was my turn now to register confusion. 'But implants have nothing to do with detecting danger. How could they? Perceived danger, the most likely type there is nowadays, is so subjective.'

As soon as I had spoken, I realized that of course she would not understand what I had just said. Sim was very far from being Tarra. More, when I had spoken to her, it had really been just thinking aloud. My mind continued to unpack a rationale almost as a reflex, as it had been trained to do. "Our worst fears lie in anticipation". We N-Ps had conquered fear by creating a world where there was quite simply no room for the unexpected and the unwanted. The Others, conversely, expected and remembered nothing, so there was nothing to fear. Surely fear only happens when your mind's eye shows you a scene, a scene where something terrible unfolds. In the dark, in different times, spirits lurked, or more material robbers and murderers were waiting for you beyond the campfire. It would start with you venturing away to tend a horse or investigate the unaccountable snapping of a twig or the alarm call of a monkey: and then a heartbeat later, a cold blade might be pressed to your throat. Blackness would descend forever as your existence ebbed away. Blackness was always the opposite to light, was always bad, always covered up bad things and bad people. Blackmail, black market, blackened names, black-hearted, black mood, black dog of depression. From what I knew about the Others, there would be for Sim no history of blackness, no myths or metaphors. Darkness couldn't exist for her as a symbol or a historic common factor betokening dangerous events. She was lost in every sense. A little piece of garish flotsam swept away and around in the vast sea of the here and now.

'Your implant is there to tell everyone else who you are, like me, now.'

'No. Stupid. Everyone knows your implant looks after your body.'

So there it was, different implants for our different cultures: mine cognitive, hers inevitably sensory. The secret, the common permissive trigger for this subsequently divergent technology, was size. Once devices were reduced to a billionth of a metre, they were transformed and transforming. Just as once a peasant in a wattle-and-daub hut in the Middle Ages would have found it inconceivable that plastics and plastic objects could exist, and that the term could even sprawl into nuances and expressions of artificiality, impermanence, and modernity, so humanity had struggled for over a century with the potential impact of the very, very small. The most invasive was into biology, breaching the firewall of the body and the outside world. Clothes and jewellery could now assert themselves, speaking up in response to shifts in physiology, or whispering back into your ear, flashing up before your eyes answers on location, on history, on anything.

But the devices crept on, ever smaller, under the skin itself and on into the blood vessels. Everything could be read out, monitored, corrected, constantly under surveillance. The instant a tooth started to decay, an artery silted or a cancerous cell divided for the first time, so the devices were meticulous in their reporting. They crept on further, into the brain: this was the basis of our Helmet technology.

I came from a stress-free world where my body consequently didn't change dramatically in its momentary levels of physiological parameters, but where constant mind read-out through the Helmet was essential – from the simple, single milestones, for example, of selecting your Breeding Partner through to logging when you entered and left the lab each day. My life goals were charted out from the time I'd been born. And each goal, as I had achieved it – be it major or trivial – had modified me further, made me who I am. Nothing could be undone: everything, by being irreversible, had a meaning. Therefore I, as a person, had a meaning, one that I had never needed to question. But a sharp thought, unbidden and spontaneous, suddenly pricked my calm complacency: that wasn't true any more.

Be honest, at least with yourself, in silence. Be honest. When you were travelling here, you realized – no, perhaps you just entertained the possible thought – that you were more than you had been back there the other side of the mountain. On the bike you could do more, had a greater latitude of thought: your mind could go sideways as well as forward. No rules held you back. You were more than a sequential series of events. There was more to you, something that could not be logged, that did not follow as a linear phenomenon to be readily documented. There was something more that was subjective and therefore couldn't be downloaded or measured: it was enduring but wasn't nameable, other than by the simple umbrella term – Fred.

'Why don't we just talk for a little while then, get to know each other without implants.'

She looked even more dismayed and confused. I tried to imagine what it must be like. For her, the wildly fluctuating turmoil of her body, in turn driven by an outside world of extreme sensationalism, would mandate different priorities. And a sense of identity wasn't one of them. In fact, its importance did not register at all. This girl, Sim, did not see herself in that way. Perhaps she didn't see herself at all. But if she wasn't aware of herself, she appeared to be aware of the Others, or at least one Other.

'You can tell me all about Zelda.'

'Zelda's my carer, in my Grouping.'

'Tell me about your Grouping.'

Again, she looked genuinely puzzled, perhaps because she assumed that everyone knew what Groupings were – indeed, I could start to imagine they were some kind of family. Alternatively, perhaps she was baffled as to why someone should be asking so many questions. From what I had learnt, and was now observing of the Others, it was not a world where anyone asked anyone anything.

'What's that?'

As quickly as the sun can appear from behind a grey cloud, she was transformed from the petrified infant into the bright, observant child. She had calmed down sufficiently to notice the bike, the novelty of which had clearly subordinated my silly questions about Groupings.

It was propped against my side, my right hand resting gently but masterfully on the handlebars. Sim had danced round my other side, from where she had glimpsed in the dark the gleam of the NanoMat, the 'nanomaterial'. Drawing closer, fascinated, she inspected the bars, the wheels, the biocube, the water outlet for drinking, all in the palest of lilac, almost transparent. The bike was indeed a thing of true beauty.

'It's called a bicycle. It helps me travel, to go from place to place.'

'I run from place to place.'

Already she was distracted again. The pale, gleaming object was inanimate and therefore had exhausted her interest: it could not compete with the dynamism of the flashing environment around her, of bright lights and movements even now, even in the dark. At home, the dark signalled the ancient time for sleeping. Because all technology was for work, away from the family, the dark time was the quiet time. Time to let the proteins in the brain replenish, to let dreams reconcile paradoxes and conundrums: it was a fixed time before the next stage of the next day. But for the silhouettes laughing on their own, swaying and singing to themselves, there was no next day, nothing to plan for, no future. I tried to persist with my mission, my line of questioning.

'When you run, do you run far from the Grouping?'

She shrugged, not knowing and not caring. 'I run away from Zelda.'

For now she was back in a state that for her was normal, in an environment that was normal. She looked around for something to look at and, for a moment, failed. Suddenly, therefore, she was able to conjure up a thought with a loose association to our staccato conversation.

'Ciro, he's my other carer. But Zelda does it usually. Zelda has red hair and her lips are pink. If she's not on caring tasks, then most of the time she sits doing old screen games with a Talking Head. But she also spends lots of time just talking into the air. She tries to tell me things. But I like running away. I like my mobile interactive.'

I was beginning to realize just how different the Others had become from us. Sim was obviously fully grown, as the prominent curves poorly concealed below the thin garment testified: but she seemed to have the verbal ability only of a small child. I made a brief mental note. Much would flow from this one basic issue: if the Others had underdeveloped linguistic skills, then poor cognitive abilities would be almost inevitable. At first, for a small child, mere naming of objects is enough. Indeed, it is the first stage in escaping the press of the moment by being able to refer to something or someone that is not actually present and in front of you.

However, it is the second step that is so crucial, and that Sim appeared to have hardly grasped. To organize those objects and people into complex interrelations – for us, that would be cognitive ability. Objects and people have more and more significance the more and more connections, associations, they can trigger. And these connections can also be in time: cause and then effect. This temporal connectivity would not just give an event, an episode a significance in your life story, but even more profoundly would enable thought itself. A central N-P principle is that the notion of sequence and order underpins thinking, thereby distinguishing it from a mere here-and-now feeling. And the best way to rehearse sequences, appreciate how one step follows from another in a constrained and ordained pattern, starts inevitably with the defined organization of sentences – first reading them, and then writing your own.

We know that children, even our own N-P young, resemble in some sense what used to be called schizophrenics. Schizophrenia was once a common and devastating mental condition, characterized by short attention spans, illogical thinking, a weak sense of identity and self, and the tendency to take things at face value. In particular, schizophrenics were similar to children in the sense that they could not interpret proverbs, expressing one idea in terms of another, more exaggerated scenario. This was because schizophrenics lacked the ability to see beyond the literal: because they did not have sufficient connections established between their brain cells, they were unable to understand metaphor. Children, with their fewer connections between brain cells, still display this inability.

'Sim, if I said that people who lived in glass Dwellings shouldn't throw stones, what would that mean?'

She looked at me for the first time, though fleetingly: for a moment I was caught unawares by the depth in the blue of her eyes.

'What's glass?'

'Stuff that you can see through, but that is very hard. However, if you throw something at it, it shatters – er, breaks into pieces. Look, there's some right here.'

Inspired, I picked up a shard, of which there were many scattered in the debris on the earth around us. She didn't even know the names of objects in her immediate surroundings: another quick mental note.

'But my Dwelling isn't made of glass.'

'But what if it was?'

'Then if someone threw a stone, it would break. You've just said so.'

By now she was fidgeting again. Stretching her neck from side to side to find something, anything, new to look at. We had eradicated schizophrenia by the time of the Exodus, with our highly controlled environment, thereby suppressing excessive emotion from infancy. The highly impressionable brains of our N-P young were trained from the outset by minimizing distractions, to ignore the sensory and to focus, focus, focus on thinking, on sequence and consequence. Any tendency to a schizophrenic mindset would have stood little chance of not being offset by such rigorous conditioning. Meanwhile, though the lifestyle of the Others was one where mental disorder would not be recognized, not least because no one would notice or care, it was an interesting thought that the lifestyle might ironically be one that induced a condition such as schizophrenia. I made another mental note. Perhaps, after all, I would be able to make progress with the mission as planned.

It was now very late into the night. I realized that if we remained stationary, Sim would soon become bored. Now that her crisis had passed, there would be no reason for her not to run off into the darkness, assuming the transformers in her footwear were appropriately powered up. She would be the perfect subject for my study and, having found her, it was imperative that I did not let her go. But I was starting to feel exhausted. Soon sleep would take over without me being able to stop it. I had to prioritize finding somewhere to stay not just for tonight, but for longer, to use as a base. Sim and I both needed to get moving, but where? It was essential that I didn't let her out of my sight.

'What about Zelda, shall we try and find her?'

'I already know where she is.' She gestured to her ear. 'My locator can tell me where to go. But my energy levels were run down so it didn't work, and my muscles weren't working well either: they were out of energy too.'

'But now both silicon and carbon are recharged.'

Her time to be silent, either because she didn't understand or rather, as I somehow suspected, my attempt at humour was so very weak. I tried a more honest line.

'Why don't we go back to Zelda together? If it's a long way and if anything drops in power again, I'll be there to help.'

This time she didn't even shrug. My presence wasn't making, nor would it make, any impact on her at the moment. She was just fine as she was. My next decision concerned how we were to proceed. One possibility would be for Sim to sit on the bike, while I wheeled it. This arrangement would ensure that she was indeed my captive and that I was in the greatest control possible. But then something in me rebelled. It was *my* bike, an extension of me, an expression of *me*, the new Fred that couldn't be defined or limited by the old pedestrian boundaries. No one else could ride my bike, ever. In need of a convenient alternative, I resorted to a pleasingly plausible suggestion.

'Would you like to see me ride the bike, Sim? When I'm on it I can go as fast as you can if you run. But I want to talk with you, so why don't I ride very slowly, while you keep up beside me, but slower than normal. That way you'll conserve your power for longer.'

She didn't bother to follow this quite tidy line of reasoning because, as I was speaking, I was already swinging my leg over the delicate lilac crossbar. She peered up at me, wide-eyed, plump red lips parted, tongue inadvertently running round their perimeter, moistening them in expectation. I was astride now, smiling down at her, already on the move.

As we set off, I noticed that she didn't have a purposeful, even stride, with one step reflecting and anticipating each stage of an argument of a thought. Rather, she seemed to dance as she moved. She was coordinated in a way that I had never seen before, her whole body syncopated: as though music was her medium rather than words.

'Why don't you laugh?'

For the first time in a long while, I was struck by the importance and truthfulness of the fact leading to the question. To my astonishment, trained as I was to unpack ideas, follow through the ripples of contingencies and potential scenarios, I could not give an immediate answer. I opted instead for the more immediate insight, that Sim had actually observed something about someone other than herself. She clearly was not uncurious, the first sign of intelligence. I ignored the question and we travelled on in a silence that seemed mutually comfortable.

I was thinking. Perhaps this chance encounter was indeed just what Hodge and I had been hoping for: casual, informal and unofficial access to the brain and mind of an Other. We had discussed how such an encounter, were it to happen, would be truly valuable, while arousing the least suspicion. And if I did have unlimited access to Sim's brain, then I could willingly formulate a neuroscientific strategy for exploration. Thankfully, we no longer needed the old whole-body tunnels of ancient fMRI machines that 'scanned' at best pale drops of residual activity long after the flash flood of a thought was over. The Helmet would work very well: I had it in my pack, of course. I felt my own body tighten in anticipation, the familiar yet rare surge of knowing that I was on the right track of discovery. I yearned to get started.

As soon as I had read-outs from the Helmet, I would feed the raw data into the Brain Institute informatics bank that placed every fact discovered about the brain into a context, cross-referencing it across different disciplines and levels of brain organization. At a glance and in a second, I would be able to evaluate the significance against the corpus of existing knowledge, concerning each of my observations. I would be able to transmit data from Sim, controlled from my watch and read-out from the Helmet, back to Hodge and the others from my implant. The implant was my lifeline to reality and even, as I was coming to realize, to sanity.

But first I had to assess Sim's real cognitive state, and before I could even do that, I had to gain her confidence in some way. It would be important to spend some more time with her before we had to meet this Zelda phenomenon. I shuddered to think of an older version of the Sim creature and what it might be like to have a three-way attempted conversation with them. Best that I focus, at least initially, on Sim. But just as quickly my thoughts swung to Tarra's grey eyes, questioning and clear, Hodge's non-smile and unblinking stare, Bill any day now about to put his chubby little hands to his head at the unaccustomed feel of the Helmet. Sim was not real, I reminded myself. She was just a subject, my subject to understand, and to own. She was a pretty plastic creature, no challenge, no genuine stimulation for me: just my subject. Her brain was what counted, and the shaping and using of it to my own design and for my own purpose.

We would not rush back to her so-called Grouping, but would spend the night outside among the dark debris and harsh fakery. I needed so much now to talk for as long as possible, before being forced to confront the uncertainty and risk of Zelda. So, first of all, the silence that had now thickened comfortably between us would need to be dispelled.

'You are curious about me not laughing, but aren't you curious about who I am, or where I'm from?'

'How do you mean "curious"?'

'It's when you want to find things out.' In order to remedy the laughing deficiency, I tried a smile.

'Why should I want to find out about you?'

The logic was impeccable, the empathy abysmal. She was already fitting a very clear and predictable profile. Part of the picture was that she clearly had no regard for past or future. The Zelda woman seemed to have been totally forgotten.

'OK, tell me more about you and your life.'

'Me? My life?'

Such abstract concepts were clearly not in her mental portfolio: it was yet another confirmatory sign of the mindset I was starting to piece together. My list of mental notes was lengthening, but I couldn't risk recording into my implant. Sim would never understand what was happening, but I couldn't take the chance of her being distracted or sensing me as any stranger than I must already appear to be.

'I'm interested in how you all live here. I want to live like you too. In the place I've come from, nobody laughs.'

I was pleased with this approach: it had a logic that Sim would understand, and it picked up on her observation, an observation about something that must therefore be important to her. And part of it was true.

'But laughing feels good. Why don't people like doing it where you're from?'

'Because it's not part of our philosophy. I'm an N-P, after all, as I'm sure you can tell from my clothes. Our idea is that it's better to think.'

All this was clearly too much: abstract concepts and general knowledge facts, even those as relevant and important about a bitter ideological enemy lurking nearby, were not available to Sim. She frowned, and I could almost see the thought process sluggishly kick-starting.

'What do you think about? And why is it better? Better for what?'

Clearly a quick-witted cleverness might be buried somewhere, deep down under the shallow sheen. Once again, I chose not to answer her questions, but veered instead on to another tack. I would never have been able to commit such flagrant breaches in the chain of logic with Tarra, just jumping ship after an important question. But, with Sim, at least there was a positive side to her infantilized brain – switching subject matter was easy and possible. I could indulge in disconnected speech patterns, and she would be completely comfortable. Then I pulled myself up short again. Be careful. Don't slip too easily into their ways. Everyone is vulnerable to environmental influence, even you. Hodge warned you of this when you had your last meeting.

'Be careful, Fred. You have a brilliant brain. You are a model N-P, among our brightest and best. But you know you have to go alone, and that will open you up to risks that we cannot evaluate as precisely as we would like. You will have no one appropriate with whom to dialogue. Your only link will be via your reports transmitted intermittently and offline to me. No other N-P has ever been so isolated. We cannot extrapolate from merely intercepting their traffic about dysfunctional bodily functions and music, exactly how it is over there, for them. You must at all times be vigilant. Don't play at being them, thinking you're inviolate. Never play at being them.' ...

'Sim, let's not go back to Zelda just yet.'

'Why not? I want to sleep now. I'm tired.'

'We could lie down here and sleep.'

I gestured to the dark, moist earth where there was a wind-blown pile of dead leaves and fortunately not too many ancient plastic gadgets and bags.

'Why?'

'Because then we could look up at the stars.'

The heavy rain had stopped, and the air was freighted with the pungent smell of damp vegetation. Sleeping out here would not be too bad. I for one was so weary by now, I could have slept anywhere, and besides, when I was cycling over the mountain, sleeping outside was yet another new experience I had discovered. One that I had just enjoyed, but for no obvious reason. It was just something that Fred the man did. Still, I hated myself for invoking the pleasure of the experience as a reason. It made no logical sense, of course, and it would make no sense to Sim. I was right.

'But I can switch on Starry Night on my simulator in the Dwelling.'

'But this time it will be real.'

'What's the difference?'

'Let's find out.'

A good reply to her impossible question. I was proud at last of how I was handling things. Dismounting with a frisson of sadness I'd already come to recognize as normal whenever I detached from the bicycle, I came back to earth, casting about for a good place. It was cold, I was tired, and Sim was my subject. I had to arrange for her to be lying next to me, on her back, not touching but near enough to talk properly, while we both looked up at the now clear sky. It was also achingly important only to see something natural: and the sky was the only place here that was uncluttered by Yakawow.

'Sim, lie down here.'

But she had lost interest again. Perhaps she had already assumed I would be telling her what to do: alternatively, it could be just that she hadn't thought through what she would be doing next. How alien to our way of setting about things. Already I was learning so much, and so quickly. Hodge would be very satisfied. Since the Others seemed to have such an immature outlook on life, then, as with small children, they would be easy to control and deal with as we eventually deemed appropriate. This was where my new research was needed. The Helmet on Sim would have the same effect as I was expecting – indeed hoping for – with my own son, for Bill. We already knew now how to bend synapses in circuits by direct micro-stimulation through the Helmet. What we didn't know as yet was the potential of the adult Other brain for change, or rather for being changed.

We had lapsed back into our friendly enough silence: me kicking leaves into a pile, she turning, skipping to an inner rhythm. Obviously all her power had returned. All her systems were activated again and she didn't need me. From what she said it was clear that Sim, as all the Others presumably, had been implanted with more than just a device in the upper arm. While we used the Helmet to enhance and stimulate thought deep inside our brains, they used invasive technology at the most peripheral gateways of ears and eyes, presumably to enhance sensation. Of course.

'Sim, could you turn your enhancer off? I would like to talk to you.'

I'd had to place myself in her direct line of vision in order for her to notice me, amid the complex and fast-paced multimodal scene that was probably playing out in her head. I wondered briefly how she might be receiving me, how my face might have been coloured, my voice transformed, my speech slowed down or speeded up. But it worked.

Like an impatient child, Sim came to a complete stop with clear frustration and irritation. Obviously she was not normally sidetracked in this way.

'Talk?'

'I want to find out more about this place.'

'But it's just a place. When you don't have enhancers on.'

She gestured to the immediate vicinity of scrubland, now starting to come alive in monochrome shades as the pallid dawn light began to push back the night.

'No, I mean I want to find out about how you live, what you think, what you do.'

She snatched for the last phrase. 'I do this.'

'But I need to know more about your enhancers, and your body-monitoring arm implant.'

She looked round and over my shoulder in a way to which I was now becoming accustomed: once again, a loss of continuing interest. 'Then ask the Fact-Totum.'

I guessed immediately that what she was referring to must be a rather simple but powerful technology to access facts quickly. Yet the Fact-Totum appeared not to feature heavily in their lives here, as exemplified by it being a mere afterthought for Sim when I prompted her with a question. Yet another mental note. What enquiries would she ever want to pose in everyday life?

'But really, Sim, I want to find out more about you.'

'But I'm here. And you know already I'm Sim.'

So there it was. Sim had no sense of her own identity, not in any way that we N-Ps would regard as substantive. The prospect of documenting her mind, and then developing it along the lines we would want, simultaneously excited and alarmed me: the task would be both more fascinating and far harder than Hodge or I could have anticipated.

'Sim, just lie down. Let's lie down next to each other and look up at the real stars.'

She looked at me now as I must have looked at her, as though I was either mad or stupid. Then, shifting her gaze to the rapidly rosying sky, devoid of stars, she just wordlessly shook her head.

'OK, Sim. Let's go back as soon as we can. But just for a little while, could you keep the enhancers off?'

Somehow, I had lost and she had won. I felt diminished and not in control. But when I reflected on how far we had come and where we currently were, it was probably for the best. The idea was simply to ensure that I had the optimum chance of studying her. The idea of lying down together was not so that the waves could lap on the beach, as with Tarra, but that I could minimize garish distractions just while I tried to talk with her further. Just talk.

This time I was too fatigued to concentrate on balancing and wheeled the bike alongside me as I plodded like an automaton, and she danced. No more to be said for the present. But I noticed Sim was starting to flick quick hesitant glances at me from time to time. She obviously felt the visual stimulation that my unusual appearance provided might, after all, be worth registering – but also I hoped it was because she was starting to feel more comfortable with me.

The day was fully up by now. Bright, unadulterated sunlight competed with the garish, multicoloured changes of patterns of a cluster of large, imposing domes. Still more people were now apparent, preoccupied and alone in ever-growing numbers. Again, a contrasting flashback of the ordered walking in pairs of measured grey figures along manicured gravel and tarmac. No one alone, all of us as a collective, all of us making progress, going forward on a clear linear path as straight as an ancient arrow or the flight of a crow. How would I survive here among debris and decay overlaid with brain-churning sensory overload? How could I, one man alone, start the process for gaining complete mastery of these sad, silly people? Hodge hadn't realized what he was asking of me. But I was strangely exhilarant: I had my bicycle, strong and real and beautiful by my side. I was Fred the man. I was doing what no N-P had ever done before. I could do anything.

Sim and I were now approaching a massive dome pulsating with bright fuscia-pink light. I took a deep breath. Now real progress was about to be made. So far, there had been no new surprises since the previous night. The onslaught on the senses was already now becoming the norm, or at least could be relegated to a level of attention that allowed me to discern signal from noise, to focus on salient and selective features of my own choosing. Now I was about to take the next important step: I was about to see what it was like underneath the vast geodesic dome roof, inside.

I followed a step behind Sim, careful that the bicycle stayed upright as we negotiated some broken glass from a long-dead champagne celebration, the history of another era. She never changed pace. I noticed she hadn't quickened her skipping in her keenness to be back; nor was she inadvertently dragging her feet. It was obviously, for her, simply the place she was headed: the place she left whenever she went on her excursions and to which she returned when she had finished. A neutral place with no meaning, no memories, no fondness, no security and no symbolism – not a home, just a place. Already, I was realizing what a strain it would be for me to see the world as they did, in purely literal terms, without any personalized or cultural connotations. In order to understand the Others, however, I would have to force myself to do just that: I would have to think like them while still observing and appreciating with my N-P brain the contrasting differences.

The sheer mental effort and the implications it carried, together with the remorseless attack on my unexercised senses, and the simple lack of sleep, were all starting to suffocate my brain. For the moment I should and would just stop thinking, step back and observe. After all, this was a crucial stage in my mission:

I had to get it right. Of course, I had no idea what was about to happen inside the pink edifice, but I would do all I could to stay with the Sim creature, the perfect subject. And so I just focused on her, on her slight, silken back with the easy loose blonde hair bouncing around her shoulders of its own accord. Her movements were natural and unthinking: as a reflex she continued right up to what I suddenly saw was an entrance panel. And also as a reflex, it readily and noiselessly slid up, leaving a sharp oblong open to us. Clumsily manoeuvring the bicycle, I stumbled in after her.

Inside it was as bright as the daylight outside, but I still had to blink and adjust to the dramatic change in my visual field. Artificial light, strange-looking, obviously synthetic objects, improbable colours: different scenes accosted me wherever I looked. I wanted to stare more closely at each object, at every angle, to make sense of it all, at least to identify what each thing might be, a face say or chair, as readily as possible. But first I had to look at everything else. Where to start? Two pregnant women were sitting separately encased in holograms, obviously more static than they would normally be to enjoy the mobile embedded technologies that I had already seen at work on Sim. But, just behind them, a good-looking man of indeterminate age was feeding a small infant in a touching age-old ritual of childcare, using his fingers to place something shiny and bright green in the child's mouth. But, like all children everywhere, this one was trying to refuse, turning its little head in an attempt at autonomy and protest. Bill. Oh, Bill. No. No. No. Look away. Just look away.

'Sim! Sim!'

And there, with a face that radiated an ecstatic smile, was a woman. Impossible, but the only possibility: Zelda.

The man stroked his thin white beard and his diamond-hard eyes glistened: so this was the start of it.

Chapter 14

ZELDA

The starry mountain sky didn't work, but the pills did. They cunningly seeped through from my bloodstream and invaded my brain: they intercepted various chemical messengers going about the relentless work of keeping me conscious. Conscious to worry about Sim. But then the drugs barricaded my brain cells, sabotaging all their networking and thereby at last consigned me to a deep, dreamless, involuntary sleep. Yet inevitably here I am now, at last finally awake: the sun is brightly filtering, unenhanced and unbidden through whatever thin slits of space exist beneath doors and around windows within the Dwelling. Wherever possible, even here, natural elements still struggle to get through. My head throbs heavy and thick: but immediately, I am revisiting the same persistent thought that kept me awake last night. With sickening turns of the stomach, I play and replay the simple fact over and over again – that Sim has not come home.

I'm too numb and churned up with loss, too drained of energy to move from where I'm lying in my sleeping zone, to know what to do. Indeed I've no real desire to do anything other than think aloud. I lie now on my back, eyes wide open, tired and tense and motionless. Will it be like this all the time when Sim leaves the Grouping for good? I might as well be dead. Time hangs slow and weighty but must be ticking by. And so I do nothing but stare upwards. I don't want any enhanced experiences, any unreal Starry Night or Tropical Beach. I just stare at the clear, white translucent surface above my head. And stare and stare.

Then at some stage, perhaps immediately or much later, across the tinkle of someone else's hologram, could that possibly be voices? In itself, that would be strange since no one usually talks to anyone else. But, yes, it's real voices in real time: a male and female. And the female voice is wonderfully familiar.

'Sim! Sim!'

I'm singing her name as I shout it. My Sim is back, back home. To me. With me. My body swings into one single, synchronized movement from the horizontal to vertical, while my hands enact their own daily reflex of pulling my garment straight. I don't care what happened last night anymore, I just care that she's now back. That's all that counts. It's only as I fling myself into the outer zone of the Dwelling to where Sim is dancing on the spot just inside the entrance, that I register the tall, male figure to which she is speaking.

'This is the Dwelling.'

She is talking, actually communicating and explaining to some stranger. She is dancing up and down and hopping as usual, but at the same time actually looking at him, directing his gaze with fast sweeps of her hands.

As I rush forward to wrap my arms round Sim and engulf her in love and hold her close forever, my face feeling split with smiles, I let my eyes dart for a fraction of a second to the man who is with her. As I gaze in relief at the perfect peach face of Sim, I can't help returning to the surprise interloper behind her, a strange-looking man with a closed, wary stare, eyes darting around at everything. Both faces turn towards me as time judders and stands stock-still. Grey eyes and blue eyes: I turn my surprised gaze up to one, and look down with love on the other. I am torn between the need for reassurance and affirmation and the impact of the new, the unexpected.

'Sim! Hello, I'm Zelda. My baby! I'm Sim's carer. You're safe! I live here, this is our Dwelling.'

'I know.'

For slightly longer now, I focus on the steady eyes staring back at me in a way that no one ever usually does. Only after some thought does he smile, showing uneven teeth that are not unequivocally brilliant white, but more cream-coloured, like teeth used to be when I was small. An asymmetry of the face too, such as is never seen nowadays: instead his appearance reminds me of that time long ago … the skin not taut like my own, and the hair not amassing as a bright single, shiny colour but a flatter, graded array of monochrome. He is a little taller than average, but that may because I've become so used to the slightly stooping Ciro. Or perhaps he seems larger because he is swathed in layers of loose and uncaring grey cloth that indiscriminately swamps his whole body, making it impossible to see his strength, to show off his muscles. And his face had a slackness under the eyes and around the chin, a blurring of the normal cut of the bones contrasting bleakly with lips unusually tight, drawn uncompromisingly in a line across his face. Then I notice that his nose has a lump halfway up and is bent slightly to one side. He looks so very different, I can't describe him by the simplistic term 'ugly': in any case such a word has fallen into disuse and I cannot remember when I last used it.

My grandfather was much older and came from an era when ageing was overt and announced in every line of the body and face; Dr Grant was more like a leftover from a very early, primitive cyber-game; and everyone else nowadays is somehow insubstantial, like holograms themselves, visible yet just not really *there*. But this man seems more immediate, somehow more male: his threadbare lack of perfection has revealed an inner and uncompromising presence that paralyzes me, roots me in front of him, waiting.

Sim is dancing round the bright interior in wider circles: she might even be pleased to be back as she shakes her hair, laughs at nothing, and glances casually around her, lingering for a moment before she restlessly shifts around in a thoughtless, purposeless choreography. He and I both stand motionless, my hands loose and weightless, his resting on an object I never thought I would ever see again, a bicycle. We let our eyes preoccupy themselves by following Sim's trajectory and finally have to look each other once again in the face.

'My name is Fred. I'm newly arrived here and met Sim while I was trying to orientate myself. She needed help, and so I accompanied her home.'

Home. A word that calls to me, warms me. How long since I have heard anyone say that word? Just that one word brings my grandparents running, arms outstretched, smiles wide open. A brief window opens on to the past.

... 'Zelda, you're home. Tell us what happened today. Soon we'll all have dinner. Now that you're home.' ...

Then the window shuts just as quickly. But that one simple, loaded word confirms what of course I had known without acknowledging from the outset. This disquieting male is not from our world, but from another time, or more accurately, another place. Where? Why? He might even be, even be, has to be ...

'I'm a Neo-Puritan, an N-P.'

The world tilts. The excitement and anticipation of a moment ago now freeze into a fear that stops me breathing. Of course. I realized what he was as soon as I saw him, but pushed the thought out of my consciousness: the unlikelihood was too great, the implications too terrible, to have in my reality, at least immediately. I need breathing space. My mind struggles to cope with a concept, one not prompted by sensory cues or rules from a game. It's an alien concept, which has no place among speed and fun and light. I twist it clumsily around, this concept, letting it slip, picking it up, trying again with mental fingers that are not nimble, are unpractised at handling the subtle and slippery. I drop it again, try and grab and grasp it harder. This concept is shadowy, has been always kept in the shadows. *They killed your parents. Your mother and father died before their time because of men like this. Do nothing. Tell nothing. Beware. Ask nothing.*

I ask, 'Would you like to see the Dwelling?'

'What I would most like, Zelda, is to eat something, if that's possible. Then, if it doesn't conflict with any of your customs, I would be very grateful if I could stay here, if only for tonight. I've travelled a long way, in every sense –' he pauses to check how well I register the nuance but I simply stare back, giving nothing away – 'and desperately need some sleep.'

His way of speaking and what he says accentuates still further the difference between him and everyone else. It is obviously a better strategy to be overtly and clearly not one of us, because it would have been impossible for him to dissemble otherwise, even for a second.

'There's not much to see anyway.' I try to explain. 'We fabricate objects with nano-assemblers as and when we want them, then change them to address our needs for which they morph each time. So you'd only be able to see what was actually being needed and used at any one particular moment. Otherwise there's just space and the Talking Heads. But then we also have the holograms and enhancer experiences, so we don't actually need anything real …'

He looks as though a thousand thoughts are racing behind his eyes.

'Nothing solid,' I add, helpfully.

By now we had reached the nearest of one of the many chilled compartment cavities in one of the walls. I gave a standard automated command for it to open and, reaching in, took the first item of food that came to hand. I had concluded by now that Fred wouldn't understand the contents well enough to choose for himself. He seemed so surprised and distracted by all the surroundings, I could predict that his reaction to our food would be similar. In any case, not asking him, just giving him sustenance of my choice, made me feel a little more in control. He might even start seeing us, me, as superior to them, since we have such awe-inspiring technology, while they apparently choose to stay perversely and deliberately living primitive lives for the sake of mere ideas and misguided principles. *And killed your parents on the way.* No, just concentrate on the food. I hand him a green triangle of sea bass.

'Perhaps you don't have food like this ... er, where you come from.'

We sit down simultaneously on two body-moulded seats. He props the bicycle against his, but extends an arm along the back of the chair, maintaining light fingertip contact with the delicate lilac frame. With his other hand he pincers the sea bass and cautiously takes small bites, even though the entire triangle would fit into his mouth all at once, as it is precisely designed to do. But he registers neither distaste nor pleasure. His hunger may have eclipsed all judgement. Alternatively, perhaps N-Ps would not ever confess to enjoyment of any type, even simple taste. For the first time, it seems he is a little more at ease, less wary. But I am tense again, unsure what he will say and what I am supposed to do now.

'Zelda, do you know anything about us, who we are, what we stand for?'

Again a dim, remote echo from long ago, when things and people simultaneously also 'stood for' other things. I feel suddenly weary, not because I crave a fresh infusion of the usual direct, simple sensation from the screen, but rather because of too many conflicting reactions to this grey, secretive stranger. I loathe what he is, but this Fred, this N-P, still stares into my eyes and beyond. I have nothing to hold on to, no easy icon on which to focus, no instant delete button to press. Nowhere seems safe now, but there is nowhere else I want to be.

'In any event, it would surely be interesting for you to hear our side, our version: comparisons, after all, allow a much better evaluation than when there is no relativity.'

How can people who have turned their back on technology and deliberately chosen a difficult life in the unadulterated, harsh real world, nonetheless speak in a way even I, with all my grandparents' special preparation, can hardly understand? I am no longer sure whether the N-Ps are ridiculous relics or very sophisticated, compared to us. I struggle now, no longer in control, dispensing a meal in my largesse: the previously warring emotions now sharpen into simple despair.

'Please. Go slower.'

Fred closes his eyes for a second, making some inner check. The smile, when it finally comes, is small, tight: the first non-genuine thing about him. But he draws a deep breath, looking at me steadily again.

'I don't know how much they tell you here, so I'll start at the beginning. Of course, stop me if you know much of this already.'

No, I will not let him know I'm different, that I'll understand and expect much more than everyone else in the Grouping. At least not yet. I want him to discover for himself how different I am from Sim. I'll tell him nothing of my personal history, just the facts he might expect me to know.

'It's an established fact that you all left because you couldn't keep up with the pace of change of technology. The Fact-Totum doesn't really say much except that you chose a life that is difficult, unexciting and unhappy. Oh, perhaps you don't have a Fact-Totum even: it's here in my ear. We all have them, they give the facts.'

'But they don't give you the ideas, do they, Zelda?'

Fred's voice is a smoky whisper that hangs suspended.

'I have a Fact-Totum but I don't use it. Not much. No point.'

Sim's voice is strident and high: an intrusive screech. Neither of us noticed her, listening in and near us. Leaning on one arm on the back of my chair, pivoting on it, swivelling back and forth, pulling a long blonde strand of hair into her mouth, alerted for a moment by the novelty of this lengthy interchange of words, but just words after all. We look back to each other. She vanishes from view. Fred wants to be serious. What he was saying is important to him, and he seems determined that I should understand.

'We favour the term N-P because it can stand for both Neo-Platonic as well as Neo-Puritan.'

This time I am not so lost and distracted by the term 'stand for'. I don't really understand, but I can suspend the uncertainty while Fred carries on trying to explain himself. And I listen.

'Perhaps that Fact-Totum device of yours doesn't have many facts on Plato: the Greek who lived thousands of years ago. He's actually very special to us because he stands for so much. At the most trivial, you could say that he was an exponent of the notion of dialogue, of one hand and other hand, of thesis and antithesis. Once you have iteration, then you have movement forward, if not in space, then at least in time: the development of ideas and ideals. And so he also stands for ideas rather than mere examples of those ideas: an abstracted generalization that is therefore perfect as opposed to the specific and thus the inevitably imperfect.'

I am on slightly firmer ground and confident enough to smile. 'But we too wish for perfection.' I tilt my face towards him: an age-old ploy that I've never used before but know very well. 'The perfect life: one full of happiness and free of pain.'

But, surprisingly, Fred becomes dismissive, almost irritated.

'No, Zelda, not some skin-deep, misplaced, self-centred absurdity: I mean perfection in the real sense, an abstraction unsullied by examples which themselves can only ever be different, incomplete facets of the whole.'

I am rebuffed, hurt in a way that cuts far deeper than the hurts of the everyday life of the Dwelling, the hurt of Sim not listening or dancing away, or the hurt of another baby walking, and then walking away. I grasp for, and then cling to, the other word he'd just used.

'So what about the Puritans?'

'Exactly.'

A real smile now. Contact. My confusion mounts, but I am still pleased.

'Zelda, you've hit on the primary connection: from perfection to purity. The abstract is unsullied, uncontaminated. We believe that life should be like that too, just like the Puritans of the seventeenth century. They were increasingly saddened and threatened by the corrupt, degenerate way of living that stripped people of their dignity, literally from the Latin, their worthiness. Above all, the escalating sensual way of life made people lose control of their own minds. When that happens, everything loses meaning. We have no point to our lives.'

Ever since my grandparents died so long ago, I had stopped wondering whether my life should have a point. I had never even thought about 'my life' as some kind of thing, what Fred might call a 'concept'. But what he is saying, much of which actually makes no sense to me, none the less starts to build a bridge to that previous time, when my grandparents were alive and I was small and children lived with just one male and female parent, and perhaps even with their grandparents. And everyone was at a very clear, different stage of their particular 'life'.

Thomas and Emma: they are now glimmering and shimmering into focus from some faraway place, my mother and father. Of course, they're always there, lodged in my mind somewhere, somehow, but sleeping. Fred has woken them up. Their voices are getting louder now, their faces and bodies coming into sharper relief.... .

'Zelda, stop playing with that screen, we're going to see Grandma and Grandpa.'

My mother's face is sunny and empty, and her voice is the same.

'Do come on.' The impatient, louder, deeper tones of my father.

At that time the computer was still something that was independent, free-standing, not embedded in other objects and clothing in the way to which we have all become so accustomed for so long. But, most important of all, the screen really was a literal screen. I still cannot take for granted the Talking Heads that anyone in the Grouping addresses whenever they want direct access for some kind of interactive audio-visual display, summoned by recognition of each of our voice patterns. Instead, those unspectacular oblongs that used to dominate the lives of so many in such a fixated way for the first half of the twenty-first century are, for me, still the real thing. Back then when my parents were still living, it was all still two-dimensional, the clear focus and starting point of everything. Either you were 'at' or 'on' a digital device, or you were out there in the real world – and right now getting into a car.

We are already different, my mother, father and I, because we have a car. A car: how odd to recall how it was still just possible to have a car in those days, and now obviously no one does. Where would they go? What would they do that they can't do in their Dwellings? What could they do in a different place other than just running around and dancing as they could do anyway, anywhere?

But then we needed to go through the mechanical motions of getting into a three-dimensional mechanical car because we needed and wanted to see my grandparents, Emma's mother and father, in three dimensions, some distance away. At that time the world was a stark place that was not enhanced or muted, but was the same standard reality for everyone, including the N-Ps. But, unlike them, most people turned their backs on the difficulties and unloveliness of it all, and drew up a chair on their own in a small room, to live instead through the little screen. Some squinted at even tinier screens embedded in their clothing, their jewellery, their watches, and turned more and more to these constant little friends to advise, to guide, to entertain: they were clumsy and simple but were filling the need that our ear and eye enhancers do now.

My mother would sometimes dismiss me without a glance, staring dreamily into the screen, but with hands and thumbs speeding over the flat, old-fashioned surface. My father, similarly at that moment now staring ahead, hands limp on the driving wheel, looking ahead as his shirt device, still externally embedded, winds its thin wires shakily up to his ears: next to my mother, but in the cyber-world that was still all on the outside. Strange to think that most people were without anything at all when they took off their embedded clothes, undid their interactive smart watches and climbed naked into bed.

Screen culture: that had been the big controversy back then.

My Fact-Totum speaks of the N-Ps as strange, deluded people who thought that the power of technology was going too far, and that to be stimulated and excited was in some way wrong. More baffling still was their rejection of the idea of physical perfection both for the inner as well as the outer body. I remember my grandparents locked in secret, grown-up conversation with my mother and father; perhaps it was just before they were killed. And I remember hearing the term 'N-P' first whispered, in fear and disbelief, but above all in complete incomprehension.

But my grandparents were always different, even back then: first they looked so unlike most of the other adults I knew. It wasn't just the whirls and sags of the flesh that festooned their chins, their necks, their arms. Most striking was the way that they looked you right in the eye: and then there was the wonderful touching; stroking my hair, squeezing my hand. I'm sitting now on my grandmother's knee, her arms firm around me, my eyes closed as though I'm asleep. I'm so young, still little more than an infant so I could never dissemble: of course I'm asleep. But I'm not asleep: I can hear everything the adults are saying.

'Well, let them go. If they want to be wretched, and in pain, and ugly, let them.' My father's voice.

Then my mother. 'It is certainly going to be a very different world for Zelda. The N-Ps are the last to have children without making use of the new reproductive programs. Mum, just as you were the last generation to have a child – me – so-called "naturally", so I'll be the last generation to use the own-egg IVF program. Zelda will not have a mother-monopoly as we both did. She'll have to choose whether she donates an egg or her womb.'

My grandmother's voice is inevitably frailer: it trembles just above my head. 'But, Emma, the rules are changing. To be an egg donor, she'll need to have a perfect genome. And she hasn't, she can't have. She was born too early, as you well know, for having

166

complete pre-implantation genetic screening. None of her genes will have been deleted or enhanced. She is already too old.'

My grandfather's warm baritone falls into line. 'Poor Zelda, what a time to be born.'

Already their concern for me had bent the conversation away from the N-Ps. And I was to hear little about them for a long time after that isolated mention. Meanwhile, as my grandfather had predicted, I was to be witness to a difficult time but one nonetheless of huge and very rapid progress – not just in the technology for bestowing an environment free of tedium, but in revolutionizing how we saw our bodies, and what we expected from them.

Then, as the generations became more homogenized into a simple, single state of continuous, monotonous adulthood, and as the body and the brain were open for all to see so, with precision timing, did the screen technologies transform into mobile ones and on to invasive embedded interfacing. All the old compartments were vanishing at once, between generations, between the internal body and the external environment, and between fantasy and reality. So it was about this time that the great backlash occurred and the N-Ps made their stand, organizing themselves into a separate and rather sinister movement. One that grew in number and intolerance: so they left, the so-called 'great' Exodus. And no one bothered to stop them: quite simply, everyone felt safer and relieved because no one had to be disturbed by them any more. There was so much more to do, so many exciting new experiences to have and technologies to enjoy. We chose fantasy. They, the N-Ps, chose reality.... .

'So what is your life like, what is it like being an N-P?

Fred angles his head slightly to one side and for the first time since he arrived, there is silence. Not a complete absence of noise because Sim is still somewhere in the background, and so is Ciro and the two egg donors, B and C. But no one actually talks, just do things that make sounds: Sim dances round and round, on her empty circuit to nowhere, while Ciro sits with a younger one at a screen. One of the egg donors, B, is methodically eating, chewing and swallowing and staring into the distance. Avril, heavily pregnant, softly snores in a light sleep. No one is bothering with, or bothered by, anyone else. As usual.

Fred finally breaks our silence. 'It is so hard to explain in just a few sentences because everything is so different. Because our ideas are so different, it means that the expressions of those ideas, the actual way we N-Ps live, might hardly be comprehensible to you.'

I realize that he is trying to understand me. 'Tell me, try me.'

'Well, the past and the future are very important to us. After all, that's what a life is: a past, present, future. My particular past was to train as a neuroscientist, so that I could try to understand the brain.'

'Why?'

'Because you have to do something with your life as you go through it, it has to mean something. Something only has meaning when it has some kind of permanence, or causes something else to occur or exist that is permanent. The longer something lasts, or isn't reversed or cancelled out, the more meaningful it is.'

'But nothing we do lasts.'

'Precisely. Nothing *you* do here lasts. When you play a game, you can just play the game again: it's meaningless.'

'But it's fun.'

As soon as I form this reply, before I actually speak, I know it was simultaneously both the right and wrong thing to say.

'That is why having fun is discouraged by N-Ps. Instead, we aim for fulfilment: it lasts longer.'

'So is working on the brain fulfilling?'

'Yes, very much so. Well, often. Sometimes. When you can prove your ideas are right.'

I once again feel wearied by these short answers, Fred's 'iterations', not because I want my old cyber-games instead, but because I feel I am struggling uphill in another, alien language with someone who is a native speaker, where I have to guess as I go along. I would have much rather he just kept talking: listening to him, watching him, just being near him, is infinitely better than sitting in front of any screen.

'What kinds of ideas do you test?'

'After I'd trained, my job was to understand more about consciousness, the inner experience you're having now and that no one else can share first hand. The experience that ends each time you sleep.'

We both, again in unison, look across at Avril, now sunk swollen in the seat, limp and deep, breathing heavily and slowly.

'But that's such a hard question. People have been asking it for hundreds, if not thousands, of years. It started with philosophers, but for the last century or so the scientists have been joining in. The problem is that we still do not know what kind of answer would satisfy the question of how the brain generates consciousnesses.'

He smiles and glances at me, but only briefly. It is as though he knows already that there will be no connecting nod. Yet he also knows, I am convinced, that it doesn't matter, that neither of us mind.

'If you wanted to understand flight, say, then you would need to build – or know how to build – something that could defy gravity. You wouldn't need to add in a beak and feathers.'.

The grey eyes sparkle, lingering. I no longer see the N-P. He is simply Fred.

'But what would you actually expect me to show you if I said I'd discovered how the brain generates consciousness? That's why the problem still hasn't been solved. We still really do not know where to start, what to aim for. So, instead of working on the difference between consciousness and unconsciousness, I work on different types of consciousness: it's rather easier.'

'What do you mean, different types of consciousness?'

'Well, for example, the different types of consciousness between our N-P society and yours. That's why I'm here, to try and understand how your brains work as you live this type of life.'

He lifts his gaze from me and sweeps the arm not caressing the bicycle over the babbling, buzzing, fragmented interior of the Dwelling. The contrast between this centrifugal man and the mindless, meaningless place in which he happens to be, slaps me in the face as only the loss of my grandparents has ever done before. How stupid and arrogant for me to assume that the N-Ps were pathetically behind us in technology, when they had gone way ahead, albeit in a very different direction.

'I want to find out what in the brain makes Sim, for example, so different from us. I mean us, the N-Ps.'

I instinctively know what he really means and what to do. 'So stay with us and study Sim's brain.'

'I was hoping you would suggest that.'

I daren't look him in the eyes, and inspect his bicycle instead.

'But I will need your help.'

Have I given too much away? Is he mocking the fact that we, the majority who thought we had the answers, are actually the silly, misguided ones doomed to eventual misery? Be careful, beware. Give nothing more away, yet. He's an N-P. Still, despite everything … And he's very clever.

'What could you possibly need me for?' Keep it simple. Don't try and be different.

'Well, Zelda, I'm not sure how happy and agreeable Sim will be to having me study her brain. It will take some time, and take up most of each day. From what I have seen so far, she will probably become easily restless, bored, impatient. Though as the experiment – I mean the study – progresses, let's hope she starts to enjoy what is happening and cooperates all on her own. Anyhow, what I'm asking is that you are with her in the early stages at least. She obviously needs and trusts you, so you can put her at ease. I cannot stress enough how important you are for the success of this, er, project. I need you, Zelda.'

Those last four words hang in the air. They reverberate over and over again, as I check that Fred has really said what I have for so long dreamed of someone saying. I'm worried that anything I now add will detract, destroy. I feel safe enough, confident enough, to have some time alone. I want to do something I haven't done since moving into the Dwelling, I want to have time without any external stimulations or distractions just to think, to savour the implications – Fred would say the consequences – of what is definitely about to happen and also what could happen, improbable though it might seem.

'Then perhaps you should get some sleep now, and we'll start tomorrow? It will give me time to prepare Sim.'

'That sounds perfect. Where is there a bed?'

A bed? Of course, he's used to fixed furniture in fixed places. 'Just stand up for a moment.'

In one fluid movement he's standing, tall above me, still holding on to the bars of the bicycle. I address the nano-assembler activator on the chair in which he is sitting, and whisper 'bed'. Smoothly the invisible molecules in the chair shuffle apart and reassemble themselves, moving this way and that, so that before our eyes, parts of the erstwhile chair swell while others contract, and others flatten. In a few moments Fred has his bed. He is smiling genuinely now, shaking his head in slow disbelief, but clearly curious and intrigued.

'Of course, I'd heard about nano-assembly, and can quite understand the theory: but we had never bothered developing it on a practical level. We just couldn't see the point.'

He extends his free hand to test out the softness of the surface where he's about to lie down. As his hand sinks lower than he obviously expected, he protrudes his lower lip, gives a quick nod. He tries to be light-hearted, humorous. A little bark of a laugh.

'But still, I'm starting to see some advantages.'

Then he flashes a quick, real smile, and bends forward over the bed. His hand still holds the bicycle upright and he looks up at me over his shoulder.

'Will the bicycle be safe beside me? It won't vanish or transform into anything else?'

Neither of us is sure how much this is a joke.

'Of course not. But if it's restricting your space, we can always put it somewhere else.'

The relaxation and warmth drain from his face, leaving it suddenly and fleetingly tight, white and alert.

'No.'

'Would you like a sleep-enhancing experience, for example, the Starry Mountain sky?'

Now he just looks weary in every sense. 'I've just had the real thing for several days now. How could anything fabricated ever be the same? So, no.' Then, more softly, 'I'm so tired anyway that I'll fall asleep instantly, without any help. But thank you, Zelda.'

I'm dismissed and know that now I should really find Sim, and talk to her about tomorrow, and why it's about to be so different from any other day she's ever had, and how it's about to change her life. Should I mention what's happening to the co-habitants of the Dwelling? I think back to the futility of the recent meeting, and cannot see what difference it would make. Ciro and the others might notice Fred, but would instantly disregard him as uninteresting.

I also know I should notify the Groupings Register that, exceptionally, Sim will now be staying where she is for the time being. After all, we have a very good reason: she needs me, or rather Fred does. But that will be broadcasting the fact of Fred's arrival. Might anyone really care who he is and why he is here? I ruminate a little. After all, the N-Ps did leave of their own accord: why shouldn't one of them come back? One man can hardly have much impact on anything here. Fred can be automatically logged, perhaps he already has been, thanks to the devices embedded in him that will inevitably give out signals: but it will mean nothing surely, to a system that is as automated as ours.

I've never really had to ask too many questions. Now my grandparents are long dead, who could or would answer them? And if I tried with the Fact-Totum, then I might be logged in some external database as curious, difficult, different. And I always try to hide that I'm all of those things. In the days when I was small, during the Exodus, terrible things happened. People would attack and even kill each other as casually as in a video game. But now the killings have stopped. No one cares what anyone thinks because everyone lives in cyber-isolation. It's easy to view our society as a result of natural evolution: everything has just happened and easily interfaced so well and automatically with technology.

But suppose there was more to it: if by doing something very wrong, then you could once again end up with blood on your clothes – your own blood. Yet I can't even envisage how such a system might operate, be so clever and utterly clandestine. No, it must simply be evolution. And – another thought – what could be regarded as 'wrong'? Where are we told or taught 'right' from 'wrong' anymore? And then, in any case, nothing any of us does has consequences. Until now, now Fred has arrived. So, suddenly, all these questions are buzzing in my brain. Best to stop, as I always do, just stop thinking.

Meanwhile, I have to let this wonderful, special day unfold and embed in my mind. I do not necessarily want to think or plan, but just to replay and enjoy the watching of it. I'm not used to having specific, important tasks to do. But still, those other things, the Register and Sim, they will wait until tomorrow. Or perhaps a few days from now. No rush. There never is. As I make my way to my own area, I realize without any strong emotion how pleased I am about what will happen tomorrow, not just because it will enable Sim to stay. A few hours earlier, and that would have been my sole concern. Tonight I shan't take the pills … .

Chapter 15

FRED

The following morning, I woke up to a day full of purpose, to a bright beginning brimming with natural sunlight. But when I propped myself up on my arm, opened my eyes properly and tried to look around, I had to squint. I realized that the natural light wasn't coming in from the outside at all, but had been fabricated as the default mood of the moment by the glowing polymer surfaces everywhere, on the walls, on the ceiling, on the floor and on whatever objects might have been manufactured, then just left overnight. The sheer novelty of these blindingly garish, gaudy surroundings for the moment trumped any thoughts or plans regarding my mission.

Had I not known better, I would have lulled myself into the fantasy that my bed was a permanent fixture, fitting well into a deep-set, almost private alcove. The bicycle was propped up on the wall near by, beaming back at me. For a moment I felt I had my own distinct place and identity, my niche. I peered out and beyond my immediate zone: my field of vision widened out to a very large but relatively empty space, with other alcoves and recesses and pillars all under an encompassing, spectacular, vast geodesic domed surface: it would have been inappropriate to have called it a 'roof', as though it was just a low, flat, functional, surface that simply joined up all the walls – as in my own home. Because the size of the Dwelling was so enormous, the vaulting domed structure above it had to be very high. It was almost like being outdoors …

I stopped myself. Was I actually starting to think like them already? I had to remember what the real outdoors was actually like. I looked back at the beautiful lilac device that had given not just a different few days of life, but had transformed me forever. But so long as I knew what was possible, who I really was deep down, then I could press on immediately with the job in hand. I had everything under control. First, explore fully where you are, I told myself. I pulled my grey garment around me and swung my legs over the iridescent bed, not daring to try the voice activator to reshape it. I was wary of the nano-assembly actually taking place, though had known for a long time about the underlying theory.

It had all started well over a century ago with microscopes a million times more powerful than the human eye, which could probe surfaces and thereby produce images of each individual atom. These devices were essentially nano-scale fingers and eyes that were soon revealing new insights into how matter operates. Soon those earlier pioneering scientists were using 'nano-tweezers'. The great challenge had been to find a way of assembling such small components together in a purposeful, controlled fashion: nano-assembly, a product of which I was currently languishing in. But for my forefathers it had been different: by then they were beginning to formulate their own priorities, driven by their mounting distaste and alarm for how the Yakawow mentality was taking hold. It was the time when they were deciding to leave in the great Exodus: all clever, impractical tricks and toys of physics and chemistry were suddenly far less important than simply safeguarding the human mind.

But here, things had clearly been different. It must have been the sophisticated automation itself – it could hardly be the infantile Others – that had developed nano-machines that could control themselves, independent of the human macro-world. The technology had just continued evolving on its own. Here self-replication would result from gears and wheels no larger than several atoms in diameter, which could give rise to atomic-size machines that would then scavenge molecules from the environment to reproduce themselves. These molecular robots, some tenth of a micrometre in size, could then manipulate more individual atoms. And, in turn, those molecular robots could be driven by voice instruction. The scientist in me was fascinated but the real me, Fred the man, wanted to explore.

I stood up and looked around. Where should I start? Where could I go first, when I wanted to go everywhere at once? It was like nothing, *nothing* I could have previously imagined. Here there was clearly no externally imposed routine, no moment when it was necessary or perhaps even desirable to interact with anyone else. Everyone I looked at, as they floated across my visual field, was in complete contrast to the sombre, soberly dressed colleagues to whom I was so accustomed. Born into a world of purpose and direction, how could I ever have conceived of these figures, humans just like me, but drifting and twirling apparently aimlessly around in multicoloured, shimmering garments? They wove their way through the spaces at different paces, some seeming to dance, yet all oblivious to each other. How could our species have diverged so much?

As I approached them in turn, one by one, each glanced by me, not registering or reacting in any way. At first I couldn't understand how there were none the less voices of different timbres and volume, all speaking – until I realized that the words were actually emanating from a range of strange-looking objects, disembodied heads of different skin tones and both genders, dotted haphazardly as far as I could see throughout all the interconnecting spaces. These heads were life-size but the necks protruded not from bodies, but from gleaming surfaces. Yet there they were swivelling and pivoting, making attempts to move what they had, to simulate real people with frowns and smiles as they spoke to whoever was passing by in front of them. But the communication seemed all one sided. No one was giving their grimaces and grins a second glance.

Then adding to this cacophony were mechanised voices from the flimsy garments themselves that the inhabitants were wearing, as each Other was living out their morning in some kind of insular bubble. However, it was a bubble that could be penetrated by read-out devices, from body temperature to choice of music: it was a modern Tower of Babel.

All this soft noise and transparent colour spun round my head and filled the vast space above it. I looked up and up to the interior of the vast geodesic roof that finally rose high and arching overhead, as an improbable, multifaceted, iridescent heaven. And when I eventually looked down and around, the brightness and gleam were unremitting: nano-assembled chairs and tables and couches competed with the Talking Heads for my attention, but were ignored by everyone else who seemed to be looking glassy-eyed and inwards, transported somewhere else.

One pregnant woman was conspicuous by virtue of the simple fact that she was actually sitting still, vacuous in a glowing chair. Another, a boy whom I had thought yesterday was unusually good-looking, was immersed in a hologram of what must have been some kind of fictional drama: the characters were three-dimensional and speaking but obviously lacked substance, as one of the infants crawled through them. Another larger child, however, was not surrounded by any overt external objects or people, but was acting as though she was: I realized that she was in some kind of virtual place, thanks to the same enhancing implants in her eyes and ears that I had so recently seen could transform Sim's world.

But just as I had derided Zelda that she could never understand our N-P way of life, so I'm sure that neither Hodge nor I could ever have anticipated just how devastatingly different reality would be among the Others. Just wandering around I was more convinced than ever of the urgency and importance of my mission. These people could be a serious threat, not because they would ever be proactive enough to mount any kind of opposition to us, but rather because, by merely existing, they remained a constant threat, a reminder of the terrible self-destructive alternative of which the human mind was capable. We needed to ensure that this alternative was rendered non-viable, forever. We had to understand how and why such a decline had been possible: then we had to take whatever measures were necessary to wipe it out.

I decided to try and make a real effort at communication and approached the woman with the swollen belly, lounging listless in the chair: at least she was static and it might be easier to communicate with her than with any of the Others, who were so incessantly on the move.

'Hello, I'm Fred.'

A silent stare in my direction, but not into my eyes.

'You look shit.'

Then she looked away, and I was invisible.

'I wouldn't bother with Avril, if I were you. She has nothing to say. Speak to me instead: tell me more about what you're going to do with Sim.'

Zelda was standing behind me, arms folded loosely across her body, head to one side, half smiling. Her red-gold curls softened her face even more than I had remembered from the previous night: but despite the flawless, smooth skin to which I was already becoming accustomed on everyone, there was somewhere, somehow, the shadow of a sadness behind her eyes and around her mouth.

'You must be hungry: we could eat at the same time.'

This kind of spontaneous decision, a mere response to a desire rather than tracking through a set routine, was strange to me. Zelda sounded like a society hostess from the literature I'd read from another epoch entirely. Was that how she really thought all the time? If so, how did she come to terms with this very different life, every single fun-filled, empty day?

The objects that she now placed in front of me were, in a bizarrely comparable way, appropriate for the sensory-laden Dwelling. Bright glowing cubes, with no indication as to what their content or provenance might be. They were there just to gorge on, to eat as much as I liked without any checks, any admonishments from the embedded sensors.

'Of course, you N-Ps wouldn't have this kind of thing. I'm sorry, I should have realized: it's all genetically modified.'

My pride wouldn't let their view go unchecked of N-Ps as some form of techno-inferiors.

'So is the food that we eat, but it doesn't look like this.'

'So how is N-P food modified?'

'Modified for enhanced goodness, not for external appearance or sensational experience.'

The difference in our lifestyles, our ideologies, in a nutshell. The N-P doctrine was to keep the body, and especially the mind, pure: hence our food resembled original, natural food as much as possible, at least to look at. However, it would have been wholly foolish to have rejected the now established technology of genetic modification. Not only was food enhanced with vitamins and other agents such as fish oils, now proven beyond question to optimize brain function, but that enhancement was engineered for the bespoke, current needs of each individual: this technology had indeed been what Tarra had worked on initially, the so-called 'neutroceuticals'. But all the ingenuity was invisible: a carrot that Tarra might place on our table still looked like it did way back at the beginning of the twenty-first century, indeed since Anglo-Saxon times, all in keeping with our simple, silent, monochrome existence.

While speaking, Zelda was rubbing her finger against a purple cube that immediately emitted a thick orange sauce, which had clearly been magnetized: her actions released it now on to her waiting fingertips, which fed into her plump pink lips. I reached for a slippery cube, rubbed it and was astonished at the slick ease of the sauce, as well as with the simple joy of sucking my fingers. The overpowering taste to which I was still unaccustomed made me reel: it was as though my tongue, my throat, my whole mouth were alive and lit up in a way they had never been, ever.

Zelda was smiling at my reaction. I had already realized that she wasn't at all like what I was rapidly learning was a generic Other, but seemed to come from another place, have remnants of something else. My analytical mind tried to localize her in one space and time compartment or the other. Without question, she could never be an N-P, one of us. Even leaving aside her appearance, from what I had seen so far, I could tell immediately that she lacked our logic and directness of thought. But she stood out so distinctly in this strange pleasure dome because, above all, she was willing to communicate, have some kind of conversation. No, it was not as directly iterative and purposeful as an N-P dialogue. But at least in some vaguer, fuzzier way she opened up avenues for responses of some kind: rather than an experience of clear, clean, verbal lasers, there was some indefinable, atavistic message in a bottle.

Chapter 16

ZELDA

That next morning, I'd had breakfast with Fred … breakfast
with Fred, how strange that was. I'd never actually sat down
and eaten with anyone since my arrival in the Dwelling and
had forgotten the demanding experience of looking, listening
and talking while at the same time, savouring and sharing food.
When my grandparents were alive, meals together had been a
key part of each day, demarcating the beginning, middle, and
end of the waking cycle but most importantly constituting major
events in their own right. How could human beings, just a few
decades later, be satisfied with simply feeding on their own?
How could I have just accepted such a major downgrading of
the quality of my life?

But now everything was different. Everything was back to
normal. As it should be. I sat across a gleaming table, staring at
a special person, someone who needed me, someone for whom
I was therefore special. Fred was preoccupied with handling the
bright triangles, already now clearly confident enough to put the
whole morsel into his mouth in one go and obviously appreciative
of the ensuing taste. I myself ate little, as I was churning too
much with anticipation: for the first time in a long time I didn't

know what was about to happen – but was convinced it would be positive, stimulating, utterly different. The silence between us was friendly enough but I recalled that it was not quite normal behaviour at meals for one person to be doing all the eating while the other just stared at them. Fred was obviously deep in thought. It was important for him to see I understood.

'Fred, I'm not that hungry. So while you're finishing, I'll go and find Sim'.

'Good idea.' His eyes caught mine for a moment, with a brief little smile: then he returned to his preoccupation with the alien objects laid out before him.

I'm not sure how much Sim understood, when I eventually found her.

'We're going to play a special game today, Sim.'

She was flicking her loose, long hair back and forth over her face by turning her head from side to side quickly and suddenly. She hadn't yet put on her enhancers, so there was the best possible chance she might listen to me. Now she was hiding her face from me behind the alternating blonde curtains. Before yesterday the thought would have troubled me that she was shutting me out: but now I just wanted to do what we needed, to give Fred what he had asked of me.

'Why? I want to play games on my own, with my enhancers.'

I persisted. 'Because Fred is staying with us and he wants to play a new and very special game. You like Fred, don't you, Sim? He brought you home yesterday.'

'Can we play a game with the mauve thing he can go fast on?'

'No, I think he may have something even more exciting that he wants to show us.'

And this wild, vague response turned out to be completely accurate. Fred stood before us, the bicycle this time propped near by in easy sight, but his primary attention focusing on a thin, silver helmet-like object. Sim and I were sitting down, me attentive and fascinated, she vibrating a leg in impatience, anxious to get going. Fred cleared his throat. He was this morning being professional, like my grandfather must have been when he was standing in front of his class. I didn't mind. He rested both hands on the helmet, glanced sideways at the bicycle, then back at us.

'This is a very special device: the Helmet.'

It was chrome-like silver, but eggshell thin: it was in two halves, to fit neatly over the two hemispheres of the brain. This design left space in the centre for adjusting the fit over the head in question via extendable, sliding connectors. There was also an adjustable grey strap, obviously to go under the chin.

'Simply put, the Helmet enables us to see into Sim's brain. It enables a read-out that we can build into a literal picture of what is happening from moment to moment.'

Sim giggled. Perhaps it was because there were strange-sounding words, or she was simply bored with being a silent observer. I noticed she had surreptitiously switched on her enhancers, but didn't wish to distract Fred with the inevitable battle that would ensue if I asked her to turn them back off. Meanwhile, I felt small and stupid. I so wanted to understand what Fred was doing and why, but the gulf between us seemed once again, though this time for different reasons, conclusively unbridgeable. I needed to take some kind of initiative, act according to my own perspective. Make a contribution.

'We trust you, Fred. I'm sure the Helmet won't hurt Sim, so we don't need to bother with the technical details. But I'm really curious to know what you're planning to do. Where will we see these pictures?'

Fred looked down at his hands resting gently on the surface of the gleaming Helmet in front of him.

'Well, that's a small difficulty, I'm afraid. We just don't have the equipment here for that. I need to transmit the data to my … colleagues, via my own implant. Just like you all, I have one under my skin, here.'

He gestured towards his upper arm, with a tentative smile. Perhaps my doubt registered fleetingly in my face. The mention of colleagues far away reminded me that above all here was an N-P, who would apparently be reporting back to them, the very people we had shunned as a society and who, for me personally, held such bitter and searing scars. But before I could respond, Fred had launched into his next statement, that clearly he hoped would compensate for not seeing the pictures,

'But really the pictures aren't that important in themselves. It would be hard to understand them anyway, if you were not used to them. It's what they tell us, and how we then intercept the ongoing mindset, and how that then changes Sim's behaviour. That is what will tell us everything.'

This was all a lot to absorb. I hadn't realized that studying Sim's brain meant changing it, and presumably thus changing her. Did I want her any different? No, no different from the person she already was; but, then again, yes, I'd like her to talk to me more, be closer. So, yes, I'd help him. I wanted to be important to Fred, and I wanted Sim to love me more. Perhaps, therefore, it was all for the good. In any case, I could hardly now walk away with Sim and tell Fred to leave. That would obviously be impossible; the very thought truly unbearable.

'How will her behaviour change?' I asked weakly.

Fred looked relieved. He leant forward on his hands, over the Helmet, the inconsequential Helmet that sent signals I wouldn't understand but that weren't important anyway.

'Well, it's a long and detailed story. But, just for the moment, let me give you a flavour of the kinds of things that might be possible. I've noted Sim has some characteristic ways of acting, ways that are more like a very small child. I don't think this is because she is only ever capable of being like a small child because there's nothing intrinsically wrong with her: I think it's because of the way she's been living. There are some strategies I've devised that could make her act more like the young adult that she is.'

'But I've given Sim so much. She means everything to me.' A confession that I would never have made to anyone else in the Grouping: but then the scenario of my ever needing or wanting to tell them, or them ever questioning or wanting to know, was preposterous.

But Fred understood. 'I know, Zelda, and it's nothing to do with you personally. It's the world that you live in here. That's why I'm here, as you know.'

I realized that there was actually much force in what he was saying. The members of the Grouping were, compared with Fred, just like very small children. I had never really faced up to this truth as such, even though there was the constant, covert comparison with my grandparents against whom no one ever, ever measured up. Now I felt obviously different from the others in the Grouping: Fred was going to share with me the reasons, and indeed come up with something that might change things. Together, he and I might transform living in the Dwelling. My life might change in ways I could never have dreamt of. I looked sideways at Sim, shutting us out with her enhancers. Could things really be about to be so dramatically different?

Fred was clearing his throat again, repeatedly and noisily. I had obviously looked preoccupied and he wanted me back.

'First of all, Zelda, people like Sim, like young children, are unable to understand what other people are feeling. They do not realize other people have feelings that are different from theirs. We need a means of helping them see these different perspectives – we call it 'empathy'. So I plan to start with a conventional visual sequence of fast-moving events, driven by the user, Sim. Slowly, we'll introduce a reduced speed of images and longer periods with speech, then conversation. We'll have voices with different inflections, so that Sim starts to experience and understand something called 'prosody', where the feeling is reflected in the tone and timbre of the spoken voice. We'll then include intermittent questions about predicting from what people are saying, and how they are saying it, what they might then actually do. Second, we need to develop a sense of privacy and an enduring sense of self with a clear narrative that Sim learns does not require feedback or comments from anyone else.'

Privacy. A word like 'home'. Words, simple single words that could restore me to a time of such different expectations and perceptions. I never thought I would hear the word again, hear anyone else say it. Did it mean that it had the same meaning for him? Was it special for him too? Had I finally met someone with whom I could share the same understanding? But he had not paused, and my first aim was to listen.

'So we shall encourage her to develop a cyber "diary" a little like the ones of previous centuries, but one that will be impossible to share wholesale with anyone else.'

'Even with me?'

'Yes, Zelda. I realize it might be hard to accept, loving Sim as you do: but it's essential no one can access her "diary". The whole point is that she must be confident she has complete control over her privacy. She can share parts of it indirectly with others if she chooses, by simply having a conversation. But direct access as it were, over her head or into her head, no. I'm sorry, but our technology will make that impossible.'

I decided to remain silent. The session was not quite going as I'd hoped. My interaction with Fred was turning out to be very different from last night. But he had already come to his third point.

'Next, we need to provide Sim with feedback, a memory bank if you like, to help give a structure to her life and to be there for her to reference until we can drive her own natural memory back into action. So this program will not be an activity as such, but simply feedback on her inputs over time. As her performance over the whole range of activities accumulates, an analysis will build up of types of her personality traits that are emerging and changing.'

He looked at me proudly, almost as if seeking approval. But I simply looked back, attentive yet blank, unable to give anything back. Too much was going on.

'Fourth, we need to build up gradually an individual conceptual framework. Sim will enter any random ideas as she has them – brainstorming, or indeed as though blogging like they did in the past. She might even include facts that are particularly interesting to her, that she might have learnt from the Fact-Totum. In this way, an individual framework will gradually grow that then feeds into other responses and activities. So an idea such as "The government is betraying us" can then be cross-referenced to a host of other examples within the existing personal framework, and then to a wider, more objective database. Evaluations can show progress on understanding of abstract ideas, but from a highly personalized and individual perspective.'

What on earth could that mean, about a 'government' and 'betrayal'? Perhaps the proposition was so abstract and refined an example, that it would have been more appropriate for another era altogether, when such concepts meant something. Perhaps the N-Ps had something they regarded as a government, and it might make sense to talk of betrayal. But the idea of Sim, *Sim*, ever, ever using or understanding such a concept, was ludicrous. I would let Fred continue his current monologue: but when things were under way, I would hope I could show him what might be realistic to achieve. Perhaps he had seen the slight exasperation on my face, because again he was pressing on hastily.

'Another problem, and one very important as I've explained, is the notion that actions have consequences. So we'll give Sim games that are permanently changed each time. For example, if someone is shot dead, they remain dead thereafter. In addition for every action, such as being shot, the program is interrupted by real-life footage with a brief report from someone on what it actually feels like to be shot, or bereaved.'

Bereaved. Perhaps Fred could use me for talking about that, about my dead grandparents, and my parents. And how they became dead, I thought bitterly. But I stopped thinking. I just needed to listen.

'Then, finally, I'd like to try developing Sim's imagination. We'll have a program with absolutely no menus! The starting point is simply a word, idea or action that freely links to anything else and is prompted by previous entries across the whole range of other programs. Icons or pictures of the entry will slowly be replaced by words or a voice. Over time, the entries will build up into an increasingly complex, evolving network of associations that can be built creatively into a story with Sim as the author.'

Fred beamed triumphantly. I felt simultaneously alive – in a way I could only remember from when I was a child, before being told I was imperfect – and full of almost pity for Fred. He clearly had so much belief in what he wanted to do, had such high and important goals: how would he react when I told him, for example, that of course Sim couldn't read a single word? Even I hadn't seen a book since I'd left my grandparents' home, and their little library, as they had called it, had been blown up along with everything else by the metallic hand of a demolition robot. The written word couldn't feature with Sim. Reading and writing were well and truly dead. But we might do something, make some progress somehow. We had to. After such a hopeful start, we – Fred and I – just had to try and realize my dream. Otherwise, life – the old life, as I already was seeing my existence prior to yesterday – would not be worth living.

Sim had not listened at all, and had surprisingly been sitting for far longer than she would normally tolerate. But now she was back on her feet, already turning the Helmet, the new object, round and round in her hands.

'So you'll really see inside Sim's brain, and change how she thinks and behaves?'

'I hope so.'

But Fred was gazing, not at me, but at his bicycle.

Chapter 17

FRED

'It's probably best if we just make a start as we've been doing. Where's Sim now?'

Zelda shrugged in a way an N-P never would if asked a direct question.

'Probably outside. Running.'

'Where would she be going?'

But now I'd had time to settle down in the Dwelling, I already knew the answer.

'Nowhere.'

'Let me go out and find her, on my bicycle.'

How I yearned to free-wheel. It had been a whole day now, since I was last able to escape.

'No. She could have gone in any direction. She'll be back soon enough, when she gets hungry, or bored, or both. So it will be quite soon. Meanwhile, why don't we eat something ourselves?'

The invitation still sounded strange and inappropriate on the lips of an Other and in the context of the fragmented, distracting environment in which any shared activity was an unknown phenomenon. From what I had surmised already, and indeed validated by what I had experienced so far in the time I had been here, Others never ate together. So when Zelda had originally suggested we share a meal, or at least eat at the same time, it must first have been as odd for her as it was a surprise for me.

It was nothing like the intimate, well-tuned, coordinated experience of eating with Tarra, of living with her. I was used to a very different existence where other people, and sharing things with other people, are a mandatory part of life. At home, my day followed an ordered and unchanging sequence. I always woke next to Tarra, copulated, then abluted and ate. Over our morning meal together there was always time, it was allocated as such after all: everything was always organized and calm as one stage or step in the day ushered in the next. Sequence and consequence in an unbroken line. Tarra would check Bill's read-out to see what he needed to eat at that time. He was still far too young to have control of his own watch, which read out from the implant and via which the calorific levels were set in accordance with the energy to be expended: Tarra would be busy, perhaps even at this very moment, she was frowning slightly as she concentrated on tapping in the correct information, her cropped head bent over her other wrist where, like all mothers, she wore her child's watch. Meanwhile, I would have helped myself to the food until my body sensors informed me to stop. I would have looked across at Tarra and known that she felt, just like me, that we were progressing along a clear and straight path, living out our lives in the best possible way. Sometimes, most times, we hadn't needed to talk at all: we looked out in the same direction, were almost one consciousness. There was nothing indirect, external.

But now, the continuing contrasts were impossible to keep simultaneously in my consciousness, and my head that morning was starting to throb as a result. That had been happening a lot recently, and was becoming ever more frequent. Merely being in the Dwelling was in any case traumatic: the strong flavours assaulting my taste buds day after day, the ever changing iridescent lighting, the sensitivity of the objects around that, at the unthinking slip of a whispered word, could change colour, shape, texture, temperature and, if needed, could talk back. Rather than being a place where people interacted with their closest Family Unit, breeding partner and child, here the interaction wasn't with people at all, but rather with things. It was as though I was living inside a three-dimensional, advanced version of an old twenty-first-century web page, fragmented and strident, multifaceted and compartmentalized with no cohesion, but each feature calling out for your attention. The Dwelling wasn't a place of sanctuary at all but an ever changing, demanding space: so much was virtual or enhanced or smart-interactive that there was no constancy, no permanency or security and most bizarre of all, no time.

The whole building was in stark contrast to what, for us N-Ps, would be the very essence of a real home where advanced technologies are shunned. Of course, we are far ahead of the Others in our science, in what we understood about the world and its now delicately balanced eco-systems – at last restored to a workable equilibrium but still requiring constant vigilance. Most importantly of all, we understand far more – and they nothing – about the human brain, which is the starting point for all control and all fulfilment. The clever little technologies, used here merely for domestic ease, we would regard as a distraction and as the wrong kind of environment for optimal intellectual development: that is why they were consigned exclusively to the laboratory and other work institutions. Beyond the implants in our arms, the essential means for establishing and monitoring the life-story of each individual, we are constantly in fear of what incessant and immediate sensual ease and physical gratification might do to the mind. But that was what I was here for now: to find out.

Eating with Zelda was a small attempt at some kind of fragile stability in my current vertiginous world, and greatly preferable to performing a mere biological function in isolation. And by now it had become part of our routine. She gestured at a nearby alcove, whispered 'seats' and two glowing golden places materialized for us each to sink into. I was taking such metamorphoses for granted now and that morning realized I hadn't registered what had been there before, and what these new objects might have been before. Don't be like them, I reminded myself. Don't start accepting an atomized, isolated moment as the norm, without a preceding link or a future permanence. Be careful. Remember who you are and where you come from. And why you're here.

'So what happens now?'

Zelda's smile was just a front: she wanted something more from me than the silent reverie into which I had sunk. Right then, I just wanted to escape on my bicycle into the fresh air. I didn't feel like dialogue all the time. After eating each morning with Tarra and Bill, I would normally have set out on the walk to the lab, the same route in reverse from the evening before, the same duration, the same steps. This was the only time I was ever alone. There was the ever-present danger after all, even for adults, of that most harmful and feared phenomenon, a strong emotion, suddenly exploding all thought from ignition by the unchecked imagination, a persistent grievance scene or a rare but possible spontaneous fantasy.

Ironic, I had reasoned quite recently, that perhaps we N-Ps shared one important prohibition in common with the Others: neither society fostered or even encouraged the wayward, and now obsolete ancient human mental talent for unfettered imagination.

The reasons were obviously very different, however. For them, it was because they had the attention spans and inner cognitive impoverishment of small children: we, on the other hand, saw imagination as self-indulgent and self-centred when it was allowed to run wild, and therefore risk being counterproductive, with no end-point. There was no point in turning in on yourself, in spending your valuable life-story in inner escapism, wasting the precious minutes and hours ticking away in conjuring up strong emotions that obstructed meaningful interactions with others: those external interactions were essential on an evolutionary level for successful survival and procreation, and on a wider social level for the collective intellectual flourishing of our society that shunned egotism.

The more attuned we all became with each other – the extreme case being a breeding partner – the less we needed actually to articulate an explanation, but rather instead only had to headline each paragraph of thought. My colleagues were a diluted form of Tarra, in that I saw them, as they saw me, as small variations along the same collective abstract theme, that of the adult, fully formed N-P. And that abstraction, that N-P perfection, was best realized at the Rallies when we all spoke, chanted, with one voice: a unified consciousness where the whole was more than the sum of its parts. At least that was what I had been told.

Now Zelda was going to be the nearest thing I had here to a colleague, which was very far away indeed. In any case, I needed her to help with Sim; she was effective at keeping Sim calm and still enough for me to fit her each day with the Helmet. The Helmet: for us, it was normally a time when you had reached a stage in your life when what was going on in your brain was considered important, both what was read out in response to set cognitive exercises – Phase 1; then how those responses were applied to everyday daily life – Phase 2; and finally how those responses could be more quickly and powerfully shaped by direct stimulation via the Helmet – Phase 3.

Although I had mentioned to Zelda that the exercises with the Helmet would inevitably change Sim's behaviour, I'd let her assume that it would be a natural consequence of experience, just as any experience had always changed the behaviour of the human species. I hadn't told her about Phase 3: I hadn't told her that just as the orchestrated hum and buzz of all of Sim's neurons could be reassembled and interpreted remotely in our Institute, under Hodge's expert gaze, that just as the delicate forming and re-forming and strengthening and atrophy of each fragile point of contact along the ever-growing and shrinking branches of myriad neuronal circuits could be reconstructed in glowing, three-dimensional images – so too could those same patterns of neuronal connections be redesigned by manipulating them with unprecedented precision through focal, targeted electrical stimulation via the Helmet.

But that was for the future. For the time being, all that was needed was to monitor Sim's brain, as I had told Zelda I wished to do. The read-out would be transmitted back to Hodge for the in-depth analysis that I could obviously not perform in my remote and traumatic location away from the laboratory. The signals were now being fed every day from the Helmet, to be amplified and filtered by my implant, and I then routinely transmitted this data to Hodge, along with my observations and interpretations, all in the form of regular reports. I was doing everything expected of me.

In the early stage, I had needed to obtain baseline readings, the control data against which all the subsequent changes and manipulations would be compared. The plan had been, therefore, that Sim would just wear the Helmet and go about her normal day, while I monitored the spontaneous output. However, I had needed to be in range to pick up the weak transmissions from her Helmet. Fortunately, the technology was robust enough for Sim not to notice that I was near by, because the distance between us could still be sufficiently generous.

On that very first morning that now seemed a lifetime ago, there had been an anxious first few minutes, with Zelda frowning between me and Sim as I adjusted the connections to fit snugly. Then it was done, and on. With her blonde hair flowing from and around the silvered metal, Sim had indeed seemed like an exotic, fantasy creature: she still did. I couldn't think of her as a real person. Because the Helmet was so light, my subject would always then forget she had it on, and dance away. During this baseline phase when we had little intervention to make, we, Zelda and I, would sit down near the exit of the Dwelling so that if Sim decided on an outside excursion, we could just follow her.

In this way, time had passed. We had established the pattern for the days and weeks to come. It would take time to introduce the cognitive programs of Phase 1 that I had described to Zelda, and their application to real life, in Phase 2. The direct manipulative stimulation of Phase 3 was still a long way off. In these early days, neither environmental nor direct manipulation of Sim's brain was required: Zelda and I had time to talk. Only she, of all of the occupants in the Dwelling, seemed capable of a real conversation.

'They are not used to communicating,' Zelda said simply one day, with a shrug.

I noted, without drawing her attention to it, that she had used 'They' as opposed to 'We'.

'But why do they not want or need to talk to anyone?'

Of course, I had long worked out my own views and explanations, but I wanted to hear how this Other who didn't think like an Other, expressed herself.

Zelda lifted her chin, enjoying having centre stage with me watching.

'They don't wish to find anything out. In any case the Fact-Totum can answer any specific questions about the world, and that would only leave finding out about each other: what would be the point? What questions would they ask?'

'They could ask the kind of questions that I've been asking you,' I suggested, and then was surprised to hear myself add without drawing breath, 'and your answers fascinate me.'

'How? In what way?' Rhetorical questions.

'When you speak of your life: I'm fascinated at how you mingle facts with objective ideas and subjective impressions.'

All true, totally true. I had never had the type of conversations with anyone as I was having with increasing frequency with Zelda. She spoke of her life as a story. But there was never a clear route, no beginning, middle and end joining a minimal three dots. Instead of the linear trajectory with a target at the end, the path that Zelda and I were treading was one that meandered, backtracked, paused, made excursions to right and left. Just as I did sometimes on my bicycle. I was indeed fascinated that, although little more than an infant, Zelda had been a first-hand witness to the great transition, the huge upheaval that had come after the N-Ps had left in the Exodus. She had been part of the change even though she hadn't understood it at the time, and was a living example of the upheaval between then and now. Then she had not been physically perfect, she told me with a smile, but she had thought that one day she might have children, by which she meant be either an egg or womb donor.

'But what about really having children?' I asked one day. 'What about copulating with a man, carrying your own fertilized egg in your own womb, then bringing the child up and caring for him or her for the rest of your life?'

'That was back in my grandparents' time.'

Zelda's face closed down. She looked away briefly at nothing, then back at me from another stage of human history. But truth to tell, I felt increasingly that she and I were starting to live a kind of life not that different from her grandparents' era. We had slipped into the habit not just of eating together, but of sharing thoughts, memories and ideas. For Zelda, it was clearly significant and special: as when she had lived with her grandparents. For my part, I welcomed this small opportunity to retain, up to point, a vestige of my normal life that otherwise seemed so improbable now. The other members of the Grouping left us to it: I was getting used to them by now, occasionally swooping by, casually helping themselves to the glistening, coloured triangles and squares and circles spread out between us. But they never spoke and never stayed. They never listened in as Zelda and I entwined our stories: she in graphic and generous detail, me through a cautious filter.

'I'm glad Sim's got used to the Helmet. I thought at first she would just pull it off. But it's so thin and light I don't think she's aware of it. And she knows that so long as she ignores it, we'll ignore her. Which is what she prefers.'

Zelda's wistful expression melted into a gaze that softened once again: she smiled in a strange way at my face, almost, odd though it might seem to admit, in a form of wonderment. I'm embarrassed to say I couldn't think of any more accurate an adjective, but it made me feel very good inside in a way it was hard to acknowledge. It was like being on the bicycle: not so much that I felt out of control – I wasn't – but rather that new, unrestricted vistas were allowed to open up. Merely doing what was expected was no longer enough. I could go wherever I wanted and be whoever I liked, yet always be the same, just myself. It wasn't that I was 'letting myself go', losing myself in Yakawow.

No: this was very different. I was actually discovering myself, being someone who had a unique presence as Fred the man, who could not be defined by sets of pre- and proscribed behaviours and responses in incessant dialogues.

'But it wasn't like that for you, was it, Fred?' Zelda prompted.

No. It hadn't been like that for me at all. How could I ever explain to her what my real life was like? Sometimes I grew weary of these questions that I could not answer fully and preferred just to retreat into my own memories of that other existence. Although much of my daily routine now was spent with Zelda, she was by no means taking up my entire waking day – it just wouldn't have been possible. Increasingly, I now needed to conduct interventions, to test out Sim's responses, and see how they correlated with her shifting brain patterns, read out by the Helmet: Phase 1. All was going well. We would soon be moving on to the set exercises of Phase 2 where I had to see how she applied what she had rehearsed in the formal sessions of the first phase, to different environmental manipulation.

I also had to take time outside on my own to report extensively and frequently back to my ever attentive superior. After all, I was normally able to use Hodge as a sounding board whenever I wished, and had taken for granted that I could make use of the checks and balances of his brilliant intellect. True, the Others seemed oblivious to me and would have no interest in any activity in which I was myself engrossed: they were speaking and singing into thin air themselves so much that it probably wouldn't register as odd me doing likewise, that is, if they registered anyone else at all. But still, here in the Dwelling I could not risk simply speaking a senseless monologue of my own, as they might well have noticed my oral reports back to Hodge. No, it was Zelda who would know. Zelda was aware of me all the time, as I was of her.

So I had developed as part of my new way of life, the essential feature of cycling off on my own. These excursions were the perfect cover for enabling me to deliver my technical and general reports in quiet and secrecy, tapping into my watch, then sending on the read-outs from the implant. As far as Zelda knew, cycling was a part of my previous world that I wished to preserve, rather like eating with another person while sitting at a table. But it was nothing like the old, grey life. I had never before felt so exultant. Being able to travel as always, yes, but this time in an arc rather than a straight line. Feeling progress, yes, but this time at a speed beyond the plodding pedestrian. Having rapid, quicksilver thoughts that could fill in vast gaps rather than map on to tight little algorithms reaching merely convergent, clever conclusions as I had been trained. To feel the impossible rather than know the plausible. Not to know quite what lay ahead, but to thrill at the thought of new horizons without constraints or boundaries, be they physical or societal. But to know that I was strong enough for anything, at the epicentre of everything. To be Fred, Fred the man in my entirety and to my full potential.

The man with the diamond-hard eyes and thin white beard pauses the recording and stares into nothing.

Chapter 18

SIM

It's funny, Fred making me do this. Talking at the Talking Head. I always choose the Dark Man one as he's the one I like best. Fred isn't dark, though. He's kind of grey. Before Fred, everything seems like a blur. It's hard now to remember what it was like before he came on his mauve thing. He's like the centre of everything – everything I do, I think. He makes everything really good. He's an N-P, which means he should definitely be different from everyone else around: but I think the Fact-Totum has been wrong about them. Before Fred, it was boring asking it about anything: what was the point? But then Fred came, and he said he was an N-P. So then I wanted to know straightaway all about them, and him.

I'd just had fun in the wash-waste and reactivated my main implant by saying 'On'. Usually, I then issue the secondary command to the ear and eye enhancers to turn on immediately. I always like it when suddenly everything changes, and then I'm really happy. It's one of my favourite times. Even if you're still inside the Dwelling, and you're just looking at the ordinary walls, the next moment you'll see them kind of melt and move. And if you've chosen the 'undulate' mode, nice sounds will start to play into your ear as you wander around. If people try and speak with you, which can happen I suppose sometimes, then it just looks like their mouths are opening and shutting in silence. And they usually slide past you, unreal.

But sometimes I feel like dancing and then will go for fast beats and loudness. When this mode comes on, everything around suddenly becomes very bright and shiny and all the colours go into red and orange. Wherever you look, things will start to glow and change with the beat. And as you like go with the beat, move with it, so every step and turn and skip brings with it a new load of colours and swirly surfaces. This is the best of the best. I don't know how anyone can choose instead to carry on walking around all quiet apart from when someone speaks. And when they do, it's just words, boring little words. Why would anyone want to stand around, to stay around?

But this day was different, the time Fred arrived. This time, instead, as soon as I'd reactivated my main implant and after it bleeped that it was back and fully operational, I spoke a different command that I hadn't used for a long time: 'Fact-Totum'.

'Please state main subject area.'

The voice is a kind female one, always nice.

'The N-Ps.'

'N-P is the dual abbreviation for Neo-Puritan and Neo-Platonic. The movement started in the middle of the twenty-first century as a backlash to the life-changing technologies that were starting to transform society. The N-Ps refused to accept the benefits of a comfortable and stress-free lifestyle, choosing instead to adopt a deliberately primitive way of life which inevitably encompassed struggle. Because they considered it impossible to continue an existence in accordance with their ideals in the midst of a society now orientated to enjoyment, the N-Ps left in a long march, referred to by them as 'the Exodus', towards the largely unpopulated area the other side of our mountain range. The N-Ps avoid excitement and any strong emotional states at all costs. For more information, see the following options: clothes; stress; depression; facial wrinkles; the backlash phenomenon.'

I wasn't really interested in finding out any more. I already could see for myself the kind of clothes the N-Ps wore, just by looking at Fred himself. And besides, from my talking with Fred even after a single day, I wasn't sure that the Fact-Totum was right. If Fred is a real N-P, then they are not boring at all. But the opposite.

It all started when we met each other outside. Everything was horrible. I couldn't run easily any more and it was dark and very wet. Not a nice warm, fresh wet like in the wash-waste, but a cold wet that wouldn't go away. And my body was aching and hurting and I just wanted to be somewhere else, but couldn't activate anything to get me there straightaway. Then this funny-looking man was talking to me, in a way that I had never heard before: instead of just saying words or moving on past me, he was looking at me and asking me a question, just like you'd normally ask the Fact-Totum something. Only this time the question was about me, Sim. He was asking if I was all right.

He said he was called Fred. At first I thought the best thing was what I now know he calls a bicycle, a mauve thing with two wheels and a large cube that makes water when it moves – only Fred makes it move by sitting on it and pushing his legs round in circles. Only Fred is allowed to get on it. But then he started to talk more with me: Zelda is the only other person who tries to do that, where you're supposed to say something back straightaway each time they say something to you. But Zelda would talk and talk and all I had to do was say a single word from time to time, and sometimes nothing really at all. And she would still just carry on speaking.

But with Fred it was different right from the start. He tried to make me, like, speak more than I ever had before. He didn't just say things, but asked me things – and that made me feel good, almost like I was dancing. But then Fred brought me back to Zelda, and it wasn't quite the same because he started speaking a lot with her instead. I was free to go, to put on the enhancers again. But I had never seen anyone like Fred before, and he wasn't a hologram experience but a solid person. A really different type of person.

On his very first morning in the Dwelling, he started out by asking me if I'd wear this funny Helmet thing on my head. Zelda was standing close by, next to him, and they were both nodding and smiling all the time. I had never seen anything like the Helmet before. It's shiny silver, and very thin. When Zelda and Fred asked me to try it on, it was like just putting air on your head: the only way I knew it was there was when I looked down at my shoulders and saw that my hair had been squashed flat against my garment as it stuck out from under all the straps. They said it would help Fred find out interesting things about me, about how my brain was working.

At first all that happened was that I had to stay more indoors, inside the Dwelling. Fred and Zelda carried on talking all the time to each other, sitting always by the exit to the outside so that I couldn't run away without them knowing and following me. So what would have been the point anyway? But sometimes Fred would check his arm implant where he said the messages from my brain, fed through the Helmet, had travelled for him to look at.

Things each day weren't that different back then, at the beginning of the Fred time: I was just doing what I'd always done. I suppose it was better because Zelda didn't hold on to me so much. It was easier just to be on my own. Sometimes, though, when the enhancement inside the Dwelling just wasn't enough, and because they wouldn't let me outside without following me, I'd have a hologram time.

All over the Dwelling, different Heads are waiting. Some are female, some male, some fair and some dark. It doesn't really matter, they're all there to do the same thing for you and answer you in the same way. Even though they'll reply to you with different voices. Implants and enhancers are used for changing how you feel from the inside, by working on your body. But the screens are for changing the world from the outside – whether it's the furniture, the lighting, the food in the chilled cavities or, most usual of all, giving you a hologram time.

To have a hologram time, you just speak to one of the screens. I knew a long time ago, from Zelda, that screens all used to be oblong and almost 2-D things that you sat in front of and watched. Zelda still did this, or used to before Fred came. She'd ask the screen for the same old hologram times over and over again. She'd sit very still with her head to one side for most of the day, half-smiling and looking almost half-asleep. All around her drifted figures in strange-looking clothes: one that she liked a lot was where the women were covered in bright-coloured fabrics that hid their legs but showed most of their top halves, and the men had long white hair, tied back, and tight shiny fabric covering their thighs with white frilly layers around their necks. Often the men and women would be holding each other tightly and pressing their lips to each other for no reason for long periods of time. I had never seen adults behave like this and thought it all a bit weird and pointless: but it was when she was sat watching these funny things that Zelda seemed to be like happy.

So, when I was still inside the Dwelling but needed something new, I'd ask one of the screens for a hologram time. Straightaway, you'd be in the middle of a different place, in the middle of a story. But you would be in control of what happened in the story, by what you did and said. Although I could still make out the Dwelling if I looked into the distance through a kind of mist, during a hologram time, you'd be busy with what was happening most immediately around you. Real-size people would appear and slide round you; they would be talking and things would be happening just as in real life. But you could put your fingers through their faces if you wanted. When I was small, I thought that was why we had hologram times: just for the fun of putting your fingers through people.

But now, of course, I much prefer thinking about the people as though they were real, because then the story is so much better. And just by speaking, I can make them do things, make whatever I want happen. One of my favourites was to be in a story where the princess is rescued from a witch by a prince. The witch was a woman with a bent body and bent nose, in black clothes, and with long, flying horrible black hair. The prince looked like any of the males in the Dwelling. I always made the witch die. This particular hologram time was one of the best, and the witch would die over and over again.

But then, I wasn't just like left on my own. Fred wanted to talk to me, and Zelda wanted to watch. I couldn't understand why Fred was so interested in finding out so much about me: it was so hard listening to all the things he was saying, and answering in the way he seemed to want. When we started our 'sessions', as he called them, he asked me about the hologram time.

'Do you like stories, Sim?'

'Sometimes. I like hologram times.'

'When you have a hologram time, do the people speak to you much?'

'No. The witch is very bad. Then the prince rescues me. Then the witch dies.'

'Why don't we have another version of the story, when this time the witch and the prince speak to you?'

'Why?'

'So they can tell you how they're feeling.'

So each day my story times changed. Things happened less quickly because the prince and the witch started speaking. The prince told me how sad he was because until he saw me he had been alone with no one to talk to. The witch told me that she wanted to keep me locked up forever because she wanted complete power over everyone. At first it was hard putting myself in their places, thinking what it might be like to feel lonely, and also to want power over everything. But, after a while, it seemed like not a big surprise that people should feel like that. I could feel like that.

I started to ask the witch and the prince questions about what they wanted to do and why. After a while, I was able to tell from the tone and loudness of their voices how they might be feeling. Then one day, I was able to guess what these two real-seeming people that I could stick my fingers in, might want to do, and what they might say, and told Fred. He smiled and smiled, checking his implant and the device round his wrist, the watch, all the time. Zelda stood behind him, arms folded across her chest, all quiet. Completely quiet.

But then the hologram time started to become not so much fun, and made me more what Fred called 'serious'. This time, he warned me, when something happened with the witch or the prince, it would stay that way forever. He told me to be careful if I made the witch die, because she would never ever be able to be in the story again.

'But if there's no witch, there's no story.'

'Exactly, Sim.'

I hadn't really thought about people dying. Obviously, in games, that was often what happened, but then you just played the game again. Zelda had talked about her parents and her grandparents, who were all dead. But since I had never seen these people, they were not real to me. I had never met someone in the Dwelling, or outside, who died and who, therefore, I would never see again. It was a strange thought that I had to turn over and over to myself.

But Fred was talking to me again. 'Why are we bothering, Sim, with imaginary people?'

Fred asked me this soon after the day I'd been guessing what the witch and prince were feeling, and they had told me I was, like, right. It was immediately after he had been trying to tell me about death, and I had answered straight back that if the witch and prince weren't real, then surely they didn't have to really die.

'I know someone much more interesting, who's actually real and who has a much better story to tell.' He was leaning back in his seat: the bicycle, as always, leaning up against the side. His hands were interlinked at the back of his head and his crooked teeth were wide and happy, strung out across his face.

'Who's that?'

'You, Sim.'

And so, with Fred's help, I started to make this, what he calls a 'diary'. It is very easy: all I have to do is talk to one of the screens each day, saying what I've done and what I'm doing – even what I plan to do, or wish I could do. But Fred says that he's arranged the technology so that no one else will ever be able to gain access to hear or see it.

'Not even Zelda?'

'No.'

At first it was strange, just sitting in front of the screen with my favourite, the dark man: I like him because he's got a deep, slow, kind voice. And I've really started like looking forward to these times, just talking into his face and knowing no one else would ever know. Apart from Fred, of course. He's always near by, watching me carefully, or checking with his watch what the messages from my brain are saying on his implant.

Next, Fred asked me to go on long walks with him. He said it was the best way for us to get to know each other, and the best way to have good talks. He would walk beside me, wheeling his bike on one side, me on the other. Most of the time he wasn't looking ahead, but his head would be almost always turned towards me, looking at me. At first it was not as exciting as talking to the witch and the prince, or talking to the screen about everything I had been doing. I now realize that this was because, on the walking times outside, I wasn't the one to decide what was said, and what we would talk about.

In any case, I couldn't see why Fred was asking me so many questions: although I tried to answer as quickly as I could, I didn't usually have to think so fast on my own. But he wanted to know more, whatever it was that I said. For instance, when he asked me quite early on what I liked doing best, I knew the answer straightaway.

'Running.'

'Why?'

'I don't know, I just do.'

Running: the feel of the air in my hair, and the sun on my face. The music in my ears and the shiny light everywhere. I couldn't at that early time of talking with Fred describe just how good it felt. The words wouldn't come, and anyhow they would have spoilt the feeling of just doing it, of the running. Fred wouldn't run with me, though. That's what I would have liked most, since I was starting to like him being there, smiling at me.

Chapter 19

HODGE

My pet rat has no name: it is easier that way, when they die and the replacement comes within a day. However, increasingly recently, I've been changing his bedding more than I need, changing his water bottle more than is necessary, vacantly watching him explore the spacious 'enriched environment' of his cage as though it were an experimental rodent gym, when all the time I should be thinking more constructively. The truth of the matter is that I am starting to get worried and trying not to admit it. Was it the odd appearance of that alien adjective in one of Fred's reports a while back, that stray term 'beautiful'? At the time I hardly registered the uncharacteristic word, one we never use: but in the light of what might now be happening, it adds to the general picture of concern.

We've learnt only too well the dangers of beauty, of something being pleasing to the eye or the ear for its own sake rather than for what it means. We've learnt to focus on the significance of people or objects, and to disregard the mere sensory conglomeration that they constitute. Some argued in the past that ideas too could actually be pleasing in this way, that 'truth was beauty' and indeed the converse: but we now know that really what they must have meant was not literally beautiful in terms of simple colours and shapes, but rather a kind of metaphor, that meant 'fine' or 'good', 'correct'. We read books, have ideas not because we wish to experience actual beauty, but because we wish to experience truth, ideas, the abstract not barnacled with gaudy add-ons.

Anyhow, I cannot pinpoint the exact time when I consciously started to feel so uneasy, when I finally acknowledged to myself the actual moment that the technical reports sent to me directly from Fred were becoming less frequent and, worst of all, were just not sufficiently thorough and thought through – I have to say, even sloppy.

As a scientist, I am used to uncertainty: it's normal, that holding of the breath as a result comes through and one is the first person ever to see that new small update on nature, that next tiny brick in a vast, endless wall. Well, I live with such unpredictability and suspense every day of my life, even enjoy being proved wrong sometimes: but it is always within certain rules and parameters. If you do your job properly, then you are exhaustively aware of all the different factors that will lead to a final net outcome. So the eventual result is always a scenario, whether you have predicted it or not, that falls within a limited range of possibilities. Yes, there might well be wider implications stemming from a discovery, but they are always constrained, always have boundary conditions.

But this uncertainty over what could now be happening to Fred … Well, I'm not used to situations like it: the relevant facts are not readily accessible, and the implications are more far-reaching than any other project in which I've been involved. If everything progresses as we hope, then our society and humanity will be secure forever. If for any reason we, I … Well, we won't fail.

Never since the N-P forefathers had finally left in the great Exodus, has such a perfect strategy been conceived. The idea of an intelligence operation also being a genuine neuroscientific experiment truly takes my breath away: the scientific findings, whatever they turn out to be, *are* the intelligence, while the need for intelligence has prompted the experiment that is Fred's mission. Perhaps never in the history of espionage or science have two such normally incompatible activities coalesced with equal importance into one single, major goal. This is no mere secret mission that needs some highly classified technical know-how, like the old James Bond stories of so long ago.

Rather, the acquisition of that technical know-how will have policy implications in and of itself. The Elders need us scientists to plan exactly what will happen, while we need them to supply the rationale and the goal. And Fred will be just the start: he is the proverbial first small step that launches the great journey. By sending him, just him, it is to be the thinnest end of what will be a mighty wedge. Fred is to be our reconnaissance, the scout I would trust more than any other. At the time, he had been the obvious choice. I had been so sure we had chosen the right man, not just for surviving amid the corrupting Others, but actually for taking advantage of them, manipulating them for the information we needed.

Now, what am I supposed to relay back to the Elders? The latest reports are hasty, too short, obviously dashed off in a way that the Fred I knew would have been too proud to even contemplate: moreover, other strange terms are appearing with increasing frequency. It is not that he is using words, concepts, of which I might never have heard from within the Others' culture. No, I am fully aware of the idea of 'fun' and 'freedom' and, worst of all, 'self': but they are notions Fred has been brought up to shun. What possible scenarios might be unfolding that we hadn't predicted meticulously in the planning? What would the Elders conclude about my judgement, and what consequences could ensue?

We had accepted from the outset that he would be far away, both literally and psychologically, immersed alone in a world that could distract him, blur his judgement. Many of us are old enough to remember the first-hand reports of our grandparents who had actually been there, and described firsthand even then the disorientation and endless confusion of the then still earlier technology of harsh colours, raucous sounds and relentless pace of ceaseless cyber-stimulation. Yet surely someone of Fred's calibre would hardly be impressed by such trivialities?

Ever since I'd first met him, I'd realized that he had an outstanding combination of scientific rigour coupled with remorseless, courageous curiosity. He had only just graduated from wearing the Helmet: you can always tell, because the young adult in question moves their head around more than is needed as they are talking, experimenting with the usual sensation of being bare-headed and unused to the absence of the strap under their chin. The cliché however of feeling perhaps for the first time the wind in one's hair is inappropriate for us, since all of us, men and women, have regulation crops close to our skulls. Back then, Fred's hair may have been a homogeneous black and his face smoother, but that expression in his eyes, that I came to know so well, was already there – the expression I always search for when I first meet someone, scan their face, and ask myself: how many cerebral lights are on?

In Fred's case, the answer was blazingly unambiguous. As I surveyed the then young man standing in front of my desk, I had found myself staring back into deep grey eyes that I knew would never give up, would never look away in exasperation or boredom, or glaze with emotion. He was none the less clearly excited but constrained as he talked of what he already knew about the brain: I had been delighted to see that the energy and the passion were already harnessed, focused on the clear goal of real understanding.

'Sir, I firmly believe that the study of the brain is the purest and best expression of the N-P doctrine.'

I nodded encouragingly, though he was hardly telling me anything I didn't already know.

'If ideas, abstract ideas are the ultimate apotheosis of the human condition, then only by concentrating on the brain will we finally escape the banal, the imperfect, the non-generalizable mandates of individual physical bodies.'

'But shouldn't we be ensuring above all that we are healthy, so that we might prolong the actual life of the brain?'

This was hardly a difficult question, but merely me fulfilling the expected role of checking and balancing in a dialogue. Fred would be used to, would expect, this kind of nudge.

'There is a big difference, sir, between optimizing and maximizing. A normal healthy body is of course a high priority, but not at the expense of mental states. If we extend the ideal for the physical body to a state of maximal physical ease and sensual gratification, then the mind will not be stretched, will not be optimized. That's where the Others have obviously gone so disastrously wrong.'

At that moment, Fred hadn't really needed to say anything to be appointed to the post in my team, after I had seen almost straightaway the enthusiasm and sense behind his eyes. But it was good to hear someone from the new, next young generation, articulate so clearly the tenets of what we all believed. By the time he first came and saw me, obtaining the position of Senior Research Neuroscientist in my Institute, our approach had blossomed into a clear and strong philosophy captured in two basic principles.

First, we should ensure that the body was in as peak condition as possible by natural means: a healthy and balanced diet was paramount, complemented by exercise, ideally from walking with each other while having dialogues. In such a way, no time would be wasted in solitary and rather pointless strengthening of muscles at the expense of valuable thinking time. Second, all new technologies would be directed at understanding and developing the mind. So now our robust economy revolves around the centrality to our society of nurturing original thought. The brain is our business. We buy and sell to each other the ever more sophisticated goods and services relating to education, research and general information dissemination, as well as devices and technologies for allowing the brain to flourish in a maximally healthy body. Meanwhile, our expenditure as consumers of material goods and objects is minimal: we have reverted only to buying what we need because what we actually want is quite simply and literally immaterial – namely, to have the best brain possible from our own individual portfolio of mental talents, and for that brain to be of maximal benefit to society as whole. Compared to the lavish, doomed economies of twenty-first-century capitalism, ours is primitive and modest. But at least it works. Everything balances.

I repeat to myself over and over again why the time is as ripe as it would ever be for applying those principles universally, and finally and completely to gain control over the Others. We have now invested too much energy, have developed too special a society, and have made too many technological breakthroughs to allow it to be in jeopardy. Until this moment, we have had no choice but to coexist with our distracting neighbour the other side of the mountains. Now we are able to take action at last. Until now, we N-Ps had been concentrating on looking inward, on defining and developing the things we thought important.

Now we have something to defend, and it is time to look out. The craving for the sensational that has been building up over several generations has surely made the Others vulnerable, open to anything that gives them excitement. They are weak now, and we are strong as never before. Most importantly of all, at the moment we can never be sure about what might happen: the all-important consequences for the future are not fixed and certain. An anathema.

I shudder involuntarily and it brings me back to the present. I've looked once again through the read-out of Fred's reports on the visual mode. I preferred this slightly antiquated way of accessing information, rather than audio output, as I am undistracted by the tones and accent of the voice vehicle used, and can more readily ponder on the written word, going at my own pace. One of my greatest pleasures is to read the ancient books which span the previous two centuries, which I have in my safekeeping. I savour turning the thick creamy paper, and still marvel at how the simple printed words can transform in the human mind into faraway places and times, sometimes so vivid that they are more real than the press of the senses from the material immediacy around me. But whether it is a fine novel or a stimulating factual account, there are times I could simply stop and stare at the wall, letting the thoughts find their place, settle into my brain against the checks and balances of my various pre-existing connections. In this way, I understand more and more.

But these reports from Fred … Well, I just don't understand them. The more I reflect, the more troubled I am than I have ever been in my life. Everything started out so very well, and as I would have predicted. Fred was living up to my opinion of him in his efficiency, under difficult conditions, to transmit regular and frequent reports. The earlier ones were very illuminating:

Have infiltrated a 'Dwelling' containing some twenty Others, of whom the central subject is a young woman referred to as 'Sim'. They coexist in a so-called 'Grouping' – a loose parody of a family containing separate gene and womb donors, carers and children.

I noticed immediately that no one else was mentioned by name. I assumed therefore that, as we had supposed, each individual, while not an individual in the N-P sense of a fully cognitively aware adult, could at least be viewed, and treated, as an isolated entity or unit. However, more fascinating still was the major observation that Fred had made early on after fitting subject Sim with the Helmet:

Subject Sim's profile for neuronal assemblies is unusually small for an adult, and certainly by our own standards. Observed by approximate audio feedback: please confirm by visual verification.

A neuronal assembly is a process in the brain that works like ripples in a puddle once a stone is thrown: tens, even hundreds, of millions of brain cells suddenly form a synchronous but highly transient working coalition that is over almost as soon as it was triggered, in less than a second. All the brain cells are, just for a moment working together, like a very short-lived choir. These highly evanescent phenomena were for many years known to be closely connected to varying levels of consciousness, the more extensive an assembly at any moment, the deeper the consciousness at that moment. But these sub-second processes had been too elusive, too fast to monitor in humans for many years, given their brief time-frames and the low resolution of the scanning equipment back then. A little like in early nineteenth-century photographs, when the camera was too slow to capture anything moving – so the sepia pictures of that bygone time could only show static objects, buildings, but never animals or people. The fast ripples of millions of brain cells operating temporarily in unison, had eluded the slow scanners of the early twenty-first century.

However, things had slowly improved over the last hundred years. Fred was referring to the fact that the Helmet now transmitted signals regarding the dynamics of assembly formation to his implant that could then be relayed on to us for display on our equipment visually. Because Fred had no such equipment in the field, he could only obtain an approximate impression of the data himself, by playing back that same electronic read-out signal through an auditory channel fed into his earpiece. He was sufficiently experienced to detect the audio-signature of assemblies of different sizes, that would reveal changing degrees of consciousness: but obviously marooned the other side of the mountains, away from all our essential equipment, he could not appreciate precisely what it would look like in terms of the intrinsic patterns of activity, changing ceaselessly like a kaleidoscope. We needed to observe these on a screen at the Institute, and then confirm and amplify Fred's interpretations back to him.

Using our very fast DNA computing methods for analysis, I was able to transmit that very night back to Fred that yes, his first impression was indeed correct: this female, Sim, had very small assemblies, indicating a limited level of consciousness. When I matched up her read-outs on our scales, they fell far short of that for a comparable N-P woman, and were more reminiscent of those from a small child.

But perhaps it was as far back as these early missives that the uncertainty started to set in and gnaw away at me ever so slightly. Fred's reports were coming back, not with the same brisk frequency as at the beginning, but still at least with an acceptable level of content – in fact it was truly interesting. Yes, Fred had attempted Phase 1, the cognitive exercises where he introduced notions of consequences and temporal irreversibility. He had started to convey the notion of symbols, not in writing since it transpired Sim was illiterate, but in simple visual imagery and metaphor. Most important of all, Fred reported he was placing most effort into developing a concept of individual identity

Everything seemed to be going to plan. As we had agreed, Fred had initially not intervened in any way. Instead he just continued to obtain baseline readings over a sustained period of time, during which all the usual daily activities gave further read-outs and eliminated the possibility that the very low index of assembly formation first recorded was not a one-off freak occurrence due to some novel and unusual activity, such as having the Helmet fitted. No, Fred's subsequent reports confirmed, it was a genuine effect: the brain of an Other, at least as exemplified by subject Sim, displayed a chronically lower index. This index was a final calculation we would make to evaluate and quantify the elaborate visual pictures we obtained. Normally, Fred would record multiple assemblies all over the brain, which would build up into a visual profile for us of the brain state, from which the final index value was averaged. However, there was one brain area that was particularly sensitive and significant: the prefrontal cortex, or PFC.

The PFC is the newest part of the brain in evolutionary terms, taking up a third of the human brain, but only seventeen per cent or so in our nearest relatives, the chimps. And, since personal development famously mirrors evolution, it is no surprise that the PFC is underactive in children, only being fully operational in late teenage years. The prediction was then that if a low assembly index was the result of a childlike, sensory-laden, fast-paced environment, the brains of Others would be characterized by abnormally small, more fragmented assemblies and, above all, an underactive PFC. And so it was, at least in Sim's case.

We are now at Phase 1 of specific exercises and I'm even starting to plan Phase 2, where what she has learnt can be applied to understanding and appreciating more about daily life. I'll introduce specific events, such as a meal, that could then constitute a 'past' and then refer back to it: in a similar way I've spoken of planned events, say walking outside as part of a 'future'. The only problem is that there have been insufficient unique or even noticeable events in Sim's life, other than eating or walking, to make the narrative compelling or different from previous days.

That was all. It was far too short given the importance of the material being described. This deterioration in length was now paralleling that in frequency. When should I have admitted that all was not as it should be? I looked back through those previous reports. In my excitement and interest, I had certainly overlooked the fact that contact with Fred was dropping from twice a day to once a day, then to only once in two days. While initially, his report back would contain a detailed response to my own analysis, now the lines are shorter and less insightful, not reacting in any way to my more detailed analysis derived from the accurate visual images that only we could inspect remotely. For the time being, perhaps, I have reasoned that the lack of feedback is not an issue – perhaps Fred agreed with everything I listed, and felt there was no need to respond simply in the affirmative. But now some of the content of the reports is in itself strange.

The nano-assembled furniture here is efficient and effective. Very comfortable and relaxing.

Only two sentences. While the surroundings of the Others held a marginal interest, there was no salient point made in the statement of relevance to his mission. Furthermore, N-Ps never put a premium on comfort; nor did we ever, ever 'relax'.

My immediate problem is that it is now time to report to the Elders in the hope that they will permit me to move Fred ahead with the next phase of our plan. I cannot spoil that plan now, just because of these minor perturbations and perhaps my own over-heated judgement. For the first time in my life I am faced with a dilemma. Yes, I have had challenges in the past, difficult issues to resolve in my work: but they have always been open, explicit difficulties that everyone acknowledged as such and could share. But this mission is a unique initiative for which I will be held personally responsible: it isn't an objective and abstracted puzzle, but rather a question of me personally risking an unwise, unsound subjective evaluation. After thinking through the implications of the two options, to admit to all my concerns or to try and make good the situation, I have been unsure. But, increasingly, alarmingly, there are interludes of complete radio silence. It is too late to say anything now. The Elders will wonder why I didn't alert them earlier. In the end, by default, I shall end up saying nothing.

Chapter 20

FRED

At the time of planning, it had all seemed so obvious and straight-forward: but now it has started to become more and more of a chore.

The man silently and slowly nods.

On one morning recently the prospect of what I had to do was particularly unappealing: my head was throbbing, even after so long, still unaccustomed to the onslaught of the Dwelling. Then what with the strong tastes of my last meal that left fiery flavours still in my throat, and what with Zelda wanting conversations and explanations, it all seemed depressingly impossible.

'I want to have fun with your bicycle. Just once.'

Sim had at last spun into view in front of us. Shaking her thick blonde hair out of her eyes, and already looking around, she had spotted my most precious possession. Already she was extending a slim, smooth hand to take possession herself.

'Just leave it.'

I was myself surprised at the loud harshness and abruptness of my own voice, and noticed that Zelda's seemingly perpetual smile conceded at last, wavering into a more genuine perplexity.

'That's not yours, it's not for you. You know that.'

I was on my feet now, jerking the bicycle from Sim's surprised and readily yielding hand. Both she and Zelda were staring at me: Zelda because she was trying to understand, and Sim because my hard voice and rapid movements created a moment of stimulation and novelty. I took a deep breath, remembered who I was, where I was, what I was supposed to be doing.

'Let's just get started.'

The kind of overture I would make to my colleagues. Try again.

'The Helmet will be much more fun.'

I held out the Helmet to Sim. The bright light caught on the silver curving surface and for a moment it became the only thing that Sim wanted to hold. She squealed in delight, as she did each morning at this juncture.

'Come here.'

I had learnt it was most effective to address her in the same kind but paternal tones as I would use to speak to Bill. And as she offered up her open, empty, unhurt face to me, I knew even more strongly this time that she was all mine: I could create a mind. So, with enormous effort, I forced myself to focus on my task: just like long ago, it was a real experiment in real time that would have to be analysed later, without all my usual backup and instant, interactive databases. It was hard and I was weary. But I had to persevere.

At some time during my earlier routine daily outings, I had to step down from the bicycle and describe to Hodge what has been happening, downloading all the lists of my mental notes as well as the latest data from Sim's Helmet. At first I found it fulfilling and stimulating to give my considered reaction to Hodge's thoughts on my previous reports, and saw it not just as time well spent but, in any event, the highest priority. Conversations in real time are out of the question. Apart from the obvious, albeit unknown, security risks of extended broadcasting periods, we both agreed each would need time to reflect on what the other had sent. I found it most productive playing back Hodge's reaction to my latest report when it was deep into the night, and darkness could envelop my alcove, with no one interested enough to come by. Because there was nothing to see. Curled up in secrecy, my implant would play softly back into my ear. And I would think and plan, just as I had been trained to do.

Yet the reports to Hodge are becoming increasingly difficult to compose, to bother with. Why doesn't this concern me more? The central problem is that it is impossible to describe what it is really like here, simply to sum everything up as an index of a neuronal assembly or an underactive PFC. Above all, I couldn't even mention to Hodge the sensation of being on the bicycle: I can hardly explain it to myself, why it is that at those wonderful times I'm cycling, I don't even want my implant on. I don't need or want any connection, any ties, any context.

And yet and yet, for some reason that defies all my usual logic, I want to be as truthful as I can with Zelda – and not just because she is getting to know me well enough to detect an out-and-out lie. In itself this is an astonishing admission to make, that an Other could not be completely manipulated. I cannot necessarily predict, let alone control, her stream of questions and comments. Sometimes responding to her is tiring and yet I am unable to end these 'conversations' naturally: all I can do is to absent myself physically, to fly away on the bicycle. But most of the time and if my head isn't aching – as it seems to be doing more and more with the remorseless Yakawow – the talks with Zelda give me insights that I could never have hypothesized back in my lab. They are telling me things and helping me think in a way beyond the N-P framework. Less surprising, perhaps, is that I am starting to understand her better too on a personal level: the result of this growing, mutual familiarity is that I have been able to bring to light something deep in Zelda, the admission of which has, in turn, tilted my new world through one hundred and eighty degrees.

It started, as such transformational events often do, without any obvious forewarning. We had just finished one of our shared meals that are now the norm: for once I didn't have a headache and felt rested. On that particular evening we were at ease in each other's company. The conversation ebbed and flowed, was lobbed and returned, action and reaction, but interspersed with companionable silences. Early on in our study, I had discovered that all the Others save Zelda, could not read. However she, Zelda, truly appreciated the value of literacy and books. So I was telling her of my own books and how, in N-P society, they were so treasured.

'Reading does something special.'

I was on my own, familiar territory. My speech already expounded many times before, in different forms, to Hodge, my colleagues, and of course to Tarra. Now I had a new, captive audience.

'It is different from the experience of the screen because you actually care about the characters – otherwise, of course, you wouldn't continue to read the book. While the screen emphasizes the ongoing experience, the book is all about content, about meaning. The act of reading a book is not thrilling in the way playing a cyber-game might be. Rather, the storyline and the people living out that story are seen in terms of what they have done and what they will do, their significance. Reading takes you away from the press of the present in every sense.

'As well as all that, I'm sure that reading, and then writing, help you think: we even say "think straight". By organizing words, then sentences, in a clear linear order, the thinking behind those words and sentences has to conform likewise. So, Sim is a good example of what happens if the human brain is just isolated in the here and now, the world of the infant, the 'booming buzzing confusion', to quote a great psychologist two centuries ago. It also fascinates me as a neuroscientist as to how the characters in a book become so real, how your mind when you read is there rather than here, how your brain can shut out the raw senses, and be somewhere else, with someone else, entirely.'

I paused for breath, and glanced sideways at Zelda. Had I got too carried away? Bored her? No. She had been paying close attention, gazing at me with that look of wonderment that I was starting to like and even expect, and that was happening with increasing frequency. Then again, these issues, the cognitive qualities that I had just listed, were those that Zelda, at least to some extent, exhibited: it was what set her clearly apart from the rest of the Others. She had once read books.

'Yes, my grandparents also had a collection of books: they called it their "little library". I used to read all the time as a child when I was living with them.'

We had finished our meal but were still sitting at the table, suspended in time. Zelda was leaning forward, almost sprawled, one elbow on the bright table, propping up her head on one side, as though it were too heavy to balance on its own on her smooth neck. The other hand was slowly and pointlessly twisting curls of red-gold hair as she spoke. And all the time she was looking and looking at me.

'I've told you already how special they were, how they taught me everything they could. Things around them were starting to change so much as I was growing up that I think they found the library, more and more, a place of retreat. The world of their books took them to places and people where they understood the values, the aims, the fears and the dreams. They just couldn't identify what was going on outside, and didn't want to.'

It was then that I made my mistake. With half a joke.

'They should have joined the N-Ps!'

Zelda's whole body sucked back, as in one movement she sat up and pushed away from the table with both hands shooting out rigid and at arm's length. Now stiff and tensed in every muscle, she lifted her chin and spoke to the space above my head.

'My grandparents HATED the N-Ps.'

She could just about keep her shaking voice under control: but it had increased in pitch and volume to the levels of panic, fear. Until finally, she spat out a small, bitter little fact.

'And me too, I also hated the N-Ps, even just the thought of them.'

'But that's to be expected. You were probably told we were some kind of enemy.'

I smiled indulgently, confident in the closeness that had silently and slowly been growing between us ever since I moved into the Dwelling.

'No, it was much worse than that.'

A slight moment of hesitation, a decision. Then something inside her welled up and burst out.

'They-killed-my-parents. When I first saw you I … I didn't know what to say or do … You, they, are against everything that my parents and grandparents prized, all that is warm and kind and loving about people. You don't realize how hard it is for me – what I've had to suppress, try and forget, every time I'm with you …'

She was sobbing now, shaking her head in private disbelief at herself, tears tracking down her rounded-apple cheeks, her voice strangled in staccato sobs. Instinctively, I wanted to put my arms round the delicate shoulders rhythmically convulsing, but I didn't dare. This was not a situation I was used to, had ever experienced. Tarra had never once, not once, broken down in tears. I tried the only strategy I knew and had been trained for: reason. I needed to pull her back from her emotional cliff edge.

'Zelda, you talk so much about your grandparents, but so little about your parents.' I was as soft as I could be, stealthily and slowly moving in, not wanting to scare, but calmly and slowly sneaking forward, as it were, on my belly.

'Tell me more about your parents.'

It worked, at least at the logistical level of restoring an almost normal conversational climate. Zelda took a deep breath and, still looking over my head, now spoke in an even monotone.

'I loved my parents and they loved me. *Very* much. We would have been so happy if it hadn't been for you N-Ps.'

This last sentence was flung at me defiantly: her eyes narrowed as we looked at each other across a seemingly widening chasm. But it felt all wrong. I wanted to be on her side, at her side.

'Zelda, do you really see me as just an N-P? I had hoped we'd grown to know each other more than that, and that you could see beneath this –' I plucked dismissively at my loose grey garment – 'and see the real person I am underneath, the real man.'

I was astonished by my own words even as I spoke. 'So, just tell me about your parents and how wonderful they were.'

This was the bridgehead, I hoped, the only one that seemed viable at the time. She sat forward again, her body deflating, put both arms now, folded, on the table, laying her head wearily on them, almost as if she would go to sleep. But of course she was fully awake, speaking into space, softly telling her story.

'I lived with my parents until I was about five. But often we would go and visit my grandparents, my mother's mother that was. We were unusual even back then in that we actually had a car. Even though, obviously, it was not using fossil fuels, hardly anyone still drove anywhere.'

'Why did your parents keep a car?'

'They liked it. My father liked driving fast, with my mother.'

'Did you like it too?'

I had lapsed into the iterative dialogue that was second nature to me.

'I didn't go with them much.'

'Why not?'

'Because ... because ...'

Something was wrong. I sensed there was now a rope bridge swaying across the chasm. All I had to do, could do, was wait, try and steady things, and hope that Zelda would walk tentatively towards me.

Then suddenly she made her decision, stepped firmly forwards. 'Because they didn't want me, they didn't want me with them.'

This was whispered, flat. Then a long silence. Then another step.

'They only wanted to be with each other. They didn't love me.'

They didn't love her. Now everything made more sense. Perhaps her grandparents had been fooled, had encouraged the easy lie of the erstwhile perfect nuclear family and the cold-hearted ones who destroyed it. But now I could see easily a little girl desperate to be impressed by love, but excluded by it. It explained the hidden hurt and the need that only I instinctively understood. As a man.

As though echoing my thoughts, Zelda was making the final step from the swaying bridge on to firm, safe ground where I stood waiting.

'Fred, you're such a special man, and you don't even realize it. You are so much more than an N-P. I've never told anyone how it really was with my parents. I've never met or spoken with anyone like you, never felt really close. I'm so happy that you've come into my life: I need you so much.'

No one had ever needed me, just for being me, a special man. But Zelda knew and understood. I was as separate from the N-Ps as she was from the Others. I was quite simply Fred. And Fred, the man, now felt he was flying, free wheeling, just being himself. I reached out and grasped her hand, a novel, spontaneous gesture I was only aware of in retrospect. Then some inner part of me all at once recognized what was going to happen.

'This is nice, too nice.'

I heard my voice whispering an adjective I hardly ever used, a weak, ineffectual nothing.

'What do you mean?'

A similarly pointless response as Zelda's lips pressed down on mine. For the first time in my life I was doing something that did not have a meaning or a long-term purpose, but just was. Fred the man was just being himself. And Zelda? As the gossamer garments slipped and slid easily apart, she was for the first time where she wanted to be: part of a story her grandparents would have recognized.

Zelda and Fred. The world narrowed to just us. No artificial iridescence, no cause and effect, no symbols, no past or future. No Tarra. No night-time reflection tonight, on Hodge's reports.

Chapter 21

HODGE

This morning I registered once again with the waxy-faced receptionist and took the journey up to the top floor of Centrum with still more nausea and apprehension than on the previous occasion. Once again, sitting in identical positions as before, I surveyed what must be the leaders of our society. This time however, there was no introductory scene-setting from the Professor with the thin white beard, or Bird-Eyes or Black-Hair. They were waiting for me to speak, silent with power. Ten pairs of eyes bored into me. Ten flat faces giving nothing away. The absence of sound grew heavy. I cleared my throat and lied.

'So far all has gone according to plan.'

In one sense, of course, it had: but in another sense, it was becoming more and more of a gut-wrenching anxiety. The first time there had been a cessation of the signal from the other side of the mountains, for a few hours, I'd assumed it was a minor technical glitch that Fred himself would soon correct. When the signal was indeed resumed the next morning, I had thought no more of it. But then I started to notice a clear pattern: the ID signal often fell off intermittently during the day, but more continuously during the night. This was no chance mishap: the only explanation was that Fred was now turning off his implant routinely at the end of the day. Yet I could still at this stage justify the reassuring half-truth I'd voiced since the science, even though it was now being reported with less frequency and less detail, was still highly significant.

'The subject, a female referred to as Sim, is showing a clearly different brain profile from a comparable individual in our society. The big question now is whether that profile can be modified to approximate our own.'

The row of lined faces for the first time nodded in small gestures. Unsurprised, but I thought they could not fail to have been pleased, inasmuch as such a term could apply. As always in N-P society, the default is that things are as they should be, as they had been planned.

'I request permission therefore to instruct our agent in the field to move to Phase 3, to attempt to modify the subject's brain.'

Professor leant forward and, stroking his thin beard meditatively, looked either side of the group to affirm consensus, then inclined his head.

'Yes, Hodge, proceed.'

And so, despite my reservations as to what might have happened with Fred, I am letting my scientific enthusiasm, or perhaps vanity, take precedence. I estimate by now Fred must have moved on to Phase 2, the application of the cognitive exercises of Phase 1, to real-life situations. But I'm not sure. This lack of any precise grasp of exactly what is happening, would have been unthinkable at the start of this mission. Indeed never before had I felt at such a loss and out of control in supervising a scientific project. But what could I do to restore the efficient communication we had once had? Nothing. All I could do now was continue as we were, and trust that Fred had good reasons. Once I've returned to my familiar and reassuring lab surroundings, I issued instructions to him to move to Phase 3 whenever he considers it appropriate.

Accordingly, when he judges subject Sim's attention span has increased appropriately, and as soon as she has become sufficiently used to him, Fred will start direct electrical stimulation through the Helmet. I'm still telling myself he must be working brilliantly and will know best exactly when the transition to the most productive and all-important final phase will commence. As a result of such enhanced input, we should see fast effects, an accelerated increase in understanding. Then again, Sim is an adult Other: just how far could we give her a 'mind', and how far could that mind be stretched and developed? This is the most crucial question of all. Ever since this initiative was launched, I have found myself awaiting the reports with increasing and quite atypical excitement. Perhaps that has obscured my judgement, my refusal to admit that the reports are becoming ever less coherent, and communication with Fred increasingly difficult.

Another possibility is inevitably looming, one that in our arrogance we have never really acknowledged as possible: if environments change brains, as they irrefutably do, then Fred's brain will not be completely inviolate. But surely he is too well trained, too well educated, too much of an N-P to be significantly impacted by Yakawow. No. there must be a reason, a sensible, scientific reason for Fred's behaviour. He is not sending proper reports for a good reason that will become evident, and similarly is turning off his implant due to some local environmental constraint beyond his control. Everything will become clear so long as I proceed as normal and don't panic. After all, I have never panicked in my life. I will be able to account for everything in due course and the Elders will be delighted. But every time I think of my next summons to the top floor of Centrum, my mind goes blank.

Chapter 22

ZELDA

I thought I would never be happy again after my grandparents had died: but gradually, as those first days had ticked by in the suddenly silent home, and as I had recognized the futility and emptiness of the silly email program for continuing to correspond with those now dead, so I had slowly started to thaw and melt back into life. Yes, everything had changed forever: but a new time had beckoned, unpredictable and open, as the big, bright new Dwelling spread out its limitless spaces in welcome. Gradually, some ten then twenty other unknown human beings were going to assemble into a new venture, an adventure of the Grouping. Anything was possible.

So, for that brief interlude, I had managed to look both forward and back with a light and eager heart. My grandparents had been old, had not suffered pain, and always had each other. What more could anyone want? And they were still with me in any case – not through a fake program simulating a flaky reality, but inside my head, sharing the present with me, giving their views, interpreting situations and people that were otherwise hard to understand. Although not alive, they were very much with me. Their deaths had been irreversible, had changed my life in one way, but, in the long run, not in any way that really counted.

But now Fred has been living with us for many months, and every day counts. I will never, ever be the same again ... . Ever since he arrived, I have felt like a different person, a real woman. From an old story in my grandparents' library, I recall a saying that a woman was only truly beautiful when she was loved. And that is me. As I go about the daily and otherwise flat tasks of picking up babies and wiping children and directing lumps of food into unwilling, wet mouths, a warm little fire glows in my deepest core. It backs me up as I look outwards and from minute to minute go through the motions of my existence in the outside world. But from time to time, I'll turn inwards from the tiny tyrannical demands and wails, and gaze into the glow. The warmth is always there, welcoming and permeating throughout my whole body as I glance in a reflective surface, a gleaming wall in the Dwelling: staring back is the same smooth face as always, but this time one that is lit from inside, pink and smiling. Truly loved. By a real man.

In the past, each day had been the same, yawning out in homogeneous monotony. But now, each day is special: at some stage I will see him, talk with him and be with him. I will discover new things about him and about myself. Today is another step forward in our adventure together. I stretch out in the wide and vast soft bed, into the vacant space next to me that, last night, had held no other slumbering body. A cool little frisson of doubt: Fred did not visit me last night. There are quite a few nights now when he doesn't come. But it is only the gentlest and briefest whisper of worry. His absence in itself should have no deeper significance other than the literal fact that he couldn't be there. Increasingly, he has had to work hard and spend more time on analysing the read-outs from Sim's Helmet. He has started on the next important phase of his study.

'It's very exciting, Zelda.' His grey eyes had shone and beamed across the table where we were sharing a meal. But he was looking into the distance, not catching my eye.

'We started off ...'

We. He had said 'we': the embers inside licked into a flickering little flame.

'... started off by just letting Sim behave and go through her day as she might normally – well as normally as possible, given our technical constraints. She had to spend more time initially inside in the Dwelling, first for us to get baseline readings and then to move on to the first real experimental phase, Phase 1, of the specific cognitive intervention.'

'You mean all those different programs you described when we first met.' I was nodding back, prompting him, professional colleague as well as lover: true soul-mate in complete accord. But Fred was looking over my shoulder, beyond and into the outside.

'Mmm ... yes, Phase 1. Then the second phase has proved crucial. Walking and talking outside with Sim: testing in normal, spontaneous conversation how her mind was changing as a result. That's what Phase 2 is all about.'

But I was no fickle little self-centred Sim. This was science and my man was, for the moment, focused on his brilliant job. I had to think just of him and his work, and show my support and approval.

'And it's working. Anyone would only have to be a minute with Sim to see how she's changing, developing.'

'Indeed.'

A minimal response and a tight smile, in self-congratulation. Then he was serious again, concentrating on the job in hand.

'But, usually, normal maturation would take a lifetime. And Sim in that sense is still very far behind. That's why we now need to move on as soon as possible to the third phase, one I haven't really discussed with you before.'

He was now lapsing into a monotone, suppressing a yawn, starting to tire.

'Why not?'

My question was rhetorical and unconcerned. I was about to be told now, in any case.

'Because there was such a lot to explain, and I didn't know how much you would understand all at once. I didn't want to worry you, if you didn't understand exactly what was going to happen with Sim. And I didn't know then that I could trust you.'

The little flame flared higher, brighter and hotter. I tried to catch his eye, catch him.

'But you do now, don't you … ?'

'Of course, Zelda.' Almost a sigh, almost impatient, almost but not quite – just a whisper. 'But this third phase *is* the most exciting, I suppose.'

He was no longer talking to me at all really. 'Phase 3 is the one that will significantly accelerate the development of Sim's mind.'

He was now almost reciting, downloading on me – I could have been anyone – what he had learnt long ago.

'Just as signals from Sim's brain can be detected by the Helmet, then filtered and fed on to my implant for further analysis – so the traffic can go in two directions. We can see the hotspots of activation as Sim is having certain experiences, can even zoom in offline and enhance the images to see in a real-time film the exact synapses that are undergoing modification, and how that modification is taking place, even what parts of each single brain cell are changing, before our very eyes. Until now, in Phase 2, those experiences involved interaction with the outside world, applying to real life the specific exercises that we had discussed for development of longer attention spans, a sense of self and so on. In effect, the exercises that Sim has been performing so far are really just distilled and speeded-up versions of real life, or how real life used to be.'

Earlier in our love, I could have caught his eye and neither of us would have needed to add, as he now did: 'How real life used to be before the Yakawow way of doing things took over.'

But now he had said it explicitly. Fred had explained to me over one of our meals together how that term was used deridingly by the N-Ps, to convey how they saw us as small children trapped in a permanent here-and-now of astonishment, be it positive or negative, dividing the world into 'Yuck' and 'Wow'. No, not all of us. By now I was used to discussing and thinking about the other members of my Grouping as types of beings who were distinct from myself. I'd always known I was different, but Fred had helped me actually realize *who* I was. Yes, I agreed with him totally. I could see readily that anyone brought up in the Yakawow way would have much catching up to do, and quickly.

'So Phase 3 is reversing the direction of the traffic in a way ...'

I pulled myself back to being Fred's concerned colleague and hoped I hadn't let my mind wander off from a vital link in his exposition.

'... we can now target the exact, critical synapses by direct electrical stimulation through the Helmet. The idea has been around from as long ago as the twentieth century, when scientists tried to stimulate the brain directly. Back in those days, however, the crudeness of the early techniques meant stimulating through the skull without any online visual guidance. All those early practitioners could do was to activate large-scale areas of brain in the most generalized way possible, without knowing the precise limits of their field of electrical current spread.'

He was speaking in unremitting chunks, hardly drawing

breath, almost to fend off any input I might have, any interaction that might ensue.

'None the less, even way back then, they did report some interesting findings: for example, some of the subjects suddenly experienced strong spiritual and religious feelings. But no one could really explain or interpret these findings: they were interesting but they didn't help us understand how the brain worked. The main problem was that everything was insufficiently controlled. Neither the time nor space resolution was appropriately high to achieve any meaningful correlation – a matching up – between what was really happening in the brain, and what the particular subject was feeling. Of course, that big issue of how the objective translates into the subjective, still defeats us, still tantalizes us …'

Fred looked far away over my shoulder, just for a second, then visibly jerked himself back to me.

'But now, thanks to our Helmet technology, we can at least match up precisely, and in real time, the exact hotspot networks of synapses in Sim's brain that we have seen are frequently activated during certain cognitive exercises. But much more impressive still, is that now we can target exactly additional ancillary areas that have been dormant, and would have remained so. We can use the Helmet to drive directly the exact parts of the brain, the highly specific networks that we ourselves select and can visualize, ideally to connect up into an ever larger neuronal assembly.'

I was completely focused now on being the colleague, sharing with my man these sophisticated concepts: backing him up, understanding and agreeing. That's what soul-mates did. Of course, I knew by now what an 'assembly' was by name: Fred had explained many times. I still couldn't quite grasp all the details, had never seen one in the way that he said was possible on special

N-P equipment. But I did know that the idea was to have a freeze-frame picture of someone's state of mind: the bigger the assembly, whatever it actually was, then the deeper the consciousness, and hence the more you understood. By activating previously unrelated networks of cells in Sim's brain simultaneously with hotspots that would be active anyway, you could make everything work together to form a new, much larger assembly. Sim would consequently have a deepened consciousness; she would make connections and see one thing now in terms of something else. She would understand more very quickly, much more quickly than letting the mere act of living capriciously activate new connections each day.

That first day, when we had implemented Phase 3, was utterly unremarkable. Just like any other start to a session, Sim had appeared fairly soon after her biorhythms had woken her and she had subsequently passed through the wash-waste. She had stood before us, clear and clean and open to whatever we chose to do to her: transparent, still lacking any real substance. By now, though, she had learnt the concepts of a daily sequence, a routine: she even seemed to enjoy the predetermined structure to her time, and knowing what activity would follow on from the next. She called it her 'identity'. I stood shoulder to shoulder next to my man: we were a team, and she was our subject.

Fred, meanwhile, had propped his bicycle against one of the walls, the nearest one, and gave a final glance at its lilac frame, static and slanted, seemingly to reassure himself it was safe, and he was safe, without physical contact or constant surveillance. By now I was used to the bicycle: it was a part of Fred that needed to be with or at least near him, all the time. I didn't mind: after all it was what he was, who he was. Just as now he was working, focused and professional, on checking Sim's Helmet. She stood motionless, staring straight ahead at nothing: knowing the routine, comfortable with it and with us. I savoured seeing him work, not minding that he was for that moment oblivious to me. We both knew we were there deep down: the embers glowed as always.

The team of two, the couple, beamed down on their subject. We both knew what she did not – that Fred was going to stimulate her brain. I hadn't asked whether it might hurt, as it truly had not occurred to me until now that it was a possibility. But I stayed silent: it was most important, as I'd learnt, not to interrupt Fred while he was concentrating on such a critical step. I trusted him to do whatever was best.

He did and said nothing different, at least as far as Sim could probably tell. But I did notice a small change once the Helmet was on, and once Fred had sat down opposite Sim, as she in turn sank into a glowing turquoise sofa: it was then that I saw Fred was more preoccupied than normal with the watch-like device on his wrist, which I knew already was interfaced with his implant. Presumably it was much easier to activate stimulation by pressing an external device on his wrist than one beneath his skin, on his upper arm. But the watch wasn't a mere on–off button: it also allowed Fred to set the precise controls and levels of stimulation needed.

By now, in any case, Sim was far less restless than she used to be: without any sophisticated or specialist analysis, I could easily see for myself that her attention span was longer, that she could now concentrate on her interactions with Fred. As he proceeded with the by now familiar cognitive programs with the screen Head, a dark man, positioned between Fred's bright red seat and Sim's turquoise sofa, so everything seemed as it always did. Fred directed Sim's responses to various presentations spoken by, or displayed on the video unit of, the dark man. I was starting to find these sessions rather uninteresting. Now that Sim was calm and content, there was very little for me to do, and Fred obviously couldn't constantly explain to me everything that was happening. They would lean forward together, grey and blonde/silver, towards the disembodied black Head, launching and returning sentences and words and sometimes smiles. I just watched. As far as I could see, Phase 3 was not that different in procedure from Phase 1.

'You'll only see the real change later,' Fred had explained to me on that night he first told me about Phase 3.

'You'll see the change when a need arises for some greater understanding of a situation. After all, this is not some little trick, some little diversion that she'll learn to play only when she's undergoing the program. That's the whole point, it's training for life. All our N-P children gain a maximal understanding this way: it's no game. It is playing to the full strength of each individual brain, improving to the maximum each individual mind with maximal efficiency. You'll only see the real change when Sim is in a complex real-life situation, one that might involve choices that are not obvious, or accepting and comprehending a difficult or unpalatable fact. Only then will you see how she behaves differently from how she would have previously.'

I had assumed that it was all part of the Phase 3 stage of the program now, that the testing of this new level of understanding apparently involved longer and more frequent excursions outside, the walking and the talking of Phase 2 from which I was excluded. I didn't really mind I suppose. It was what my soul-mate had to do, and I had to let him focus on his work. He had explained to me even at the beginning that I would be a distraction, that if I were there too, he would want to talk with me instead, not have difficult and clumsy conversations with Sim. And rather than walking with Sim, he would want to be holding me. I understood. I didn't mind. Anyway, I have my own gentle, trivial tasks in the

Grouping. I still have to look after some of the infants at least part of the time.

And yet ... Again the chill, whispering worry disturbing so slightly my happy equilibrium. These experimental explorations outside with Sim are increasingly taking up his time during the daylight hours. She must be generating a large amount of data. And that's what he said. He needs to analyze and plan and reflect on what his implant reads out in a stream of numbers and technical concepts that come too thick and fast for me to ever understand, or dare ask to understand. Fred is busy, doing his job. I have to accept that. The quiet night hours when Sim eventually sleeps deeply and instantly, all energy spent on fresh air and understanding – that is the time Fred needs to do his work. And that is the time I lie dreaming, awake, staring at the ever-changing colours of the muted lights above and around me.

Of the many transformations Fred has made in my life, one is just that: the ability to stand back and appreciate what has happened, to measure it up against previous experiences, even previous thoughts, to place it into a 'context' – one of Fred's favourite words. Only when something can be set in a context, only then does it have a meaning, a real significance for you: only then do you 'understand' what it means. Apparently, that is why the normal way of training N-P children is to ensure that they read while their brains are simultaneously being directly stimulated in the Phase 3 protocol. The context will then be the most extensive possible. I smile to myself. Sim will never be more than just a subject. Her brain will never be as fully developed as those of Fred's world. She cannot read, and never will. The way we now live means we have no books and no concept of time.

But when I was growing up, I had both those commodities – it's what makes me different, so different that Fred recognized it almost immediately. Books for me are still there, like my grandparents, in my mind. Lined up in dim shades marshalled on shelves and piled on tables, static and unchangeable – fixed and constant voices offering the same message, the same journey to whoever turned the pages. But still no one would make the same journey, or at least feel that they had. Each person would make the journey in the context of their own mind. They would apply their own checks and balances and associations. For each reader, the words, the sentences, the journey, would have a meaning that was as individual as their own brains and as the mechanical neuronal connectivity that Fred told me underlies that mental personalization.

Yes, I at least know all about books and the quiet, explosive power that they could contain. But they had already fallen into disuse for everyone else, for everyone apart from me, everyone who did not have parents who had died before their grandparents. The Fact-Totum will confess that books used to be the building blocks of thought, information and entertainment, long before the screen technologies encroached and everyone went Yakawow. But everyone apart from me was born far too late. Their time, indeed my time, was, and still is, interactive, multichoice, non-linear – never to step back.

Unlike before the Fred time, there is now a part of me that appreciates this time on my own, lying in the vast bed that we sometimes share: this silent gap in space and time gives me the chance not so much to think, at least not in the sense of solving a problem or understanding a fact. Rather the moment can fatten, swell, become bloated with the reliving of recent times with Fred, looking and listening to that creased smiling face with the loving, dancing grey eyes. I can savour and savour again the recent shared moments, nurturing and feeding them, all the time comparing them with the dry, thin times of my previous existence: I can luxuriate in the wonder of having achieved something I have always wanted, even though I have never known what it really was. Whenever I'm not with Fred, just as I once expanded the thoughts from reading a book, so now I want to be with him in my mind over and over again in that engorged moment suspended in time.

Chapter 23

FRED

'Take just one, Fred, you'll find it might really help.'

Zelda is lying beside me naked. She is propped up on one elbow, looking at me with tenderness and concern. Our lower limbs entwine of their own accord. Her breasts are plump and swelling, exposed and pale in the dark light. It is the middle of the night. But my brain refuses to shut down. It needs to carry on working. There's so much for it to do, so much work to be done and, above all, compartmentalized, keeping everything clear and separate. I must keep things separate. So much Zelda mustn't know and so much that I can share and learn, provided that I stay alert and vigilant. But Fred the man is still in control. So long as I don't sleep. But my whole body is aching, my eyes are pricking with the pain of staring and looking and processing. I must close them, I want to close them, but I can't. I turn to Zelda. She holds out her hand, flat. I take the thing, swallow it. Then the next I know is that Zelda is leaning over me, still smiling, and running one finger lightly along my arm, telling me it's time to wake up.

For some time now the path ahead of me that was once so clear and so perfect, so right, has no longer been any of those things.

The episodes of each day no longer provide a means to an end: instead they have taken on a completeness in themselves. They jerk and jump like ancient frames in silent movies. You know that any apparent continuity between them is an illusion, a trick of the brain. The times with Sim and the times with Zelda are totally different, distinct, and therefore not related. And I feel confused and disturbed that it should be like that, that the two people and the events that they create with me should not be cause and effect, are not complementary, do not join up. And if times with Zelda and times with Sim are not a sequence, but disconnected, then where is it all leading? Nowhere. Each freeze-frame in time simply justifies itself, is of itself. Which makes me just the consumer, the hapless participant in the moment. A bit player, not the overriding narrator. Impossible. I need to clear my head. I need to sort this out, to see how they could, they must, relate to each other: compare and contrast.

On the one hand, the times with Zelda. Zelda needs me in a way Tarra never has. While Tarra is an extension of me, the waves lapping and covering the shore, blurring the line between the two of us, so Zelda is a distinct entity, the opposite or rather the complement to me: she is a woman and I am the man. The world of romance that I'd visited only in the literature of other centuries was one I could conceptualize but not really understand: a word like 'love' was so overworked and, without any context, truly meaningless. And then in any case it was the context, the situation, the interactions themselves that counted: the admittedly indirect, but at least demonstrative read-out of what someone felt. Not the over-used, over-blown, empty word. Yet Zelda did love me, she said so frequently, and referred always to our 'making love'. This love was incessant, unremitting, unconditional, free of context. I just had to be the object of it, the male partner in Zelda's dance.

We are not following the preordained ideas and guidelines that made Tarra's and my life perfect, at least N-P perfect, where our main aim was to discuss ideas to reach an abstract truth. Rather, Zelda and I eat and talk and look into each other's eyes, just being together, with no other purpose at all, no end in sight. This is time out, a suspension in time that I've never experienced before. It was at first a novelty for me to learn about her past, not as a linear rationale for extrapolating some generalization about the Others, but just so that the woman I held in my arms was fuller, more open, more of a complete entity. And as we just looked at each other and held each other closer, so I unfolded the easier parts of my own history. I laid out before her the story of an N-P living out his life as he had been told: it could have been anyone's story from the other side of the mountains. The things that are special to me and me alone, my own theories of the brain, Tarra and Bill, and now my growing confusion as to how all these things could fit together with the overriding feeling I had on the bicycle – none of this could be shared with Zelda.

My thoughts soar back to the other side of the mountains, to the beige box that was the Family Unit, to the bed that was just and always had been just a bed, and would never be nano-assembled into anything else. We had been just fine. Tarra's quiet face lying on her side, next to me each morning, slowly smiling: then me snaking an arm round her waist and pulling her to me in the warm half-sleep that opened up into the start of another day as she opened up to me. The lacy white foam spreading forward on to the compacted tan sand, then sucking back, only to surge forward with a gentle sigh: Tarra and me. Then a raucous cawing, but not a seagull …

'Fred, you must wake up. Are you all right? Is everything fine, my darling? Why don't you say something? You don't talk to me like you used to …'

Talking with Zelda is becoming increasingly hard as there is so much I cannot say. However she seems so content with so little that I realize my mere presence, my existence, is actually enough. Zelda's imagination seems to do the rest. My own thoughts are in turmoil, but she doesn't seem to notice. On and on go her monologues and smiles. The fragmented moments of heady sensuality are now coming with a price that is heavier by the day. They are no longer interludes of amusement, brief moments snatched along the wayside of the journey that is my mission, my life-story: now I am unclear as to where I am headed. The times with Zelda have become a complete detour from which it is ever harder to rediscover the main path.

On the other hand, there are the times with the Sim creature, as I still think of her. Sim needs me in a way that Tarra never has. Ah, at least one similarity with Zelda. But all the rest is completely different. Sim looks up to me. When I'm with her, I'm the master, the Magus: under my control and guidance she is flourishing into a cognitive being. Now we have shifted to Phase 3 of the program, the effects of the direct stimulation could be striking. Before that, during Phase 1 of the indirect cognitive program, and Phase 2 of the walking and talking outside, Sim had already started to acquire an identity of sorts, though of course she herself over-uses the term in an endearingly overly generalized way.

'That's my identity.'

She smiles a big beam that splits her face wide open, white even teeth savouring and mouthing the word over and over again. And all she was doing was recalling something that she had done yesterday. I only realized after some time that of course Sim, like all the Others, didn't actually own anything. Although she lived in the Dwelling, and used and transformed the objects around whenever anything was wanted, nothing belonged to her and her alone. Why should it? What would she need, if she lived from moment to moment? If she has physical ease and sensual gratification, then objects are otherwise superfluous: they could have no intrinsic interest in themselves as, say, books did for us. Nor would external objects actually symbolize, stand for, anything since Sim, as all the Others, has lived only in a literal world. She would not need an object to 'say' anything about her, to denote status or, in the words of a much used clichéd slogan from advertisements of the twentieth and twenty-first centuries, to be 'as individual as you are'. Sim had not needed to own anything because she hadn't been an individual. Now she is. *Her* identity. Sim isn't aware of what the word really means. What is more important to her, is that it is hers: something she owns for the first time.

But now we are on to Phase 3, she will soon realize. As the growth of her neuronal connections accelerates at my command, stimulated and activated and spreading through her brain as I command, so her conceptual framework will grow and strengthen. She'll realize that an identity is not a possession, but it *is* her, and that she exists as a consistent entity through space and time. And then she'll realize that things and other people also endure beyond the here and now, that they can be compared and connected, and fuel generalizations, ideas and abstract concepts that could not be seen or heard or touched. At last Sim will be able to formulate plans, at least under my guidance. She is the product of my insights, my ingenuity, my power.

But no, that's not quite right. Not any longer. Do I really want power? What I really want is to escape on my lilac bicycle. When I'm alone, as I fly past the gaudy, silly, pointless domes to trees and sky, only then do I feel I'm whole and complete, I suppose at peace: what an odd phrase, one I've never used before. At peace. Alone, I need react to nothing, please no one, report to no one. Increasingly, I enjoy the moment, just being alive and elemental, an integral part of the universe. But then what significance do I have? My whole life I've defined myself as a brain scientist, or I used to. Still, I cling to that: that is what I need to be as it gives me a meaning. Not for Hodge, not for the mission, but for me. I need to have, to find, a meaning to my life because I'm no longer sure who I really am.

So I'll focus on Sim and the work that still fascinates me. Yes, I'll suppose I'll carry on going through the motions of recording these reports: I'm doing so now, aren't I? And I'll also report to Hodge because otherwise things may become even more difficult. I can't think how exactly: there are too many variables to cope with putting them all into different hypothetical permutations. But from this point, whatever I do is not to please or impress Hodge:. His wise, lined face is staring at me now, slightly frowning, not quite sure, perplexed. But I truly no longer care about Hodge: there is too much else to worry about. He doesn't care about me, about Fred, the man, the real person. He doesn't even know me, even though we've worked together forever. He wouldn't understand how hard it all is, once a path bifurcates and bifurcates, and bifurcates again, and you need to go down all the roads, but then the roads don't meet up and there you are on your bicycle wondering where you're actually going … .

The sleep enhancers help. Drugs. A word from a previous century – a flashy, romantic world of razor blades and mirrors and white powder. Above all, a world that overrode reality, defied it, mocked and manipulated it. In the years before the Exodus, even before the screen technologies had so effectively created a new reality, so increasing numbers of people had sought refuge in the invasive chemical forerunner. But even before the N-Ps had formed themselves into a distinct group with a clear ideology, so my predecessors had already started to worry what might happen to a society where en masse most of its members were saturating their brains with these synthetic agents.

Of course, we now know far more about how drugs work at the level of neuronal connections – how some strengthen, and some weaken, how some stimulate more of the naturally occurring transmitters, while others block their action. Yes, we can be far more precise in cataloguing how and by how much, and when and for how long each of these many different chemicals bends and turns to shape the connections of cells within the brain. But now I've experienced first hand a phenomenon I've known about since I first was a student of neuroscience, and I realize that just to know a fact without experiencing it falls far short. So even more poignant now is the question that endlessly tantalizes: how that biochemical chicanery, how those different transient bends and shapes in the brain actually translate into a subjective state. How and why do those little sleep-enhancing pills actually remove my consciousness?

There would have been a time when I could have concentrated on that question to the exclusion of everyone and everything around me. But now, the most important thing is that they work, and continue to do so night after night: they have to carry on freeing me from the agitated, sweaty torment of lying on my back, mouth desert-dry, eyes wide open, gritty and sore, with no escape. Those little pills have to give me some remission from the too loud, too fast confusion that is increasingly closing in on me. All that raw colour and noise, and at last my adrenaline responding to the call of its evolutionary mandate to adapt and be part of it. I'm half afraid and half excited. I can no longer shut out the outside world of Yakawow: it is starting to break down the walls of my mind, trample into my brain and take over. Glaring, unsure, dominating with one simple question: what happens now? Right now? And the only response has been to close everything down, to shut down my brain, to fall into the soft, black oblivion.

The neat little conceptual polarizations of Zelda and Sim, the tidy compartments and classifications of my thoughts and reasoning of which Hodge used to be so proud, are no longer working as they should. My concentration has drifted yet again, as it is doing increasingly these days. I clench my jaw and summon all my energy to focus, to get back on track with arguing things through: I have to hold all the swirling hopes and fantasies and memories back in firm check, to think of the future. I feel I'm in different pieces, fragments and, more than anything, I need to be whole.

Chapter 24

SIM

Over time, it has become easier to use words more quickly to answer Fred, to help him see how I am feeling, just as the witch and prince once told me what was happening inside them. The more I speak to Fred in this way, the more he says it helps him. He says he is able to record all that I am doing and saying and feeling into some kind of database that he can't show me, that would tell me what kind of person I am.

'So who am I?' I asked one day. Immediately the words were out of my mouth, I knew that they sounded different and strange. But Fred was pleased. These days, he always seems happy and pleased with me. So I was starting to expect that whatever I said would make his mouth widen, and his eyes so shiny.

'You've just taken a big step, Sim. You've asked a very big question that children never ask, but that mature humans have been asking for thousands of years.'

'So what's the answer?'

Fred laughed. A deep gurgle from the back of his throat that I had never heard before.

'That's what each one of us is trying to find out, Sim, apart from all the rest of the Others of course.'

'Do you mean everyone in the Dwelling?'

'Yes.'

'Zelda, as well?'

'Well, no.'

He looked briefly away from me and the bicycle, eyes going into slits as if looking hard at something in the distance. Then he sighed and looked back at me.

'But soon, Sim, I'll try and share with you what my program says about you, how it describes you as a person, an individual.'

Meanwhile, I was really enjoying this walking and talking outside. Soon, we were spending most of the time not in the Dwelling with Zelda but, with our backs turned on the groups of large domes, would make for the trees and the open spaces.

One morning, it had started to rain heavily while we were outside: the big dollopy drops had pounded down suddenly on my Helmet, and streams of water slid down the back of my neck, under all my clothes. It was becoming cold and windy: we both realized without needing to say anything that we would have to stop and find somewhere out of this wetness. The problem was that we had wandered far beyond the Dwellings, as had become our normal way. Looking around, the only obvious possibility was a ruined building from a previous time: some walls leaning against each other made of brown-coloured oblong blocks that Fred said had been called bricks.

There was no dome overhead, but because the walls were still quite high we both automatically moved towards the space inside. It was probably an ancient Dwelling of some sort. The floor area was uneven, with slabs of some hard, unrecognizable material, and earth and the usual broken glass and strange, old smashed-up plastic objects. But we had settled into a corner, huddling close just to stay warm and dry, and started to have one of our dialogues. Fred put his arm round me.

'Did everyone used to touch each other like this all the time?'

Perhaps it was the simple act of touching that was, to me, the strangest thing. Adults touched children because they had to, and Zelda had carried on trying to touch me, hold me, for much longer than was normal. But adults in Groupings – well, everyone in a Dwelling was free, on their own, unconnected in every way. It made me think of how it must have been in the other times that Zelda used to speak so often of. It was hard to imagine what it was like then, before the N-Ps decided to leave.

'No, not everyone.'

His pale face had flashed a smile. A flash of lightning and a smash of thunder stopped him for a second. Then the rain drummed on.

'But they did look into each other's eyes, just as I'm doing with you now. And sometimes they would put their arms round each other just like this, to show that they understood how the other person was feeling. At that time, it was often a far more powerful action than words.'

'How would you know how someone else was feeling?'

'I've told you before, Sim, how the brain will be changed by whatever it is you experience and actually do. The more you practise thinking in a certain way, or even thinking at all, the easier and better it will be. But the opposite is also true: if people never do something, they will never be good at it. So, as people in the middle of the twenty-first century spent more time communicating via their fixed-screen technologies, they never learnt to interact with each other, as we're doing now and even when we're just talking, not even touching. It's hard to look someone right in the eyes for a long time, and equally upsetting if you're talking to someone and they are always looking somewhere else. You have to learn, all of us have to learn, how to talk face to face with another person and how those interactions change according to how well you know them.'

'But how would you know how someone else was feeling?' I had repeated yet again.

'That's a hard but good question, Sim. You never can get right behind someone else's eyes and see the world, first hand, exactly as they do. One day we might be able to so understand the process of consciousness, though, that eventually we could manipulate things and intervene to do exactly just that. It's my ultimate research project ...' His voice had softened and he had swallowed in a conspicuous movement of his throat. 'Well, it was what I wanted to work on. I don't think it's so likely now.'

He tilted his chin up defiantly and took a deep breath,

'But given that we can't yet experience someone else's consciousness first hand, the answer to your question is that we have to try and work out what's happening in another person's mind, from indirect evidence. The most established way is to have real-time conversations where you can ask lots of questions and both see as well as hear how the other person responds. The more you see and have an idea of the kind of experiences they describe, the more you can imagine what it must feel like to be them. Imagination and curiosity, Sim: that is the key. And then if, as people used to do, you go on to read books, you can see the world from the perspective of those long dead, or living in very different conditions.'

I remembered then ... .

'Await instruction for hologram display of item: Book.'

One day I'd tried to investigate books on my own, with a Talking Head: the Dark Man had tried to be helpful like he always was, but had just shown rows of oblong objects that all looked just the same: a bit like those 'bricks' but not quite the same shape. I'd turned away, irritated that my investigation without

Fred had led nowhere. But as I had hoped and trusted, as we'd continued with our conversations, so I had learnt in a way that I never could from the Fact-Totum and the Head. Now I had some idea at least of what books could, or rather couldn't, do.

'But you can't ask a book a question.'

A smile: that tight, tiny smile that Fred used a lot. 'No, but you can ask yourself questions about what is in the book, as you go along.'

I was truly puzzled. 'But how does asking yourself questions help you understand what someone else is feeling?'

Fred had looked away and shaken his head. 'Dear Sim, let's hope that one day you'll understand. You have to make such a journey away from all this sensual, saccharine muck where no one knows or cares about anything or anyone at all. We have a lot of work ahead of us.'

Our trips outside were certainly very different from running and Fred was starting to point out and say things that made me ask questions without him prompting me.

'What do N-Ps like to do?'

This was on another day and, as always, we were heading away from the Dwellings, Fred wheeling the bicycle on one side, me on the other. I was getting used to talking in step, to looking ahead, searching for trees without admitting it, or for ruined buildings where we would sit for a while. Both trees and ruins were not that unusual, but they were not that common either. And as we walked, moving further away from the bright domes, so there were fewer things to watch out for underfoot. We were less likely to trip up or stumble or stub our toes on debris, so I could look forward more easily and into the distance. Far, far away on the horizon, when it wasn't raining and the sun made everything bright, I could see the mountains where the N-Ps lived on the other side.

'We like to think.'

'Why?'

'For the same reason you like to move. A very clever man once said, over a hundred years ago, that thinking is movement confined to the brain. So, really, we both like doing the same thing.'

'But that's silly. When I run, I just run. What do you mean by thinking?'

'Thinking is when you go on a journey: so it is like running after all, you start in one place and end up somewhere else. One step follows on from the next.'

'How do you mean?'

'Something happens, and that makes the next thing happen. It's what we N-Ps call a sequence: when you walk, or when you run, things happen in a certain order, just like when you talk, as we're doing now.'

I was starting to see what he meant. 'So, one thing can make something else happen?'

'Exactly. In fact, that's usually how everything in life works. You don't just live in the moment: what has just happened to you, or what you've just done, will determine what is about to happen. That's what's so important, at least to us N-Ps: making the right things happen.'

I started to think about how things happened all the time, every moment. It was a new and exciting way of seeing everything, that each moment could be somehow hooked up to the one before and the one that was coming. It felt good, but a different kind of good feeling from running.

'Zelda doesn't make things happen.'

Fred's face, which was normally a unique grey-white, suddenly looked like it was lit up from inside by a red light.

'I think you'll find she does, Sim – it's just that you've never really noticed before. You've been too busy running, and dancing. Zelda loves you very much. She has cared for you ever since you were small. You are the sunshine of her life.'

'How can I be sunshine?'

Fred had sighed very deeply, with his eyes closed. 'I'm saying that you are *like* sunshine. It's a way of talking and thinking, to see one thing in terms of another.'

At the time it had all been very strange. I hadn't really understood what Fred was getting at. But the more we walked and talked, the more I started to see my time with him as fun, and to look forward to the funny and strange things he said. Even when I wasn't with him, I started to think of things he had told me, and to ask myself the kind of questions he liked to put. They were usually all about me, what I did, what I liked. But then one day, things changed.

'Now it's time for a new game, Sim.'

We are back in the Dwelling, in front of my favourite Dark Man. As always when we are inside, Zelda is there. She is leaning close to Fred, her body leaning towards him, but not touching. She is looking from me to him and back again, and I don't feel she's listening as attentively to what he's saying as I am. But then, of course, this is my game, not hers.

'The time has come for you to learn about meaning, how things that are nothing to do with you personally, can still have significance. All I want you to do, Sim, is to tell the screen any ideas that you might have, about anything.'

I am confused: not quite sure what an 'idea' is.

'What do you mean?'

'Well, let's just say anything you've seen or done or heard that you might like or dislike. It would be especially helpful if you could say why you liked or disliked it. What will then happen is that any term you use, for example, 'happy' or 'running', will then be linked via a large database to other examples people have had over hundreds of years of, say, being happy or even –' the slight smile – 'running. Gradually, as you use the same term over and over again but in different contexts, so the connections that the term triggers will have a greater meaning, a significance beyond what the term means just to and for you, but what it means in terms of the wider world.'

'Why is that good?'

'Because it will help you appreciate being happy, or indeed running, even more.'

I couldn't understand why seeing how other people might have run or been happy, would make me feel any different. But by now I'm starting to trust Fred, and realize what a big change he is making to every day of my life: so I just let his last words sort of hang in the air.

Chapter 25

TARRA

Solitude has always been viewed in our society as a seriously suboptimal condition for the mind: thoughts can wander unchecked by the balance of another perspective or, worse, just circle round in obsession without any advance at all. I wasn't used to being on my own after finishing my day at the Institute. I'd always had someone with whom to talk whenever I wanted, or indeed even when I didn't. Initially, of course, it was my parents. Just like everyone else with their respective families, I had sat between my mother and father at the meal-time table, walked between them to Rallies, always looking up to them. Always I'd had a physical and mental boundary on all sides. Always I had known where and who I was, defined by those around me.

Then, when I first met Fred, things changed. Instead of being surrounded and protected by secure, high walls, vast uncharted vistas opened up that would have scared me on my own. But now I had a reference point, a constant and consistent presence with which to make new, brave excursions. Instead of looking up, I could look straight ahead, knowing that I didn't need, ever, to turn my head to check that Fred was at my side: I knew he would always be there.

But then, suddenly, he wasn't. On that day he left, we were up earlier than usual. It was well before Bill would wake, and still dark. Fred was leaving very early, noncommittal and preoccupied. Since his sudden announcement earlier, we hadn't spoken of the Others at all: this was partly because neither of us had access to any new information, apart from the standard reference material, that would fuel an appropriate discussion – but also partly because the very mention of them made them more real. Where did you start with people who, apparently, just lived for the pleasure of the present? If people didn't plan, then presumably nothing was important. And if so, then they didn't care what happened. So what would happen to Fred when he was there, alone, among them? If he was thinking as I was – and I always assumed that was the case – then he would be as sick with fear and apprehension as me. It was a minor selfishness on my part, one that I refused to nurture, a whisper of regret that Fred was not sharing his dread with me.

The only subject he seemed willing, even excited, to discuss before he left, was some strange contraption he was due to collect from the laboratory: his transport over the mountains. I had obviously learnt about the bicycles of the previous few centuries, but had never seen one. I couldn't understand why this banal object, rather than the science of the mission itself, not to mention the danger, was so dominating Fred's thoughts. But, unusually on that last black, pre-dawn morning, he had just talked at me in long paragraphs and, equally atypically, I had just listened as a half-interested audience. Eventually he paused for breath, looked me in the eye for longer than was needed, pressed his lips tightly together in resignation, turned and opened the door. And left without looking back.

The sudden thud of silence was heavy and suffocating. But I knew I had to concentrate on Bill. Besides, it stopped the obsessional, pointless circle of thought. I went into our son's room and, for the first time ever, woke him up. It is widely established as highly important to benefit from the full quota of sleep: normally, our lives are so well ordered that the natural sleep time is timetabled in, and Bill, like everyone else, would be able to sleep to the full, only waking when fully rested: and he would still not be late for the next stage in his day. The old concept of unpunctuality is only one that we encounter indirectly now in the literature of previous eras.

But I needed to anticipate the obvious question Bill would ask at the newly asymmetric breakfast table: it was important that he felt things were under control and planned. I needed therefore to tell him about Fred before he asked. I looked down at my motionless little boy and stroked my fingers through his silky but shorn brown hair as he lay on his side, thumb in mouth, eyes shut.

'Bill, you need to wake up, I have something important to tell you.'

No endearing terms of address, ever, as in previous times: emotions and sentiment were no help to an infant N-P. An individual should always be called by their name, whatever their stage in life, however young they were. It gave them a solid continuity and enhanced their sense of a single identity. And no words like 'surprise', however 'special' or 'exciting' I could have dressed it up to be: surprise was yet another concept that no longer featured as an everyday phenomenon in our lives. Bill opened his eyes, unfocused, at the sudden, cruel blast of consciousness. He looked at me, still silent with half-sleep, waiting and trusting.

'Your father has had to go away to do some very important work: you'll have to be a big boy now as there's just the two of us and we need to look after each other.'

I could almost see the idea, this unexpected sequence of events, and my conclusions, trickling through Bill's wakening brain.

'When will he be back?'

The inevitable question.

'Soon.'

I could have told him it was a secret, but that would have led to many further questions: when one is Bill's age, secrets are for sharing after all. Or I could have told him a precise date, with an exact number of days to go; but then he might have wanted to count off each of those days, given that he was already becoming very agile with his numbers. Or I could have told him the truth, that I didn't know and that strange, overpowering feelings of what must be fear and anxiety were taking me over, already preventing me from acting and thinking as I should. But how would that have helped him? My kind, easy half-lie that led to no further interrogation and that might, just might, turn out to be the truth – that was the best I could do for him at the moment.

But Fred didn't come back soon. The dramatic change in every moment of my daily life at home, mercifully perhaps, took up much of my energy and attention: no one had trained me to adapt to a sudden transformation in circumstance. I only knew an existence where everything was planned and predictable, where events followed on one from another in a calm and logical sequence. Now I was completely on my own and unsure what the future held, not knowing when Fred would return. I had never spent one night alone, without any other adult near by. Initially, therefore, just the mere difference, the loneliness, and not knowing the best strategy for coping with change – all that preoccupied me as I did my best to carry on as normal.

All the time I was fully aware that there was no one else, had never been any other N-P of my generation, experiencing the strange unprecedented lifestyle that had suddenly been thrust upon me. Now, even after so long, I was still having great difficulty in adjusting. And even though much of the time I could be preoccupied with the logistics of the new routine, the periods of solitude stretching over hours, when I could only talk to myself, were still an arduous novelty. I was so accustomed to dialogue that it was strange to generate conversations in a more one-sided manner, either with a book, or with Bill.

Bill was the one incandescent spot of light in my grey home: inevitably, my first worry was the effect that Fred's absence would have on him. Every single morning of his young life, Bill had eaten breakfast with his father smiling down at him, just as Fred and I had each done in our respective Family Units a generation earlier. It was a given of N-P life, as predictable as the sun rising. What long-term effects would now be caused by the empty seat at the table? I tried my best to build the walls high and protective around my little son, to ensure that he still had boundaries.

So our days settled down to a lopsided version of normality. I worked as always, while Bill had now started his first Helmet sessions at the Young N-P Institute, the YN-PI. This, the first most important stage in development, the fitting of the Helmet, had happened without his father being present: to prevent my sadness over this, I tried to blot it out of my mind. Rather, I forced myself to concentrate on practicalities, and introduced an innovation to our domestic routine: as well as eating breakfast together, I now joined Bill for the evening meal that normally he ate with me just watching, while I would have dined later with Fred. He was still too young to stay up for when his father returned: eating in the evening as a trio was planned for a later stage, in some three years' time. I had checked with my superior that my taking the meal early would not compromise my metabolism, and he confirmed my own assumptions that we wouldn't need to modify my calorie schedule for the short shift in timing, but we should keep the issue under review.

I'd also needed to notify Bill's supervisor at the YN-PI that I was planning this alteration in his routine, since every possible input to Bill's brain, every experience he had, was anticipated according to our meticulously arranged system. Any potential change needed careful evaluation and consideration. Here, the interview was not quite as cursory as at my own Institute.

That first morning Fred had left, all I could manage was to limp through the rest of the day, trying not to feel anything but just to think about the problems at work that I was indeed tasked to think about. This strategy turned out to be easier than might have been imagined, perhaps because, I now realize, in those early days I was in the state of delayed shock that was often described in the archive news reports from the twenty-first century. The enormity of the worry and the strangeness of experiencing an overwhelming churning had taken over my consciousness as Fred walked out: next had been the gnawing anxiety when I woke Bill, then finally the feeling of being just empty, exhausted, numb. All I had done was get through the first day, making the required movements and responses, trying not to think. Just behaving in a way that wouldn't make anyone suspect anything was wrong with me. But then all my lifelong training asserted itself: I started to plan. So it was that not too long after Fred's departure, I requested an interview with Bill's supervisor.

The YN-PI was like all other buildings, beige and square, and in this instance quite squat. It bore no resemblance whatsoever to the schools that I had read and studied so much about evolving over centuries in previous civilizations. There was no concession to youth: no colours, no kindly pictures, no ebullient noise. No face-to-face instruction took place. There was no teacher as such equipped with their incomplete corpus of information,

274

relaying on second hand and imperfectly their own small version of facts and theories in a standardized broadcast to a sea of faces. Now, all 'teaching' was supervised by an individual who was an expert on Helmet technology: instruction was bespoke, coherent, interconnected with other areas of information already locked into each individual personalized brain.

Phase 1, the non-invasive, indirect cognitive program, took place as soon as a child could talk, with Phase 2, the application of the mental processes that had been learnt, being practised each evening in the Family Unit. The Helmet was usually introduced intermittently during these stages, merely to observe the brain activity and patterns as they reflected the maturing cognitive abilities. Depending on the progress of the individual child, but normally between the ages of three and five, Phase 3 was introduced: direct stimulation to accelerate the learning process, and in particular to maximize understanding. The Helmet allowed personalized traffic of information into and out of each young brain, transforming it into a corpus of knowledge that would never, ever be standardized from one child's mind to the next. How different from the old idea, and practice, of education when it was an effort to learn and to teach: even then it didn't necessarily result in real understanding, in true knowledge.

Bill and I walk to the YN-PI each day over the even, dark grey paving, him holding my hand as he learns to put one foot in front of the other in a steady, even pace as we begin the dialogue that is explicitly prescribed. He looking up at me as I had once looked up at my mother, walking in time, one little soft hand holding tightly on to mine, the other cradling the precious Helmet that he would wear once inside the building, for the rest of the day. By now a slight breeze could just about ruffle the pale brown close-cut hair. It would need to be shorn again very soon.

My own long legs contrive short, slow steps to help him keep up. For the moment, Bill is so small that his sentences are very simple and still only statements of facts relating to his immediate present. However, I can see that his first Helmet has already been helping a lot with the embedding of those facts in a greater conceptual framework.

'That tree is very big.'

He is pointing to a gnarled and twisted veteran of the centuries, generously branching out in all directions, dappling the path we are taking as it stretches out between us and the weak morning sun.

'But some trees are small,' he continues unprompted.

I am delighted that he has acquired the ability to generalize and apply this to the generic concept of trees, as well as to compare and appreciate the diversity within the category, particularly as there are no smaller trees within our immediate field of vision.

'What do trees do, Bill?'

I ask slyly, knowing that the question is too hard really for a child at his stage. But again, asking the occasional, impossibly difficult question is what we are required to do. The program thus avoids learning by rote or even simply responses that are not backed up by maximal thought and appreciation for the significance of what one is actually saying. And, who knows, a hard question for which there might not be an immediate, easy answer could none the less still take root, set up questions, perhaps forge improbable, and potentially innovative, links within his neuronal networks.

But by now we have arrived. All around us similar pairs of a grey-clad adult of either gender, quietly hand in hand with a Helmet-bearing smaller figure, are converging on the functional, wide, simple entrance. At the sound of a clear bleep the children, almost in unison, release their handholding and form into a line, at the same time starting to fasten on their

Helmets. Everyone is now silent as they have been trained to be: just occasionally, one or two of the parents step forward to help adjust and buckle as their offspring glance over, mutely requesting a little help.

Now a long line of identical, shiny Helmeted heads marches off. The parents too file out almost with the same quiet precision and order. None of us knows each other and cannot see the point of establishing superfluous, supernumerary relationships that will not necessarily advance ideas effectively. In any case, we shall all be together, celebrating our latest achievements, at the next Rally. But, that morning shortly after Fred has left us, I alone hang back, to see Bill's supervisor.

He is immediately standing in front of me: N-Ps are never late.

'Greetings Tarra, Mother of Bill.'

A monotone that gives nothing away. We have no need of surnames, as in the past, since everyone has a unique ID number and indeed an implant corresponding to that number that provides all biographical information. Names now are simply for giving a sense of individual identity to oneself, rather than as a reference term for anyone else – for giving each person a continuous strand from when one is even younger than Bill now, right through to the time that they become an ex-breeding pair with the progeny on to the next stage. The use of the phrase acknowledging my relation to my son is the formal form of address, employed on the relatively rare occasions when one meets someone for the first time and states the stage in the life narrative that they have reached. I nod my head quickly and equally unnecessarily.

'Greetings Adam, Ex-Father of James.'

It is a statement rather than a question because I have, obviously, done all the research I could on Bill's supervisor. Like many who are entrusted to oversee and plan the particular

Helmet programs for the very young, Adam is of a generation where his own child would have left home. This generation is considered optimal for the task due to the additional time they can now give, undistracted, to this vitally important job, as well as bringing to their decisions and plans the benefits of a longer lifetime of accumulated experience. I am not surprised therefore that Adam is wrinkled, slightly stooped, with his cropped hair admittedly still thick but as grey as his garments. He is not smiling as perhaps people meeting for the first time may have done in a different era. It is pointless, so it is not our way. We are here simply to reach a consensus over a specific issue. But given my continuing numbness, perhaps a smile would have helped me frame my request more effectively and less bluntly.

'I would like to eat my evening meal with Bill rather than just watch him.'

The face, almost eye-level with mine despite its fleshy folds, seems constituted of granite.

'That would be most unusual, in fact unprecedented. Why would you no longer share the evening meal later with your breeding partner, as you should?'

'Bill's father is away.'

For a moment the stone-grey face is caught unawares, the ghost of a start flits briefly across his composure. I know that Adam, the model N-P, will be amazed that Fred is not there but will never ask why he is absent. Educated though we all are to be intellectually curious, we are equally disciplined never to ask extraneous personal questions, never to challenge the rules and guidelines of our society. If Adam needed to know, for professional reasons, why there had been such an unlikely event as Fred leaving, then he would have been told by someone other than me. Obviously, no one predicted my current request, and hence the need for anyone else to know of Fred's departure.

Adam has turned already, however, to the specific question in hand that is his business.

'But if Bill sees you eating, it may deter him from sustaining a continued line of thought in train with his own eating. We know, at this early stage, the young brain can be readily distracted and deviate from a linear line of thought very easily.'

I have anticipated this very real concern: after all, Bill's welfare is my top priority. He is all I have now.

'I would like to request he keeps his Helmet on during those meal sessions. It will help him focus even though he sees me making minor movements at the table. And only until his father returns.'

'When will that be?'

At last a genuine reason for asking the question he had wanted to ask from the outset.

'Soon.'

'I suggest we proceed as you request for a limited period, reviewing the situation every month. Do bear in mind, however, that this is a very radical departure from the optimal program for someone at Bill's stage. But I can understand your rationale: eat with him then, but keep his Helmet on. Just until his father returns.'

So my son and I start to eat together. The food in front of us looks unchanged since the twentieth century, but is actually supercharged with natural additives as well as being neutroceutically modified. Obviously, my portion is larger than Bill's: as we eat, slowly the watch on my left wrist counts up my calorie intake, constantly monitored by my implant, while the comparable device on the right wrist gives me a similar read-out for Bill. We are both drinking water in limitless amounts. No other fluid is consumed by N-Ps, since a valuable lesson has been learnt about the addictive and health-threatening properties not just of the infamous alcohol, but also of tea and coffee and synthetic fizzy drinks.

We are strongly opposed to all forms of psychotropic drugs because they distort the senses, thereby reducing the brain as well as the body, to a suboptimal state: however, there is also the economic argument. These non-water drinks were expensive and time-consuming to produce. We have better use for our time and indeed for our lean budgets, equipped perfectly for the supply and demand of commodities that aid mental processing rather than impair it. I sip slowly and thoughtfully, as I have been brought up to do. Bill is also drinking his water, holding the adult-sized cup with both hands, eyes bright over the rim. He is so small and the rounded white half-sphere of crockery is so large it almost collides with the smooth rim of the Helmet. He's thinking and drinking. That's good. Then he carefully places the emptied cup down in front of him.

'Adrian's got red eyes.'

He peers up at me, blinking, with the grey eyes of his father. He is referring to the albino rat, Adrian, which we keep as the system prescribes, in order for him to learn interaction, even at that young age, with a consciousness that is much more modest than his own, and over which he has control.

'But some rats have black eyes.'

Admittedly a generalization over the diversity of rat eye colour is only a small step in the great cognitive voyage that awaits him: but it is a start. Soon he will progress to understanding how rats fit in with the ecosphere and the rest of the animal kingdom. Then eventually – on the far more distant horizon – he will be able to grasp metaphor, to connect rats to despicable human behaviours that in the narrow literal sense are actually completely outside the rodent repertoire. For now, however, the amount of dialogue that we could exchange is very limited. In any case, his

Helmet has read out to me that his synaptic circuits have had enough for the time being. A small amber light starts to wink just above Bill's left ear. Time is needed for consolidation, for the replenishing of key proteins that would enable the manufacture of the requisite neuronal branches, the dendrites along with their tiny, protruding spines: time also is needed for the exhausted pools of transmitters that serve these newly formed, personalized circuits to be replenished. The monitors on Bill's Helmet indicate the imminent abolition of consciousness: hence suspension of all further new inputs, is needed.

I have a choice. Either I could keep the Helmet on him, and activate the intervention program whereby micro-currents would fragment the large-scale coalitions of brain cells, 'assemblies', so that consciousness is no longer tenable: within a few moments such treatment would result in a read-out of a delta-wave EEG pattern that was a blanket, uniform and undifferentiated sign of a brain on hold, recognized for centuries as an index of deep sleep. Alternatively, I could allow Bill to just drift away naturally. This 'natural' sleep option is advisable for roughly half of the time, to allow a degree of individual, spontaneous final formation of neuronal circuitry. The analogy that was always used in N-P doctrine was that it was a little like a tree: constrained in a certain place under certain conditions, the final arborization of a tree of a certain species would be, in general, predictable. But the micro-configuration, the eventual twist and turn and precise angles of its branches, would always show small variations from each other that could never be strictly planned.

So it was for the human brain: N-P belief was that we did not want everyone to have identical brains, down to the very last synapse, the very last spine on the dendrite. By allowing for limited variation, we would be able to develop new ideas between people as they eventually had dialogues with each other. But the crucial concept here was the limited degree for this spontaneous fine-tuning. The 'natural' option was only to be used with careful planning. Gently, I unfastened the strap anchoring Bill's Helmet, and ran my fingers through the soft hair that had been flattened for hours by this extra skin of metallic silver. Bill stared up at me with an already unfocused gaze, put his thumb in his plump little mouth, obediently shut his eyes, and left me for the night.

My only company now were the books. Because Fred and I were senior ranking, we had the great privilege of acting as custodians of those very precious commodities. Not every household was allowed to protect and care for books, especially a collection the size and age of ours. When our forefathers had left, escaping just in time from the fun-filled suffocation of the Others, they took with them as many volumes as possible. They worked in pairs, carrying the heavy, precious chests between them like the treasure that they were. By that time the Others had long forsaken reading, even from a screen: so first the demand, then the primitive process and attendant culture of producing and acquiring books, had fallen into obscurity. We had lost the art, and no longer had the time, for the ancient practice of publishing books. All information was relayed via the screens of our cyber-devices in the workplace, following on from the Helmet education that everyone had. Home was reserved for development of ideas by spoken dialogue within the Family Unit, without any technological aids. All pleasure was derived from talking and thinking with one's Breeding Partner and, as time went on, with one's child. Only senior-ranking N-Ps with the highest brainpower evaluations were allowed to be the custodians of this additional source of external stimulation: the books, to read and savour and discuss. The higher the rank, the greater the number and diversity and indeed value of the volumes left in one's charge.

Of course, we now have superior ways with our endlessly updated informatics banks of accessing the thought processes of others long dead: but the static, fixed book is still valuable to us as rare and fragile because it isn't viral, isn't just fed simultaneously into thousands of Helmets and on to those receptive young circuits. To hold a book in your hands is to hold a particular moment fixed forever in the swell of the passing of time. This thought, this passage of thought, is there always, unchanging, leading you on a journey inspired and constrained through the narrow agenda of another time and place. Small wonder that only those who had high commendations for their complete adherence to N-P ideology were allowed to turn these powerful piles of pages. But still, as I cradle a revered volume in my hands, I have no desire at all to read.

Chapter 26

SIM

Gradually, the days have settled down to a certain way of doing
things, in a sequence: Fred explained that was how it was with
the N-Ps all the time. But although I started to know what to
expect, it didn't prevent each day bringing some new surprise.
Most days, we will walk and talk outside, but every so often
we'll stay inside so that I can learn a new game with the Dark
Man screen. The latest is the strangest activity of all. I simply
have to say a word or an action, or even what Fred might call an
idea, and pictures or icons will seem to appear spontaneously as
a result, but actually as a result of rapid cross-referencing from
all the inputs I've been making in all the other games. Fred says
that, in this way, I'll be able to see how the 'general' significance of something relates to my own 'personal conceptual
framework'.

'Don't mind so much about all the fancy words, Sim. The
point is that everywhere you go, everything will start to mean
something in two ways, first that it stands for something other
than the object it is – that it has a kind of life-story of its own –
and, second, the world itself will start to mean special things to
you, both the objects and the people in it.'

As the icons and pictures slowly gave way to spoken words, I started to understand what Fred had been describing. He said it was 'unfortunate' that I didn't know how to read, because then we could have had 'written' words rather than spoken ones, and that this would have been much better still.

'Why?'

'Because then you travel entirely at your own pace, you're in complete rather than just partial control of your journey. Because, Sim, reading a book is going on a journey. Sometimes you want to stop and just stare around you for a while, and sometimes even retrace your steps. That's harder to do when the words are spoken. But always, you end up finally going forward. And because your eyes have to be fixed on the words, you cannot let them stray off or be distracted. And by reading rather than listening, the voices of all the different characters speak to you alone in a way that they never could through someone else's actual voice.'

'So teach me to read, Fred.'

I had seen books and pages displayed by the Fact-Totum, and by the Talking Heads, and really could not see why Fred found reading so special. I still couldn't understand what the process of just staring at black squiggles on a white surface would feel like: I couldn't see how the squiggles could be turned into things and people in ways that were more exciting than dancing with enhancers, or even a hologram experience. If I was bored with Zelda actually speaking words, I couldn't see how long periods of time just staring at pages would be any better, when surely it could only be worse. Still, if he did think it was important, then I wanted to please him and show him I could learn to be like him. But Fred just smiled and shook his head as though I'd said something truly impossible.

'You're doing well just as you are, Sim. Very well.'

He was right. The games and then the walking and the talking have all had a big effect – I can tell. By knowing now that things were important to me, and why and how those same things might be important to other people, and also knowing how other people might now feel and think … I've started to make up my own stories, ones that are not just about the witch and the prince, but about what *I* have done and what *I* want to do. Fred said this was me developing an 'identity'.

In any case, I've started to feel very special: different from how I used to feel when I ran a lot, and before Fred came into my life and turned it into a story. My life: there was the time when I was small with Zelda, then the time before Fred, then the Fred time. The Fred time was best as I started to link up the times we were together, to remember what we had been talking about so that we could carry straight on.

Now I'm wearing the Helmet all the time. I like it because it reminds me of Fred when he isn't here. Fred doesn't wear a Helmet, but I noticed that he accesses his arm implant and his wristwatch a lot. Sometimes when I say something that makes him laugh, and especially if I say something that makes him smile and nod, he will quickly look down at his arm and hand. He doesn't think I notice. But I do.

I watch him a lot. I suppose, out of all the things and people I am learning to see as 'significant', Fred is the most important of all. Cause and effect: just like he told me to see things. I begin to understand how Fred thinks, how he sees things differently from me. And it isn't just because he is an N-P, but because he is Fred.

I actually told him that one day, trying to put all these feelings into words so that he would see things as I did and understand. It was starting to be important to me, that Fred knew how I saw things, understood my 'identity' and, most of all, that he liked me.

'It's good being with you so much. You make me feel special.'

'And I like being with you, Sim. You are a remarkable young woman. You learn so fast.'

We were on one of our many walks. The bright sunshine would have almost persuaded me not to turn on the enhancers, even in the days before Fred. Now I didn't even think about it. I tried to remember the occasion when I had last activated them: even the thought of doing so now seemed unnecessary and strange. Instead I felt a warm glow of comfort from thinking about things I had recently done: that's me, Sim, doing things, living the life that is mine, that is my 'identity'.

The sun blazed down unenhanced and sweltering. Because it was hot anyway, the thermo-sensors in my dress had made it as light as possible, so light it floated like air around my legs and billowed as I walked, keeping step with Fred.

'But you've made me see everything so differently. You've changed everything: I have an identity –' the term was still novel enough for me to enjoy saying it, whenever I could – 'I never really knew what identity was, what it meant, until I met you.'

Fred looked down at me as we carried on walking and at the same moment I stared up at him. Normally, when we talked and walked, we stared straight ahead or at the things that he pointed out to me. And at that moment I felt as I used to when I had enhancers inside me going on to maximum mode. It was a feeling that had been growing – these new enhancers that I never knew I had, had been slowly turning themselves up on to stronger and stronger mode every time I thought of Fred, and all the fun and wonderfulness that was there each time I was with him. But now all that suddenly was so strong it was unbearable, and I didn't know what to do.

Fred stopped and so did I: he put his hand under my chin and tilted it up further, so all I could do was look into his eyes. His voice had changed, had become so soft I could hardly hear him.

'I have never taught anyone as beautiful as you before. Sim, you make me feel so worthwhile.'

I didn't really understand this last bit. What did 'worthwhile' mean, and why was it good that someone else could make you feel you were something? Surely you were or you were not a certain type of person: how could an outside person make any difference? Especially me, Sim. Fred knew everything, told me everything, and was always right. What effect could *I* ever have on *him*?

My head went round with these silly questions. But it didn't matter because I was feeling so strange, as though I was melting, melting into Fred's eyes, and into Fred himself. Then he said something very unusual indeed.

'Sim, let's take off your Helmet.'

He had let the bicycle just fall on the ground. Another thing that was very unusual. It lay on its side, the wheels still slowly revolving, suddenly awkward, unloved, and lovely no longer. But in an instant Fred was like a different person. I had never seen him before in such a rush, and it was all especially strange since there was no reason for him to be. Nothing was happening around us, and there was no one else to be seen. But Fred was already loosening the Helmet strap with the other hand that wasn't angling my chin. Although he was staring right at me, not even blinking, he seemed not to see me any more. His voice was coming in strange, short breaths now, almost as an afterthought to some kind of other urgency.

'And let's take off this, this dress thing.'

I had got so used to the Helmet, I'd almost forgotten what it was to be outside without it, and to feel the air blow the long strands of hair across my face. But it was still stranger now to step outside of my garment: I only did so in the wash-waste, and never outside. I could feel the heat of the sun on my skin all over, and then my hair became damper and I felt it sticking to my bare back. It reminded me a bit of the feeling I used to have when I ran all the time, only this time it was so much stronger, nicer – much nicer.

What happened next was something I could never have imagined, not even since Fred had taught me how to think, and indeed how to imagine. In all the databases and fact-finding and learning about significance and meaning, what happened next was something I couldn't understand at all. By now, Fred had also unwrapped all his layers of grey clothes: they lay about us like little colourless hills. He came up very close and stood right in front of me, looming over me, so our bodies were almost touching. And then they were. Then he gently but firmly pushed me down on to the coarse, thick fabric – pushing down and down. And then in me.

Time stopped. My identity stopped.

Afterwards, after he had started to breathe normally again, his voice finally came back. It was still croaky and soft.

'Sim, do you know what we've just done?'

'I think so. I think the Fact-Totum says it's what people used to do before the reproduction programs made everything so much easier. Or perhaps it was Zelda who told me.'

My voice came out in strangled little gasps. Fred was lying on top of me and was very heavy, his whole body pressing down so I could hardly breathe. But then he sat up and ran both hands over his stubbly grey head.

'Sim, I'm going to say something very important now.'

His voice had returned to the familiar tones I loved: yes, 'loved' would be the right word for what I now felt, but not for how he had been a moment or so ago. Fred was speaking again in way that was so much back to the teacher's voice that

I recognized, that I suddenly felt very stupid lying on my back on my own, with no clothes on at all, squinting at the sun. I propped myself up on an elbow and looked back up into his eyes. But he had looked away, was looking around everywhere as though he had lost something, was now pulling on his rumpled grey clothes.

'Sim, you must not tell Zelda about what we have done. It's our very special secret.'

A secret. A new word. Another new, shiny idea: something else that I couldn't see or hold, but that was very important. But the hardest thing of all to understand was that it, this secret, was something that Fred and I owned. I still found even this idea hard, that a person 'possessed' something, some object that wasn't part of them, didn't even interact with them, but was still special to them and no one else. But I knew that even though I didn't 'own' anything myself, it could be possible: Fred with his bicycle was what I thought of every time he spoke about 'having' something. But now it was almost impossible: how could Fred and I both 'own' the same thing, and especially something that didn't appear to exist?

'What's a secret?'

Now Fred seemed to be angry, perhaps angry with himself. 'Is there no end to the work to be done?'

But I knew he was asking himself the question, not me. Shaking his head, he sighed and finally looked at me.

'Dear Sim, a secret is one of the most special and important things in the world. A secret is something that some people, like Zelda, must never know.'

This was the strangest idea yet. Everyone could know everything, after all. Fred had told me about the special computers that the N-Ps had, 'quantum' computers that meant, or so I thought, that no one could hide anything. And why should they want to? It seemed to me that having a secret served no purpose at all. Why shouldn't everyone know everything? Even here, anyone who wanted could access the Fact-Totum for any question they had. And the Fact-Totum knew everything.

'But how can we know something and the Fact-Totum not know it?'

'Because the Fact-Totum only knows facts.'

A throwaway, flat, fast voice now.

'But what we've done is a fact.'

Fred's mouth was now a tight straight line. He leant down and put both hands firmly either side of my shoulders.

'Listen, Sim. It's very simple. Even for you. Just don't tell anyone. Now put your dress on, and your Helmet.'

He had turned his back on me and was gathering up the crumpled last bit of grey fabric on which we had been lying so recently. I felt sticky and sore, and most of all, sad. Fred didn't seem to like me any more, seemed to think even that I was not special or clever. The most hurtful thing of all was that he hadn't needed to ask me not to tell Zelda anything anyway. It was always Zelda telling me things, always just her talking. Even before Fred moved into the Dwelling, I didn't tell Zelda anything really. Anyhow, what did she need to know from me that she couldn't have asked the Fact-Totum?

And until I had met Fred, there was nothing inside me, nothing about what it felt like inside me that I wanted or needed to tell anyone else. The secret would stay our secret if that was just a funny way after all of saying that I wouldn't tell Zelda. Of course I wouldn't. Fred was now paying all of his attention to the bicycle. He had pulled it back up to its normal, upright position, and was gently dusting a thin coating of earth from it with his bare hand. Almost caressing it with care and concern. Finally wheeling it on one side, Fred walked back with me on the other side as we might always have done, not touching, but also not talking.

'I'm sorry, Sim,' he said eventually.

The luminous, multicoloured roofs of the Dwellings came into view. The figures that were always dancing and turning around outside became more distinct, though always looking the same and identical to each other. Apart from one, a familiar figure with red-gold hair still gleaming faintly in the now fading light: Zelda. Arms folded, waiting for us, squinting into the setting sun, looking for us. She and Fred smiled at each other. I went alone into a corner of the Dwelling, just as I had done all my life, and for the first time for a long time deployed a hologram experience, fast and loud and bright. Sometimes previously, I had taken to imagining that the witch was a bit like Zelda while the prince, of course, was Fred. But now I was sick of that story. I didn't feel like telling the Dark Man all that had happened, but I knew I had to. Then I wanted to select a hologram-time just of dancing with lots of other people, which wouldn't be a story at all.

Chapter 27

FRED

The past, the present and the future ... let me get organized and try to think of the Hodge communications like that. Until a while ago, the past was predictable. My reports, though a bit less often I suppose, and with less detail of my daily life, had none the less told of a story we had expected, and what I had once really hoped for.

Phase 3 making a clear impact: estimate assemblies now showing a very different profile. Effects of direct stimulation increases assembly size and reduces overall number even in adult. Overall index, higher. Subsequent observation that even after extensive period of direct stimulation, assembly still continuing to grow with heightened control from prefrontal cortex (PFC).

Surely Hodge could be content with that. Anyway it will have to do. Let him have his reports when I feel like it, not when I'm commanded. I need to be a free man. He can have the data, but he'll have to work it out all by himself from the raw, basic facts: my heart is no longer in lengthy explanations.

There is nothing in Sim's read-outs to suggest that Phase 3 is not going to plan, yet I've described to Hodge nothing that indicates what is really happening to Sim's behaviour as her cognitive powers have grown. The assemblies in Sim's brain are now gradually expanding on their own, having been primed by direct stimulation: in particular, her prefrontal cortex is steadily more active and seems to play a role in ensuring cohesion with the other transient assemblies that ceaselessly form and re-form every moment. These bigger assemblies will mean an ever deeper consciousness. Hodge will already know this: why should I waste precious time giving him actual examples? And anyway I have other things to think about. There is something that is starting to trouble me, something that just won't go away.

At first I had made sure to remove her Helmet before I touched the Sim creature: but then I suppose it was a strange mixture of carelessness and personal curiosity that tempted me to leave her Helmet on occasionally, to see what happened in her brain during copulation.

As Hodge and I had discussed quite often, the mature and healthy human brain could always revert to the sensational mode of 'wine, women and song', of 'drugs and sex and rock 'n' roll. Since these were times of extreme feeling and no thought, no self-consciousness, no identity, I predicted that just for those few moments 'letting herself go', literally, that Sim's brain would revert back to the state of pure joy and abandonment, the mindless sensuality that had characterized her mental state as a generic Other, before I came into her life.

For my reports to Hodge, I already had my explanation cut and dried: I would tell him that during these periods, Sim was doing something else highly sensory and non-cognitive – the easiest and most plausible scenario could be eating – when she felt a pure pleasure that I assumed was a pale echo of what she experienced with me: but enough to show how the human brain could revert to a more childlike state during times of extreme emotion and hedonism.

In such cases, I would have predicted a complete shutdown of the frontal part of her brain, her PFC, and an ensuing pattern of much smaller, more fragmented assemblies: the profile would once again resemble the initial pattern we saw in her as a typical Other, namely that of a small child, schizophrenic, or a compulsive eater – anyone who put the physical sensation at a premium over a cognitive stance. But here was my worry: even at the climax of the copulation act, I was astonished to observe she was not reverting to the mindless mode, that Sim's brain remained in its new, developing mode of an ever active PFC with fewer but much larger assemblies.

She clearly was unable to unlearn, however transiently, what she had learnt from me. Her conceptual framework, realized as the literal network of neurons that enabled that heightened cognition, had evidently become very robust, even obstinately persistent: but at those special times, surely she should have been ecstatic, literally outside of herself. Yet curiously, despite the most extreme circumstances, she could not 'let herself go'. It meant she was now *always* in control of herself, self-conscious and dispassionate, as I rode the crest of the wave, as I surmounted this elemental being, she wasn't with me.

She would be the self-conscious observer.

This thought, slow and taunting, was now lurking there, creeping in from the periphery of my mind, to centre stage. She was not mine after all to create, shape and develop, not completely. But what *is* really happening? My thinking darts sideways, looking for an alternative to the most obvious conclusion. But face the cold truth: Sim cannot, or will not, ever experience passion. She is not carried away with ecstasy when she is with me, her creator. And that can only mean that I am no longer in complete control of her. I am failing as an N-P, failing as a neuroscientist in my own right and now … the terrible conclusion looms in front of me, massive, undeniable: I am failing as a man. I am less of a man. Fred the man is diminished. Who now is he?

All I can do is to shut out the past and the people in it that I am betraying, and the empty future where I have no significance. I now feel too sad and too small to ride the big, carefree bicycle. I no longer have anywhere to go. Nothing new to discover. But I keep it with me at all times as it is all that I have left. I can only go through the motions, the occasional and minimal scientific reports, the now mechanical sex act. And when I tire of doing what is expected by Hodge, by Zelda and by Sim, and by what I still expect of myself, then, mercifully, I can always reach for the pills.

Chapter 28

SIM

The day following the secret, it was as if nothing had happened. In fact it all seemed so unlikely that I could have imagined it, fabricated a new story about myself to help 'define my identity' as Fred would say. Yes, I could have made it up had it not been so very improbable. In any event, just as before, perhaps now more so, our walking and talking outside continued, me with the Helmet, Fred increasingly checking his implant.

'What is so special about your arm implant? I never need to look at mine.'

I was back to asking questions again, just as Fred required me to do.

'That's because the implants read out different things. Yours tells you about your body and ensures that it is working correctly. Mine tells me about my mind.'

'Mind' – another special word that Fred used a lot, but not in the same serious way he spoke of our secret. He said that the mind was all that made you different from everyone else. This mind was when your brain changed as a result of what happened to you and you alone. Fred said that it was this process that he knew so much about, and that had enticed him over to live with us in the Dwelling. He had shown me a picture on one of the Talking Head screens of what it looked like inside our heads: a wrinkly, lumpy thing that didn't move but could make me feel and now think. It made me who I was, Sim, living Sim's life, because the 100 billion tiny parts, the cells inside, were connected in a way that was changing all the time according to whatever I was doing. So the more I experienced as I lived out my life, the more the connections changed in a way that was increasingly special to me. This meant that as each day went by, and the connections changed again and again, so I became increasingly different from everyone else, more *me*.

I had never before thought about each day following on from the next, since before Fred they had always been the same as each other. I'd never thought of them kind of building on top of each other, at least in my brain, that is. But still, that's what the Helmet monitored: Fred told me what all this actual living would look like in the read-outs from the Helmet that we couldn't see because we didn't have the equipment. But he said we could imagine at first lots of bright patches all over my brain. That's what it would have looked like before Fred took over. But as we walked and talked more, the picture would be changing. There would be fewer patches lighting up: but the ones that were there were much bigger, and getting bigger each time. Fred called these patches 'assemblies' but didn't explain further what they were or what it all meant. But it was because I wasn't ready yet to understand. It wasn't because it was a secret.

Our secret, the real one, was still there: it happened again, and then again, bringing us close together and keeping us apart at the same time. It became a normal part of our daily outings, not every day, but quite often. Fred would always be the one to decide. Whenever he asked me to take off the Helmet, he seemed to change: he didn't speak so much, in fact hardly at all. And when he did, it was as though he didn't know anything about me or who I was: he no longer cared at all about my identity. It was almost as if he didn't actually like me. Not in the same way as when we talked all the time, and I was wearing the Helmet and my dress. But although Fred seemed like someone else during those secret times, I gradually found them less uncomfortable and strange. Sometimes he made me keep my helmet on. And because Fred seemed to become happy in a different sort of way, I was happy enough to let him. It wasn't important.

'I'm teaching you something more, something you would never have learnt or experienced if I had never appeared.'

Fred had told me this one day as he was lying back afterwards, his grey curly hair on the folded grey clothing, staring up into a sky with grey clouds forming and re-forming, a bit like the 'assemblies' in my brain. I lay next to him and said nothing. I had learnt also that during these secret times, if Fred spoke at all he didn't like me to say anything back. So we both looked up at the sky, high and wide and cloudy above us. The moment seemed to last forever, with nothing else happening.

Until Fred came into my life, I would have thought it strange, boring, to just be lying there without even my enhancers on, and not moving. But because Fred was my special teacher, because he had changed me and my life so much, I would lie there for as long as he wanted – until he told me to stand up. Somehow, Fred knew this – that I would lie there until he told me the secret time was over and that I should stand up and put my garment and Helmet back on.

One day, as we lay there, his breathing became heavy again like it did at the beginning of our special times. But now it was slow and regular. I turned my head and saw that his eyes were not looking at the sky any more, but were tight shut. He was asleep. This no longer surprised me, Fred sleeping in the daytime.

He said it was because he had to work a lot and think during the night: but I knew it was because he sometimes took sleep enhancers, like I used to see Zelda do. Ever since we'd started playing the new game inside, I realized I understood a lot more.

So I stared at the sky again, then looked back at Fred, his brain now working in a different way, in a lesser way. It was interesting to see him without all the grey clothing hiding everything. As he lay with his head now turned, resting on one crooked arm, I noticed the other arm, flat and open, limp by his side. Nothing special. Just an arm really, with his grey-white skin, black hairs – and the tiny scar under which lay the implant.

I gently brushed my fingers along the arm: Fred didn't respond at all, and the breathing continued slow and deep and regular. He'd said that our implants were different: but just because they registered different things didn't mean they worked in different ways. The read-out would come into his ear via the nano-device that everyone used, or would be converted into a visual signal via nano-interception in the retina. But since he was asleep, and since we had just had one of our secret times, his monitors would be turned off. I turned mine on. Because no one's body in the Dwelling ever got close to anyone else's any more, there had been no need to safeguard each person's individual read-out. In any case, everyone could know everything about everyone else, probably because there was so little to know anyway. So, I wondered, would my monitors pick up Fred's read-out? Would I be able to look for myself at Fred's wonderful mind?

The slow, heavy breathing continued. I leant near to the implant, a small pucker of skin where it had been inserted when Fred was born. Gently and silently, I brought my upper arm to almost touch his, so that now the skin surface under which my implant was starting to buzz, was in direct contact with the faint pucker on the white skin below. His wristwatch was starting to display numbers and then squiggly words that I didn't know how to read, let alone understand.

But yes, I was getting a signal direct from under the skin: on my own system I would have as default anyway the audio read-out. I'd preferred that because staring at any visual images on a read-out about my body would slow down my running. And because the visual enhancers made everything around me look so exciting, it meant that visual read-outs of blood pressure and heart rate and glucose levels weren't much fun. If I looked at images, that would only be inside the Dwelling with a Talking Head. Like Zelda used to do all the time. But the implant was just for helping your body, and for that the audio worked best if you wanted to dance and run.

My ear monitor buzzed into life. The signal was strong enough for me to sit back on my heels, near enough to Fred but not so near I would wake him up. I waited while the menus were assembled. Then the voice listed the options. It was a very different voice from the one of my own implant. Mine was a soft but clear woman's voice: usually she would say simply that my body was too cold or too hot, or my energy levels were getting low. But this N-P voice was male and uncomforting: a distant, clipped articulation of words without any feelings.

'One: Basic ID details. Two: Early life. Three: Training and expertise. Four: Current life. Five: All professional and personal relationships. Six: Personal traits. Seven: Behaviour patterns over last ten days. Eight: Secret mission – Hodge direct.'

I had been about to select the option that covered personal relationships, to see if I was listed as the special one, the close one who shared a secret. But the last option suggested that he already had a secret with someone called Hodge. Was it our secret or a different one? Could you have more than one secret or share the one secret with more than one person? I had to find out straightaway.

'Eight,' I whispered as softly as I could, just in case Fred woke. A new, very different man's voice now spoke into my ear. This voice was not so much a clipped, clear sequence of syllables but a long drone, without any ups or downs. The words came out as facts, even less friendly than the Fact-Totum.

'Hodge communication number five-one-eight. Early progress in Phases 1 and 2 was as anticipated and desired: refer back reports numbers one through three-zero-five. Subject Sim performing well and according to plan. Cerebral assembly size clearly expanding, suggesting possible to adapt and start direct intervention via Helmet. PFC now much more active but still hypo-functional compared to normal. Clear correlation between increasing PFC activity and much increased assembly size within an overall reduced number of assemblies throughout the brain. Clearly indirect interventions through programs successful. Now appropriate to proceed with direct stimulation, full Phase 3.'

None of this made any sense. Perhaps there had been some kind of malfunction that resulted in words being strung together without meaning anything. I fast-forwarded.

'Hodge communication number five-two-zero. Phase 3 apparently as anticipated so far: but much concern here that your accounts now becoming increasingly intermittent and less detailed: refer reports three-zero-six to present.

Insufficient explanation as to why you are no longer in constant communication and why communication block with your implant increasing periods of time each day. Insufficient explanation as to why your reports lacking in any further progress or interpretation. Essential you respond now immediately, or whole mission could be in jeopardy, and recall only option. Next few days are critical in deciding on future use of, and status of, subject Sim: options will include being Boxed.'

I heard no more, but unfolded my legs: they felt weak and insubstantial as I shakily stood up and the implant synchrony was broken by the wider gap now between us. Fred still lay motionless and sprawled with his implanted arm flung loose and still untroubled, white-skinned and black-haired against the grey fabric. The metallic clouds continued to scud above us, him sleeping, me standing and wondering. As the signal had shut off, I had shut down my monitors both as a reflex and as a precaution. It would be all right if he woke now. But I felt very unsafe and unsure. I had intercepted a proper N-P conversation. They obviously talked differently to each other than when Fred the N-P spoke to either me or Zelda.

Who was this new person, Hodge? Why was I 'subject Sim'? Perhaps Fred was keeping a secret from me, just as we did from Zelda. Perhaps I wasn't the special one after all. If Fred talked about me to Hodge and planned how my brain was going to look, then how did he really think of me? In any case, what was a 'mission' and what was this particular mission? And then there was the biggest question of all: what could it mean for me to be 'Boxed'?

My throat was dry and my hands were damp and trembling, then all over my body I started shivering. All I knew was that

SUSAN GREENFIELD

I had to get away from Fred as quickly as possible and reached down for my Helmet, cast casually on one of the grey mounds of clothes. I pushed my head into its smooth, welcoming cavity and fastened it, all in one movement, practised and habitual: but was it even now transmitting messages to Hodge? I turned my implant back on as the rule was always to have it operational, apart from in the wash-waste. Immediately it started to admonish me in soft tones:

'Stress response, stress response: breathe deeply and remove immediately from current location.'

Obeying the instruction, again out of unthinking habit, I walked away, leaving Fred still unconscious on his grey pretend bed. Not so long ago I would have run, but now I needed to think.

306

Chapter 29

ZELDA

Looking back, it seems odd that there was no warning, that I had noticed nothing that could have been a harbinger of disaster and tragedy in the days, even the weeks, beforehand. Even that last morning there was no premonition as I opened my eyes in a sleepy, sweet haze, that I was to be blown apart, and that the embers of the little fire at my core would be stamped out forever into ashes. As my mind seeped into wakefulness, the past and the future coalesced, the happy, random thoughts of times with Fred and the prospect of what lay ahead that particular day.

That day, the day that was to be the worst day of my life, I was luxuriating in the early morning of half-sleep and half-thinking – no, not really thinking, just being. The walls around me complemented my mood via my body sensors by turning a soft, luminescent pink. In the days before Fred, at a time like this, I would probably have even switched on the audio-enhancers and closed my eyes to engorge the moment, but for a different reason. But before Fred I had wanted to escape from the world; now I wanted to bathe in all the experiences it was giving me. The escaping had never worked: I was too much of a previous time. The thinking would sooner or later trump the sensational – the understanding of who and where I was constantly kept me a prisoner. My only escape had been more drastic measures, the strong, blunt assault on the brain that only drugs could accomplish unconditionally and indiscriminately. My relentless understanding had once been a curse, a trap. Now it was the opening to a new life, a life with my soul-mate. It was all because I was different from the Others, as Fred now dared to refer to them to me, and indeed as I now thought of them. I was especially different from Sim.

Sim. My thickening moment, which had actually been swelling round and round Fred, now started to contract. My thinking embarked on straighter, simpler lines and moved forwards: undoubtedly, she was transformed. Fred had taught me well how and why such a change was inevitable, given the 'plasticity of the brain', another of his favourite phrases. But neither of us, in our more professional and scientific discussions over meals, would have been able to predict exactly what would happen, or to what extent. Why else bother embarking on such a great and strange adventure, if the answers were already known down to the last detail? After all, that was the whole point of his visit.

Ever since we had implemented Phase 3 and started stimulating Sim's brain directly, enhancing and giving ever more meaning to each of her experiences, so she was responding and behaving even more dramatically than during Phase 2. For example, she was no longer using her enhancers at all. She no longer danced, and she rarely laughed. When she wasn't with Fred – which was increasingly rare – I would often see her suspended in time, head to one side, looking inwards. She had never been affectionate: now she seemed downright cold. Outwardly, anyone observing would have said she was far more curious: but I who knew her would have doubted whether she could ever understand other people, or relationships such as the one I had with Fred. I smiled to myself at the very use of the term.

A relationship was a concept, a way of life that, just like reading, had faded into extinction with the end of my grandparents' time. But I now had a relationship. Unlike all the Others, I at least knew that a relationship was like a thought process, like the iterative walks on which the N-Ps apparently placed so much importance. It was an interaction: on the one hand, then on the other. It was each modifying the other, being a separate component, but where the end result was more than merely the sum of the two. It was being A Couple, recognizing your soul-mate in an ever changing action-reaction that went on and on … I felt little flames strong and bright inside me spreading a warm glow to my fingertips and toes.

Even as those last few minutes of happiness were ticking away, there was still no alarm bells: I don't remember actually doing anything or looking anywhere in particular as I just lay smiling to myself on my back, limbs spread-eagled. The immediate past, the almost definite future, it was all there, all mine, ours – mine and Fred's. Then the moment shrivelled as fast and as completely as a burst balloon. Sim burst everything. Her shrill siren wail swirled into my ears and deafened my brain.

'Zelda, where are you! Where *are* you!'

Then she was standing, panting, in front of me. The pink bloom on her face had been washed out and bleached white. Her eyes were reddened and frantic, darting everywhere and seeing nothing. Although rooted to the spot in front of me, everything about her was on the move: her fingers pulling at the strands of damp hair, plucking at her thin tunic, and her whole body racked and heaving with primeval sobs that punctuated her urgent speech.

'Fred, Fred. He has secrets. Hodge. With Hodge. He wants me Boxed. I'm not special. Not at all. Just a, a subject. Not Sim. Just subject Sim. And Fred doesn't really like me. He tells Hodge about me. So I'm not special, not to him. He doesn't care. He doesn't care about, about my identity. And he said he did.'

This last series of statements had been escalating in pitch and ended in a wavering, drawn-out whine, as though she had been physically wounded. But it was the very last, the final, statement before her garble collapsed into complete incoherence that pitched me forward and over into the abyss. As I was falling, the words echoed from a long way off.

'He doesn't care. AND HE SAID HE DID.'

I had fallen all the way and was at the bottom now, in a narrow, black, suffocating place. I was all on my own. No one could get me, no one could hear me. Only over a very, very long distance. My stomach churned and my throat went dry: my implant started to bleep that I was undergoing a stress response. But I couldn't even bother to turn it off. Any movement would have been too much effort, too much distraction from this single, simple thought. Of course. His long absences with Sim. The increasingly frequent absences from me at night. I now remembered from the time of bright romance that there was that other story too, the darker one that so very often overshadowed couples: someone else lurking in the shadows to spoil things, to tarnish the shiny ending. You never knew what had happened or how or when: but as soon as you knew, you realized you'd known for much longer already.

Sim had been there for a long time, betraying me. The baby, the beautiful little girl who had once been the centre of my life, had paid me back with casually wrecking everything that was worth living for. With a shake of her yellow hair and a flick of her flimsy clothes she had stamped on my life-story with Fred.

Like a malign fairy she had slid in, insinuating herself between me and my soul-mate, stealing his soul from me.

And the worst of it, I realized, even though I was suffocating at the bottom of the abyss, was that of course she didn't understand what she had done. I hated her then, not so much for the careless, powerful perfection of her face and body, but more because she was so stupid. She understood nothing. Every fibre in my being ached, every part of me knew with absolute certainty now what Sim had done. With Fred. But still, I needed to be sure. Would she hear me shouting up from such a long way down in my dark, dark prison that was also a sanctuary?

'Sim, have you and Fred touched each other? Has he been very, very close to you?'

My voice indeed sounded muffled and a faraway echo from someone else's misery. But as the air closed around me like a solid fog, silencing and softening and distancing everything, I could still make out her eyes widening, could see that she was looking around for an answer. In contrast to my deep, slow, distant murmur, Sim's voice was sqeaking and tinny, short-distance, short-term.

'It's a secret. I wasn't to tell you. But now he has the secret with Hodge. So I can, well I will anyway. And because I'm scared. Help me: I'm scared of the boxing secret. What will happen to me?'

My throat felt sick, but my stomach was rock hard. Where once the little fire had flickered and glowed, now there was just the dirty hearth and a hard, cold slab of hatred. All dead, all still, all nothing. I was finally able to focus, look around my new prison at the bottom of the abyss. The significance of what Sim had done with Fred obviously couldn't register with her still limited brain capacity. And lacking any imagination or interest in anyone other than herself, she obviously would never have envisioned that Fred and I, Fred and I ... I focus again: had to stay focused in order to get my bearings down there in the darkness, to find a direction. I pushed my mind to think of this new name, a name that held no pain, this entity called Hodge. An N-P inevitably, a colleague of Fred's, obviously. Someone with whom Fred was in dialogue, but whom he had never mentioned. Why not? Why couldn't he have told me more about what he was reporting back to the N-Ps? He shared everything with me, meals, the past, plans. Why hadn't he shared the reports with me, his one true partner?

If it was that the content was too technical, too hard for me, even though I was learning so much so quickly – then surely he could still have merely mentioned Hodge, and described a little the conversations that he had with him. No, he couldn't. Because he was betraying me. Because he wasn't the person I thought he was. He is only what he said he was, an N-P. Nothing is what I thought it was. Relationships don't exist, not any more. This is why they died, when my grandparents died. It was all a story. Better to be an Other. This is what happens when you think so much: it's all just in your head. Nothing is real any longer. So now I have to make real things happen.

'Nothing at all will happen to you. You will just carry on with your pointless little life and your empty brain.'

My own voice sounded flat and very distant: it was someone else who was still speaking. From a long, numb distance, I saw Sim's lip tremble and her trashy, flashy round eyes became red and watery. Her chin wobbled as her lower lip trembled convulsively.

'But that's not true, Zelda. I have a good brain, a mind that's growing. I have an identity.'

The last word came out almost as a scream. Now her whole face was reddening, her voice louder.

'Listen, just you listen.'

And with that she fumbled around, one hand reaching around beneath the hampering gossamer, grasping for that special place on her other upper arm: her normal grace turned clumsy with her sobbing, as she at last activated her implant. Why? Why, at a time like this, when I was at the bottom of the abyss, and had just smashed her precious, pathetic little identity into ruins? Why activate the implant? But she was concentrating now, selecting something to play me, as she turned up the volume for third-party access.

'Hodge communication –' fast-forward, she needed something very specific – 'Subject Sim performing well and according to plan. Cerebral assembly size –'

Fast-forward again … of course, in her normal self-centred way, she was searching in some kind of report for the places where she specifically was mentioned.

'Essential –' too soon, more speed forward – 'whole mission could be in jeopardy, and recall only option. Next few days are critical in deciding on future use of, and status of, subject Sim: options will include being Boxed.'

I understood now. Crouched, hunched in the abyss, it was almost a relief to have a simple and immediate problem to solve, just piecing together facts, making sense of an incomplete flood of consciousness from a self-obsessed child. Obviously, Sim and Fred had been in such close proximity that her implant had picked up messages from his device. But messages from whom? Who *was* Hodge? Not a high-priority question, though. Not just now. Not when I'd just heard how the person I had truly loved – I realized that now – was not after all simply planning, but plotting. He wasn't a high-minded scientist who had found a soul-mate and shared with her secrets of the brain and secrets of his own life. Instead his skills were somehow being twisted for some kind of sinister purpose beyond the pure one of simple understanding. Far from sharing and building, he was rejecting and destroying. And all possible because of the snivelling, meaningless, pointless slut in front of me. She had indeed become an irrelevance. I needed to focus, to plan, to turn Fred over and over in my mind. She was just an irritation and a distraction. I wanted rid of her.

'I never want to see you again, Sim. This is all your fault. Go off and be an egg donor, or a womb donor. That's all you're good for, all you'll ever do. That's what boxing means'.

I suddenly had an inspired, spiteful way of hurting her, 'It means packing you off, out of Fred's life. Because he doesn't want you near him any more.'

I stared at her, through her. She wasn't my daughter, after all. I thought I could guess what boxing might really mean. However the phrasing in the communication had been ambiguous: was it an option for Fred or for Sim? Yet I no longer cared. Perhaps I even welcomed that prospect for Sim. Or perhaps not. The numbness was so great, the silence down there at the bottom of the abyss so all-enveloping, that nothing really mattered, certainly not her. But she carried on, doing nothing, standing swaying slightly on the spot. Still whining and sniffing. An unlovely trail of colourless fluid was inching unchecked from her nose; her eyes were puffy. But her chin was still pointed upwards, though perhaps teetering on defeat.

'My brain is special. It makes me special. I have an identity, my own identity. And I have special secret times with Fred.'

The last sentence wounded the most, even though I thought I was completely numbed. I screamed up the echoing abyss walls: I had to be heard. I couldn't risk these words being lost and absorbed within the high, black rock walls.

'None of that is true. Fred hates you. He wants you to go away. Just like I do.'

She heard. Silence at first. She was calmer now. I could tell that she was trying to make the most of her new-found ability to think, to understand.

'You're saying that because you want to be like me. You want to have a secret with Fred. You want to be special too, but you can't. So you're spoiling it. Zelda, it's *you* that should go away. You come from a different time anyway, the time that the Fact-Totum says there were old people and they died slowly. You're old and I wish you were dead, dying right now.'

She was shaking her head slowly as though the power of this reasoning was a novel and heavy process. The sobs had stopped, had given way to deep breaths. She realized, perhaps too late, that she couldn't say anything more final. Tossing her knotted hair, she bit her lip in some kind of resolution, turned and stumbled out of my life. So much for my baby, my princess. So much for all the stories and the enchantment. I would care later, perhaps I would care later. Right now, just now, I was no longer an entity that felt anything. I was heartless: I was just one single, pure, uncontaminated thought. I knew exactly what I had to do, and whom I had to see. And yet I was still crawling along in the blackness at the bottom of my abyss. I stumbled outside, oblivious to the bright day, the normal scenes of bright twirling. I wasn't sure where I'd find him. It didn't matter, since nothing else did.

I have no idea how long it took as I wandered aimlessly with no direction, searching for that very familiar, very distinctive figure. It was still daylight, though, when eventually I saw him. He was sitting on his outer garment, grey as all the other clothes he wore: the lilac bicycle was propped up against a nearby tree, but all his concentration appeared to be directed towards his implant. He was hunched over his upper arm, head and face close up to the exposed flesh, occasionally glancing back and forth at the external watch device on his wrist. He did not see me, walking slowly now, towards him. Only when I was standing right over him, blotting out the bright light, casting a long shadow, only then did he look up. It took a moment for him to register what was happening, who I was, and why I might be there. The creased face was wary, waiting, deliberately blank.

'Zelda.'

He spoke my name softly, almost as a question.

'I know. I know everything.'

In contrast my own voice sounded metallic, grating, unloving and unlovable. Like the machine that I had now become. But at least I was in control. For a short time, a time period of my choosing, I knew things of which this N-P was still unaware. I would play slowly: after all, the stakes were high.

'Hodge.'

I dropped the name, the one word like a stone in a puddle, and watched the ripples spread out through Fred's brain. The one betrayal would suffice for now; hold the other one, the most painful one, back awhile.

'Yes, Zelda, Hodge is my senior colleague.'

He was now on the defensive, building walls around his body, his eyes, his words. With a casualness that was poorly feigned, he asked, 'How do you know of him?'

'Because I've heard the reports he sends you. I know everything about your secret plot.'

For my part this was, of course, not strictly true. But I came from a time before imagination had not been completely suppressed, and the relationship with Fred had enabled me to rehearse and practise the old skills from when I sat on my grandmother's knee. I had imagined the witches and the princesses with an evil and a beauty that wildly surpassed any reality: and then as I matured to complex plots and interwoven storylines, I had guessed the anonymous miscreants well before my grandmother – or so she allowed me to believe at the time.

As I'd crouched and hunched my body foetus-like in the abyss after Sim had left, I'd thought of logic and likelihoods rather than, rather than … Anyway, it was neither hard nor improbable to guess what the N-Ps wished to do. How stupid I had been to believe him: of course, they would never have 'just studied' Sim's brain without a clear purpose. The final goal was to do us harm in some way, to destroy us or, at the very least, our way of life. Studying Sim's brain for a purpose other than mere study. 'Sequence and consequence,' he would have been the first to recite, to take comfort in the phrase – in any other situation. But for now he was silent, trying to gauge how much I really knew, how to play it.

'So what are you going to do?'

What would indeed be the consequence? That was the all-important issue for him, I noticed, not the evidence and how I had accessed it: that was the past, now leading up to this uncertain, unpredictable present. And it was the present, indeed the immediate future, which had to be his highest priority.

'It depends, Fred. On you.'

Even now, even after the betrayals with Hodge and with Sim, even now I wanted him to lie, and for the lie to be the truth. If he said we were a couple, wonderful, close, lifetime partners, then we would pave a way forward together. I was back on my grand-mother's knee, with stories where anything was possible, and it all came right in the end. I spoke quickly: there was no time to lose.

'We could escape, go away from the Dwelling and the Grouping. You could forget you were an N-P, and I could forget I was an Other. We could be together properly: just be ourselves. You and me. We wouldn't need anything else, or anyone else …'

I was almost believing it, the fairytale that I could now so readily conjure up, when abruptly Fred stood up, and placed each of his hands either side on my shoulders, but with no affection.

'Zelda, stop it, just stop it. You don't know what you're saying. In so many ways you have it so wrong.'

Exasperated, he took his hands from me, ran them through his hair and looked up at the sky, then desperately and longingly at his slumbering dream bicycle.

'You don't understand about us, about N-Ps. I could never, *ever* cease being an N-P because it's not just a name, not just a way of life: it's the whole purpose of life. Do you really think I could stop thinking and believing in and about everything that mattered to me?'

A mirthless laugh.

'And in any event, we are not like you Others, dancing around with nothing mattering. Everything matters, everyone matters. There could never be escape. They will always find you. And anyway, where would I go and what would I be? Why on earth would I want to leave? '

Clearly, I was back in the enemy category. We were no longer working together. The divide was clear between us. I felt as though the ground had crumbled away from under me.

'For me.' A barely audible squeak. 'You could change your life for me.'

Then I just stared at the ground.

'Zelda, we have had a special time together. When I first met you, you made me feel a different person, and we had conversations and a kind of mental and physical experience that I had never had with Tarra.'

'Tarra?'

'My Breeding Partner. She is an extension of me. We fit together, go together. That's how it's supposed to be. She's my soul-mate and we have a little boy, Bill. That's what real life is.

With you, I had a brief and powerful insight into being someone else, discovering new ways of seeing the world. It was like reading a book, a very good book. For a while, until you come to the end, the real world can be put on hold. But now we've come to the end, Zelda'.

I hadn't really listened fully to the last few sentences: they had been eclipsed by two words. Two words that hurt even more, if that were possible, than Sim: soul-mate. Someone else was his soul-mate, someone I'd never met and never knew existed. Fred had never spoken of how he personally lived among his own people. Perhaps I has just assumed that N-Ps, like us, had no one special in their lives. In retrospect, I now realized, I should have found it strange and suspicious, at least questioned Fred about it. But perhaps I already was suspecting something I didn't want to hear. And that's why I'd never asked. He wasn't my soul-mate, though. Could never have been: how could you have two? It had all been a sham. His past, present and future – his life – was nothing, *nothing* like I had perceived it. I had loved someone who had never existed.

'So, I'll tell you what I'm going to do.'

Now I was angry, unloved, blighted with bitterness. It had slipped his mind that I knew about the plot. For a moment he was so busy defending himself to me, playing the model N-P, the model 'Breeding Partner', someone else's soul-mate: and he was unaware that I had also learnt that he was no longer exemplary in the eyes of Hodge.

'I'll tell Hodge.'

I was almost laughing, mocking.

'Your reports are failing, you're not staying in contact and he'll know why now. Oh yes, he'll know it's because you have had sex with your subject, the precious Sim. You've been carried away by your emotions. You've told me that's the worst offence possible. You're unreliable. But now everyone here will know:

I can announce it on the screens in the Dwelling and everyone will know very soon. Someone will get you. One of us Others will get you. Then Hodge's plans will fail, and all because of you. The N-Ps will lose, even though you all give up so much just so that you can think all the time and think you know everything. You don't.'

My voice reached its crescendo, cracked on the last sentence, then stopped. Fred had become silent and white, almost grey. The creases in his face had deepened as I was speaking, and his shoulders rounded.

'Zelda, let me tell you how it has been since I arrived here, how hard. You Others stood, stand for, everything we despise, that we know threatens the advance of the human species to reach its full potential. Just think, if the brain could understand itself – it just *might* be possible.'

For a moment he had forgotten the bleak plight he was in, transported by pure thought. He was resorting to stereotyped sentiments, a reflex strutting like a decapitated chicken. His voice stated to lift, lighten, even bubble slightly with excitement or perhaps hysteria.

'And most amazing of all, we might eventually understand consciousness itself – how the brain in a body reports to something inside that can only be the brain in its body …'

It was a rote speech from another time in his life, now surfacing out of context. A stereotyped response. Absurd. But the inability to take this thought further brought him back to the dire reality.

'But when I came here, it was indeed to understand how your brains worked differently from ours. That is still true, it's just as I informed you. I didn't tell you what Hodge wanted, I know: but that's because you didn't *need* to know, Zelda.'

He was almost pleading with me now.

'You see, you would have ended up having a better life, you

still could. You're right: I must stop copulating with Sim. She obviously told you our little secret: perhaps that was inevitable, given you're her carer. But I wonder if you'll ever understand how she was so different from Tarra, and of course from you. Sim is wild, elemental, a creature. Being with her is not like being with another person, someone who's the same as you. She's an experience: being with her is pure feeling, but in a new and powerful domain. It's all feeling. At least for me.'

He sighed, shook his head in disbelief at what was happening.

'But I do need to get back in control. I don't know what's been happening to me. I don't know who I really am any more. The reports are getting harder to write, and I'm confused over the interpretation of Sim's brain processes, her neuronal assemblies. It's because of the heightened sensationalism here – I always knew it would be a problem anyway – but now I've had such an experience with Sim, I can't think for long periods of time alone, as I used to.'

'What about the experience with me?'

'That was just a story, Zelda, a fairy story.'

We had started to walk back towards the Dwelling. Our bodies moved in step and at the same pace, but our shoulders and arms didn't touch. The cold dead heart inside me grew heavier and heavier until I was entirely just that, a cold heavy lump. Plodding towards what end?

'You are a wonderful heroine, of course. Especially given your age: I mean, an N-P woman of your years would never, ever look like you, be like you.'

So Fred, like Sim, found me misplaced, an anachronism. Story over. And we had no future. It was as though my time with Fred had never been. I was back at the beginning again, just like in the screen games: everything had been so readily reversed. But this time I couldn't just play the game again.

Fred would not come back to me. Fred no longer loved me, even liked me. I was now an irrelevance, or perhaps worse, an impediment to him and Hodge – grey, cold, uncaring N-Ps – doing something terrible.

Well, at least I could be that: an impediment. I could do something that would be real, that would show him I wasn't just a story, show Sim, both of them, that I might be finished as someone else's story, but I could still do something that would have significance, long-lasting significance. Despite my confident threat, I had no idea how anyone in my own careless, hedonistic society would ever get round to 'getting' Fred. Perhaps something so threatening to our way of life, once broadcast via the screen network, would activate some automated retaliation. But I had no idea, like everyone else, how everything worked so well. Better instead to let his own people follow their procedures.

'I'm reporting to Hodge that you have disobeyed the basic N-P rules: you've put pleasure and experiences where you let yourself go, above the ideals of purpose, of consequence, of final and ultimate goal.'

'If you try and communicate with Hodge, Zelda –'

Fred's voice was monotone and strong now: he was emphatic, though it obviously took great effort – 'if you try and contact him, then you will be putting yourself in great danger. This mission is too important to fail: the ensuing plans are long term and large scale. We are at the threshold of our destiny. You will be the only person standing between much planning and the step-by-step coordination of the final goal. Just think about it.'

It was true in part. Although Sim knew about the communication with Hodge, she didn't understand it. All she cared about was herself. So, after all, I was indeed unique: in this regard alone, I would be distinctive, memorable. Someone who made irreversible things happen. I could press my Fact-Totum input facility, something that was rarely used but enabled us to feed in facts and issue instructions. Since we normally were receptive rather than proactive, it was a procedure that I was not completely swift at performing. But good enough. When Sim had played me the message, it would have been stored in my own incoming sensory information bank. Replying back to Hodge would be easy now that I had his original message. My reply message need not be long and I had already drafted it in my mind while searching for Fred. Once it was sent it could not be reversed. This was, after all, no game. Fred's face was frozen with fury.

'You fool. You'll have us all dead. I wish you were, I truly do. It's what you deserve, all you are good for.'

Our fate was sealed then: whatever it was, there was nothing else we could say to each other. The sequence of dialogue was over. The consequences would now unfold. Condemned, we walked in silence, further apart but still in the same direction. We were, after all, both walking towards the Dwelling. Eventually the lurid multicoloured glow of the buildings came nearer, in cruel ridicule of all I had wanted, and lost. As usual, isolated figures gyrated and twirled in their own spaces in the area outside. As we approached, I could make out that one was Sim, but she wasn't really moving. And as we drew nearer still, I could see that she was bent over, clearly unwell. Of course, no one was bothering to help her. Now she was on her knees, on all fours, her back humped in convulsions. Her implant was issuing instructions but she was obviously not in a state even to hear what they said. She was actually being sick, vomiting over the earthy ground.

'Like Tarra with Bill,' Fred muttered almost to himself.

But I heard as though he had spoken at five hundred decibels. I was deafened, and the abyss cracked apart to open up yet further depths: I tumbled down blinded into a blackness that was utter, complete, final. Sim a mother. The mother of Fred's child. The child that should have been mine, but that I could never, ever have. I stopped.

Fred carried on walking without looking back, wheeling his bicycle, as though I no longer existed. I waited until he was well out of range: just in case, just in case he turned back. All I needed now was for him just to turn his head even, and look over his shoulder. But I was no longer of the present time. Staring at the retreating grey figure, asymmetric with the lilac gleam on one side, I pushed up my flimsy sleeve and whispered into my implant the short missive, ready and already so rehearsed in my head, that by now it was fluent, fast, word perfect.

Chapter 30

FRED

The sun was bright and high in the sky. But a cold breeze had been strong enough to awaken me. I immediately pulled my loose grey clothes tighter and closer. They felt rough on my bare skin. The loveless landscape around me was empty. As usual, I'd made sure we had walked well away from the Dwellings. No solitary figures danced in this empty place. And so I looked around with no particular urgency. And no real purpose.

It didn't strike me as particularly odd that Sim wasn't there. It didn't really matter. She didn't really matter much any more. When I filled her up, emptied myself into her body as well, I once thought my power over her was absolute, both mental and physical. But it wasn't. What irony that my own technology, my own experiments, had revealed how inadequate I was. But it didn't matter. Why should it matter? Surely it was the feeling of the moment that was reality, not thoughts about other people. Insubstantial absurd thoughts doing nothing but flitting around inside your head.

Before I'd reached for the little capsule, I remember culminating that last time just as I had always done, with the abandonment of pouring and pouring into her, evacuating myself so that the other absence, the darkness of complete sleep, could then take me over. But now I was awake, I was alone. The light hurt my eyes. She wasn't lying next to me as usual, staring into me, silent and pretending she wanted to please like normal.

Sim had gone, but I hadn't been alone after all. I now remember Zelda had been there instead. Standing in front of me, saying strange things. Suddenly she knew about Hodge, knew about Sim. I tried to answer her as best I could, get back on top of things. Be the N-P who knew everything, who could anticipate and plan. But there was so much that I couldn't understand. I didn't know what branch of the bifurcating roads I was on. When I woke up, I wanted to stop and look around, but Zelda wouldn't let me. She was talking so quickly, leaping from one fact to the next, concluding things and suggesting things. Talking and talking. On and on and on.

As we had walked back, with the sun burning right in my face and making me screw up my eyes in the glare, I had been concentrating only on shutting out Zelda, on drawing a line, or rather a wall between us, of wrenching apart the Yin and Yang that had locked us in so tightly. I had wanted only to disentangle myself from her tight grasp, and fly away, smooth, solitary, and perfectly balanced and whole on my bicycle. I just didn't need her to complement me any more: it wasn't real. The gleaming lilac always at my side was all that there was and all that was necessary. So the immediate task ahead was simple, to arrive at the Dwelling and leave Zelda there behind its walls so that I could fly away – but that clear sequence of events dissolved as soon as I saw Sim vomiting.

My unthinking remark, my brief comparison to Tarra when she was carrying Bill, had stopped Zelda in her tracks. She had become a statue, every curve and colour of her body turned to hard monochrome. Her eyes unblinking and staring into nothing. I backed away as her temperature seemed to fall to such an extent that the cold blasted beyond the confines of her body. A silence like death. I knew not to try and speak, not to explain, not to suggest. I just had to leave her. All I could do was turn and continue to the Dwelling, to Sim bent over the earth, now transformed into the eternal earth mother. All that fevered cellular activity that was now going on inside her, shaping into a unique, individual being that was already making itself known: my seed, my final drop of power ... my fault.

As I walked away from Zelda, I knew I would never see her again. I knew I had to keep my eyes rigidly focused in front, and face up to what was confronting me: Sim was having my child. But the problem was that I couldn't face it. My insides were churning so much that I too felt like kneeling down on the earth and vomiting all the toxicity of this mission and these people out of my system. I wanted to be pure again. How had it all gone so wrong? Why did I let myself break all the rules that had been proven to give human society the only chance of a truly fulfilling life? I was a good man, a model N-P, a brilliant brain scientist, trusted with a truly vital quest. Where could I turn now, and to whom?

As if reflecting my thoughts, my feet started to slow down in their purposeful striding, hesitant, wanting to step sideways. I knew that Zelda was still glaring and staring after me, even though I had put a good distance between us. I could feel the fury burning into the back of my head, while my eyes strained until they were sore with holding their unblinking fixation on the humpbacked quadruped that was Sim, looming closer and closer into view. I couldn't sidestep, I couldn't evade the taut axis along which I was walking between these two women. I had to see Sim, talk with her, explain what was happening and how I would take control, of course I would. And look after her, as I always had with everything I've been expected to do.

She may not even have realized that she was pregnant. Although she would be used to swelling bellies and subsequent babies, Sim would link the process only with an IVF treatment, which of course she'd never had. And I now realized belatedly that although all her body had of late curved and fleshed out, there was still no unambiguous convex stomach, no obvious sign that my seed was actually taking root inside her. The more I thought on it, the more I realized that Sim's current sickness would in all likelihood seem merely that to her: a sort of sickness. Zelda herself hadn't even guessed what was happening, until I had blurted out my revelation. She, the only person who could have shared with Sim the wisdom of another era, would never have seen this as the remotest possibility.

Zelda knew about sex with Sim: it seemed to upset her very much. The betrayal of our little secret was easy to guess. Silly little Sim had obviously been too excited, too overwhelmed to keep our special times to herself. Obviously, she would have eagerly gushed about her experiences to her carer, her mother figure. She would have told her it was like nothing else she had ever experienced. Of course, she would have said that. She must have. I couldn't believe she might not have felt that. But then Zelda and Sim lived in a world where a mother figure wasn't really a mother, and someone of another generation looked like anyone and everyone of the same adult stage in life. What would Tarra say about how things here were turning out? And what of Bill? What was he doing now? Perhaps playing with his pet rat, Adrian … A shutter came down. Just don't go there, in circles, go there to the tree instead, anywhere, think of anything else, in a straight line.

As we interlocked in bed, Zelda had kept saying that she 'loved' Sim 'with all her heart'. But Zelda's reaction to Sim and my baby would not have been maternal: such a generation and such relationships no longer existed here. First problems first: what to do about Zelda? It was true, what I had told her. We had come to the end of our story. She had said, repeatedly, that she loved me until the statement, the feeling, had been devalued to the level of a casual greeting: and in any case I had never been sure what this 'love' actually meant. My extensive, accelerated Phase 3 education of early thought, literature and philosophy had equipped me well to encounter love in all its guises, in the mouths and minds of men and women of all ages and eras. Even then, it had seemed unclear to me what they were each actually feeling firsthand. The interaction itself was what fascinated me. So Zelda might as well be Eve, just as I was Adam the man, Fred the man.

But as this 'love' of Zelda's 'grew', so I was expected to say and do certain things at certain times with a monotony that reduced me to a generic player, acting out a stereotyped role. No, I had never 'loved' Zelda. And now the Yin had been wrenched away from the interlocking Yang, a clear truth remained that I had to act on: she had to be prevented from communications with Hodge. What might he be planning even now? That last, briefest instruction gave no clue as to what might now happen.

Imperative you establish contact immediately. Immediately.

So I tried to focus on the next sub-problem: what would Hodge do about me? Here, it *was* easy to predict what would happen. It wasn't so much that I knew Hodge well, but rather I knew how he, and I, had been trained to reason. He would compartmentalize the issue of Fred the Problem into two parts: (a) and (b). Part (a) would cover the general strategy and the continuing goal and how it may need to be modified. The original mission would, presumably, obviously proceed, but perhaps with different operatives or using different methods. They certainly wouldn't risk sending another lone individual into what would be perceived as such a perilous and unpredictable environment. To have happen to them what was happening to me …

But more immediate was the Part (b) of the problem, the personal one of that lone individual who was failing so miserably, who had let down his colleagues, his society and, above all, its ideals: Fred, the ex-N-P. Such a clearly substandard individual had never before existed: the occasional 'bad' people of whom my father had spoken would never have been this bad, an N-P who had betrayed both his people and his ideals. The rhythm, such as it is, of my stumbling walk was helping: it helped me to work things out, or at least to try. My implant for direct broadcasting was turned off – an obvious precaution, as Hodge would have found copulation with anyone other than my Breeding Partner utterly unbelievable, least of all with an experimental subject. He would be disgusted both as an N-P and as a scientist.

But now I had to get back on duty, to reactivate my implant and re-establish some sort of contact with Hodge. His reports were becoming increasingly angry. I seemed to be no longer capable of producing the detailed and meticulous accounts that he was expecting, and I didn't really want to write them anyway, even if I could. So instead I had simply been shutting him out, putting him on hold. Because I had nothing better to do, I thought I might as well turn on my implant. Just for a second. I stopped and fumbled: even this oh so familiar reflex was now clumsy, unpractised. There was an immediate soft bleep.

Your dereliction of mission and failure to deliver according to instructions will now have profound consequences. Unprecedented event of an Other, name withheld, reporting on knowledge of mission and of your copulation with experimental subject. Immediate instruction to cease all interaction with subject Sim and with unknown Other. Imperative you re-establish contact immediately. Repeat, immediately.

Instantly, I turned it off, terminated the harsh intrusion with my fingertip. So Zelda had carried out her threat. That was how much she 'loved' me. What a shallow, lying world she lived in. No mention by Hodge, of course, of the pregnancy. He presumably didn't know of the baby. Zelda had been so stricken by the fact itself, when I passed my offhand comment on Sim's vomiting, that perhaps she hadn't wanted to admit it, make it a reality in the report. What she had said must have already been more than enough. But even if my logic was faulty, Sim's experiences were in any event obviously of sufficient uniqueness for her brain to present an interesting subject for neuroscientific investigation. My last report had described Sim as at last having insight into who she was, and thus perhaps into the society in which she lived, and even the alternative one that I represented: yes, she would be an interesting case study, but the same unique set of circumstances that made her so, also made her a security threat.

But then again, to whom would Sim have spoken in any case? Zelda would have been the most obvious, the only person for her to go to with her story, as she eventually did. Zelda knew as much as Sim, indeed more, in that ironically she was the only one of the two women who would have realized that Sim was pregnant. No one among the Others copulated. Ever. I was sure their prized Fact-Totum would have given some version of events of the reproductive biology of the sex act but as some out-dated, now obsolete process of the past. But I already knew from Sim's reaction when we first started sharing our secret that it no longer was part of their mindset. For her the sex act was something that previous generations had done but it's link to the possibility of she, Sim, now reproducing in this obsolete way, would never have occurred to her. Reproduction via IVF for the Others was like milk in milk cartons had been for many urban children in the early twenty-first century. The original method, the true story involving grass and udders, was hazy and unimportant, didn't touch people's daily existence any more. Sim may or may not have known that copulation could lead to pregnancy. But she would never have applied that fact, even in her now sophisticated cognitive state, in connection with her own real life.

It was up to me to tell her that she was now different from all the Others: she was having my baby. And I would take control. I had to. I would be someone again, a father. But my feet felt frail and useless now, as though great stone weights were tied to my ankles. Every step required huge effort to drag and pull one leg after the other. No, don't look sideways. Focus, just like you used to. Focus on the problem before you, and its resolution.

'Sim, is everything all right?'

Obviously, it isn't. Sim's body convulses one more time, and an unlovely, primeval croaking sound delivers this time only a few spots of glutinous fluid dribbling around her mouth: she pushes herself upright, sits back on her haunches, looking at me with weary, wary eyes.

'I've been very sick. I don't know why. Normally, my body works perfectly.'

Then a cloud comes over the already dulled blue eyes, making them still more cloudy, as the lull in her all-consuming physical discomfort allows her perhaps to remember our last encounter. I'm not sure what has really happened as my own memory isn't working as it should, as it used to. It hasn't been right for some time. Everything is misty and the harder I try to recall what might have happened, the more my mind fogs up. I find myself lurching towards Zelda's second-hand version, not my own. But Zelda had told me what she knew, not what had happened when Sim and I were last alone together. I hesitate therefore. Standing over Sim, impotent. She looking up at me, sitting back on her heels, quizzical and defiant.

'You want me Boxed. Who is this Hodge, that he can have absolute power over you?'

Her voice is steady and calm, preoccupied with a very different priority from the one inside her that will soon be taking her over mentally and physically. Perhaps it is the force of the now self-evident fact that she really is unaware she is having my child, or perhaps it is the familiar name of Hodge, utterly out of context on Sim's lips, along with a verb that makes me shudder. Whatever it is, it leaves me with a dry mouth and no words for it to say.

Boxed. A long ago childhood memory of my father, stern, sitting across the table from me in a completely silent room. Him leaning forward, cold-steel eyes staring at me in a way that made me feel like squirming and looking away, yet left me utterly transfixed.

'Sometimes, Fred, just occasionally, there is a very, very bad person who breaks the rules. And even when everyone tries to help them, they carry on being disobedient, so as a final answer, they have to be Boxed. They are taken far away to a little box without any windows, below the ground, where they no longer can talk to anyone at all. Along with air their food and water is delivered automatically, and their waste cleaned automatically so they never see another human ever again.'

'Wouldn't it be easier for them just to die?' asks the young Fred, already hardened to, and by, logic. My father smiles a smile that has no humour behind it whatsoever.

'Yes, and that's why it doesn't happen. Remember, Fred, we have seen the silliness of romance and martyrs and high emotion. We know the power of conversation and ideas about death. By depriving the very bad person, who is no longer really an N-P, of everything, he or she would then have a living death. As I said, Boxing hardly ever happens because our society is so well run. But it's important you know what the term means.'

Should I too now be fearing it? I'm looking back at Sim, waiting for her answer, wanting to know what will happen. Fred the N-P, the insightful and original scientist – he would have known what to say now; he would have had a plan, a carefully thought-through strategy of sequential steps. But no longer. For the first time, I think I must face up to the reality that Fred the N-P no longer exists and I'm unsure who is now in his place. I carry on just staring back down at Sim, simply because I don't know what else I can do. The baby, being Boxed, the wrenching of the Yin from the Yang, the mocking but irrefutable data from Sim's brain, the mists of my once clear past and the uncertainty of my once bright future all are converging on me and driving me away.

I clutch the bicycle tighter. I daren't ride it, of course. It's too big, I'm too weak, and I'm frightened now to travel fast. But I have to get away. Clumsily, I wheel it round so that it, and then I, are turning away from Sim. I look back at her one more time over my shoulder. She is still staring up at me: head now to one side, waiting for an answer. The only sign that she is truly anxious is that her breathing is deep and visible, her chest rising up and down heavily beneath the gossamer.

'I'll explain later. It's complicated. I need to be on my own first. I'm sorry.'

Even before I've finished speaking, or rather mumbling, I'm pushing the bicycle away from the Dwelling. Trying to see a way forward … I cannot be bothered to make any more recordings like this. So I'm giving up. Who would ever be there now, in the future, to listen to them anyway?

The man with the thin white beard and diamond-hard eyes sighs and imperceptibly shakes his head.

Chapter 31

SIM

As I watched Fred's retreating back, I knew he wouldn't turn round, not even to glance at me one more time. His head was bowed and his whole body stooped forward, leaning heavily on the lilac bicycle as a support. But I stared after him none the less, until his slowly diminishing silhouette had become a distant, amorphous shape, then a speck, until it was nothing at all. But still I sat there, kneeling back in the earth outside the Dwelling, in suspended animation. Not only was I not sure what to do next, but I was feeling weak in a way I never had before. I was sick and tired in every sense.

What was happening? What would happen now? Clearly, the walking and talking sessions with Fred were finished forever, as were the secret times. It was all part of my identity, of having things happen which then ended, but which transformed permanently how I then perceived everything around me. That was a valuable lesson that I had learnt – that although something was over, a single event that would never occur again, it was somehow fixed and constant: it would in some way have become part of my brain, part of me after all.

I don't know how long I was just sitting there, generating minimal energy, my life on hold: but I knew that something had to happen. What was there left for me, Sim, actively to do? Of all the objects and events and possibilities that were swirling around me, how might I gain control and be effective? Near by was the gleaming Helmet. I had got into the habit of having it always with me. First, it had been a reminder of Fred when he wasn't there: and then I enjoyed the fact that he had come to trust me enough with it, to put it on or off whenever I liked, even when he wasn't close. And, finally, I suppose it had become so much a part of me, it would have seemed wrong somehow not to have it there. It was, after all, *mine*. The first thing that I had ever owned, an extension of my *identity*.

Yet Fred had explained that in order for the Helmet to 'work' – an abbreviated term for helping me learn so much so quickly – he had to be within a certain range with his own implant active, as well as a device around his wrist, which he referred to as his 'watch'. Apparently, watches were used in previous centuries to enable the wearer to be aware of the precise passing of time. I had never appreciated why it would be important to monitor one moment following after another: but Fred had tried to explain that in previous times, as with the N-Ps even now, each day you were alive was very different from any other, and every moment could be different too.

'Different events occur at different stages of the day, Sim.'

This was long ago, but not at the very beginning of the Fred time. We had started the secret by then: however, this was when I was wearing the Helmet and we were on talking mode. We were just walking nowhere,

'It's odd here for me too, Sim. In my case, it still feels strange not to have to walk somewhere specific within a certain time.'

We were in easy step, me close on one side of him, without touching but perfectly synchronized: on the other side, inevitably, the shiny lilac bicycle that was almost an appendage of his body.

So it was that we moved on to talking about specific episodes in a life, in a day, that occurred at precisely anticipated moments, for which other people at other times, for many centuries, had used watches, precise monitoring devices strapped to their wrists.

'So we still call things like this –' Fred dismissively gestured to his own wrist – 'we still call them watches, even though they are nothing of the kind. It's a little like you referring to the devices that are external cyber-nodes, those Talking Heads dotted around the Dwelling, as 'screens', when they are not screens at all.'

'Yes, but they still function in many ways like the screens from Zelda's time. But your thing there, it has no function at all comparable to the old watches, does it?'

By that time, I was starting to sustain a dialogue with Fred quite well, and he had told me already, at the beginning of the previous secret session, how pleased he was with me. We had carried on walking as Fred explained about his watch. I knew him well enough at that stage to see and hear, as he spoke, that he considered his watch very special.

'No, it does much more than tell the time, Sim. This watch is interfaced closely with my implant: the two both need to be operational for me to give your Helmet the precise instructions it needs, and indeed to filter back, analyze and transmit the signals it emits from your brain. Without me –' he smiled with the tight, lips-only smile that was becoming very familiar – 'the Helmet would not be of much use.'

So there I was, sitting crouched in the earth: since Fred was now far away, the only purpose the Helmet currently had was as an inanimate object, to gleam and contrast in all its artificial beauty with the natural brown, pungent earthy reality that was crumbling in between my toes and already under my fingernails. Finally, I stood up, dusted myself down as best I could and moved towards the wash-waste. My first decisive action, the first thing

I would now do, would be to stop wearing the Helmet. Instead, I would hide it away in the Dwelling. I would find a secret place until it could be of use again – until I could access Fred, or more accurately his watch and his implant.

And so my life changed yet again. I was still living with the Grouping in the Dwelling: once I'd had Zelda grasping and grabbing me, then next there had been Fred, who had given me a completely new life. Now suddenly, for the first time, there was no one either giving or taking anything to or from me. I was on my own. But here I am, talking as Fred had wanted, still talking to the Dark Man: perhaps this is the very last time I'll address him and his fake, meaningless face.

So then … As time passed, there was an increasingly pressing problem: what to do each day. Initially, I was content just to stay still and stare into empty space, but in reality seeing Fred, replaying our times together, hoping that with each iteration, I might make sense of all the things that he had said. He taught me that true understanding meant seeing one thing in terms of something else. But I couldn't place Fred and our secret and the dialogues into a bigger world, a context where it all fitted in. The only context I had was the bright world around me: and the more I tried to compare and integrate the smart, interactive objects and the vacant, isolated people into the same space and place as Fred and me and my continuing identity, the more I failed to link and connect everything together: there was no overarching idea, no frame of reference for me to 'understand' the people among whom I had grown up. But why this need for comprehension? What difference would it make to my current life? Each day I saw Ciro and Avril and everyone in the Dwelling doing the things they had always done, and that I have always done myself: dancing, eating, wondering and wandering. But of course that wasn't enough any more. 'Understanding' wouldn't have changed what I or they did, but I realized now that I just did those things without thinking. Then, surprisingly, I realized that I was no longer happy. I needed something more than fun. I did try once to learn on my own from the Fact-Totum, but was not sure where to start, what questions to ask. Without Fred there to guide me, to be my partner in the kind of brain dances that we used to have, I found the isolated, disconnected facts on their own very uninteresting. Why care about the height of a mountain, or the date of a battle, or the name of a long-dead leader? Fred and I had joined facts together, made connections that he proudly called 'ideas'. Without him, it was much harder to generate ideas, when all I could get were one-word answers or single-sentence responses from either the Fact-Totum or one of the Talking Heads – answers that were really just more facts that led me nowhere further on.

Had this situation continued unchanged for much longer, I'm not sure what I would have done. Yes, there was food and warmth and colour and music and thrilling sights and sounds. No one bothered me. But it wasn't enough: yet I didn't know what could have filled the void. Only continuing conversations with Fred? No, not now: the Fred of the present wasn't the same as the Fred of the past. Just as a seemingly fleeting episode could become permanent because it had modified your brain and expressed itself in your subsequent behaviour and speech, so the converse could happen – something, or someone, that you thought was permanent could, over time, end up being something or someone utterly temporary, provisional, ephemeral.

The Fred of the past had created, and then filled, a void. My mind drifted back over all the special episodes – the clear, special, distinct memories in space and time that were different from any other, but that could connect up to each other like their own kind of logical argument or progression. At that time everything seemed so good. Back then, there was the still unfamiliar awareness that there was something to look forward to each day, as each day I was to learn something new. But then we never got to finish our work, did we? I had discovered the real Fred, the Fred who had walked away, the Fred who didn't care that I might be Boxed or even explain what it meant, the Fred who was calling me 'subject Sim' and discussing me with someone called Hodge, obviously another N-P. That alternative Fred was someone who could in some way I couldn't even articulate or understand – well, that Fred might destroy me in some way.

Gradually the ill-defined ill ease that the thought of Fred was starting to elicit, was shaping into a single idea: I had to approach from different angles, come up close and squint and then stand far away and look at it from a wider angle. I had to walk all round this idea to make sure it was what I thought it might be. Then I had to accept it. And I needed to plan, carefully. There was certainly time to do so: after all, it would have been very difficult to move forward with any scheme, while Fred was actually absent.

It was about this time, however, that I started to feel so strange that my fevered plans in any event became less central. The thinking process that Fred had taught me, the linear progression and clear, clean steps that led from one to the other, started to be overtaken by the messy discomfort of my actual body. I had been feeling sick for some time, and now I was starting to feel swollen and bloated. I was getting heavier. Interestingly enough, however, my implant did not register signs of acute physiological danger; nor did the wash-waste deviate from its daily announcement that all was well. However, its flat, factual report was now ending with the puzzling sentence:

'All proceeding as normal.'

I should have questioned this new word, 'proceeding', but had no idea how I could do so. There was no facility for challenging the statements: only if something was wrong, would you then be told what you had to do. You didn't have to think for yourself.

Then one day, it was just a day merging now like they all did into debilitation and fear and boredom and anger, when I would previously perhaps have been dancing away my agitation: but I was feeling too weak to focus on anything, even standing up. As I sank into one of the glowing gold seats that wrapped itself around me, and switched on warming emissions, so an unusual thing happened: someone, it happened to be the womb donor Avril, actually approached me. Normally, until Fred's arrival had changed everything, each of us in the Grouping would encounter each other in the periphery of our daily activities. A fleeting sight of someone dancing or eating on their own, of talking within holograms, but sometimes more. Sometimes, someone would interact with one of the infants: Ciro or Zelda would often have a baby on one hip, or be wiping their faces, or aiming food into their mouths: after all, that was what the carers did. And, much more rarely, we would try communication with each other: no one really liked conversing unless they had to because, for whatever reason, you were being prevented from continuing with your own activity, such as moving in a certain space or accessing a favourite Talking Head.

Obviously, Avril, like everyone, was completely unused to initiating real conversations in real time, one on one, but it seemed that on this occasion that was precisely what was going to happen. Clearly, there was something about me that was so pressing that it could necessitate overcoming the difficulty and unpleasantness of having a face-to-face conversation.

'Who were the genetic donors?' Avril blurted, staring at my stomach. By now she had had her child, handed it over to Ciro and knew that she soon would need again to open up her womb. Suddenly, the recent moments, the isolated events since Fred had left, when I had felt sick and found that my body was expanding, connected up into a logical progression. How could I not have realized earlier? 'Proceeding' would be what the wash-waste would report to a womb donor like Avril, in a healthy but progressive condition. I was giving the same readings as a womb donor ... Why hadn't I applied what I knew from the past to what was happening in the present, as Fred had taught me? All the old stories that Zelda had told me, about how her grandparents had lived in families, as people did back then. Of course, of course ...

'So who were they? And why are you having a baby in this Grouping? That's what I do, not you. You know we're full here. You'll have to leave.'

Avril was now sitting on a deep blue sparkling seat directly opposite. She was reclining back, as though her womb was indeed full to bursting, though her hands were cradled over a flat, silky tunic. She tried to stare into my face but when I looked back at her, I noticed she needed to talk instead to a space above my head. But that didn't stop her lip curling up, her chin tilting, her face getting redder and redder as she made herself angrier and angrier. She tossed her long black hair away from her face as though it belonged to someone else.

'You're obviously almost halfway through. You'd better start seeing where you can go. Then just get out.'

All this conversation had clearly run the full gamut of Avril's initiative and communication skills. She had even failed to realize that I hadn't actually answered her opening question about the identity of the genetic donors. But, in any case, whatever she said was sounding as though it was a long way off. I was just trying to make sense of the new information, to embed it as Fred had shown me, against existing facts, previous episodes, comparable events: it was this process he had referred to as 'appreciating the significance'.

'This is how you convert information into knowledge, Sim.' He had smiled and smiled at me and gently placed the palm of his hand against my cheek. The Fred of the past, the unsecret Fred who spoke to me.

Now the words 'pregnancy', 'baby', and intermittently, 'Fred's baby' echoed round and round my head as information. They were facts and I just couldn't digest them, come to terms, understand. Worst of all, I had no idea what I should do. The first move was clear, however: to escape from Avril and her sneering face. She had told me to go, so I would. At least for a brief moment. As always, I thought better outside, when I could make the environment as exciting or as ordinary as I wished, and had to navigate round fewer people and their ongoing experiences. Nowadays, I also liked looking up at the real sky, which still couldn't be really simulated in the Dwelling, and breathing real air even though it was sometimes windy and wet.

Baby. Pregnant. Fred's baby. The words were like a mantra now as I walked firmly away from the Dwelling as fast as I could, looking straight ahead but with no sense of direction whatsoever. I had to slow down, my brain had to slow down to a linear path, to iterate sequence and consequence as Fred had taught me. But it was so much harder on my own, not to just repeat the same words over, not to be distracted by a bird now cawing overhead, and most of all not just to stall in despair. I thought of myself trying to think about myself but my implant was already bleeping that I was showing the first signs of distress. So I walked on and on as the bleeps became more demanding and as the night started to darken my excursion.

How far had I walked? It didn't matter because the main

point was that I was starting to tire in a way I would never have previously and the reason for this was at last reassuringly obvious. My purposeful stride became more hesitant, allowing me to observe the jagged edges of the usual broken glass gleaming in the growing dimness, an unusually large pile of white and blue plastic bags flattened and earthy, a lone clump of tired yellow flowers, a human figure hunched up near them, head bent under folded arms, arms folded round bent knees, foetal, rocking. Even in the dark I could see the matted hair on the buried head would have been red-gold. Zelda.

'Zelda. It's me, Sim.' I stood near her, over her.

'But you're no longer mine.' The voice came deep from inside the rocking balled-up body, toneless and factual.

'Why are you here, Zelda? What are you doing?' Meaningless questions, a child's questions.

'I'm here because there's nowhere I want to go.'

Finally, she showed me her face, tilting up that white oval bleached of emotion, staring hard at me, hurting me.

'And I'm doing nothing. What can I do, when you've done everything.'

'What do you mean?' Again I hide behind the child I always was, with her.

'You have Fred's baby inside you.' Now there was not so much a sob, but a sudden, sharp intake of breath. Then the rocking resumed as she looked away.

'Zelda, you are not well. You haven't been in the Dwelling for a long time. You must be cold and hungry.' So now I am the mother: my new identity.

'Sleep. I want sleep. I can't sleep.' It was almost a chant. 'Just bring me my capsules, my drugs. That's all I want. Then I don't want to see you ever, ever, ever.'

Her voice was now escalating into a wail.

But I was in control: I was Sim and I could understand a situation.

'Zelda, I'll bring you food. You should switch your implant on so that you get instructions on what you need to do for your body. To get well again.'

The Zelda that had suffocated me, drained me, talked at me, was no more. But perhaps it was my current, transformed state that made me want to do something. In the old days, before Fred, it would have been easy just to walk away, perhaps like many passing by here had already done. But now I understood about life and consequences and life-stories, I felt I should help Zelda. In any case, it would be more interesting and meaningful than having fun every moment in the Dwelling. But before I set off, there was still something that I didn't understand.

'Why don't you want to see me, Zelda, ever again?'

'Because. You. Have. Fred's. Baby.' It was hard for her to speak clearly while sobbing and rocking.

'But you like babies, Zelda. You're a carer in the Grouping, after all.'

Not a serious counter-argument: just a small nudge in the process of dialogue, as Fred had taught.

'But it should be mine. Not yours. I was the one Fred loved. Really loved.'

My knees buckled and I struggled to keep standing in my superior position, fighting to be the one still in control and command.

'No, Zelda, I was the special one. Hodge, this N-P Hodge might have said to … to Box me. But I know I was special to Fred, when we shared our secret time. He said I was beautiful.'

Why, of all the dialogues we'd had, of all the teaching and explanation and excitement that had so transformed my life and given me an identity – why should I first only remember that generic, banal statement that was no evidence at all of what had happened with Fred and what he felt.

'And he said the same to me. Of course.' The white oval was tilted back up at me again. The rocking had ceased. She was completely still, waiting, holding her breath for me to respond. Empowered once more, at last.

'So Fred and you, Fred and you …'

'Yes, Fred and I were in love. Until you distracted him with your tedious, endless innocence and fertility.'

I didn't understand the second part of what she said: but the first part fitted into a context without difficulty. I realized immediately what must have happened. That Fred and Zelda had also had a secret, one that they kept from me all the time while I trusted both of them. Neither had told me the truth. They had both betrayed me. Zelda was not my carer, after all. My earlier, just possible plan for Fred now all at once solidified and hardened to an implacable and impregnable rock-solid resolve. I knew without question what I would do. But I had to wait. Meanwhile, Zelda was already here, right in front of me.

'I'll go now, Zelda, to get you food and help. But I'll be back. And I'll also bring you your sleep enhancers.' It was just a statement, no longer a dialogue. I wanted no reply.

So each day I returned to see Zelda. She was always in the same place, always rocking. She was occasionally drinking rainwater that accumulated in the crevices of the dirty plastic bags, but apart from that had clearly eaten nothing for a very long time. She was much thinner, weak, and obviously more and more confused. Each time I visited her, she rocked more, hunched up more, and said less. I didn't actually bring her much of the food I'd promised: but I did bring her a large supply of her sleep enhancers.

Yes, I visited her each day to see how she was, just to check that she really was dying. More and more often she would be unconscious, but sometimes in a tearful conversation with her grandparents, telling them about Fred, saying she was going to have his baby. Then one day, as I approached, I saw that she wasn't hunched up, but sprawled out flat. On her back, mouth slightly open, and eyes wide open. Not breathing. At last, perhaps, she had died the kind of death that she was always reading about.

Now I can really focus on what lies ahead, for me alone. Yes, this has definitely been the last one-way conversation I'll ever have with the Dark Man.

Chapter 32

FRED

As Fred wheels the bicycle away from the Dwelling, Sim and Zelda and Hodge all blur into one, into a three-faced something he wants to blot out. He just can't cope with them, with it. If only he could ride away on his bicycle. But he can't. He would be lost. Anyway, what he really wants to do, more than anything, is sleep. The enhancing agents are the best, the most important thing in his life. That last day with Sim, that day just gone, he thinks, they put him into such a deep, wonderful darkness. Then when he woke Sim wasn't there. He knew that was the way things were. People just came and went. He was no longer sure how the past fitted together.

Perhaps if he walks some more, he can sort things out, just as he always used to. But when he was an N-P, he never had problems like this. There was no fog in his brain then. Before, he had needed only to concentrate on a defined scientific goal: yes, the problems had been hard – impossible in the case of consciousness. Even the very word seems unhelpful and ugly now: just a word. He remembers the particular problem was something that had mattered to him a lot, but he can't remember why it was important or what he was doing about it. Then all other parts of his life were in little boxes of time and space and they piled up on each other, to make a big wall. A big, solid wall that was Fred. But it wasn't so solid after all: all the little boxes have come tumbling down.

He tries to walk purposefully – measured, even steps and, above all, in a straight line – while the bicycle trembles and wobbles beside him: but where is he going? He spots a tree on the horizon, a natural feature stretching back a century and disappearing into the distance away from the fakery of the Dwellings. Fred likes trees. He remembers a long, long time ago, when he thinks he must just have arrived here: the first thing he did was to find a tree and sit against it. So he keeps looking at the tree and starts walking towards it, trying to think, to think and not feel lost and frightened.

He tries to pretend he's still an N-P. Here he is walking in a straight line: that's good. So start thinking in a straight line. Let's start with the basics. He has two problems, and they are separate. One issue is that Zelda knows about Hodge and his plans; the other is that Sim is pregnant with his child. He focuses on the tree, has to keep just looking at the tree.

But just as he had been unable to tell Sim the truth and had backed away, scurrying and scared, not even able to ride the bicycle – so now it is with Hodge. He has not replied to Hodge's instruction. What can he say? What is he to do? He is so used to receiving instructions where he knows he can deliver the expected answer or desired response that now he has no reserve of experience, no wider repertoire from which to draw. Now the possibilities, the outcomes, seem boundless, and threatening. They frighten him. He is completely powerless, with no defences, no excuses: he is nothing. All he can do is to wait and think, to imagine what might even now be happening. All he can do that is purposeful, is to keep his implant turned firmly off.

Hodge will probably need to discuss this unexpected impediment to their plans, Fred's silence, with the Elders. Fred has, of course, never been in their presence, never seen or heard them. But their power is felt like the strong wind in the trees, though never seen: it was known, was all-pervasive. Invisible maybe, but the effects could be devastating. So they didn't need flamboyant shows of leadership or personality like those bedevilling certain societies in the previous century. The Elders will sit quietly with Hodge and list the options, calculate and evaluate the implications of each, and then reach the consequent decision.

The big uncertainty looms as to what Zelda has told Hodge. The fact that he has been told anything at all means that Zelda has prioritized revenge against Fred for not loving her, over preservation of the Others' way of life. After all, she could never possibly imagine that the N-Ps would just abandon the whole mission, just give up because they know one woman is aware in some way, of their plans. Zelda has not been thinking straight. Even now, even though Fred feels his mind clouding over, even now, Zelda is not as clever as he is. Zelda is reacting to him, not planning ahead: she has not been equipped with the right mindset like he has. But why think of Zelda? Fred has more immediate and real problems to deal with, not least his own survival.

By now he has reached the tree. He takes comfort in running his hands down the bark: this at least is real, not manufactured or enhanced. Simple, rough, hard and brown: it is non-interactive, unconscious, just there. This is a world he is used to, or used to be, at least within his own home: this is the world that all human beings, since the dawn of time, used to exist in, where objects did not change shape or interact in a personalized 'smart' way with the user.

Now he has become the only inconsistent element in a consistent and stable world. How he yearns now to be back at home, yes, with Tarra and Bill – though his whole body winces at the sounds of those names – back where objects are not nano-assembled but are solid and real and permanent and exist, have a justification, a meaning independent of the consumer or end-user. A tree could of course be many things – a source of shade and of food, a home for birds and squirrels, a metaphor for family relations and indeed for life itself. But all those uses and applications stem from an inherent tree-ness. A tree is quintessentially a tree, not some slippery unidentifiable smart device that is all things to all people: clever but with no identity of its very own. Just as he was.

Nice tree. He sits down with his back against the gratifyingly insensitive, unresponsive trunk, and tugs his thinking back to the more immediate issue of what to tell Hodge and what to do about Zelda, and to try and imagine what Hodge might wish to do about Zelda. With slight surprise rather than sadness, he realizes that he does not care about what might happen to her in the sense of her suffering, but only in the sense of how her fate will impact on his own. Has it always been so, between them? Perhaps, yes. Perhaps the appeal of Zelda was simply how she had made him feel, how she existed in relation to him, and not as an entity in her own right at all. So when she is no longer a part of him, then she is no longer the cause, or object, of any strong feeling.

It doesn't matter how she is stopped, or by whom: but it would be in no one's interests, neither Fred's nor Sim's, and certainly not Hodge's, for Zelda – disenchanted, bitter, talkative, unloved Zelda – to be allowed to weave any further her own version of malevolence. Clearly, she will be silenced in some way, will have to be. Not his job now, not his problem. So much for romance.

Was it hubris that he once thought he would be uniquely impervious to any outside influence? Was it because he'd actually seen an alternative way, stupidly thinking for a moment that it was a better way? How arrogant that seems now, to think that he, Fred the man, would have a better solution than generations of his forefathers, of Elders, who had systematically laid the plans, for the optimum way to live and be fulfilled. At least face up to it, the situation. At least admit how bad things are, and where you are. Try and think like the N-P you once were.

He has failed himself, Hodge and the whole N-P ideology in various ways. First, and most simply, he has not obeyed instructions and completed his reports as and when requested. Second, he has deviated from his mission and allowed himself to become distracted by trivial, emotional events. Third, he has started to adopt the Others' way of life: he has been taking enhancing agents and indulging himself in sensationalist experiences. Fourth, he has gone even further than the Others in this regard: while they were so infantile and autistic-like, lacking any natural disposition for forming interactive relationships with each other, no such privations applied to him. Not only has he copulated with two women outside of his Family Unit, but one has been driven by that intimacy to endanger the all-important plans, while the other has become pregnant.

Sim. Pregnant. With his child. His N-P mind starts to jerk away, to flinch, to seize up. The new but welcome fuzziness, the meandering, vivid images that are increasingly taking over his consciousness, now once again fur up all logic and abstract reason. A brother or sister for Bill. No one in his world has siblings. One child per Family Unit ensures maximal attention, maximal resources directed in the optimal way with minimization of spontaneous and therefore uncontrollable experiences. But what might Bill have done, what games might the two of them have played? A shutter comes down through the pain of the image like the guillotine. Deep breath. Try and think. Think again.

At the very least, the child with Sim will be a good source of new genes, which is after all one of the goals. This will be a small drop in the genetic pool that needs urgent replenishment. Then again, such reasoning assumes that the child will live, and thus that Sim will live, at least for a while. Hodge's report has mentioned the possibility of Boxing Sim, of her ceasing to exist in every way other than the literal one. Will the fact of her pregnancy hasten or slow down that option?

How much time is going by? The sun has been very hot and the tree has been shady: but now the sun is lower, seeping in its death throes into his skin, into his eyes. He realizes that he has been banging his head against the bark and now it has even subconsciously increased in vigour. Now it hurts, might even be bleeding. So he stops. What will they do to him? N-Ps never disobey instructions. They have been too well trained, too carefully brought up, for that scenario to occur spontaneously, just for no reason: an effect without a cause. Unthinkable.

But it has happened: all that carefully orchestrated arranging of his synapses with daily, clever guidance through the Helmet, has ultimately failed. Somewhere in Fred's brain, there has been an unpredictable rearrangement of his neuronal connections, driven by the happenstance of his new environment and the people within it. They have given him a different mindset, different size and shape and duration of assemblies, and hence a different consciousness. He is not who he has once been, at least not an N-P. There has been a break in the narrative of the life that defined him, that made him who he was. So who is he now?

He no longer conforms to the N-P profile; nor can he define himself by his scientific position, by his Family Unit, or his relations with Bill, Tarra and Hodge. Just as the connections in his brain that enabled logical, progressive thought are dissolving, so he's sure his assemblies are becoming increasingly diminished. As a consequence, his consciousness is less and less orientated to the past and the future, as it should be. Yes, and so here he is, reduced to the present moment and banging his head against a tree. But then again, perhaps that is all that is left to him: perhaps he has no future. He certainly has no choice, no options. All he can do is sit against this tree, this uncomplaining, non-interactive, non-judgemental tree. The bicycle, propped up against the bark, as always within a fingertip's reach, stays static and lilac and shiny, the promise of flight locked into its every molecule, but utterly motionless, not delivering.

Riding the bicycle was the perfect balancing act between emotion and thought, between the past that made him who he was so far and the future that lay ahead that could and would continue to offer possibilities for further change – but always evolving as Fred the man. Above all, when he was on his bicycle, Fred the man could not be pinned down: the elements might be so mixed in him that there was more – that fifth elusive element, that quintessence, that emergent property that is surely what being an individual should be all about.

His head starts to spin with excitement. Perhaps it will be all right, after all. Perhaps, even now, he can just swing his leg over the beautiful frame, and take off on his own, Fred the man, just a man. Surely he would be impervious to problems? Surely no one could hurt him? He would be inviolate. He looks again at the wheels not turning, at the pedals devoid of his feet. And he knows he can't. He just can't. He doesn't dare try to ride the bicycle.

He stares around into the gathering gloom. The natural world is growing monochrome, with bits of invisibility encroaching. Is that what death would be like? A gradual dimming, a slow loss of energy as the battery finally ran down and no one or nothing could recharge it. He stares again at the biocube on the bicycle that contains the ingenious fuel cell, elegantly allowing the flow of ions, the generation of electricity and the happy corollary of crystal-clear water. He has no more energy to be part of that. Then again, he sees the coldness, darkness, the permanent unconsciousness, of not being, which he supposes is death, but which is a path he is not ready to take. And yet that path is the clear and only logical one that he will be expected to follow. Once again, the new feeling of being at a loss, of not knowing what to do, of needing help. Stranded in the present.

His synapses have broken loose and are falling apart. Dismantling themselves, opening themselves up to the immediacy of the cold, black air on his face, the hard bark against his bleeding head. As his neuronal assemblies shrivel, and his prefrontal cortex shuts down, so his body swells with unknown and unseen hormones, as chemicals flee from his brain, speeding up his heart, turning his stomach to an aching, watery presence, pushing up the blood through his veins, lathering the palms of his hands in sweat, drying out his mouth.

Think about that, just about that. No, don't think. There is no longer a past: it can only ever be in his head, unreal. And there is no future, is there? Where is it? Can he touch or feel it? All this time he's been his own prisoner, trapped by this unreal inner brain-world. Better to be in the real world, right now. To give up to it, to surrender, to open up, just to feel. Just give in.

Chapter 33

TARRA

I stared out of the window at the other homes, uniform as ours, and wondered what was happening behind all the other blank windows and the grey doors. Everyone I knew had a child, albeit in a range of various ages. I could imagine, with a sad emptiness, each of the neighbouring Family Units passing the evening now, just as Fred and I used to do. If the child was Bill's age, then, like Bill, they would by now be asleep, most with their Helmet on, yet a few perhaps, like Bill now, with their hair spiking and sprouting up loose around their little heads in the rare but limited freedom of free neurogenesis, the unfettered growth of brain cells. But unlike my current bereft state, the parents would be in vigorous dialogue: they would be attuned and chiming thoughts in the way that was possible and indeed prescribed during that time of the day, the evening, when work was done and the young did not need supervision. I could instead have challenged some of my existing conceptual framework with a book: but I preferred to stare and stare out of the window, at nothing.

I'm not sure how long I had been like that in suspended animation, when suddenly there was movement in the otherwise muted and monochrome scene of early evening that was black-ening the gentle green outside world to invisibility. A man was walking purposefully towards our home, and indeed turning into the short stony path leading to our door. His heavy black boots crunched rhythmically and urgently as he strode towards me waiting there, watching. But he didn't see me: his head was down, his thin grey hair fluffed by a slight breeze. He was a man lost in deep thought, just as was to be expected. But also he was clearly a man with an immediate purpose. Fred? Might it, could it, possibly be, Fred? No Fred didn't walk like that …

A cursory, hard-fisted knock on the door. Of course: not Fred. Fred would have just opened the door and entered. I quickly recalibrated my response from expectation to emptiness and now on to unease. I wasn't sure what to do, how to react. Visits such as these were not part of the plan. Never before had a stranger appeared outside our home. Homes were reserved for Family Unit time, bonding with partner time. All other interactions took place in specified collective professional or social fora, most usually the Rallies. This stranger clearly had a different set of rules: he would know what to do in these unusual circumstances. He knew he had to start off by knocking: I would just watch, and listen. My mouth was very dry.

'Greetings Tarra, Mother of Bill.'

I wasn't surprised that he knew who I was. Why else would he be there?

'Greetings.'

'I'm Hodge, Ex-Father of Amy. I know Fred will have spoken of me.'

'Of course.'

Hodge. Fred's immediate superior. Fred had referred to him many, many times, since, apart from his dialogues with me, this was the person with whom Fred had the most frequent conversations. I looked into watery eyes that tried to smile back at me. The lines in Hodge's face were deep grooves set and rehearsed in the process of deep reflection, not in the upward curves of a smile. But he was trying to be gentle.

'We need to talk about Fred.'

'Yes.'

A whisper. I was listening. So carefully. Hodge had embarked on this highly unusual visit because obviously something had happened to Fred's mission, or even to Fred himself. He looked uncomfortable: someone in his position, and of his way of thinking and living, was not used to improvising dialogue. Then again, none of us was. He sat down and stopped fidgeting, mind made up. He cleared his throat, then spoke in a long, low, steady tone.

'Fred would not have been in contact with you because he was under instructions to focus entirely on his mission. Any interaction with you would obviously have introduced environmental variables that would have hampered the most effective interpretation of the data he was collecting. I know he explained to you before he left that he was being sent to study the brains of the Others, and he would also have explained why he had to remain in complete radio silence.'

Fred had not actually discussed why he would not be able to communicate. He had simply said that he wouldn't, that it was completely secret. Then he had returned to the thrill of owning the bicycle. But I nodded, waiting and wanting Hodge to fast-forward to the things I didn't know and that really mattered right now.

'The work was going well: I knew it would with Fred. He is, after all, the top neuroscientist of his generation. And he is a model N-P. We couldn't have sent him into that Yakawow maelstrom if we didn't believe he would be impervious to it.'

I was straining forward, silently willing Hodge to come to the critical consequences of this scenario.

'Well, I must tell you now, Tarra, that things have gone badly wrong. We underestimated just how dangerous the Others can be, even for someone like Fred.'

He took a deep breath and now quickly set about the clearly unpalatable task of telling me the details of what I had immediately realized, as soon as I saw him stride up to our home, would be unexpected and very bad news. I allowed myself a freeze-frame moment in time to see how hard this was for Hodge. But freeze-frames can't last forever. At some stage you have to press forward.

'Fred's main subject, a female named Sim, was the perfect choice for monitoring the underdeveloped status of the Others' brains. Indeed, we were starting to see interesting results as Fred developed a clear cognitive, phased program for the overly sensationalized brain. Her assemblies were growing, just as we had predicted, and her prefrontal cortex was starting to approximate the same level as our older children here –'

'Yes, I know a little about the prefrontal cortex and Fred's prediction: he used to talk about it quite often.'

I had hastily and rather inappropriately interrupted, yet again playing for time almost by instinct. By reverting to a more normal conversation, one about science and facts and ideas, I was making the situation itself normal. At least for a brief moment it would give me a breathing space. Hodge for his part looked somewhat flustered by my interjection. He was now torn between pressing on with his unpleasant task, or taking the more familiar and welcome opportunity of elaborating on his all-consuming favourite subject. Hodge sighed and looked briefly away. Once again, he seemed overtly uneasy, briefly licking his lips, and staring down now at his hands, loosely clasped on the table.

Then, taking a further deep breath, he did what he had to do: look me in the eye.

'So it was an exciting finding that, after all, the underactive prefrontal cortex could indeed account for the childlike behaviour of the Others. But then the reports from Fred became less frequent, and I was astonished to see that he was switching off his implant increasingly for substantial periods each day. I started to realize that the interaction with subject Sim had obviously been two-way, that Fred was being significantly influenced by his experiences of experimentation. This deduction was confirmed by a third-party report.'

'But I thought Fred went alone. I thought that a larger team would have been too conspicuous and less effective, and of course more dangerous.'

My voice was a flat whisper, an unnecessary interjection. But Hodge looked me again in the eyes, clearly uncomfortable, and I noticed his throat motion a silent swallow.

'The third party was actually an Other.'

My neuronal circuitry was not up to the task. It struggled to accommodate this fact, this concept, into the existing frameworks of associations, precedents, expectations. And failed. The idea that an Other would report on Fred to Hodge was impossible: too many questions crowded in to justify the necessary premises, were that to be the case. I needed more information, some qualifying context. So I just waited, quietly nodding at Hodge to get on with his incomprehensible account, hoping that soon it would make more sense.

'This third party reported something that will be hard for you to understand, Tarra, because you would never have been able to predict it, because it is illogical.'

Hodge was now talking without any more intakes of breath, seeing at last that soon he would soon reach the end.

'Fred has contravened many rules, Tarra. Not only has he failed to maintain contact apparently due to the influence of the Others, but he has succumbed in the most extreme and degenerate way possible to their solid sensual assault. He has violated the objectivity of scientific observation and ... and has broken the deep code by which we live. He has engaged in an activity that the Others themselves would normally shun and that was such a cause of societal problems in the old days.'

The muscles around Hodge's white jaw were starting to jerk.

'I have to report to you, Tarra, that Fred has indulged in recreational copulation with subject Sim. The report from the anonymous Other is unequivocal and entirely validated by the information we were able to track from his implant before he turned it off, apparently for good.'

My circuitry shut down, locked down: the mind that it constituted, my mind, was unable to encompass the onslaught of so much unexpected and unexplainable information. Rather than trying to understand and digest what I had just heard, I focused instead on simply finding out still more facts.

'But the Others do not behave like that. They are incapable of reports of events that are in the past, since they live just for the present moment. And in any case, they are only interested in themselves, not in what anyone else may be doing. Is this third party really an Other?'

'That was precisely my immediate reaction. The read-out that I have been able to track back from the implant that they all have for physiological homeostasis, reveals from the low level of testosterone that the individual was a woman: the overall hormonal profile is being supplemented, as it seems is normal with the Others, by an infusion implant of high levels of oestrogen, suggesting she is at a stage that would have been referred to in the old days as a post-menopausal age. But of course the

Others' implants give no facts, register no information regarding individual identity and personal history, mainly because they don't usually have any.'

Hodge stood up and paced round the small grey space, then, just as I had done, he stared out of the window. Not looking at me appeared to help him think aloud.

'I could not exclude the possibility that this individual was indeed not a typical Other, even though she carried a typical implant and is receiving typical hormonal supplementation. In fact, the most likely explanation for this uncharacteristic behaviour would be that either she was an N-P infiltrating by pretending to be one of them, or that she was in some way and for some reason, atypical. I excluded the first possibility since I could check at the highest level, and indeed across all other departments, that Fred's mission has been the only one operational. So I'm left with the inevitable conclusion that she was a deviant Other. As such, she was very dangerous to our plans.'

Something started to trouble me as Hodge continued to speak in the past tense.

'Is she no longer dangerous then?'

I posed my question to the wide grey expanse of Hodge's back: he carried on addressing the window.

'No. No longer a threat. Her implant now registers she can no longer be cognitively active: she might as well be dead. In all likelihood she is.'

For just a moment I felt a small ache. We accepted death as a natural conclusion, indeed the wonderful culmination of a lifelong journey. When an N-P died they were at their most individual, their most unique, at the height of their wisdom. But this woman – this unknown woman who had uncharacteristically taken an impartial, third-party interest in my breeding partner

– well, she had not finished what she was doing. She had not finished explaining.

The ache I felt was born readily, easily, out of the frustration of ignorance. Had she possibly died simply of old age? If so, then Hodge would have mentioned as critical information that her implant had been monitoring the physiological decline. Could someone have actually killed her? Now my unpractised imagination was being pushed unwillingly into action. No one killed people any more. Not deliberately and actively stopped their heart beating. But then actual killing took us back again to the old days. That was before we understood the mind so well that such actions became unnecessary; alternatively, as for the Others, the minds had been lost to such an extent, that again, there was no reason to terminate that particular individual consciousness: it was already ineffectual.

But this woman had been different, and so what happened to her had been different. Perhaps Hodge had ordered her Boxing or indeed her actual death. Then again, they would need to find her. Pointless to raise all the questions as he would obviously deny it. So equally pointless therefore to show anger: I wouldn't know anyway how to express such a hypothetical feeling. And why was she so dangerous? Reporting back on the inadequacies and weakness of a neuroscientist seemed hardly to deserve such an extreme end. Then again, my Fred could have somehow caused it to happen, perhaps as a consequence of her reporting him. But Fred was in the business of thought, of developing minds and consciousness, not destroying it.

Another possibility was subject Sim. But why should someone whom he was studying and with whom he had copulated, however illegitimately, then wish to remove one of their own people who had been purely tangential to their actual activities? The only other scenario that I could conjure was that, bizarre though it might seem, this strange, unknown Other had for some reason killed herself. But no one – neither the Others nor the N-Ps – did that, not any more. We had clear goals and purpose, while the Others had fun. Neither was a reason for death: quite the opposite. None of this made sense, but then again, I was not good at imagined scenarios, especially ones based on such a flimsy and incomplete factual framework. Best to stop this circular reasoning: we had been taught that as soon as circular thinking took place, it had to be terminated immediately. Stop and break away: attempt a linear thought process. Stop, then start, then go on to a middle and eventually to an end. Where could I begin?

What of that other woman, the Other who was the subject, Sim? I tried to imagine Fred copulating with someone who wasn't me. And couldn't. Perhaps that was why, at least for the moment, I felt no pain, nothing. But I had always suppressed spontaneous feelings, ever since I could remember. Calm, rational thought always solved the problem. So all I could do was reason, yet there would be no reason, and no compatibility. If she was a typical Other, subject Sim would be a gaudily coloured, self-centred child inside an adult body. There would be no connection between her and Fred. Besides, Fred was a wonderful N-P: he would never have broken such a fundamental ruling that ensured the integrity of the Family Unit.

Since none of this made sense, I was unable to evaluate the situation any further. Perhaps I should just continue asking Hodge more questions, in the hope that the fragmented facts could eventually form some sort of framework that I might understand.

'What is happening to subject Sim now?'

'She might still be retaining the Helmet: if only we could access the read-outs via Fred and his implant and watch, to gain further information. In addition, the intervention Phase 3 mode, again due to Fred's absence, can no longer be activated, so I am unable to drive her connections or shape and steer her thought patterns as much as I might like. In any case, given we have no idea of her physical environmental context at any time, it would be counterproductive. And offset against all this potential is the hard truth, Tarra, that Fred is proving unreliable. Better to have no data than false data.

'But who knows how we shall move in next: the subject has proved useful so far, embodies valuable time spent on her and has vitally important equipment with her that must not fall into anyone else's hands. For the time being, subject Sim is of more value to us remaining as she is, rather than being Boxed – that is even if they could find her.'

In any case, it was odd to think of the same term used for what could almost be called 'killing', of purposefully ending the complex, interactive physiological processes within a normally functioning physical body. The end of killing, the uselessness of it, had been the prime justification for the generation some while ago, to rush ever more enthusiastically into the numbing culture of the cyber-world, with all its comfort for body and brain. But the 'Boxing' that, for N-Ps had replaced killing, meant a living death.

It would mean isolation, removal to an underground box so small you could only pace several steps and could easily touch the ceiling without stretching. There were intermittent, unpredictable periods of bright lighting. So no ready cycles of sleep. And nothing whatsoever to do. Only to stare at the blank wall. I strained to imagine it. Above all, there would be no contact with any other living being for the rest of your life. You would pass the time staring at the walls: no books, no sounds, no inputs to your brain of any kind. Forever. The same, just sufficient food delivered automatically; waste cleaned by the same ruthlessly efficient but impersonal technology. Until your implant registered that you had died. I shuddered at the inhumanity of such a situation. The absence of Fred, the few hours I now spent alone in the evenings with my books, felt a truly difficult time. Physical, immediate death must surely be better than the complete, continuous isolation of Boxing … .

I imagined being led underground and towards that isolated room. I would be looking for the last time, the very last time, at real people – my escorts taking me, marching with me either side, towards the place where we would descend underground. I would study every feature of ears and hair and lips, knowing I'd never see such again. Of course, there would be no mirrors inside … . Why was I doing this? I'd done nothing wrong. But what if Fred … .

My brain, trained as it was to make connections and to seek justifications in order to make predictions, was in disarray. There were too many unlinked facts. A nameless woman coming from a culture that lived in the moment, none the less stepping outside of the present to conceive a future plan based on past events. Another woman with a name, but also faceless, stepping outside of that same culture to engage in what would have been perceived by her society as a deeply aversive and outdated act. The first woman dead or effectively dead, killed by someone, or by herself, for no reason that fitted with our N-P society or indeed that of the Others. The second woman alive because she still served some kind of purpose. I seized on this last fact with some relief: it was a possible starting point.

'So is Fred's mission still to carry on, after all? Is subject Sim somehow to be monitored, even though Fred is no longer reporting?'

'Tarra, I'm sure you'll appreciate that the mission is to be much bigger than just Fred. All you need to know is that it's important to the very survival of N-P society, and the triumph of thought and knowledge. Other plans are being made. We will not stop now; we, or someone, cannot. This business with Fred only proves that the Others are indeed a true threat: just look at what they can do.'

I had never thought of the Others in such a proactive sense. Once more I wondered whether there was indeed a consciousness guiding the shallow, hedonistically disconnected ephemera that was all they knew as a life – or whether it was after all the mere sequelae, the inevitable consequence of increasingly sophisticated technology regulating, reporting, controlling and ensuring that physiological subroutines were maintained in healthy working order: the end result would emerge automatically. One outcome being that my breeding partner had been distracted from his mission, from the N-P ideals ... and from me. I just couldn't accept that. I was finding it hard now to concentrate, but there were still some urgent questions that needed answers.

'How did it all go this far? Were there no warning signs?'

Hodge turned his back on me completely, lowering his head. A voice came slowly from behind the expansive grey back.

'Tarra, if at any stage I slipped into talking about "we", about "us" monitoring Fred, I really meant just me. The reports were coming to me and me alone.'

'So it was your decision to carry on?'

'Yes. I thought it would resolve itself, that I knew Fred well enough to be able to control everything. And the data was exciting and encouraging. I knew the Elders would be pleased, that it was what they wanted. It was, is, difficult for me, Tarra. Really difficult.'

He turned round, and I realized Hodge was, after all, human. Rather than think about Fred and unleash floodgates of despair, easier to divert a small channel of pity for the man in front of me.

His lined face had rivulets of tears trickling surreptitiously down the grooves. He knew he had to give up at last, and had given himself up: we both knew what would, in all probability, now happen to him. The worst possible imaginable. The living death.

'And, Tarra, I decided to tell you in person before anyone else. Once I've made my formal report, who knows to whom I'll be able to speak, perhaps ever again.'

He brushed a brief, brusque hand against his damp cheeks, businesslike, and looked me straight in the eye. A real N-P to the last. I realized I could have felt angry with Hodge for not intercepting the problems that Fred was having much earlier, and of taking some kind of pre-emptive action. But when I looked at this once distinguished man, this great intellectual, and realized what probably lay ahead for him, how could I have felt anything other than a wistful sadness? I was also impressed that despite his own terrible, impending fate, he had thought of me, of Bill, and the need to visit us. In any case, I had to ask the obvious question now, the one that had been lurking, sinister and large. The question that would tilt my world, would redirect the clear path I thought I was treading.

'What is happening to Fred?'

Hodge flattened his lips into a hard, straight line, perhaps relieved to be the professional again, objectively talking about someone else.

'I think you already know, Tarra. He was instructed to return, and he has disobeyed. His implant is now, it seems, off permanently and it's therefore impossible to track him. Unless or until things change, he is lost to the Others.'

These facts were not as hard to comprehend as some of the previous information Hodge had given. At least I could understand the concepts, and the sequence; the logic of his account was robust. Now I had to plan where I would go with these facts. The most immediate issue to resolve was Bill's welfare, and restoration of the continuity of his and my life together.

'I realize that this unpredictable event is a significant one for you, Tarra. But the way ahead is clear, that was one of the reasons why I came. You are aware, of course, of the Partner Substitute Program, for when one partner in a Family Unit, albeit very rarely, actually dies prematurely. The program enables you to register your vital personal information for maximal pairing with a male in the small pool of those in a similar position, where a female partner is deceased. Because of our excellent healthcare, as I say, the pool is modest, but I'm sure there will soon be someone with whom you can re-partner. First, you just need to register: in fact, I need to remind you that it's actually mandatory …'

The voice was still speaking, but as an echo from a very long way off. I was finding it hard now to pay attention: I heard sounds, distant and flat, but my thoughts had taken on their own, more strident central position. I struggled to articulate the main point, the point that was both the start and the end.

'So I'm to regard Fred as dead?'

'Yes.'

Where to look? What to say? And Bill? What could I possibly tell Bill?

I peered at a loss around the grey foggy nothingness. Adrian the rat blinked two red eyes and, flicking his thin, scaly tail, retreated to the back of his newly cleaned cage.

Chapter 34

SIM

This is the first recording through my own implant, but it appears to be functional .... My plans were solidifying well. The normal pattern, the one that Avril would have judged as the only option, would have been to register in a new Gathering and then, as in her case of womb donation, to be informed to await implantation of a fertilized egg. Like everything in our lives, all necessities, such as food, are delivered to the Dwellings automatically. So it was with body treatments, on the rare occasions when they are needed. Because illness was a phenomenon mainly relegated to the previous century, mostly 'body care' is concerned with reproduction.

There is a special zone within the Dwelling reserved for telemedicine: in the normal course of events, I would have accessed this special zone when my implant bleeped it was time to do so, and laid down on the flat, functional, narrow bed provided. Under the guidance and instructions of the Talking Head, the fertilized egg that had been delivered would then be implanted by the robotic arms that occupied and operated in the Body Area, in turn under guidance from remote systems monitoring everything on an array of screens set up around the narrow bed for that purpose. Everything about the baby that was to grow within my womb would be registered: the genetic donors, the donor of the emptied egg allowing IVF, and me, the womb donor.

But I was no longer part of this system: I was the entirety – the gene, the egg and the womb donor. And I have not undergone the normal implantation procedure under guidance from a central, automated source. I had unwittingly embarked on something that no one has done for a long time: an act, perhaps a precedent, which might even threaten the smooth running of our fun-filled lives. And, worst of all, the sperm donor was an N-P, someone who would hate all that we stood for. Yes, an N-P for whom I wasn't special after all, an N-P who wanted me Boxed, perhaps therefore to harm me in some way.

I couldn't project any conceivable sequence of events into the future that would enable me to live normally in any Gathering. The Plan that had been slowly taking shape over all this time was a way out, the only way out. But because this next step was so unlinked to what I knew, had experienced, or even what Fred had told me about N-Ps, I refused at first to walk up close to it, and once again to inspect it. So I flinched and twisted away my head, screwing my eyes shut. But now The Plan was here to stay and it wouldn't leave. It was part of my existence, indeed it was my whole life … . I had to face up to it.

Gradually, each day, as my stomach stretched and arched taking on a life of its own, as I had to sit more often and for longer – so, gradually, I started to open my eyes and confront the difficulties of all the details of The Plan. I began thinking through each step, leaving the Dwelling, leaving all the Dwellings, leaving everyone. But if I was to be on my own, then I would need to be allowed to be on my own. I couldn't let anyone block my intentions. Fred was the problem. The Fred of the past who saw me as a subject for study, who talked about me to the N-Ps, who would now try and track me down. The Fred of the present who wouldn't answer questions and had just turned his back on me. All I had to do was remember him and Zelda, as if I had ever let it slip my mind. I just had to remember my resolve, and then go over everything again and again, very carefully. I had to make sure I had worked out, and catered for, all the possible implications: the consequences.

But there was a barrier, transparent though it may be, that stood impregnable between what I wanted to do, and what I could do. My mind was swimming in circles, in a glass bowl that kept the hypothetical plan clearly separate from the reality. Though I could easily peer out from my bowl, I couldn't break out. Then one day the glass was shattered: the idea at last merged into reality. Fred returned.

I was sitting, as I often did nowadays, ostensibly interacting with a Talking Head, apparently playing a game. But in effect my responses when I spoke them were random, and the only mild bemusement I had was vaguely to observe how the responses of the Head, what he said and showed me, could vary at the casualness and randomness of my command and reactions. It was the Dark Man who had featured so much, long ago when Fred and Zelda stood watching me always, a time when I had never experienced a moment being on my own just because no one cared. The Dark Man was my only friend now.

'Sim?'

A familiar voice behind me, but resigned, muted, quieter than I ever remembered it. Almost a croak, framing almost a question. I let myself turn my head slowly, and then my whole heavy body.

'Where have you been?'

'Everywhere, nowhere.'

'What do you want here?'

'I don't know.'

We looked at each other, but not as we used to. I looked him in the eye, but now there was no sparkle, no challenge. He wasn't seeing me, just his own helplessness.

'You might be here to get me Boxed.'

Fred's face rippled at the mention of the word, then went blank again. He turned his head slightly, but warily kept his eye on me. He appeared not to know what I was talking about. Most of all, he seemed to be suspicious of me, perhaps not really to remember even who I was. Only my name seemed like some kind of mantra.

'Sim, Sim, I need help. I'm tired. But I can't sleep. I've run out of sleep enhancers.'

Rather unnecessarily, he extended his arm, palm up, and showed an empty vial that would normally contain an ample supply of drugs. Now it was easy to piece together the sequence of what most probably had happened over the last few months.

In my mind's eye, I saw Fred stumbling away from me, bicycle as a crutch. I saw him at his limit physically, hungry and tired. I saw him staggering around from one Dwelling to the next, ignored and inconsequential, uninteresting and harmless. Just left. I saw him foraging for bits of food. As people danced and ran outside, they might often take handfuls of roast beef or trout or chocolate mousse with them and, once satiated, drop what was left on the ground among the rest of the rubbish of the decades and the centuries. I saw Fred on his hands and knees, half sobbing, reaching for whatever shiny bright triangle, half-eaten, he might find, brushing off the earth, and biting into it. Drinking always the clear water by-product from the bicycle. Surviving. I saw him craving oblivion, and finding it in the sleep enhancers. But then they ran out. Unlike food, they were not discarded; nor could they easily be discovered on the ground. He'd had to come back.

But as I looked at him, the old admiration, the respect for Fred of the past, had not lasted into the present. The present Fred had discussed with another N-P that I might be Boxed, though now it genuinely seemed that was not his plan. The man before me, leaning forward now, with his head in his hands and his bicycle propped up beside him, had no plans. But I still hated him. The understanding he had given me, the identity he had taught me, now hated him. But the hatred, I now reflected, was not emotional; not the kind of hatred that Zelda may have had. It was the cold hatred of calculation and deduction, of betrayal, of disgust. And when you felt disgust for someone, then you had to exterminate them to stay healthy and uncontaminated. And in any case, he might be being watched. Perhaps he could still have me Boxed, or block my way ahead. My way out. My only way. As the glass of my little bowl shattered, so The Plan became the only reality.

'First you must sleep, Fred. Just get some sleep.'

Of course, I knew where Zelda had kept her supply of enhancers. In any case, there was a large reserve in the Body Area. And when those supplies ran low, as with food, there was always an automatic delivery of more.

In a few seconds, he was unconscious. And, in the weeks to come, when he woke each day I was there. I was there always to help him with more drugs, perhaps to amuse him a little with a Talking Head or a hologram experience. I was there to give him thrilling food and incessant music. He started to seem happier. At some stage early on, I had stripped him of the reeking, filthy grey rags and wrapped him in shining, clinging gossamer, smart with sensors for staying in tune with all his body functions. Gradually, the face that had once been creased with curiosity and passion, and was then crumpled with worry and fatigue, now smoothed out with baby-faced beams of sheer pleasure. Finally, it was time.

I had ensured that the enhancers were plentiful that evening. By now Fred took whatever I gave him: he trusted me, looked up to me, and to me, to help him. As his body inflated and deflated rhythmically, the first step was easy. Very gently, I unbuckled his watch. Now I needed to synchronize his implant with my own: not just the single menu option of last time, that time when I discovered about Hodge, but this time everything had to be downloaded. Because the N-P implants were cognitive not sensory, it wouldn't matter that such non-physiological information from Fred's implant was now transferred on to the implant in my body. If I chose to activate the implant, then I could, mentally, be Fred. I would need to do this in order for the watch and Helmet to work. But I couldn't do it often, in case Hodge were able to track me down. Whatever Boxing was, I knew it was bad. I knew I needed to escape it. But I also knew I needed to learn more and that I needed the Helmet and the watch, and the downloaded information from Fred's knowledge-base implant, to be able to succeed.

I leant forward and as before, a lifetime ago, pressed my own implant next to his exposed upper arm, turned outward and upwards from his head as he lay on his back, vulnerable and trusting. I touched the watch as I had been practising and studying and experimenting on all those other nights when, like this, Fred let the drugs unplug his brain. But this time it was for real. As my own implant trembled and hummed, as the watch registered stage after stage of option downloaded, so I realized it was, yes, it was going to work.

Fred was snoring slightly now, more like a cat purring, innocent and gentle. Emasculated. It was done. I leant over and turned off his implant by the slight pressure on the skin. Everything was just as I'd thought through. Earlier that day, it had been so easy to select a piece of jagged glass from outside, among the piles bearing witness to an earlier time when glass was everywhere and did so much. We no longer needed implements for cutting, those scissors and knives I'd none the less learnt about from the Fact-Totum: the glass would suffice.

As gently as I could, as the snoring now grew a little louder, slower, deeper, I lowered the sharp edge to the white, soft skin to slit a fast small incision in his arm so that Fred's implant would not just be inactivated as it was, but destroyed forever. But I couldn't do it. It seemed such a primitive act: and in any case the simple 'off' mode meant that Fred was no longer in contact with that world beyond the mountains. And I had the watch, so it would be impossible, even if he tried. Whatever still slumbered in the silicon of Fred's implant could not be accessed, at least not readily. And there was no one who would really try, either now or in the future. In the first place, how would they ever find him?

Another week and I had grown so large that I knew I couldn't delay much longer. And because I was now so overtaken by this swollen belly, it came as no surprise when Avril, unusually, suggested a meeting. The meeting with the Grouping was not normal. Zelda had summoned one up long ago, I think, when I had been running outside and then found Fred. Zelda: just a name now. Perhaps only a word. And Fred: saying his name now, just thinking his name, became less and less painful each day, as the Fred of the past faded against the Fred of the present, who in turn was becoming increasingly insubstantial as any Fred of the future.

No. Meetings were very rare. Of course, usually the way of life in a Dwelling was to glance by each other, for perhaps our bodies to brush in passing, our eyes even to meet, fleetingly, our attention or focus to alight for a second on someone else, before fluttering on to the next colour, sound, smell, shape. But

379

now, on that special day, we all had to be in the same space at the same time.

Sometimes, in the times before Fred, I had wispy recollections of such events. But they had usually meant that Zelda did most of the talking, that they had been Zelda's idea, and her instructions. But Zelda had gone. After our last time together, when she had found out about my secret with Fred, she had been suddenly so aggressive that I had never wanted to see her again. But I did still think about her, how she used to be when I needed looking after. But that was Zelda in a different time, when she and I had been different. That much I had learnt – the past was somewhere different and separate, so that you could visit from time to time, and then leave. The difference in time was the same as a difference in space.

So we were all to meet. What everyone needed to know, rather than discuss as if there was an alternative, was that I had to leave the Grouping. Avril wanted support to make me go. When we had spoken so long ago, she had summoned everything, every drop of never used courage and dislike, to tell me to leave. And I hadn't. Now she would make sure that her wishes were granted, that the normal pattern was once again followed. That life could return to being exactly as it had been and was meant to be. Even before Fred, Zelda had said that I wouldn't be living there forever, that it made her very sad but she couldn't see what we could do to stop it. Soon I would have to donate eggs or my womb and be part of another, new Grouping before the results of my contribution, some kind of baby, meant that we would be too numerous. There simply would not be enough space for us all to be happy all the time.

We had gathered in a luminescent area of the Dwelling that was plain white, perhaps reflecting the multicoloured range of different sensations and read-outs of the different members.

Often, I could now predict quite accurately what people were going to say: since Zelda had gone, however, I had little opportunity to practise since no one else ever really said anything. I looked down at my swollen belly, just like Avril's had been. Soon Avril would probably ask how I had become pregnant, who the genetic donors were. The Grouping didn't need me, when they had her.

'It doesn't matter.' Ciro's deeper, calmer voice was next. 'Sim needs to leave anyway.'

'I'm glad.' Female A – for so Zelda had always called her – was almost snarling 'She's been talking all the time. Trying to talk to us, watching us. She's shit. I'm glad she's going.'

I wasn't quite sure what I was meant to say or do. Perhaps it was because I would not have finally left just by deciding all on my own one morning, and walking out. I wasn't following the normal procedure. I'd had no instructions about the location of a male gene donor, or any of the usual information sent that would then guide me in finding my new Grouping. Then the young male gene donor, still a child, but very beautiful and obviously with a clear brain, almost shouted at me in accusation.

'Where's Zelda?'

I realized that so much had *not* happened as usual, that not only was I pregnant in a way that no one could understand, but also that a key member of the Dwelling was just suddenly not there. In my obsession with the two big ideas, inactivating Fred and escaping on my own, the repercussions of Zelda's absence had never had a chance to occupy my thinking. Now, of course, such a big change in the environment would impact on even the sensitivities of the other oblivious members of the Grouping. After all, the situation was unprecedented, that one of us should just vanish. For a brief, silly moment, I wondered if I could offer to substitute for Zelda, which would make the numbers right and provide the service Zelda had done, the part she had played.

That was, after all, all that they cared about. But no, impossible. With the baby now kicking inside me, my fate was clear: I could never be accepted as a carer. In any case would I really want to be another Zelda?

No. Never. Clinging fleshy arms, a sad smile, watery eyes, inner worlds that were locked away forever. No, I could never know, despite Fred's training, what it felt like to be her. But I was certain now that I didn't want to live as she had. And unlike everyone else there in the Grouping, I knew for certain that Zelda was never going to come back. Not ever.

But there was nothing I could say, nothing I could tell them about Zelda, if indeed that was the purpose of the meeting. Zelda had tied me down, imposed herself on me, stood between me and Fred at first, and then had not understood, had not been glad for me when I told her of the secret. No, for some reason she had despised me for it all the more, had been the one that told me that Fred really detested me. Zelda, like Fred, had first shown only love but really, all the time, it had been hate. But I took comfort now: neither of them would love or hate anyone ever again.

Because no one here ever thought of different types of outcomes, of making plans to change the future, I had the opportunity to decide for myself how and when I would leave, where I would go. No one would have come to this meeting because they wished to make suggestions or had a strategy as to what to do with me. At most they would obey their implants: and these only ever issued positive instructions, to do something that wasn't obvious from the immediate situation you happened to be in, or more usually relayed the retaliatory action needed if the body was exceeding its physiologically homeostatic constraints. Now the collective gathering of the Grouping convened by Avril was, after all, to tell me unambiguously the simple negative: to go.

'Just go, Sim.' Ciro nodded in agreement with himself. The kindest voice: my remote carer, always secondary to Zelda. But he had cared as much as he could.

'Go! Go! Go!'

Now collectively everyone had taken up the chant. The rhythm had assumed its own purpose, the experience of making noise together, a novel pleasure. Louder and louder. Everyone got on their feet, as one. How much longer would they just be jumping up and down on the spot? Would they soon discover some ancient, long-buried behaviour and actually touch me, actually push me out? Would they, any minute now, go back to the time that Fred had mentioned, when you did to real people what you usually did to the enemy in video games? When the best of all was to show off your clothes soaked in someone else's real blood?

There was nothing to keep me there, and no large amount of objects that I needed to collect or pack. The way we lived was not based on possessions in the way life had been in the previous century. Back then people had defined themselves by what they owned, in that clothes or their cars were claimed to 'say something about them'. Of course, these objects were not smart or interactive as everything is today, so it's hard to imagine how those ancient static, silly, pointless objects could ever have 'said' anything. Now we focus on the here-and-now experience and only require technologies that allow us to feel as happy as possible. Since everything we touch, from clothes to walls to objects, is interactive and mutable, what reason to have piles of possessions?

But it was no time for such musings. Since the Fred time I'd noticed my increasing tendency to step out of the moment, into somewhere that wasn't anywhere – neither the past nor the future, but a general, continuous Sim that was neither pure fantasy nor hard, likely reality. This Sim had made it possible to deal with Zelda and her disappearance, and the realization that I was to have a baby, and to accept what had happened to Fred. But I couldn't think of Fred just then: there was no place for Sim-out-of-time, because I had to respond to the press of the moment. I had to move as quickly as I would have done before Fred, and before I had swollen up to be so large and clumsy and slow.

I checked on the important objects, however, that I needed to take. First, there was the Helmet. I was quite familiar now as to the process for using it to stimulate the brain, and how the events in the brain could then be read out and transmitted long distances if need be. Oh yes, I knew all about Hodge. But the crucial issue was that these emissions would be jammed, analyzed, intercepted and filtered by first routing through the local links in Fred's implant, in turn controlled by the watch, the second important possession. I fastened the strap now around my wrist, seeing immediately the contrast on my small bone, compared with how it had been dwarfed on Fred's fleshy white forearm.

My own implant was the third vital tool I needed to take. Obviously, it was coming with me: it was, after all, embedded in my arm. But my implant, like me, had changed. The essential commodity that it now encapsulated was the huge database that I had managed to synchronize and download from Fred's implant. In the time to come I hoped I would be able to download this information into my own brain through the Helmet, to learn and understand so much more, and to continue the journey that Fred and I had started together. Perhaps I would eventually be able to analyze my own brain, downloading it back and forth with the implant, as though the implant was another person. In essence, of course, the implant *was* another person: since it was material all about Fred, then surely, if it was Fred, I was now Fred? But I doubted that could be the case. Fred was more than a list of general and personal facts. But what else had he actually given me when we interacted? When we slipped into the secret times, Fred the actual person had vanished: in his place there'd been a silent man doing what all men used to do for millennia, until we were transformed by technology.

But this reasoning was no good, not helpful, even dangerous. I shook myself from thought into action. Finding the nearest of the ubiquitous reflective surfaces, I grabbed fistfuls of my pointless yellow hair and hacked with the glass shard that had previously been procured to slice into Fred's flesh. I needed to survive and all those lifeless strands in my eyes, blowing into my mouth, tangling up everywhere, anywhere, was suboptimal. Checking my implant one final time, I tightened the Helmet around my cropped head, simply because it was safest that way and would make it easier to run, if I had to, especially because of the baby heavy and squirming in the core of my being. The Helmet was inactivated, just a kind of hat like people used to wear: a protective helmet in the ancient, military sense.

The chanting had ceased now because I had already removed myself from their immediate visual fields, and the thrill of shouting in unison had given way to brighter, faster, external surprises and sources of fun, via each enhancer, the screens or even just the room. No one would be killed just for the sake of it, after all: my blood wouldn't be a trophy. Things had returned to normal. I was already forgotten.

Carefully, I lumbered around the preoccupied people with whom I had spent my entire life, working my way towards the oblong square of natural daylight that was the exit and simultaneously, for me, the entrance into something so vast I couldn't find the right word to describe it. The shapes that hummed and swayed and laughed were some small, some adult, some female, some male: one was Fred.

'Fred. Goodbye.'

At first he didn't look up. He was in a rosy-coloured hologram cloud. His eyes were shut and he was humming softly to himself.

'Fred. It's Sim. I'm leaving, and I won't see you again.'

Dreamily, he half opened his eyes and I caught a sliver of grey below the heavy lids. He was still wearing the iridescent, multicoloured garment that I had dressed him in and his warm body had activated it to be light, translucent. I could see the familiar muscles and corners and angles of his body, now no longer touching mine. His face was still uniquely undulated; but it was less grey, almost as pink as the light within which he danced. But the biggest change was the expression: the clear, rigid thought that had blazoned through the imperfect features had given way to an empty peace. He was impregnable.

'Goodbye then. Thank you.'

Why was I thanking him? What had he done for me? I was utterly and completely isolated. From the moment I had been born, there had always been someone or something there: Zelda, my enhancers, my implant, the Fact-Totum, all the technologies of the smart Dwelling, the chance brushes and background presence of the rest of the Grouping, and then finally, Fred. Either they had vanished, or I no longer had use of them: it amounted to the same thing. For the first time there was just my identity.

I ran my finger against Fred's implant: it didn't vibrate or bleep in synchrony with mine. I had indeed inactivated it successfully It was now just a silent part of Fred's body. The slight pressure of touch was enough, though, for Fred to pull his arm slowly away: my finger hadn't been painful or irritating, he just didn't like touch any more. But he was not in a hurry.

Yet I was. I needed to escape into the fresh air. Stumbling now, even clumsier in my haste, I broke out into the outside. I set my face against the wind that was blowing, not severely but enough to notice, and strode off into the grey cloudy vastness. I pulled a thick grey outer garment, which Fred had long discarded, around me. I had grown out of the gossamer smart clothes as well as the silly long hair. Appearances were nothing: thinking was all that mattered, thinking ahead.

I realized that even though I had ensured that Fred and Zelda could no longer communicate or read out to Hodge, that Hodge would not have forgotten me. He knew about me, had contemplated having me 'Boxed' and in any case probably now had larger plans, a mission in which the N-Ps in some way came back, not to me, but in some way against me. But what did it matter? I was different now from all I had been brought up to be. Why should I care if a way of life I could no longer live was in any way threatened?

So could I become an N-P? Could I travel to their place and pretend I was one of them? I laughed bitterly to myself. If I assumed that everyone looked like Fred, with careworn creases in body, face and clothes, my genetically programmed face like glass would draw immediate attention. And when they looked beneath the skin to the brain, they would find that it nurtured a mind far different from theirs. And even if I was able to, to live in a corner of their world without them noticing, would I actually want that? Did I want only to think, to reduce myself as much as was biologically sustainable to an abstract entity?

I was Sim. No one else was. But who was she? First I had been defined by Zelda and her story, then by Fred and his facts. Zelda perhaps indeed had 'loved' me, and wished to build up the fiction, the old-fashioned lie, that I duly loved her back. But I had loved Fred, until my love had turned him into another person that no one could love, because no one was there any more: only the facts had remained. In different ways, both Fred and Zelda had been destroyed by me. Or perhaps they had run away from me. Or driven me away? I stopped striding and stared up at the deeper grey sky closing in and glowering down. All of these statements could be true, and they all amounted to the same outcome: I was alone.

I started to walk on once more. Some heavy large drops of rain had started indiscriminately and occasionally to splatter on my clenched hand, my metallic-skin helmet, my upturned face. But it wasn't only the rain that was making my face wet. I discovered I was crying. Not racking sobs, not fearful screaming, but a slow and steady sadness, welling up and out through my eyes, tracking in well-ordered streams down my cheeks. I resolved then never, ever to cry again.

I had to escape the rain, though, now beating down, drumming on the helmet, down my neck and back, stinging my eyes still more. And from deep inside me, an answering kick, then another. I placed my hand over my stretched belly and remembered that I was not, after all, alone. This baby and I would have to find a direction, but we could do so together. It would be a new way, one like no other. But, now cursed and blessed with a past, a present and, above all, a future, I had no choice. I opened my mind and breathed deeply the fresh air outside as though for the first time. As I turned my back on the Dwelling and the bright blinking cluster of domes, I stepped heavily round all the usual glass and plastic. It was important that I didn't trip. Near the incandescent walls, there were always the densest piles of rubbish. On top of one, upside down, spattered with earth and splattered by muddy rain, was a lilac bicycle, one wheel revolving slowly and pointlessly in mid-air. I paused for a moment: should I take it with me?

AFTERWORD

'...Might man become a mere parasite of machinery, an appendage of the reproductive system of huge and complicated engines which will successively usurp his activities?'

So wrote the brilliant biologist J.P. Haldane in 1923 when he read a paper 'Daedalus' to the Heretics' Society at Cambridge University – a paper that was to be the inspiration for Huxley's seminal work: *Brave New World*. Some people think it's just a waste of time to try and predict the future. They sneer at examples of the seeming arrogance of previous generations, now rendered misguided and risible in the glory of hindsight: one of the most popular examples is the alleged quote by Thomas J. Watson, boss of IBM from 1914 to 1952, asserting that there might in the future be at best a market for five computers in the world. But notice that the inaccuracy here is not the technology itself, rather the lack of foresight as to how that technology would be used. Even if it's unrealistic to try and predict with any precision and detail the prowess, and most significantly the cost, of an invention itself, the basic scientific concepts can indeed be envisioned, and often with chilling accuracy. For example, George Orwell's *1984*, written back in 1948, makes for eerily uncomfortable reading in envisaging a world of surveillance and manipulation of thought that some might say is now growing daily and where the key concept of Big Brother has been hijacked by contemporary TV world-wide. So although we may not be able to predict the precise technologies, it is possible, as Haldane, Huxley and Orwell have shown, to articulate the underlying idea, observe its realisation currently operational in some nascent form, and then extrapolate where such technology might be headed in impacting on human existence, society, and thought.

2121 is a fictional prediction of life in the future. The story is set just over 100 years from now, and the actual date was intended as a play on 20-20 perfect vision, with the paradoxical prospect of going even beyond that optimal state. By setting the story in the not too-distant future, it was possible to link the dramatic changes in lifestyle to one that would be much more familiar: hence the character Zelda is technologically reconstructed in a way that enables her to span these two time periods.

My aim has been to lay out two very different portraits of individual identity, relationships and hence of society as a whole that, caricature through they may be, could well be the all-too inevitable outcomes of the twenty-first-century lifestyle. One of the enduring central themes of my professional life has been to explore the continuing questions of identity, relationships, and the human condition through the prism of neuroscience. But ever since I can remember, I've also been much influenced by those two transformational dystopias of the twentieth century (*Brave New World* and *1984*) and the various future scenarios possible when the human mind meshes with new technologies, not just as an abstracted thought experiment but more as a cautionary tale. So, although this is a work of fiction, many of the ideas and the science expressed through the main characters, in particular Fred, are not wild flights of fancy but have already been discussed in my non-fiction books, such as theories of consciousness, the mind and identity not to mention attitudes to pleasure, child development and home life.

Anyone wishing to find out more, please see: *The Human Brain, A Guided Tour* (1997, Orion Books), for basic informa tion on the brain; *The Private Life of the Brain* (2000, Penguin Books), which outlines a neuroscientific theory of consciousness; *Tomorrow's People: How 21st-Century Technology is Changing the Way We Think and Feel* (2003, Penguin Books), which is a survey of the impact of future technologies; *ID: The Quest for Meaning in the 21st Century* (2008, Hodder & Stoughton), in which I discuss possible options for the twenty-first-century human mind; *You & Me: The Neuroscience of Identity* (2011, Notting Hill Editions), which talks about the neuroscience of identity.

Despite my original education in the humanities (Classics then Philosophy), the transition to a non-scientific writing style proved slow and painful and I needed an enormous amount of help and moral support through countless iterations of various drafts. First therefore, I would like to thank my agent Caroline Michel of PFD, who believed in the book even at its most clunky and unmarketable initial stages, and to Tim Binding of PFD who then gave detailed and invaluable advice on the major changes needed in the first few drafts. I'm also hugely grateful to Mathilda Imlah and Anthony Cheetham at Head of Zeus, who had the courage and conviction to sign up the book when it was at an embryonic stage of development, and to my friends who have made really significant contributions in various ways. More specifically, I'd like to thank Professors Alex Thompson and John

Stein who ploughed through early versions and did not shrink from giving their tough-love comments. I'm also very grateful to Sim Scavazza, for letting me use her name, which seemed so perfect for the futuristic, cyber-integrated character: but I must stress that any similarity stops with the name and that the real Sim has all the qualities that, even at the end, the fictional Sim still lacks. I also owe a big debt of gratitude to Professor Nick Rawlins who actually first suggested the title, and a colossal thank you to Carolyn Lloyd-Davies, who persisted in reading and commenting on the various incarnations of the text right up until the final version. However there was one friend who has been unable to read *2121*: Winston Fletcher.

From 1998 Winston served as Chairman of the Royal Institution (Ri), taking up office in the same year that I was appointed Director. For both of us the challenge was formidable: Winston was about to oversee an organization that had in certain respects fallen into a genteel slumber, whilst I for the first time was venturing beyond conventional university life to encounter the private sector, the charity world and the rigours of the more structured world of committees and organizational governance. From the very beginning Winston proved a tireless source of wisdom through this turbulent time. He was always there at the end of a phone, be it weekends or evenings, to steer and develop ideas, to act as a sounding board and to provide the experience accumulated over decades. His attitude was always one of humorous de-bunking and ensuring that I never got too carried away, whilst at the same time always being constructive in his reservations. After 2008, when Winston finally demitted office after ten strenuous years, we remained in close contact, and I greatly looked forward to our lunches where I could benefit from his extensive knowledge of the London gastronomic and social scene. He had the ability, granted to few, to make you laugh out loud until your face ached, and at the same time feel that you were getting to grips with interesting and important subjects. He was a true friend, both professionally and personally. Tragically, Winston died unexpectedly in the autumn of 2012, leaving many of us in shock and with a sense of acute loss. Above all, Winston was a prolific author and man of letters and a true wordsmith: even the sight of his name in my email inbox would trigger a small thrill at knowing that however banal or logistical the reason for his writing it would always be amazingly witty. It therefore seemed particularly appropriate to pay tribute to Winston by dedicating this book to him. It is by sheer coincidence that he bears the same name as the central character in *1984* – a fact which I hope now is making him chuckle, wherever he is… .

Susan Greenfield
Oxford, March 2013